COLD CASE IN CHEROKEE CROSSING

BY
RITA HERRON

Published in Great Britain 2014
by Mills & Boon, an imprint of Harlequin (UK) Limited,
Eton House, 18-24 Paradise Road, Richmond, Surrey, TW9 1SR

ISBN: 978-0-263-91378-1

46-1214

Harlequin (UK) Limited's policy is to use papers that are natural, renewable and recyclable products and made from wood grown in sustainable forests. The logging and manufacturing processes conform to the legal environmental regulations of the country of origin.

Printed and bound in Spain
by CPI, Barcelona

Award-winning author **Rita Herron** wrote her first book when she was twelve, but didn't think real people grew up to be writers. Now she writes so she doesn't have to get a *real* job. A former kindergarten teacher and workshop leader, she traded storytelling to kids for writing romance, and now she writes romantic comedies and romantic suspense. She lives in Georgia with her own romance hero and three kids. She loves to hear from readers, so please write her at PO Box 921225, Norcross, GA 30092-1225, USA, or visit her website, www.ritaherron.com.

To my beautiful daughters who, as counselors,
are the real heroes.
Love you,
Mom

Prologue

Blood splattered the wood floor and walls. So much blood.

A scream lodged in nine-year-old Avery Tierney's throat. Her foster father, Wade Mulligan, lay on the floor. Limp. Helpless. Bleeding.

His eyes were bulging. The whites milky looking. His lips blue. His shirt torn from dozens of knife wounds.

The room was cold. The wind whistled through the old house like a ghost. Windowpanes rattled. The floor squeaked.

Horror made her shake all over.

Then relief.

That mean old bully could never hurt her again. Never come into her bedroom. Never whisper vile things in her ear.

Never make her do *those* things....

A noise sounded. She dragged her eyes from the bloody mess, then looked up. Her brother, Hank, stood beside the body.

A knife in his hand.

He grunted, raised the knife and stabbed Wade again. Wade's body jerked. Hank did it again. Over and over.

Blood dripped from the handle and blade. More soaked his shirt. His hands were covered....

His eyes looked wild. Excited. Full of rage.

She opened her mouth to scream again, but Hank lifted his finger to his lips and whispered, "Shh."

Avery nodded, although she thought she might get sick. She wanted him to stop.

She wanted him to stab Wade again. To make sure he was dead.

A siren wailed outside. Blue lights suddenly twirled, shining through the front window.

Hank jerked his head around, eyes flashing with fear.

Then the door crashed open and two policemen stormed in.

Hank dropped the knife to the floor with a clatter and tried to run. The bigger cop caught him around the waist.

"Let me go! Stop it!" Hank bellowed.

The skinny cop moved toward her. Then he knelt and felt Wade's neck. A second later, he looked at his partner and shook his head. "Dead."

The cop turned to her with a frown. "What happened?"

"Don't say anything!" Hank yelled.

Avery's cry caught in her throat. She didn't know what to do. What to say. She'd seen the knife in Hank's hand. Seen him stabbing Wade over and over.

Something niggled at the back of her mind. Something that had happened. Wade had come into her room.... She'd heard a noise....

"Where's your mother?" the policeman asked.

She didn't know that, either. The foster homes had been her life.

"Stop fighting me, kid." The big cop shoved Hank up against the wall, pushed his knee in Hank's back, then jerked his arms behind him.

Tears blurred Avery's eyes as he handcuffed her brother.

"It'll be okay, sis," Hank shouted.

Avery let out a sob. Hank was all she had.

What were they going to do to him? Would they take him to jail?

If they did, what would happen to her?

Chapter One

Twenty years later

"Thirty-four-year-old Hank Tierney is scheduled for execution in just a few days. Protestors against the death penalty have begun to rally, but due to Tierney's confession, his appeals have been denied."

Avery stared at the local television news in Cherokee Crossing, her heart in her throat as images from the past assaulted her.

Hank holding the bloody knife, Hank repeatedly stabbing Wade Mulligan...

Her doing nothing... She'd been in shock. Traumatized, the therapist had said. Dr. Weingarten had tried to protect her from the press. Had sat with her during the grueling forensic police interviews. Had tried to get her placed in a safe, stable home.

But nobody wanted Hank Tierney's sister.

Especially knowing their father was also in prison for murder.

That fact had worked against Hank. The assistant D.A. at the time had argued that Hank was genetically predisposed to violence. The altercations between him and their foster parents hadn't helped his case.

A couple of the neighbors had witnessed Hank lashing out at Wade when Wade had reprimanded him.

Wade's wife, Joleen, their foster mother at the time, had testified that Hank was troubled, angry, rebellious, even mean. That she'd been afraid of him for months.

Avery had been too confused to stand up for him.

But she'd secretly been relieved that Wade was dead.

And too ashamed of what the man had done to her to speak out.

"Hank Tierney was only fourteen at the time he stabbed Wade Mulligan. But due to the maliciousness of the crime, he was tried as an adult and has spent the past twenty years on death row. His sister, Avery, who was nine when the murder occurred and the sole witness of the crime, has refused interviews."

The nightmares that had been haunting Avery made her shiver. Hank's arrest and the publicity surrounding it had dogged her all her life, affecting every relationship she'd ever had.

Just as Wade's abuse had.

She was shy around men, reluctant to trust. Cautious about letting anyone in her life because once they heard her story, they usually ran.

A photo of Hank at fourteen, the day of the arrest, flashed on the screen, then a photo of him now. He was thirty-four. Not a teenager but a man.

His once thin, freckled face had filled out; his nose was crooked as if it had been broken. And he'd beefed up, added muscles to his lanky frame.

There were scars on his face that hadn't been there before, a long jagged one along his temple. But the scars in his eyes were the ones that made her lungs strain for air.

Still, he was that young boy who'd stepped in front of her and taken blows for her when Wade was drinking. Who'd sneaked her food when Wade was on one of his rampages and she was hiding in the shed out back to escape his wrath.

Hank had spent his life in jail for what he'd done. For taking away the monster who'd made her young life hell.

She should have told.

Although the therapist had assured her it wouldn't have mattered, that the number of stab wounds alone indicated Hank suffered from extreme rage and was a danger to society.

But Hank had killed Wade in self-defense. And Wade had deserved to die.

Still, her brother would be put to death in just a few days. It wasn't fair.

She looked outside the window at the dusty road and woods. The prison was only an hour from Cherokee Crossing. Subconsciously she must have chosen to settle back here because she'd be close to Hank.

Or maybe because she'd needed to confront her demons so she could move on.

Just like she had to see Hank before he died and thank him for saving her life.

TEXAS RANGER JAXON WARD took a seat in the office of Director Landers, his nerves on edge. He'd just gotten off a case and his adrenaline was still running high. Beating the suspect the way he had done could get him kicked off the job.

Hell, he didn't care.

He was ready to hang up his badge anyway. Maybe open his own P.I. agency. Then he wouldn't have to play by the rules.

"You asked to see me?"

"Yes, I've decided to grant your request to work the domestic-violence team."

Jaxon tried not to react. The director knew his background, that he'd grown up in the system and that domestic violence was personal for him.

In fact, it had been a strike against him. The director had expressed concerns that Jaxon might allow his own experiences, and his anger, to cloud his judgment, and that he'd end up taking his personal feelings out on the alleged abusers.

The director had good reason to worry.

Today was the perfect example. When he'd seen Horace Mumford go after his kid with a wood board, Jaxon had taken the board to him.

"Thank you, sir." Jaxon stood, waiting on the reprimand.

But it never came. Instead the director cleared his throat. "Your first assignment is to make sure the Tierney execution goes forward."

Jaxon frowned. "I didn't realize there was a problem."

Director Landers ran a hand over his balding head. "Some young do-gooder attorney wanting to make a name for herself is trying to get a stay and a retrial."

Jaxon had seen the recent protests against the execution in the news. Not unusual with death row cases.

"Go talk to Tierney. Make sure everything stays on track."

Jaxon's gut tightened with an uneasy feeling. "Why the interest?" According to the news, the guy was only a teenager when he murdered his foster father. And he'd been railroaded into a confession.

"Because that case was one of the first ones I worked when I was a young cop. It built my career."

Now Jaxon understood. The director was worried about his damn job, not whether or not a man was innocent.

"Wipe that scowl off your face. I didn't screw up. Hank Tierney was as guilty as his father was of murder," Director Landers said. "The kid was caught with the bloody knife in hand, blood splattered all over him. Hell, even his sister said he stabbed Mulligan."

"Fine. I'll go talk to him myself." He'd also ask about his motive. He didn't remember that being reported, only that the police thought the kid was violent and dangerous.

Director Landers gave him a warning look. "Listen, Ward, I know your history, so don't go making this kid out to be some hero or I'll can your ass. Your job is to make sure that case does not go back for a retrial. If it does, it could affect all the cases I worked after that."

That would be a nightmare.

Still, Jaxon silently cursed as he walked out of the office. Was this some kind of test to see if he followed orders?

Or did Landers just want to make sure nothing happened to tarnish his reputation?

AVERY SHIVERED AT the stark gray walls of the prison as the guard led her to a private visitors' room. Apparently the warden had arranged for them to actually be in the room together versus being divided by a Plexiglas wall.

Because she was saying a final goodbye to her brother.

She twisted her hands together as she sank into the metal chair, guilt making her stomach cramp.

She should have visited Hank before now. Should have come and thanked him for that night. Should have made sure he was all right.

The door closed, locking her in the room, and her vision blurred. Suddenly she was back there in that cold room at the Mulligan house. Lying in the metal bed with the ratty blanket...

Joleen was gone. She'd left earlier that day to take care of her mama. Avery knew it was going to be a bad night. Wade had started with the booze as soon as he'd come home from his job at the garage.

She clutched the covers and stared at the spider spinning a web on the windowpane. Rain pounded on the tin roof. Wind whistled through the eaves, rattling the glass.

"Get in there, boy."

"Don't tie me up tonight," Hank shouted. *"And leave Avery alone."*

Avery fought a scream. She wanted to lock the door, but she'd done that before, and it hadn't stopped him. It only made him madder. He'd broken it down with a hatchet and threatened to kill her if she locked it again.

Something slammed against the wall. Wade punching Hank. Grunts followed. Hank was fighting Wade, but Wade would win. He always won.

Footsteps shuffled a minute later, coming closer to her room. Hank shouted Wade's name, cussing him and calling him sick names.

She bit her tongue until she tasted blood. The door screeched open.

Wade's hulking shadow filled the doorway. She could smell the sweat and beer and grease from the shop. His breathing got faster.

He started toward her, and she closed her eyes. She had to go somewhere in her mind, someplace safe where she couldn't feel him touching her.

Then everything went black....

The sound of keys jangling outside the prison door startled her back to reality. The door screeched open, a guard appeared, one hand on the arm of the man shackled and chained beside him.

Hank. God… Her heart stuttered, tears filling her eyes. She remembered him as a young boy—choppy sandy blond hair, skinny legs, eyes too hard for his age, mouth always an angry line.

But he was a man now, six feet tall with muscles. His eyes were cold and hard, his face and arms scarred from prison life. He was even angrier, too, his jaw locked, a vein pulsing in his neck.

He shuffled over to the chair, pulled it out, handcuffs

rattling as he sank into it. The guard stepped to the door, folded his arms and kept watch.

She waited on Hank to look at her, and when he did, animosity filled the air between them. He hated her for not visiting.

She hated herself.

A deep sense of grief nearly overwhelmed her, and she wanted to cry for the years they'd lost. She'd spent so much of her life struggling against the gossip people had directed toward her because of her father's arrest, and then Hank's, that she hadn't thought about how he was suffering.

For what seemed like an eternity, he simply stared at her, studying her as if she were a stranger. He shifted, restless, and guilt ate at her.

"You came," he finally said in a flat voice. "I didn't think you would."

The acceptance in his tone tore at her. Maybe he didn't blame her, but he was still hurt. "I'm sorry I didn't visit you before. I should have."

Hank shrugged as if he didn't care, his orange jumpsuit stark against his pale skin. But he did care. He'd always acted tough, but on the inside he was a softie. When she was little, he used to kiss her boo-boos to make them better.

No one had been here to soothe him the past few years, though.

"I'm so sorry, Hank. At first, there was so much happening—the Department of Children and Family Services the foster system, your trial…" And then she'd had to testify to what she'd remembered.

Her testimony had sealed his fate. "I should have lied back then, said I didn't see anything."

Another tense second passed. "You were only a kid, Avery."

"So were you."

His gaze locked with hers, the memories of the two of

them huddled together out in the rain after their mother had left them returning. *I'll take care of you,* Hank had promised.

And he did.

How had she paid him back? By abandoning him.

He cleared his throat. "I tried to find out what happened to you after I got locked up, but no one would tell me anything."

Avery twined her fingers on the table. "Nobody wanted to take me," she admitted. "I wound up in a group home."

He made a low sound of disgust in his throat. "Was it bad?"

Avery picked at her fingernails to keep from rubbing that damned scar. "Not as bad as…the Mulligans." Nothing had been as bad as living with them.

Of course, Hank might argue that prison was.

"They told me you didn't remember the details of that night." Hank lowered his head, then spoke through gritted teeth. "I'm glad. I hated what he did to you. He was a monster."

Shame washed over Avery. She'd never told anyone except the therapist the truth. But Hank knew her darkest secret.

Avery reached across the table and laid one hand on his.

"I'm so sorry for everything, Hank. I know you killed Wade for me." Tears clogged her throat. "I…should have spoken up, told someone about what he was doing. Maybe it would have helped get you off, or at least they'd have given you some leniency and a lighter sentence."

Hank studied her for a long few minutes, his expression altering between anger and confusion. "You still don't remember?"

She swallowed hard. "Just that he was drinking. That you fought with him, and he tied you up. Then he came in my room." She pressed a finger to her temple, massaging where a headache pounded. The headaches always came when she struggled to recall the details. "Then everything went black until I saw you with that knife."

Hank pulled his hand away and dropped his head into his hands. "God, I don't believe this."

Avery watched him struggle, her heart pounding.

"Hank, I'm sorry. I should have lied about seeing you with that knife. You always stood up for me, and I let you down." Her voice cracked with regret.

The handcuffs clanged again, as he reached for her hands this time. The guard stepped forward and cleared his throat in a warning, and Hank pulled his hands back.

"Look at me, Avery," Hank said in a deep voice. "I didn't kill Wade."

"What?"

"I didn't kill him," Wade said again, his voice a hoarse whisper.

Avery gaped at him. Was this a last-minute attempt to save himself from death? "But...you told them you hated him, that you were glad you'd stabbed him."

He leaned closer over the table, his look feral. "I did stab him, but he was already dead when I stuck that blade in him."

"What?" Avery's head reeled. "Why didn't you tell the police that?"

"Because I thought *you* killed him," Hank hissed.

Avery gasped. "You...thought I killed him?"

"Yes." The word sounded as if it had been ripped straight from his gut. "He was in your room, and there was no one else there in the house. And you had a knife. It was bloody."

"What?" Avery looked down at her hands. "But I don't remember that."

Hank rubbed hand down his face. "I...I took it from you. You were...hysterical, in shock."

Avery tried to piece together the holes in her past. "But…I didn't kill him, Hank. At least I don't think I did."

Hank's eyes narrowed. "You said you blacked out?"

She had lost time, lost her memory. Because she'd stabbed Wade herself?

Her pulse thundered. Had she let Hank go to jail to cover for her?

God… "Hank, tell me the truth. Did you see me stab him?"

"No, not exactly." Hank rolled his hands into fists on the table, his scarred knuckles red from clenching his hands so tight. "But I heard him going into your room that night. I knew what he was going to do. I'd known it when Joleen left that morning and I'd been dreading it all day."

So had she.

"So I sneaked a knife under my pillow. But he tied me up like always. I lay there and heard the door open, and I got angry." His cheeks blushed with shame. "Then I heard you crying again, and I got madder and madder. He was a monster, and I was your big brother. I had to do something."

"But you did," Avery said, her heart aching as memories surfaced. "You tried to pull him off me before, and he beat you for it." She paused, struggling with the images hitting her. Wade on top of her. Wade holding her down.

Or was that another night? So many of them bled together….

Nights of Wade shoving Hank against the wall and beating him with his belt. His fists. A wooden mallet. Anything he could get his hands on.

"I *wanted* to kill him," Hank said, his voice gaining force. "So I twisted in the bed until I got hold of that knife and cut myself free. But when I made it to your room, Wade was already bleeding on the floor. His eyes were bulging, and he wasn't breathing."

Avery's head swam. "He was already dead?"

Hank nodded. "I thought you'd stabbed him. You were crouched on the bed, crying and shaking. I tried to get you to stop crying, but you wouldn't. And you wouldn't talk, either. You just kept staring at the blood, and I heard the siren and was afraid they'd take you away, and you didn't deserve that."

A cold chill enveloped Avery. "Oh, Hank, what have we done?"

Silence fell between them, fraught with emotion. They were both lost in the horror of that night.

Finally Avery swiped at her tears. "This is unreal.… You went to jail for nothing. I should have come forward and told everyone what he'd done to me." Rage and pain suffused her for all Hank had lost. For what they'd both lost. "I'm so sorry.… We have to make this right. We have to get you out of here."

Despair settled on Hank's face, the scar on his temple stark beneath the harsh lighting. "It's too late now. My execution is already set."

She couldn't let him die for a crime he hadn't committed. "No, I'll find a way," she said. "I'll talk to your lawyer."

Hank grunted. "Not the one I had in the beginning. He didn't give a crap. But there is a new lady, just out of law school. She came to see me a few weeks ago."

"Did you tell her what you told me?"

Hank shook his head. "I was afraid they'd come after you and arrest you. There's no way I'd let you end up in this place."

Avery's throat burned with regret, yet her anger gave her strength. "What was this lawyer's name? I'll talk to the warden, and then I'll call her."

"It won't do any good," Hank said, defeat in his voice. "I told you, it's too late."

"No, it's not." Avery took a deep breath. "What was that lawyer's name?"

"Lisa Ellis," Hank mumbled. "But I'm telling you, it won't make any difference." He gestured around the room, then at the guard. "I know how things work in here."

Avery's voice gained conviction. "I'm not going to let you die for something you didn't do, Hank. I'll talk to that lawyer and if she can't help, I'll find someone who will."

Avery stood, anxious to make the phone call. Hank had given up hope long ago because she hadn't been there for him.

No one had.

It was time that changed.

JAXON IDENTIFIED HIMSELF to the warden, a chuffy bald man with thick dark brows and ropes of tattoos on his arms, and explained that he wanted to visit Hank Tierney.

"Yes, you can see him, but this is odd," Warden Unger said. "Tierney has only had one visitor in the past twenty years until today. Today he's had two."

Jaxon straightened his shoulders. "Who else came to see him?"

"His sister." The warden scratched his head. "Obviously with the execution date approaching, she wanted to say goodbye."

Or perhaps that lawyer Director Landers had mentioned had spoken with her.

The warden twirled the pen on his desk. "What brings you here?"

"My director wanted me to make sure the execution is still on."

Warden Unger nodded. "Good. Thought you might be working for that pansy-ass attorney out to get a stay."

"I take it that means you think Tierney is guilty."

Unger shrugged and dropped the pen. "A jury convicted him. My job is to make sure these animals in here don't slit each other's throats, not argue with the court."

A buzzer sounded on the warden's desk, and his receptionist's voice echoed over the speaker.

"Warden, Avery Tierney insists on seeing you right away."

Unger glanced at Jaxon and Jaxon nodded in agreement. "Send her in."

Jaxon had studied the files on the case before he'd driven to the prison. Avery Tierney had been the only person at the house when her brother murdered their foster father.

She was nine at the time, and according to the doctor who'd examined and interviewed her afterward, she'd been in shock and too traumatized to talk.

The door opened, and the warden's secretary escorted Avery Tierney in.

Nothing Jaxon had read in the file prepared him for the beautiful woman who stepped inside. Avery Tierney had been a skinny, homely-looking kid wearing hand-me-downs with scraggly, dirty brown hair and freckles. She'd looked lost, alone and frightened.

This Avery was petite with chocolate-brown eyes that would melt a man's heart and curves that twisted his gut into a knot.

Although fear still lingered in those eyes. The kind of fear that made a man want to drag her in his arms and promise her everything would be all right.

She looked back and forth between him and the warden. "Warden Unger," Avery said, her voice urgent. "You have to help me stop the execution and get my brother released from prison."

The warden cleared his throat. "Why would I do that, Miss Tierney?"

A pained sound ripped from Avery Tierney's throat. "Because he's innocent. He didn't kill Wade Mulligan."

Chapter Two

Jaxon forced himself not to react. Avery was obviously emotional over losing her brother, and desperate now that his execution was less than a week away.

Warden Unger gestured toward Jaxon. "This is Sergeant Jaxon Ward with the Texas Rangers. Sit down, Miss Tierney, and tell us what's going on."

Avery's brows pinched together as she glanced at Jaxon. "You came to help Hank?"

Jaxon gritted his teeth. "I came to talk to him," he said, omitting the fact that he'd actually come to confirm the man's guilt, not help him.

Avery didn't sit, though. She began to pace, rubbing her finger around and around her wrist as if it were aching.

His gaze zeroed in on the puckered scar there, and his gut tightened. It was jagged, ridged—maybe from a knife wound?

Was it self-inflicted or had someone hurt her?

AVERY TRIED TO ignore the flutter in her belly that Jaxon Ward ignited. She had never been comfortable with men, never good at flirting or relationships. And this man was so masculine and potent that he instantly made her nervous.

His broad shoulders and big hands looked strong and comforting, as if they could be a woman's salvation.

But big hands and muscles could turn on a woman at any minute.

Besides, she had to focus on getting Hank released. Sorrow wrenched her at the thought that he'd been imprisoned his entire life for a crime he hadn't committed.

"Miss Tierney?" Sergeant Ward said. "I understand you're probably upset about the execution—"

"Of course I am, but it's not that simple. I just talked to Hank and I know he's innocent."

That was the second time she'd made that statement.

"Miss Tierney," the warden said in a questioning tone, "I don't understand where this is coming from. You haven't visited your brother in all the time he's been incarcerated. And now after one visit, you want us to just believe he should be freed."

"I should have come to see him before," Avery said, guilt making her choke on the words. "I…don't know why I didn't. I was scared, traumatized when I was younger. I…blocked out what happened that night and tried to forget about it."

"You testified against your brother," Jaxon said. "You remembered enough to tell the police that you saw him stabbing Wade Mulligan."

A shudder coursed up her spine as she sank into the chair beside the Texas Ranger. "I know," she said, mentally reliving the horror. The blood had been everywhere. Hank had been holding the knife, his T-shirt soaked in Wade's blood.

"But Hank just told me what really happened." She gulped back a sob. "He said he found our foster father on the floor, already dead. He thought I killed him, so he covered for me."

Jaxon and the warden exchanged skeptical looks. "Hank is desperate, Miss Tierney," Jaxon said. "At this point, self-preservation instincts are kicking in. He'll say anything to convince the system to reevaluate his case. Anything to stay alive."

"But you don't understand—" Avery said.

"He confessed," Warden Unger said, cutting her off. "Besides, the psych reports indicated that your brother was troubled. Other foster parents testified that he was violent. Mulligan's own wife stated that Hank was full of rage."

"Yes, he hated Wade and so did I." Avery's anger mounted. "We both had good reason. Wade used to beat Hank, and he…" She closed her eyes, forcing the truth out. Words she'd never said before. "He abused me. Hank was only trying to protect me that night. He took beatings for me all the time."

Jaxon leaned forward. "Protecting you and hating his abuser give him motive for murder," he pointed out. "Although I'm surprised Hank's attorney didn't use that argument in his defense."

"So you read his file?" Avery asked.

Jaxon shrugged. "Briefly."

"It doesn't matter," Warden Unger said. "Hank Tierney confessed."

"Because he thought I killed Wade," Avery admitted in a broken voice. "That's the reason he confessed. He thought I stabbed Wade, and he didn't want me to go to jail."

JAXON'S PULSE JUMPED at the vehemence in her voice. "Why would he think that you killed Mulligan?"

Avery stared down at her fingers, then traced that scar on her wrist again, a fine sheen of perspiration breaking out on her forehead.

"Because Wade…was coming into my room that night." Avery's voice trembled. "Joleen, our foster mother, left earlier that day, and Hank and I both knew what that meant."

Jaxon had a bad feeling he knew as well, but he needed her to say it. "What did it mean?"

She visibly shuddered. "It meant we'd have a bad night," she said in a faraway voice. "That Wade would be drinking."

The pain in her eyes sent a shiver of rage through Jaxon. "He'd hurt you before?"

She nodded again. Which meant Hank could have planned the attack, that it was premeditated. According to the transcript of the case, Hank had never expressed any remorse for what he'd done.

Hell, Jaxon couldn't blame Hank. Knowing his foster father was hurting his sister could make a fourteen-year-old boy stab a man to death and not regret it.

Avery sucked in a shaky breath. "I tried locking the door, but that only made Wade madder and he tore through it with a hatchet. And that night…I heard him yelling at Hank. Hank tried to fight him, but he tied Hank in his room."

Jaxon's jaw ached from clenching it.

"Then I…heard the door open and…"

The images bombarding Jaxon made him knot his hands into fists. But he didn't want to frighten Avery, so he stripped the rage from his voice. "What happened then?" he asked softly.

She lifted her gaze, her eyes tormented. "I don't remember. I… Sometimes when Wade came in, I blacked out, just closed my eyes and shut out everything."

The warden was watching her with a skeptical look. But Jaxon had grown up in the system himself. He knew firsthand the horrors foster kids faced. The feelings of abandonment, of not being wanted. The abuse.

"What *do* you remember?" he asked.

She ran a hand through the long strands of her wavy hair. Hair the color of burnished copper. Hair that he suddenly wanted to stroke so he could soothe her pain.

"The next thing I remember was seeing Hank holding that knife." She straightened and brushed at the tears she didn't seem to realize she was crying. "But it could have happened the way he said. Someone else could have killed Wade. Then Hank came in and thought I did, so he stabbed him and took the blame to protect me."

"But you were the only two people in the house," Jaxon said. "You and Hank both said that."

Avery looked up at him with a helplessness that gnawed at his very soul. "But there had to be someone else," she said. "Hank only confessed because he thought I stabbed Wade. I can't let him go to the death chamber for protecting me."

Jaxon wanted to believe her, but there hadn't been signs of anyone else at the house.

And without evidence or proof of her story, there was no way to save her brother.

AVERY SENSED THE warden was not on her side. He'd obviously heard hundreds of inmates declare their innocence.

Death row inmates in the last stages of their lives probably always made a last-minute plea of innocence.

But she believed her brother and had to help him.

Because the person who'd really killed Wade Mulligan had escaped.

Her heart hammered.

What if I did kill him?

The thought struck Avery like a physical blow. Hank must have had a reason to think she did....

He'd mentioned that she had a knife.... She didn't remember that.

Did she have blood on her hands?

For a second panic seized her.

What if she discovered she had stabbed Wade, and that she'd let her brother take the fall?

Bile rose to her throat.

"Avery, are you all right?"

Sergeant Ward's gruff voice made her jerk her head up. His deep brown eyes were studying her with an intensity that sent tingles along her nerve endings. It was almost as if he were trying to see inside her head, trying to read her soul.

She felt naked. Vulnerable. Raw and exposed in a way she hadn't felt in years.

Because she'd just confessed about the abuse, which meant others would be asking questions. And if Hank's case were reopened, she would have to go public with her statement.

Shame mingled with nausea. Could she open herself up to that kind of publicity? Then everyone would know....

"I'd like to talk to Hank myself." Sergeant Ward turned to the warden. "Can I do that now?"

The warden's scowl cut Avery to the bone. "Sure. But you're wasting your time. In all the years Tierney has been here, this is the first time he's ever claimed innocence."

"What kind of prisoner has he been?" the Texas Ranger asked.

The warden pulled up his record on his computer. "A loner. Kept to himself. Got into fights a lot when he first got here." He scanned the notes. "Prison psychologist said he kept saying he was glad Mulligan was dead."

Avery's chest ached with the effort to breathe. "Was he abused in prison?"

The warden folded his hands on his desk. "Lady, this is a maximum-security facility. We do our best to protect the inmates, but we've got rapists, murderers, pedophiles and sociopaths inside these walls. They're caged up like animals and have a lot of testosterone and pent-up rage."

Avery bit her lip. She'd heard horror stories of what happened to prisoners, especially young men. And Hank had only been a teenager when he was arrested. Not able to defend himself.

"When he was sentenced, he was only fourteen." Sergeant Ward said. "Why didn't he receive psychiatric care and chance of parole?"

Warden Unger grunted and looked back at the computer. "The prosecuting attorney showed pictures of the gruesome, bloody crime scene, a dozen stab wounds altogether. That was enough for the jury to see that Tierney was violent and dangerous enough to be locked away forever."

Avery rubbed her wrist, a reminder of her past.

And how far she'd come.

At least she thought she'd survived. But she'd been living a lie. Never moving forward.

Ignoring her brother who'd fought and lied and risked his life to save her.

The system had failed them by placing them with the Mulligans.

Shouldn't the fact that she and Hank were being abused have factored in to the court's decision? Hadn't anyone argued for Hank that he'd been protecting himself and her?

JAXON STOOD, BODY TAUT. Avery Tierney was obviously upset and struggling over her visit with her brother. Had Hank Tierney manufactured this story as a last-ditch effort to escape a lethal injection?

Was he guilty?

An uneasy feeling prickled at Jaxon's skin. If Avery didn't remember the details of the murder, could she have stabbed her foster father, then blocked out the stabbing?

Damn. She'd only been a child. But if the man had been abusing her, and she'd fought, adrenaline could have surged enough for to fight the man and inflict a deadly stab wound.

Not likely. But not impossible.

The more believable scenario was the one the assistant district attorney had gone with when they'd prosecuted Tierney. They had concrete evidence, blood all over the boy and his hands, and those damning crime photos. For God's sake, Hank was holding the murder weapon and had admitted to stabbing Mulligan.

And Hank and Avery were the only two people in the house at the time.

"Talk to Hank and you'll see that he's telling the truth," Avery said. "Please, Sergeant, help me save him."

Man, that sweet voice of hers made him want to say yes. And those soulful, pain-filled eyes made him want to wipe away all her sorrow.

But he might not be able to do that. Not if Hank were guilty.

Avery touched his hand, though, and a warmth spread through him, a tingling awareness that sent a streak of electricity through his body.

And an awareness that should have raised red flags. She was a desperate woman. A woman in need.

A woman with a troubled past who might be lying just to save her brother.

He'd fallen into that trap before and almost gotten killed because of it. He'd vowed never to make that mistake again.

But the facts about the case bugged him. Considering the circumstances, the kid should have been given some leniency. Offered parole. He'd been fourteen. A kid trying to protect his sister.

Unless those circumstances hadn't been presented to the jury.

But why hadn't they?

His boss would know. But hell, Landers wanted Hank Tierney to be executed.

Because he believed Hank was a cold-blooded killer?

Or because he'd made a mistake and didn't want it exposed?

Chapter Three

Jaxon tried to reserve judgment on Hank Tierney as a guard escorted the inmate into the visitors' room, shackled and chained. Hank's shaved head, the scars on his arms and the angry glint in his eyes reeked of life on the inside.

A question flashed in Tierney's eyes when he spotted Jaxon seated at the table.

"Hello, Mr. Tierney, my name is Sergeant Jaxon Ward."

The man's thick eyebrows climbed. "What do you want?"

"To talk to you, Hank. I can call you Hank, can't I?"

The man hesitated, then seemed to think better of it and nodded. For a brief second, Jaxon glimpsed the vulnerability behind the tough exterior. But resignation, acceptance and defeat seemed to weigh down his body.

"I just talked to your sister, Avery." Jaxon watched for the man's reaction and noted surprise, then a small flicker of hope that made Tierney look younger than his thirty-four years. Maybe like the boy he'd been before he was beaten by Mulligan and he was locked away for life.

"I can't believe she called you. I just saw her." Emotions thickened his voice, a sign that he hadn't expected anything to come of their conversation.

That he hadn't expected anything out of life for a long time.

"She didn't," Jaxon said, knowing he couldn't offer Hank

Tierney false hope. In fact, all he really knew was that a jury had convicted him.

And that he and his sister might have concocted this story to convince a judge to order a stay of execution.

"I came at the request of my director. But your sister showed up at the warden's office while we were talking."

Cold acceptance resonated from Hank at that revelation. "So you came to make sure they stick the needle in me?"

He *was* world-weary.

Jaxon folded his arms and sat back, his professional mask in place. "I came for the truth. Your sister insists you're innocent."

Hank's chains rattled as he leaned forward. He ran his hand over his shaved head, more scars on his fingers evident beneath the harsh lights. When he finally looked back up at Jaxon, emotions glittered in the inmate's cold eyes. "You believe her?"

Jaxon scrutinized every nuance of Hank's expression and mannerisms. According to his files, he'd been an angry kid. And according to Avery, he'd been abused.

Twenty years in a cell had only hardened him more. The scars on his body and the harsh reality of prison conditions attested to the fact that he'd suffered more abuse inside. But judging from the size of his arms and hands, he'd learned to fight back.

"I don't know," Jaxon said. "I read the file. You confessed. You were convicted."

Hank shot up, rage oozing from his pores. "Then why did you come here?"

Because your sister has the neediest eyes I've ever seen.

He bit back the words, though. Avery Tierney had survived without him, and if she were the victim she professed to be, she might be lying now.

Worse, his boss wanted him to make sure the conviction wasn't overturned. Wouldn't look good on Director Landers if one of the cases that had made his career blew up and it was exposed that he'd sent an innocent man to prison on death row.

But something about the case aroused Jaxon's interest.

Because Avery had created doubt in his mind. Just a seed, but enough to drive him to want to know the truth.

"I had my reasons for confessing." Hank turned to leave, his chains rattling in the tense silence, his labored breath echoing in the room.

"Did you kill Wade Mulligan?" Jaxon asked bluntly.

Hank froze, his body going ramrod straight. Slowly he turned back to face Jaxon. The agony in his eyes made Jaxon's gut knot.

"I wanted him dead," Hank said, his voice laced with the kind of deep animosity that had been built from years of thinking about the monstrous things Mulligan had done. "I hated the son of a bitch." He shuffled back to the table and sank into the chair.

"Every night I lay there in that damned bed across the hall from Avery, staring at the ceiling just waiting. The old lady would take her pills and pass out. He'd wait a half hour or so, wait till the house was dark and he thought everyone was asleep." Hank traced one blunt finger over a fresh bruise on his knuckle. "But I couldn't sleep, and I knew Avery couldn't, 'cause we both knew what was coming."

Jaxon gritted his teeth.

"Then I'd hear that squeak of the door...." Hank's voice cracked. "At first, I was so scared I crawled in the closet and hid like a coward. But one night...I heard Avery crying and something snapped inside me." He balled his hands into fists, knuckles reddening with the force. "I couldn't stand it anymore. I had to do something."

Jaxon's stomach churned as he imagined Avery at nine, lying helpless at the mercy of that bastard. "What happened then?"

"I ran in and tried to drag him off her." Hank's voice shook, his eyes blurry with tears. "He knocked me off him and beat the hell out of me. Used a belt that night."

"It happened more than once?"

Hank dropped his head as if the shame was too much. "Yeah. After I started fighting back, I couldn't stop. But the beatings got worse. Then he started locking me up at night, tied me to the bed so I couldn't come in and stop him." He groaned. "I had to lie there like a trussed pig and listen to that grunting, the wall banging. I wanted to kill him so bad I imagined it over and over in my head."

Hank lapsed into silence, wrestling with his emotions. Sweat trickled down the side of his face.

"Tell me about the night of the murder," Jaxon finally said.

"The old lady was gone, left for a couple of days." Hank sucked in a deep breath, his eyes glazed as if he were thrust back in that moment. "I knew it was going to be bad that night, that he'd stay at it till dawn. So earlier, I hid a kitchen knife in my bed, under my pillow."

"He tied you up?"

Hank nodded. "But then Avery screamed, and I got mad. I twisted until I got that knife and cut the ropes." He jerked his hands as he might have done that night. "Then I tiptoed to the door and peeked into the hallway. Avery's door was cracked.... I could hear her crying...."

Jaxon swallowed. If he'd been Hank, he would have killed the animal, too.

"Then what happened?"

Hank pinched the bridge of her nose. "I had the knife in my hand, and I tiptoed across the hall. I wanted to sneak up on him, stop him once and for all. Make him feel pain for a change."

He paused, his expression twisting with horror. "But Mulligan was on the floor at the foot of Avery's bed. He...was staring up at the ceiling, his eyes wide like he was dead. Blood soaked his shirt, and he wasn't moving…."

Jaxon leaned forward, trying to visualize the scene. "He'd already been stabbed?"

Hank nodded. "Blood was on his shirt and the floor. One of his hands was covered in it where he'd grabbed his chest."

"Where was your knife?"

"In my hand." Hank slowly lifted his head, eyes cloudy with confusion. "Then I…saw Avery holding one."

Jaxon would have to check the police reports to see if there was any mention of a second knife. And he needed to look at the autopsy reports. "Then what happened?"

"She was pitiful, crying and rocking herself back and forth." He gulped. "So I ran over and took the knife from her. Then I wiped it off."

"If he was dead, why did you stab him?"

Hank gripped his thighs with his hands. "I don't know. Avery was sobbing, and I thought she'd get in trouble, and I couldn't let that happen. She was already suffering enough."

Jaxon felt for the kid and his situation.

"I wanted to cover for her. And I don't want to get her in trouble now."

"Let me worry about that," Jaxon said. "I just want the truth. Tell me about stabbing Mulligan."

Hank shrugged. "I was so mad. I had to make sure that monster never got up and hurt her again, so I lost it. All that rage and hate I had for him came out, and I went after him. I just started stabbing him, over and over and over."

Hank closed his eyes, pressed the heels of his hands against them and sat there for a long minute, his shoulders shaking.

Jaxon understood the man's—the boy's—rage. He'd felt helpless. Had felt responsible for his sister.

But there were still unanswered questions, pieces that

didn't fit. "Hank, what happened to the knife you brought into the room?"

He looked confused for a moment. "I…don't know. I think I dropped it when I ran to Avery."

"Did Avery have blood on her hands? On her night clothes?"

Hank shook his head. "I don't think so."

Jaxon breathed a small sigh of relief. If Avery had stabbed Mulligan, she would have had blood on her. She was only nine, too young and traumatized to have stabbed someone and clean up the mess.

Hank made another guttural sound in his throat. "Then Avery didn't kill him?"

"I doubt it," Jaxon said.

"That's the only reason I confessed, to keep her from being taken away." Hank gripped the edge of the table. "But if she didn't kill him, then I've spent my life in a cell for nothing."

Jaxon knew his boss wasn't going to like it. But he actually believed Hank Tierney.

"There's one major problem with your story," Jaxon pointed out. "You and Avery both claimed there was no one else in the house that night."

Hank pinched the bridge of his nose again. "There had to have been. Maybe someone came over after Mulligan tied me up in my room."

Jaxon gritted his teeth. That was a long shot. But it was possible.

Even if the man had killed Mulligan, Mulligan had deserved to die. Hell, Hank Tierney was a hero in Jaxon's book.

He didn't deserve a lethal injection for getting rid of a monster.

He should have been given a medal.

And if he hadn't killed Mulligan, then someone else had. Someone who was willing to let Hank die to protect himself.

AVERY WAITED IN an empty office for the Texas Ranger while he questioned Hank. She was still reeling in shock over her conversation with her brother.

She hadn't realized how much she'd missed him over the years. She'd been too busy trying to survive herself, working to overcome the trauma and shame of her abuse and the humiliation that had come from being a Tierney, born from a family of murderers.

Therapy had helped put her broken spirit and soul back together, although she still bore the physical and emotional scars.

But she had been free all this time.

Her brother had been labeled a murderer and spent most of his life behind bars, living with cold-blooded killers, rapists and psychopaths.

Hank didn't belong with them.

She had to talk to that lawyer. The guards had confiscated her cell phone when she arrived and would return it when she left, so she stepped to the door and asked the mental health worker if she could use the phone.

"I need to call my brother's lawyer."

The woman instructed her how to call out from the prison, and Avery took the card Hank had given her and punched the number. A receptionist answered, "Ellis and Associates."

"This is Avery Tierney, Hank Tierney's sister. I'd like to speak to Ms. Ellis."

"Hold please."

Avery tapped her shoe on the floor as she waited. Through the window in the office, she could see the open yard outside where the inmates gathered. Only a handful of prisoners were outside, four of them appearing to be engaged in some kind of altercation.

One threw a punch; another produced a shank made from something sharp and jabbed the other one in the neck. All hell broke loose as the others jumped in to fight, and guards raced out to pull them apart.

She shuddered, thinking about Hank being a target. How had he survived in here? He must have felt so alone, especially when his own sister hadn't bothered to come and visit him.

How could he not hate her?

"This is Lisa Ellis."

The woman's soft voice dragged Avery back to the present. She sounded young, enthusiastic. "This is Avery Tierney, Hank Tierney's sister. Hank told me that you came to see him and are interested in his case."

"Yes," Ms. Ellis said. "I've looked into it, but unfortunately I haven't found any evidence to overturn the conviction. And your brother wasn't very cooperative. In fact, he told me to let it go."

Avery traced a finger along the edge of the windowsill as she watched the guard hauling the injured inmate toward a side door. Blood gushed from his throat, reminding her of the blood on Hank's hands and Wade Mulligan's body.

"Miss Tierney?"

"Yes." She banished the images. "I just talked to Hank. We have to help him. He's innocent."

A heartbeat of silence. "Do you have proof?"

Avery's heart pounded. "No, but I spoke with a Texas Ranger named Jaxon Ward and he's going to look into it." At least she prayed he would.

"I read the files. You were the prime witness against your brother."

"I know, but that was a mistake," Avery said. "A horrible mistake. I was traumatized at the time and blocked out the details of that night."

"Now you've suddenly remembered something after all these years?" Her tone sounded skeptical. "Considering the timing, it seems a little too coincidental."

Frustration gnawed at Avery. The lawyer was right. Everyone would think she was lying to save her brother.

"I didn't exactly remember anything new," Avery said, although she desperately wished she did. "But I just spoke with Hank, and we had a long talk about that night. It turns out that he confessed to the murder because he thought I killed Wade."

Another tense silence. "Did you?"

Avery's breath caught. That was a fair question. Others would no doubt ask it.

And if she had killed Wade… Well, it was time she faced up to it.

"I don't know," she said honestly. "I don't think so. But Hank said when he came into my bedroom, Wade was already lying on the floor with a knife wound in his chest. He saw me crouched on the bed, crying, and he thought I killed Wade in self-defense, so when the police came, he confessed to cover for me."

"That's some story," Ms. Ellis said. "Unfortunately without proof, it'll be impossible to convince a judge to stop the execution and reopen the case."

Despair threatened to overwhelm Avery. She understood the lawyer's point, but she had to do something.

"Can't you argue that someone else came in, killed Wade Mulligan and left?"

"With you in the room?"

Avery closed her eyes, panic flaring. If only she could remember everything that had happened that night…

"The social worker and doctor who examined me afterward can testify that I was traumatized, but that it was possible."

"I'm sorry, Miss Tierney, I want to help. But I need more."

Determination rallied inside her. Then she'd get more.

Footsteps pounded the floor, and she looked up and saw

the handsome-as-sin Texas Ranger appear in the doorway. His square jaw was solid, strong, set. Grim.

His eyes were dark with emotions she couldn't define.

He didn't believe Hank. He wasn't going to help her.

She could see it in his eyes.

Hank's scarred face haunted her. She'd let him down years ago when she told the police she'd seen him stab Wade. And then again when she stayed away from the prison. When she let holidays and birthdays pass without sending cards or writing or paying him a visit.

If Ranger Ward wouldn't investigate, she'd do some digging around on her own.

Chapter Four

Jaxon's insides were knotted with tension. He believed Hank Tierney.

But he would be in hot water with his boss if he challenged his opinion and the verdict that had landed Tierney on death row.

Landers also knew Jaxon's past and would question his objectivity regarding the situation. Hell, the man had practically dragged Jaxon from the gutter himself.

Jaxon owed him.

But…Avery had sounded upset, and the way she described that night sounded so heart wrenching that she couldn't have made up what had happened or been acting.

Could she?

Unless…she'd been so traumatized that the details of the evening were distorted to the point that she believed the story she'd told.

Or…there always the possibility that she and her brother had concocted this story at the last minute to create enough reasonable doubt that the governor would have to grant a stay and retry the case. And if they both stuck to their story, it was possible they could garner enough sympathy to convince a jury that Hank was innocent. That they were both victims.

Which he believed they were.

Avery dropped the phone into its cradle. "You aren't going to help me, are you?"

Jaxon's lungs tightened. Damn if she didn't have the sweetest voice.

He scrubbed his hand over the back of his neck. What the hell was wrong with him? When had he become such a sap?

"I will investigate," Jaxon said, knowing he was jeopardizing his career, but that he had to know the truth. "I'd like to talk to the foster mother you lived with at the time."

Avery's eyes widened in surprise. "I have no idea where she is. At the trial, she said Hank and I ruined her life."

They had ruined her life? "What happened to you after the trial?"

"They placed me in a group home. I never heard from her again."

"She and her husband should have been prosecuted for child abuse and endangerment." And the old man for rape.

"Did you tell the social worker about the abuse?" he asked.

Avery averted her face. "No. I was too ashamed at the time. I thought…that I did something wrong. And Wade said if I told, he'd kill me and Hank."

He wished Wade were alive so he could kill him himself.

Worse, if the social worker hadn't documented evidence of abuse, then it was Avery and Hank's word against a dead man's. A prosecutor would argue that they'd invented the story to save Hank.

But he didn't think Avery was lying about the abuse. That kind of pain was hard to fake.

Besides, any woman who stood by and allowed abuse of any kind to take place in her home was just as guilty as the perpetrator.

Although psychologists argued women were too afraid physically of their abusers to leave or stand up to them. And they often felt trapped by financial circumstances.

Worse, if a woman sent her abuser to jail, when he was released he often went straight home and took his anger out on her all over again.

It was a flawed system, but if it were his child, he'd die to protect him or her.

"I'll find her," Jaxon said. "I'd also like to speak with the social worker who placed you and Hank in that home."

Because that social worker should have realized what was happening and stopped it.

AVERY COULDN'T BELIEVE the Ranger's words or that his voice sounded sincere. But something about the man's gruff exterior and those deep-set dark, fathomless eyes, told her that he was a man of his word.

Not like any other man she'd ever known.

Don't believe him, a little voice in her head whispered. *Men who make promises either lie or have their own agenda.*

He'll want something in return.

She was not the kind of girl to do favors like that.

"You really are going to talk to them?" she asked.

He tipped his Stetson, a sexy move that spoke of respect and manners and…made her heart flutter with female nerves.

Good heavens. She had to get a grip. Jaxon Ward was a Texas Ranger. And she needed his help for Hank.

Nothing more.

He took a step closer, his masculine scent wafting toward her and playing havoc with her senses. "Hank said he stabbed Wade Mulligan, but that he was already dead. If you didn't deliver the deadly blow and Hank didn't, that means there was someone else in the house." The silver star on his chest glittered in the harsh lights. "Who else might have wanted the man dead?"

Avery had desperately tried to forget everything about

the man. But if she wanted to help Hank, she had to confront the past.

"Avery, can you think of anyone?"

"His wife," she said, her heart thundering. "If she knew he was coming into my room, maybe she tried to stop him."

Jaxon's expression was grim. "That makes sense, but didn't she have an alibi for that night?"

Avery's head swam. "She claimed she was at her mother's." Panic began to claw at her chest. "Maybe Joleen lied about going to her mother's. Or she could have come back for some reason, and she saw Wade tie up Hank and come into my room. Then she slipped in and killed him."

Although even as she suggested the possibility, despair threatened. The problem with that theory was that Joleen hadn't cared for her or Hank.

She certainly hadn't loved them enough to kill her husband for them.

JAXON GRIMACED. DISCUSSING the case would definitely reopen old wounds for Avery, but questions had to be asked and answered. "Do you know if Mrs. Mulligan continued to take in foster children after her husband was murdered?"

"I have no idea what happened to her," Avery said.

"What about the social worker who placed you with the Mulligans? What was her name?"

Avery rubbed her forehead as if thinking back. "I...think it was Donna. No, Delia. I don't know her last name."

"There should be records," Jaxon said. "What do remember about her?"

Avery shrugged. "Not much. She gave me candy on the ride to the Mulligans' the day she dropped us off." Her voice cracked. "But I don't remember her coming back to visit."

Jaxon bit back a response. "Did she testify at your brother's trial?"

Avery rubbed the scar around her wrist. "I don't think

so. But I was so young that they didn't let me inside for some of the trial."

That made sense.

"I'll pull the transcripts from the trial and review them, then question her."

Avery squared her shoulders. "I'd like to go with you to see her."

He hesitated. "I'm not sure that's a good idea."

Avery folded her arms, a stubborn tilt to her chin. "I may have been a child then, Sergeant, but I'm not anymore. My testimony put my brother in prison, and got him the death penalty. Now that I know he's innocent, I have to make things right."

Jaxon lowered his voice. "Avery, do you think it's possible that Hank twisted the truth because he's afraid to die?"

She shook her head. "No. Hank's not like that. He always owned up to things he did wrong. Even if it meant he'd be punished for it. Besides, he just said that he confessed because he thought I killed Wade."

Oddly it sounded as though Hank Tierney had character, that he wasn't the bad seed the prosecutor had painted him to be.

And if a jury heard his testimony now and heard Avery's story, they might let Hank Tierney go.

So why hadn't the D.A. and Tierney's defense attorney pleaded not guilty and put the kid on the stand?

Dammit, he needed to see the autopsy report for Wade Mulligan. If someone else had delivered the fatal stab wound before Hank Tierney had unleashed his rage, it might show up in the autopsy report.

AVERY'S PALMS BEGAN to sweat at the idea of dredging up the details of the past. Already she felt drained from the day's visit with Hank and now this Texas Ranger.

And if she helped Hank—and she *had* to help him—this

was only the beginning. Everyone in the town—hell, everyone in the state—would know her sordid story.

Taking a deep breath to fortify her resolve, she lifted her chin. "Please. It's time for me to face the past. Maybe seeing Joleen Mulligan and the social worker will jog my memory of that night."

"That's possible." Sergeant Ward's dark eyes met hers. "But are you ready for that?"

No. She wanted to run as fast as she could and as far away as possible. But Hank's troubled voice claiming he was innocent, that he'd taken the rap to save her from arrest, echoed in her ears. There was no way she could allow him to be put to death when he'd confessed to protect her.

"Yes. I have to do this, Sergeant."

"All right. Give me your number, and I'll call you when I locate them."

Avery recited her cell number, and he entered it into his phone.

The dark, handsome Ranger tilted his head to the side. "One thing, Avery—I will look into Hank's story, but I can't promise anything. It's almost impossible to get a murder conviction overturned this late in the game."

"It's not a game," Avery said, her senses prickling. "This is my brother's life."

A heartbeat of silence stretched between them. "I know that. But I don't want you to get your hopes up." He pierced her with a dark look. "And if I find out either of you is lying and using me, I won't hesitate to tell the judge that, either."

Her heart hammered against her breastbone. "Hank and I aren't lying," she said. "Hank didn't kill Wade Mulligan. That means that the real killer has been walking around free for twenty years thinking he got away with it. And I can't live with that."

A muscle twitched in his strong jaw. "You may have to. Sometimes the justice system fails."

Yes, it had done so twenty years ago.

But she'd do everything within her power to change that now.

JAXON'S PHONE BUZZED as soon as he left the prison. His director.

Still contemplating what to tell him, Jaxon let the phone roll to voice mail.

Wind whistled across his skin as he climbed into his SUV and pulled from the parking spot. He'd worked in law enforcement for ten years, yet the razor wire and armed guards made sweat bead on his skin. He liked the law, thought the system worked for the most part.

But occasionally a case went wrong. An innocent victim fell through the cracks.

Hank Tierney had been locked up since he was a teenager. Should he have been free all this time?

Had his life been stolen from him by someone who'd murdered his foster father, then walked around free for twenty years while he lived in hell?

Chapter Five

On the way to Cherokee Crossing, Jaxon stopped for lunch at a barbecue joint, wolfed down a sandwich, then looked up the number for the attorney interested in Tierney's case. The receptionist patched him through immediately.

"Sergeant Ward, I talked to Avery Tierney earlier. She said you were investigating the murder conviction."

"I am," Jaxon admitted. "Did you find anything that might exonerate Hank?"

"Nothing specific," Ms. Ellis replied. "I just had a feeling when I read the story that there was more to it. Foster-care kids get bum deals. I wanted to know more."

"You may be right."

"Listen," Ms. Ellis said, "if there's anything I can do to help, let me know. If that man is innocent as his sister claims, he deserves justice."

He agreed with her on that. "Thank you. Call me if you learn anything that might be helpful."

He hung up, then used his tablet to access police databases and search for Joleen Mulligan. It didn't take long to find her. She had a rap sheet.

Two DUIs and an arrest for possession of narcotics. She'd also been dropped as a foster parent after Mulligan's death, so she'd resorted to government assistance and project housing.

Jaxon phoned a friend with social services—Casey Chambers, a young woman in her twenties whose parents had been killed when she was twelve, throwing her into the system. She'd seen enough of it to want to help other kids get out like she had.

"Hey, Jaxon, what can I do for you?"

"I need some background information on a case that came through the social service agency twenty years ago."

"What's this about?"

"The Hank Tierney murder conviction."

"You're looking in to that?" Casey made a soft sound in her throat. "I've seen the protestors, and I heard some young lawyer was asking questions, too. Is that true?"

"Yeah. I was at the prison and some questions have come up regarding the conviction. I need contact information for the social worker who placed Hank and his sister, Avery, in the Mulligans' home. Her first name was Delia."

"That was a long time ago and the agency has a pretty high turnover rate. Burnout and all."

"I understand. But can you find it?"

"I'll see what I can do and get back with you."

"Thanks, Casey."

"Jaxon, what do you think? I read about the murder and the guy's confession. He admitted to stabbing the man. But something doesn't ring right to me."

Avery's pain-filled eyes taunted him. "I know. That's why I want to talk to the social worker."

A hesitation. "Jax?"

"Don't repeat that to anyone," he said. "Just get me that information."

"You got it."

The waitress brought his check, and he paid the bill and left her a nice tip, then drove toward the courthouse. The land seemed even more deserted with winter taking its toll.

Everything looked desolate, deserted, dry, almost like a ghost town.

Cherokee Crossing looked like a throwback in a Western movie with a bar/saloon in the heart of town, and a tack-and-boot store beside it. Life moved slower here. Residents told stories about the Cherokee Indians being the dominant tribe in the area, and the canyon that had literally and fig-uratively divided the Native Americans and early settlers.

The town had been built to bridge that gap.

Jaxon parked in front of the county courthouse, noting the parking lot was nearly empty. It was four-thirty; people were heading home for the day. He parked next to a pickup, then strode up the sidewalk to the courthouse steps. He identified himself, then went through security and headed to the clerk's office.

He greeted the secretary, reminding himself to use his charm. Death penalty cases were always controversial and stirred emotional reactions on all sides.

Alienating people would not get him what he wanted. Av-ery's tormented expression haunted him. He hoped to hell he wasn't being a sucker and being lured into believing an act.

Maybe the social worker could shed some light on the sit-uation. He also needed to review the trial transcripts, study the way the lawyers handled the case, make sure nothing was overlooked or evidence hadn't gotten lost, misplaced or intentionally omitted.

Roberta, the clerk in charge of records, was always friendly and knew more about the goings-on in the court-house than anyone else. She'd also worked with the court system for thirty years.

Jaxon had only been a year older than Hank Tierney when Hank was arrested. That was probably one reason he remembered the case so well.

It had been all over the news. Jaxon's uncle, the only living relative he'd had at the time, was disabled and had watched the story with him, then had a come-to-Jesus talk with Jaxon. He'd told him he was going to end up like Hank Tierney one day if he didn't get his act together.

Unable to raise him, that uncle had shipped Jaxon to a military school, where he'd learned to be a man. He'd hated it at first.

But looking back, he now saw that that school had saved him from going down the wrong path.

"Hi, Roberta, I need some help. Can you get me a copy of the transcripts of Hank Tierney's trial twenty years ago?"

Roberta's eyebrows climbed. "The Tierney man who's about to die?"

"Yes. My director wants me to review the matter because of some young lawyer looking to get the conviction overturned."

Roberta sighed. "I always felt sorry for that boy and girl. Folks said the boy was scary, that he stabbed that man a bunch of times, but if you ask me, something else was going on in that house. Something nobody wanted to talk about."

"You remember the trial?" Jaxon asked.

"Of course." She reached for a set of keys in her drawer. "Never forget how terrified that poor child looked when the reporters pounced on her. That young'un was scared to death. Something bad happened to her, I tell you. Children don't look like that unless they've seen real-life monsters."

True.

She ambled around the side of the desk. "Those files are old, Sergeant. They'll be archived downstairs."

"That's fine. Can you find them and make a copy for me?"

"Sure. But it might take a few minutes."

"No problem. I'll be glad to wait."

She maneuvered her bulk toward the door and walked down the hall. Jaxon phoned Avery. She answered on the third ring. "Hello."

"Avery, this is Sergeant Jaxon Ward. I found an address for Joleen Mulligan. I'm going to visit her tonight."

Her breathing rattled in the silence that fell between them. "I'll call you after I talk to her," he said.

"No," Avery said in a shaky voice. "I want to go with you."

Jaxon gritted his teeth. "Are you sure you're up for that?"

"No," she said softly. "But I'm the reason my brother is in this mess. It's my place to get him out."

A wealth of guilt underscored her words.

Jaxon found himself wanting to erase that guilt. But that might not be possible. Chances were slim that they could get her brother's execution postponed, and even slimmer that they could prove him innocent and free him.

AVERY LOWERED HER head between her legs and inhaled slow, even breaths just as her therapist had instructed to do to ward off panic attacks.

That had been years ago, although occasionally old fears swept over her when she least expected it. The least little thing could trigger a reaction.

A sudden dimming of lights. A noise. The sound of someone breathing too hard. The smell of smoke or…body sweat.

And cologne, the one Mulligan wore. The musty smell hadn't mixed well with the rancid odor of his beer breath.

"Avery?"

The Texas Ranger's voice startled her, jerking her back to reality. "Yes."

"Do you want me to pick you up, or do you want me to meet you somewhere?"

Her first reaction was to meet him. She didn't like to be in enclosed spaces with men. But Jaxon Ward was a law officer, and he was trying to help her.

He'd think she was strange, rude, maybe paranoid or unstable if she balked at riding in the car with him.

"I'm almost to my house if you want to meet me there."

"Fine. I'm at the county courthouse. It'll probably be a while before I leave. I'll pick you up in an hour."

"That works." She needed that hour to pull herself together. Maybe do some yoga to relax and focus her energy on her well-being.

On the fact that she had survived the Mulligan abuse and family years ago, and she was an adult now. Joleen Mulligan couldn't hurt her.

She wouldn't let her.

BY THE TIME Roberta returned with the files, it was already getting dark outside.

"I had to dig deep," Roberta said. "But you have to sign in to have access, and that took a while. The guard in charge asked a half dozen questions. Said you were the second person in two weeks to ask for a copy of the trial transcripts and copy of the police investigation report."

"Did he mention who else made the request?"

"That lawyer, Ellis. Said she was gonna talk to Hank Tierney, too."

"Thanks, Roberta," Jaxon said. "You take care."

Roberta caught him by the arm before he could leave. "You do right by them, Mr. Jaxon, you hear me? They were just kids when all that went down."

She was obviously sympathetic to Avery and her brother.

"I will," he said, although he couldn't make any promises to her, either. When Landers found out what he was up to, he might pull him from the case.

Or fire his butt.

Tension knotted his shoulders as he carried the file through the building and outside to his SUV. The sky had turned a dismal gloomy gray while he was inside, the sound of thunder rumbling.

Texas temperatures could drop quickly, and the chill of the night was setting in.

He checked his phone for Avery's address as he climbed into his SUV, his pulse quickening when he realized she lived only a few miles from the government-funded project housing where Joleen Mulligan had spent the past few years.

As he expected, traffic was thin. The storm clouds gathered and rolled over the horizon, making it look bleak for the night. He maneuvered through the small town, around the square, then turned down Birch Drive, a street lined with birch trees.

The houses were small, rustic and quaint, but even with winter, the yards looked well-kept. A few had toys indicating small children, a Western theme evident in the iron mailboxes that all sported horses on the top of the barn-shaped boxes.

Avery's house was the last one on the right, with flower boxes and a windmill in the front yard. He couldn't see the back, but it was fenced in, which surprised him since the land didn't back up to anything else. Then again, she might have a dog.

He pulled up behind a Pathfinder and shifted into Park, then climbed out, reminding himself that he was here on a job.

Not because meeting Avery Tierney sparked an attraction that he hadn't felt in a long time.

Hell, the woman had been abused as a child. That fact alone warned him to keep his distance. He had no idea what kind of scars she carried inside her, but he'd bet his life trusting men wasn't high on her list.

A bad side effect of foster life—kids grew up learning not

to get attached. They were shuffled around so much, and it hurt too much to leave friends and people behind.

Besides, Avery was a case, nothing more. At least if he investigated, maybe he could sleep without those wounded, pain-filled eyes haunting him, telling him that he should have done something other than accept everyone's word that Hank Tierney deserved to die.

He punched the brass doorbell, then heard footsteps clattering inside. Seconds later, Avery opened the door.

He grew very still when he saw her pale face. Obviously today's visit at the prison had done a number on her.

What would facing the woman who should have protected her from that monster Mulligan do to her tonight?

AVERY PASTED ON a brave face, determined not to let Sergeant Ward see how the idea of confronting Joleen Mulligan was affecting her.

"Are you ready?"

She clutched her purse strap and nodded, but her heart was pounding as she locked the front door and followed him to his vehicle. She reached for the door handle and startled when he beat her to it and opened it for her.

Her nerves raw, she twisted her head up to look at him.

"I'm just opening the door for you," he said. "Relax, Avery. I'm trying to help you."

"Why?" The question flew from her mouth before she could stop herself from asking.

His dark eyes met hers, a sea of emotions swimming in the depths. She knew nothing about him except that he'd come to see Hank today.

She didn't even know the reason for his visit.

"Because I want justice served," he said in a gruff voice. "If it turns out your brother is innocent, I'll do whatever I can to free him. If it turns out he's guilty or if he's lying and using me, I'll watch while he dies."

His words hit her like a physical blow. Yet she admired his honesty.

If a man said what he meant, then maybe he'd do what he said.

She was counting on that.

Chapter Six

Jaxon wasn't sure if he made Avery nervous or if it was just the situation. He probably shouldn't have been so harsh. But he had to be honest.

Besides, he was fighting his own attraction toward her. Trying not to let her sweet but tortured look tear at his heart and make him do something he'd regret.

Like start to care for her.

Caring was way too dangerous for a man who lived his life working case to case. Besides, the only thing he knew about families was that they were messed up. Couples stood and made promises and vows that they didn't keep. Men strayed. Women strayed. Both got bored with each other.

The kids suffered in the end.

He didn't intend to travel down that path.

"Sergeant Ward?"

Then again, if he wanted her to be more comfortable, maybe they shouldn't be so formal. "Why don't you call me Jaxon, Avery?"

She gave him a wary look. "All right, Jaxon. Does Joleen know we're coming?"

"No. I didn't want to give her a chance to decline talking to me."

"She probably would, you know."

"Yeah, I do." He threaded his fingers through his hair as

he made the turn onto the road leading to Joleen's. Scrub brush, dry parched land and ranch land stretched out for miles, but the development had been built close to town for the residents' convenience.

He turned into the complex, scrutinizing the beat-up trucks and weathered cars scattered in the parking lot. A group of construction workers had gathered at one end by two trucks parked close together. Other families were grilling burgers while the children played tag.

"Joleen lives here?" Avery asked, surprise in her voice.

He nodded. "Apparently she lost her house after her husband's murder."

"I...didn't know."

Jaxon glanced at her with a frown. "Don't feel bad for her. Apparently she got some DUIs and had a drug arrest. Not to mention the fact that she didn't take care of you and your brother as she should have." And that was putting it mildly.

Avery nodded, her long hair spilling around her shoulders as she turned to look out the window.

"You want to tell me about her before we go in?"

She shrugged. "She was just one in a long line. But just like always, I hoped this one would be different." A bitter laugh escaped her. "But it was worse."

"Did she hurt you?"

Avery's sigh filled the silence. "She didn't hit us," she said softly. "She just...sat and drank and watched."

"Just as bad," Jaxon said.

Avery sucked in a sharp breath and reached for the door handle. "I'm not that scared little girl anymore," she said, her voice filled with determination. "In fact, this visit is long overdue."

AVERY WRESTLED WITH her nerves as they walked up the sidewalk. All the units were identical. The complex was situated next to the little store on the corner so residents could walk if they didn't own an automobile.

She was grateful Joleen wasn't still living in that run-down house where she and Hank had lived with the Mulligans. She hoped they'd burned down the place.

Jaxon knocked on the door while she studied the surroundings. Dirt marred the doorstep, and the flowers in the hanging basket had been dead for ages. Joleen had never been a housekeeper, one of the things that had triggered Wade's temper. He'd ranted that since he paid the bills, the least she could do was wash the dishes and have a meal on the table when he got home from work.

Considering the fact that her grocery money paid for her booze and her meals had mostly consisted of vodka, Joleen hadn't cared if any of them went hungry.

Jaxon knocked again, and finally they heard footsteps shuffling. The door screeched open, and Joleen peeked outside. Avery bit back a gasp at the woman's stark features.

The years and alcohol hadn't been kind to Joleen. Dark circles lined her glazed, bloodshot eyes; her skin looked yellow, deep wrinkles sagging around her chin, mouth and eyes.

Her graying eyebrows drew together in a frown. "What you want?"

"We need to talk to you," Jaxon said.

She pinched her lips together as she glared at Avery. "Who are you?"

"It's me, Avery Tierney," Avery said.

"Go away," Joleen snarled. "I don't have anything to say to you."

Jaxon caught the door when she tried to close it. "Actually it's Sergeant Ward with the Texas Rangers. And you do need to let us in."

Joleen ran a shaky hand through her scraggly hair, her eyes piercing Avery. "You got a lot of nerve showing up here after what you did to my family."

Jaxon shouldered his way past her, and Avery followed, stunning Joleen. She staggered back toward the couch in the den as if to escape them. The strong scent of booze assaulted Avery, mingling with the musty odor of the apartment, which looked as if it hadn't been cleaned in months. Dirty laundry, magazines and food-crusted dishes were everywhere. A coffee cup with something moldy in it sat on the coffee table beside a plate dried with eggs.

"We need to ask you some questions," Jaxon said.

Joleen picked up her tumbler and swirled the vodka around. "Why you coming around?" she asked Avery. "You want me to say I'm sorry your brother's about to get the needle for what he done?"

"My brother is innocent," Avery said.

"The hell you say," Joleen muttered. "You saw him stab my Wade."

"That's true," Avery said. "But I talked to Hank, and he told me that your husband was already dead when he stabbed him."

A bitter laugh escaped the woman. "Yeah, he would say that now that he's going to die—"

"Mrs. Mulligan," Jaxon interrupted sharply, "I need you to tell me what you remember about that day."

Joleen huffed, then tossed back a swallow of her drink. "Why? You trying to get that boy off?"

"I'm simply verifying the facts," Jaxon said. "So the sooner you answer my questions, the sooner we'll be out of your hair. Then you can get back to whatever you were doing."

Which would be finishing the bottle, Avery thought.

Joleen's hand shook as she reached for a lighter and pack of cigarettes on the table. "Got up same as usual. Wade went to work at the garage like always. I got a call from my mama saying she was ill and needed help." She tapped the pack against her hand, pulled out a cigarette and lit it. Once she exhaled the smoke, she continued, "I left Hank in charge." Another bitter laugh. "It was a mistake ever trusting that kid. Something was off about him."

"What? Because he was angry?" Avery said. "He had a right to be angry. We were tossed from house to house, and you and your husband made it clear that the only reason you took us in was to get that government check each month."

"We took you in 'cause nobody else wanted you," Joleen roared back. "And after what happened, I can see why. Hank was a mean kid, violent." Her hand shook as she took another drag on the cigarette. "I was so scared of him I used to lock my door every night."

Avery bit her tongue to keep from defending her brother. "You closed your door when you were passed out so Wade wouldn't come in and bother you. You closed it so you wouldn't have to hear what he was doing to me."

"You always were a little troublemaker," Joleen snarled. "Flaunting yourself in front of him. Asking for it."

"I was nine years old. I never asked for anything," Avery said. "Except for a home and a family. One that didn't use and abuse me."

"You ungrateful snit," Joleen quipped. "You wanted Wade to come in there, wanted him to love you. That's why he did it."

"He did it because you let him," Avery snapped. "You didn't want him touching you, so you let him turn to me for that."

Joleen's eyes blazed with rage. "I was afraid of him just like I was afraid of Hank."

Avery was trembling all over. She started to retaliate, but Jaxon caught her hand and squeezed it. His soothing look gave her comfort.

Still, all the anger and hurt and humiliation she'd felt over the years threatened to make her explode.

JAXON WANTED TO pull Avery into his arms and comfort her. He also wanted to get her as far away from this horrible excuse of a woman as he could. To protect her from the woman's vicious accusations.

But he'd come here for answers, and he didn't intend to leave without them.

"Why exactly were you afraid of Hank?" Jaxon asked.

"Because that kid was mean as a snake," Joleen growled.

"Hank wasn't mean," Avery said. "He was angry at you and your husband for the way you treated us."

"We gave you food and a roof over your head," Joleen snapped. "But you didn't appreciate anything."

Avery started to protest again, but Jaxon gave her a warning look. "Mrs. Mulligan, did your husband ever hit you?"

The woman tapped ashes into a dirty coffee cup. "No, but he came at me a couple of times."

Avery's eyes widened, but she bit back a response.

"Did your husband ever hit Hank?" Jaxon continued.

Joleen tossed back the rest of her vodka. "He had to," she muttered. "Kids need discipline, and that boy needed plenty of it."

"Where were you when these beatings occurred?"

"Making dinner or taking care of the house."

Avery's sigh suggested the woman was lying, that she'd probably been passed out.

"How about Avery?" Jaxon asked. "Did Wade ever hurt her?"

Joleen fidgeted, stubbed out her cigarette and poured herself another drink. "My husband was good to her," she said when she finally answered. "He loved Avery. That was his only flaw. Then those kids turned on him, and cost me everything. My Wade. My house. It's their fault I ended up here."

Anger surged through Jaxon. "Wade loved Avery so much that he molested her?"

Joleen jumped up, shoes clacking as she paced in front of the couch. "You got a lot of damn nerve speaking ill of the dead. That boy killed him, that's all there is to it." She swung her hand toward the door. "Now get the hell out."

Avery stood, rubbing her hands down her jeans as if she couldn't wait to leave. Jaxon stood as well, but he fisted his hands by his sides to keep from shaking the woman. She was a pathetic drunk, but that didn't excuse the fact that she'd allowed her husband to mistreat Hank and Avery.

"You said you went to see your mother. Is there anyone who can verify that you were with her all night?"

"You," Joleen shouted. "You trying to make me look bad? Like I killed Wade?"

"Just answer the question," Jaxon said.

Joleen crossed her arms. "My mama could. But she's dead."

"Was she in the hospital at the time?" Jaxon asked.

"No, at home."

"I suppose she lived alone?"

Joleen nodded. "Now, I'm done with you. If you wanted to pin this on me, you're way off. Hank killed Wade, and he's going to die for it."

Avery's expression bordered between rage and disgust. "I should have known you wouldn't help, just like you stood by and let your husband molest me. You're nothing but a sorry drunk, Joleen."

Joleen lunged toward Avery, but Jaxon stepped in front of Joleen to prevent her from touching Avery. "She's right," Jaxon said in a low voice. "In fact, if Hank did kill your husband, I don't blame him. The legal system got it wrong this time. They should have put you in jail as an accomplice to child abuse, child endangerment and rape." He balled his hands into fists. "And I'm going to do everything I can to see that the truth is exposed and that Hank Tierney goes free."

Barely able to control his rage, Jaxon coaxed Avery toward the door, before he strangled the woman to death himself.

AVERY SANK INTO the passenger seat, her heart hammering.

When she was little, she'd been scared of Joleen, not because she'd ever hit her, but she'd yelled and cursed and said horrible things to her. Had told her she was worthless and that was the reason no family wanted her.

And after Wade started coming into the room at night, she'd accused Avery of being a dirty girl.

She had *felt* dirty back then. Had felt as though she must have done something wrong to have brought that man to her bed.

Looking back, she realized that she hadn't done anything wrong. She was a child caught in a terrible situation.

In fact, she'd covered herself in clothes, long baggy shirts and sweatpants.

Anything to keep him from looking at her.

But it hadn't made a difference.

"Are you all right?" Jaxon asked as he slid into the seat beside her.

Avery leaned her head on her hand. "Yes. I...can't believe I used to be afraid of her. That I let her make me feel like I was nothing. She's pathetic."

"Yes, she is." Jaxon angled himself toward her. "I know it took a lot of courage for you to face her."

His praise nearly brought her to tears. She'd grown so accustomed to people being cruel to her or judging her by her past that when someone treated her with kindness, it touched her deeply.

Jaxon started the engine. "She was lying. She knew her husband was coming into your room."

"Of course she did, and she allowed it to happen," Avery

said. "Like I said, she didn't want him touching her, so she was happy to let him use me."

A muscle ticked in his jaw. "She might have not minded," he admitted. "Then again, if she was afraid of him, maybe she sneaked back and killed him, then let Hank take the fall."

"You think that's possible?"

"I think she might be more cunning than you gave her credit for." And if she had killed Mulligan, she needed to pay.

Chapter Seven

As Jaxon drove away from the complex, he contemplated the theory that Joleen had actually lied about being with her mother or returned home that night. Money hadn't been a motive.

But she could have come in, realized her husband was at it again and snapped.

Or could she have planned it—lied and said she was going to take care of her mother, waited till night, then sneaked back and stabbed him.

Maybe Avery had witnessed the murder and been so traumatized that she'd blocked it out. When Hank had seen Wade dead on the floor, he'd assumed his sister had stabbed Mulligan, and lied to protect her.

The scenario made sense. Not that he could sell it to a judge without proof.

More questions nagged at him. If Joleen had been drinking as much back then as she was now, would she have been able to pull off a murder without Avery or Hank knowing she was in the house?

Hell, could she even have driven?

But if Avery were right, that the woman welcomed the fact that he used her for sex instead of his wife, then she had no motive.

"I don't know, Jaxon," Avery said. "Joleen was really

meek around her husband. I can't imagine her standing up for me by killing him. I don't think she cared enough."

That was even sadder. "I can't believe that social worker placed you with that family."

Avery sighed. "She said she didn't have a lot of options. Joleen was right. No one wanted me and Hank, not with our father incarcerated for murder."

"Tell me about him," Jaxon said.

Bitter memories washed over her. "I was four, Hank nine. My father was upset over my mother leaving. He got in a bar fight and killed a man the same night."

"So you lost both your parents at once?"

She nodded, remembering how confused she'd been. Hank had been her rock.

But the stigma of being a jailbird kid had made her life more difficult. And then her brother had ended up in prison for homicide, as well.

Jaxon's pulse kicked up. "Did the lawyer bring up your father's history at the trial?"

Avery shrugged. "I don't remember. I wasn't in the court for the trial, just when they called me to testify."

"I'm going to study the transcripts, then talk to the prosecutor and the attorney who defended your brother. Do you remember him?"

"Not really," Avery said. "Just that he was young, a public defender."

The kid had probably been overloaded with cases, and considering Hank's confession, he hadn't dug very deep for a defense.

Jaxon turned onto the street leading to Avery's house, again struck by her home's neatly kept lawn and fresh paint. Obviously growing up in a rat trap had made her appreciate her home. "I'll let you know when I get the social worker's information and set up a time."

She handed him a business card. "You have my cell number, but this is my work number."

He glanced at it with a smile. "You work at a vet clinic?"

She nodded. "As an assistant. I like taking care of animals."

Because they gave unconditional love.

"Does that mean you have a houseful of cats?"

She gave a self-deprecating laugh. "No, no pets."

Probably went back to the attachment issue.

Amazing how easy she was to read. Yet how complicated she was at the same time. She'd lived through hell, but she'd survived and managed to make a life for herself.

"Avery, were there other foster children placed with the Mulligans when you and Hank stayed there?"

Avery rubbed her forehead in thought. "There was another girl there when we first arrived. I think her name was Lois. I'm not sure what happened to her, though."

"I'll look into it," Jaxon said. "You know, Mulligan may have abused other girls before you."

Avery's face paled. "I suppose you're right. I never really thought about it."

"It's another question for the social worker."

Anger flashed in her eyes. "Yes, it is."

He almost regretted suggesting the idea, but Avery wanted the truth, and if she hadn't been the first girl Wade had molested, the social worker might know.

Even if she hadn't known, though, another victim meant someone else had a motive to kill Wade.

"Don't think about it too much tonight," he said gently. "Just get some rest."

She reached for the door handle, then turned to face him. "Thank you again, Jaxon."

Her thanks made guilt mushroom inside him. He hadn't

done anything yet. Worse, his efforts might not make a difference at all.

Her brother could still be put to death if he didn't find some answers fast.

AVERY LET HERSELF inside her house, disturbed at the idea that Wade had hurt others before her.

And that the social worker might have known and placed her and Hank there anyway.

If Wade hadn't been murdered, he would have continued the pattern.

She wanted to thank whoever had killed him for saving future victims.

But whoever had killed him had let Hank rot in prison for his crime.

The house seemed eerily quiet tonight, making her think about Jaxon's questions. She worked at a vet clinic, but had no pets of her own. That might seem odd to him. But she'd gotten attached to a dog at one of her foster houses, and it had ripped out her heart when she'd had to leave it.

She'd vowed never to get attached to anything else again.

At the clinic, she could pet the animals, but she knew they'd be going home with their owners.

She made herself a salad, then slipped on her pajamas and turned on the television. But the news was on.

"Today, protestors against the death penalty rallied outside the prison objecting to Hank Tierney's upcoming execution."

The camera panned the crowd of protestors, who were chanting and waving signs to stop the lethal injection from happening.

Guilt plagued her for waiting so long to visit her brother. If she'd done so sooner and he'd told her the truth, she would have had more time to help him.

What if she'd waited too long and it was too late?

AVERY'S FACE HAUNTED Jaxon all night. In less than a week, her brother would be executed.

He reminded himself not to let things get personal, but he couldn't help sympathizing with her. Her eyes were like a sensual magnet drawing him to her.

He stepped onto the porch of his ranch house, pausing to listen to the creek rippling in back. He'd bought the land because he liked wide-open spaces, enjoyed riding on his days off and fishing.

Only tonight it felt quiet. Maybe too quiet. Lonely.

Hell, he liked to be alone.

But for some reason, he imagined Avery beside him, maybe sipping wine on the porch. The two of them talking in soft hushed voices. Her fingers roaming up his neck, her kisses feathering against his cheek.

Then he saw her on the ranch, riding across the pasture, her hair blowing wildly around her face. She was laughing, a musical sound that made him want to drag her off the horse and make love to her.

Dammit. He forced the images from his mind.

He had to work. Making love to Avery was not in his future.

He grabbed a beer when he went inside, dropped the take-out burger he'd picked up on his way home onto the table, then spread out the trial transcript.

The prosecuting attorney in the case was the assistant D.A. at the time, now the D.A.—Snyderman. Due to the viciousness of the attack and number of stab wounds, he'd pushed to have Hank tried as an adult. He displayed pictures of Wade Mulligan's mutilated body, showing the brutality of the crime, no doubt shocking the jurors into convicting without hesitation.

Witnesses against Hank included Avery, age nine, Joleen Mulligan, and two other foster parents, Teresa and Carl Brooks, and Philip and Sally Cotton. Both had testified that

Hank was an angry kid, that he exhibited episodes of lashing out, and that he hadn't been a good fit in their homes, that the younger children were afraid of him.

Avery's account of the events of that night read just as she'd told him. When asked if she'd been afraid of her brother, she'd said no, that he always protected her.

Neither the prosecutor nor the defense attorney had pushed her for more when they could easily have encouraged her to explain her comment. Why had Hank felt the need to protect her?

If they'd pursued that line of questioning, the truth about Wade Mulligan would at least have been exposed, garnering sympathy from the jury.

But the attorney had skimmed over the details and focused on Hank's confession.

The public defender, a new graduate barely out of diapers, had argued against the death penalty, claiming Hank was emotionally disturbed.

The A.D.A. had agreed that Hank was disturbed, but because he exhibited no signs of remorse, argued that he was psychotic. He ended his closing arguments by reminding the jurors of the number of stab wounds he'd inflicted on Wade Mulligan, arguing that Hank was not only dangerous, but also had no rehabilitative qualities.

Jaxon heaved a breath of frustration. The public defender should have requested Hank undergo a psychological exam, should have had both Hank and Avery medically evaluated and should have introduced the abuse factor. He should have researched past foster children placed with the Mulligans to see if there was a history of problems with the family.

Jaxon had hoped Casey would call with the social worker's name, but he found it in the transcripts—Delia Hanover.

According to Delia, Hank Tierney had anger issues related to his father, had trouble adapting and fitting in and he had hated Wade Mulligan. He'd asked her to move him and Avery from the home, and she was searching for another family to take them, but he killed Mulligan before she could find another placement.

Hank's attorney should have pushed her for more details on the reason Hank had requested a change.

Jaxon scrubbed his hand over the back of his neck, then sipped his beer.

At the least, the public defender should have cut a deal with the A.D.A. for an insanity plea and had Hank moved to a psychiatric hospital.

He studied the photographs of Mulligan's body, the dozens of stab wounds, and understood why the jurors had voted him guilty.

But they hadn't had all the facts.

Would these revelations be enough for a judge to grant a retrial?

He doubted it.

He needed a look at the autopsy report. But it wasn't in the file.

He would get it, though. If there were evidence of a second perpetrator, maybe that would be enough to convince a judge to stop the execution.

AVERY SHIVERED AND *dug her feet into the covers. She wished she could just disappear forever.*

Maybe if she pulled them up high enough over her, she could hide underneath and he wouldn't find her.

The ping, ping, ping of the rain on the tin roof sounded like nails driving down. Footsteps sounded.

Then his voice mumbling something she couldn't understand. But she knew what would come next.

"Leave her alone!" Hank shouted.

"Shut up, you little bastard."

Then a slap across the face. She'd heard the sound so

*many times she should be used to it, but it still made her
stomach heave.*

"Beat me, but leave her alone," Hank bellowed.

*Tears leaked down Avery's cheeks. Hank was always
taking care of her. She clenched the sheets, sweating all
over. She had to tell someone. Get her and Hank out of here.*

*She jumped from the bed and rushed to the door. Wade
slammed his fist into Hank's stomach, but Hank lunged at
him. They wrestled and fell to the floor. Hank kicked at
Wade, his foot connecting with Wade's knee.*

*Wade grunted in pain and punched Hank again, this time
so hard blood spurted from Hank's nose.*

*Avery covered her scream with her hand, terrified, as
Wade dragged Hank to his bedroom.*

*He was going to tie him up. Hank wouldn't be able to
help her.*

*She slammed her door and tried to lock it. Looked for the
stick she'd sneaked into the house to try to fight him off with.*

*Wade shouted an obscenity, then began to pound the door
with his fists. The door jarred. Wood splintered.*

*Avery jumped back against the wall. She was trembling
all over. Felt sick to her stomach.*

*The door splintered and Wade stormed in. His face
looked red, his eyes full of rage. He swung his hand out
to grab her.*

"Come here, girl. You got to earn your keep."

*Avery screamed, "No," and swung the stick out. She hit
him across the face, and he staggered. The rancid smell of
his breath struck her as he lunged toward her and grabbed
the stick.*

*Then he shoved her onto the bed. She looked up and saw
the stick coming at her, and she covered her face with her
hands and screamed again as he delivered the first blow....*

Avery jerked awake, shaking all over and clawing at
the bedding.

It took her a moment to realize that she was having a nightmare.

That Wade Mulligan wasn't here now, and that he could never hurt her again.

Her phone jangled, a trilling sound that sent a shiver through her. Hand trembling, she reached for it, praying Jaxon had good news.

But another voice echoed back. One that sounded garbled.

Only the words were clear.

"Your brother is a killer. He deserves to die. And you'll die, too, if you try to get him off."

Chapter Eight

Jaxon's phone buzzed, waking him at 6:00 a.m. "Sergeant Ward."

"Jaxon, it's Casey Chambers. I have some information for you."

He sat up and grabbed a pen and pad from his nightstand. "What is it?"

"I found the social worker who placed the Tierney kids with the Mulligans."

"Delia Hanover," Jaxon said. "I saw her name in the trial transcripts."

"Right," Casey said. "She left the office where she worked a couple of years after Hank Tierney was arrested. Now she works with the local school system."

"Give me her contact information."

"I'm texting you her phone and address now."

"Thanks. Anything else?"

"I did some digging around and discovered four other foster children who lived with the Mulligans before the Tierneys."

"Good work. I'd like to talk to them. Send me their names and contact information, as well."

"It's on its way. Although one of the girls, Lenny Ames, killed herself a few months after she was removed from the home."

Jaxon's heart pounded. "Is there any more information about her suicide?"

"Not much. The report was short. Said she went from the Mulligans to a juvenile center for troubled kids. She slit her wrists one night and bled out before anyone noticed."

"Did she leave a suicide note?" Jaxon asked.

"No. But the house parents at the time said she was deeply disturbed, withdrawn and depressed when she arrived."

"I suppose nobody bothered to run a psychological checkup on her?"

"Doesn't say here. But my guess is no. She was another kid who got lost in the system."

"Or died because Mulligan abused her to the point where she hadn't wanted to live anymore."

She mumbled agreement.

"Thanks, Casey. This has been very helpful."

His phone was buzzing again, another call coming in, so he pressed Connect. "Sergeant Ward."

"Jaxon, it's Avery."

Her voice sounded shaky. "What's wrong?"

"Someone just called here and threatened me."

Jaxon went still. "Stay on the line. I'll be right there." He grabbed jeans and a clean shirt and dressed quickly, stuffed his weapon in his holster and snatched his badge and Stetson.

"Do you know who the caller was?" Jaxon asked as he hurried outside to his SUV.

"No." Avery's breath rasped out. "It sounded like a man, but it was muffled, and I couldn't be sure."

"Keep the doors locked. I'll be there in a minute."

She hung up. He started the engine and drove onto the main road leading into town toward Avery's house. The sun was fighting its way through the clouds and failing, the clouds hovering above and casting a dismal gray to the land.

Avery's neighborhood was like a breath of fresh air in comparison.

But the fact that she'd been threatened made his instincts kick in, and he scanned the streets and yards in case anyone was lurking around watching her. But the street was quiet with only an occasional neighbor venturing out for the morning paper or to get in their car and head to work. Two joggers ran by, while a trio of young mothers were already strolling their babies.

Nothing suspicious.

He pulled into the driveway and parked, then hurried up to the door. Avery opened it before he could knock. "You didn't have to come," she said, although her face looked pale and she'd obviously been upset by the call. She wasn't dressed, either. She looked as if she'd hastily thrown on a robe. Her hair was tangled from sleep, her cheeks flushed.

She looked sexy as hell.

And frightened.

"Tell me exactly what happened."

She turned and walked to her kitchen. She went straight to the coffeepot, poured two cups and handed him one.

He thanked her, then blew on the steaming brew, waiting until she was ready to talk.

"I had a nightmare about Wade Mulligan," she admitted.

He gritted his teeth. Naturally asking questions about what had happened that night would stir up old nightmares for her.

"When I woke up, my phone was ringing."

"Was there a name on the caller ID?"

She shook her head. "Unknown."

"What exactly did the caller say?"

"That my brother is a killer. That he deserves to die. That I will, too, if I try to get him off."

Jaxon fisted his hands in an attempt to control his anger. Who the hell would want to scare her like that?

The only person he could think of was the person who'd killed Mulligan.

AVERY TOLD HERSELF that the call had been a prank, but still it was difficult to shake the fear that had snaked through her at the sinister words.

There had been three other calls since. All from reporters wanting an interview about her brother's upcoming execution.

"I'm going to put a tracer on your phone in case he calls back," Jaxon said.

"You think he was serious?"

Worry flashed in Jaxon's eyes a moment before he masked it. "Could be. But there are already protest rallies for both sides of the death penalty. It's possible some overzealous fanatic is trying to scare you."

Avery's pulse began to steady. "I guess you're right. I mean, how many people even know that I'm trying to reopen the case?"

"The warden, Lisa Ellis, a social worker I asked for information, the clerk at the courthouse and Joleen Mulligan. But I can trust the social worker and clerk."

"You think Joleen would threaten me?"

"I wouldn't put it past her." Jaxon sipped his coffee. "There's another possibility."

Avery tensed at the anxiety riddling his tone. "Who?"

"The person who murdered Mulligan."

Her breath caught. "That means the threat is real."

Jaxon sighed. "I didn't mean to scare you, but we have to face the facts. If Hank didn't kill Mulligan, then whoever did is not going to want the case reopened and another investigation."

"You're right." Avery drained the rest of her coffee and

set her cup in the sink. "But it's not going to stop me. And neither are the reporters who keep calling for interviews."

"When did that start?"

"Last week. I've refused them all, but twice I saw someone stalking me with a camera."

"Dammit. They're like vultures."

"I can handle them," Avery said. "I've been doing it all my life."

"But you shouldn't have to," Jaxon said in a voice laced with wariness and something else…maybe admiration.

No. She was reading too much into things.

Jaxon's gaze raked over her, and Avery remembered she hadn't dressed before he'd arrived. She'd been so shaken by the phone call that she'd immediately punched his number, thrown on a robe and searched the house in case whoever had phoned was inside.

"I know where Delia is," Jaxon said. "If you want to go with me, I'll wait while you dress."

Avery frowned. "You found her?"

"Yes. She left social services and is employed with the school system now."

"Does she know we're coming?"

"No. I want to surprise her."

Avery didn't bother to ask why. She didn't care. All she wanted was to hear what Delia Hanover had to say.

And if she'd had any idea what kind of people the Mulligans were before she'd sent her and Hank to live with them.

JAXON SIGHED WITH relief when Avery went to get dressed. Good grief, that thin little robe barely covered her. And that short gown showcased legs that he wanted wrapped around him.

But that was never going to happen.

The shower water kicked on, and he had to step outside for some fresh air to keep himself from thinking about how Avery would look naked with water glistening off her bronzed skin.

He had a case to solve, and the clock was ticking. He didn't have time for distractions.

Besides, Avery was not interested in him except for his expertise.

A van rolled by, slowing as it passed, and he saw someone take a picture of the house with his cell phone. Irritated, he headed toward it.

He waved at the van, and the driver pulled over to the curb. Two young men were inside, the camera guy snapping shot after shot of Avery's house and lawn.

"What are you doing?" Jaxon shouted.

The camera guy grinned. "Isn't this where the Tierney woman lives? The one whose brother's going to be executed?"

Dammit, the gawkers had already started.

"No, it's not." He flashed his badge. "What do you want with that woman anyway?"

"Just some pics. Heard she refused interviews, so I'm gonna catch her coming out and put it up on YouTube."

Then everyone would know where she lived, and all the crazies would come after her. "Get out of here, you scumbag," Jaxon said. "And if you bother Avery Tierney again, I'll arrest you for harassing innocent citizens."

The front door opened, and Avery stepped out.

"It's her!" the driver shouted. The other guy raised his camera.

Jaxon snatched the phone and deleted the pictures.

"Hey, you can't do that!" the guy shouted.

Avery apparently realized what was happening and stepped back inside the house.

"I can and I did." Jaxon shoved the phone back in the man's hands. "Now get out of here before I arrest you."

The guy cursed, but he ducked back inside the van and the driver sped off.

Jaxon waited until the van turned off the street, then went to the door.

Avery stood in the entryway, her purse slung over her shoulder.

"I'm sorry about that," he said.

Her frown deepened. "It's happened all my life. It's their last chance to get some drama out of Hank's conviction."

And make her life hell.

Avery didn't say it, but it was true. And not fair. But the media and curiosity seekers were seldom fair.

He was not going to let her be hurt by them again, though. Or by that threatening caller. He would guard her until this mess was over.

Until Hank was free and the real killer was locked behind bars.

AVERY TUGGED ON a hat as she and Jaxon left her house. She kept her head low as they drove from the neighborhood.

She'd kept to herself since she rented the house two years ago, had liked her privacy.

Publicity over the investigation and execution had robbed her of that now.

She'd considered changing her name over the years, but had decided that she wouldn't run from who she was.

By the time they arrived at the school, she'd summoned her courage. Jaxon identified himself to the receptionist in the school office.

"May I ask what this is about?" the redhead said.

"It's police business," Jaxon said.

The woman looked curious, but she refrained from pushing for more information and escorted them down the hall to the counselor's office.

She knocked on the door, then cracked it open. "Ms.

Hanover, Sergeant Jaxon Ward with the Texas Rangers is here to see you."

Jaxon stepped in, and Avery followed, twisting her hands together as she contemplated what to say. Delia Hanover was not what she'd expected or remembered. Of course, she hadn't seen her in twenty years.

Which meant Delia had been young, maybe early thirties at the time she'd known her. Her hair was slightly graying now, her eyes wary.

She rose from her desk, her face paling as her gaze latched with Avery's.

"Oh, my goodness, Avery," she rasped out. "I…guess I should have expected you to come."

Avery swallowed hard. "I saw my brother, Ms. Hanover. He's innocent."

The woman's brows pinched together. "I don't understand…"

Jaxon cleared his throat. "That's why we're here," Jaxon said. "We need your help to find the real killer, Ms. Hanover."

"Please call me Delia." She sank into her chair, a weary look in her eyes. "But Hank confessed, Avery. You said you saw him stabbing Wade Mulligan."

"Hank lied to protect me," Avery said. "He thought I stabbed Hank, so he tried to cover for me."

"Oh, my God, that can't be true," Delia said.

"I talked to him myself," Jaxon said. "And I believe his story." He planted his hands on top of her desk. "Which raises the question, who did kill Mulligan?"

The social worker's face turned ashen. "How should I know? I believed Hank."

"Think, Delia," Avery said. "Do you know anyone else who would have wanted Wade Mulligan dead?"

Chapter Nine

Jaxon studied Delia's shocked expression, searching her face for some clue that she knew more than she'd revealed. "Can you think of anyone else who would have wanted to hurt Mulligan?"

She shook her head. "No. No one that I can think of."

"What about his wife? Do you think she was capable of murdering him?"

Delia drummed her fingers on her arm. "They had their fights," she admitted. "Of course, I didn't know that when I placed Hank and Avery in the house."

"You had conducted follow-up visits to the home, didn't you?"

"A couple," Delia said, although a frown darkened her expression. "I was swamped at the time and should have gone by more often."

"Couldn't you tell that something was wrong?" He glanced at Avery and saw her bite down on her lip. "Couldn't you see the children were unhappy?"

She released a pained sigh. "None of the children I placed in foster care were happy, Sergeant Ward. Hank and Avery had already suffered the trauma and stigma of their father's arrest and their mother's abandonment. And they'd been shuffled through a half dozen other homes before I moved them to the Mulligans."

"Why were they moved from those homes?"

"Various reasons. The first family said they couldn't keep both of them. The next one, the mother had health issues. Another family claimed Hank was an angry kid and that he hit one of their own children."

"Were any other children in the Mulligan home when you placed Avery and Hank there?"

"No."

"What about Lois?" Avery asked.

Delia rubbed her forehead. "That's right. I forgot. She was there, but only about a week at the same time you were."

"What happened to her?" Jaxon asked.

Delia shrugged. "She was sent to a group home a few hours away."

"How about other children who lived with the Mulligans prior to Hank and Avery's placement?"

"I don't know much about them. I inherited the file from the former social worker, Erma Brant."

"There were no notes about abuse by the Mulligans in that file?"

Anxiety streaked Delia's face. "No. I…wish there had been."

Irritation shot through Jaxon. If she had known and had put them there anyway, she was partly responsible for what happened to Avery. "This is important, Delia. A man's life depends on it. What happened to the others?"

Delia stared at her hands, picking at her cuticles. "A couple aged out of the system. One boy was moved to a juvenile facility because he was caught stealing from a convenience store."

"Did any of the children, male or female, complain that they were abused?"

"No." She bit her nail. "And like I said, I didn't see any notes regarding abuse. I wouldn't have left Avery and Hank there if I had."

"But he abused me and my brother," Avery said. "I can't help thinking that we weren't the first."

The woman turned toward Avery, sorrow in her eyes. "I'm so sorry this happened to you, Avery. I should have seen it sooner, should have picked up on something."

"I should have told you what he was doing," Avery said. "But I was too ashamed."

"You were just a child," Delia said softly. "Mr. Mulligan was supposed to take care of you, but he took advantage of you instead."

"He said he loved me," Avery said with a bitter laugh. "That if I told anyone, he'd kill me and Hank." Her voice cracked. "It's my fault Hank went to jail. If I hadn't been so scared—"

"You had reason to be frightened." Delia walked around her desk, knelt in front of Avery and squeezed her hand. "So don't blame yourself. You were an innocent little girl, and all the adults in your life let you down. Including me." Self-recrimination underscored her voice. "If I'd known what Wade Mulligan was doing, I would have gotten you and Hank out of the house before Hank stabbed Mulligan."

Jaxon inhaled sharply. So she believed Hank was guilty. "You left your job shortly after Hank's arrest. Why did you switch jobs?"

Delia looked tormented. "Because I realized I'd made a mistake with Avery and Hank and decided I couldn't be responsible for something like that happening again."

Jaxon studied her for another long moment, then handed her a business card. "Thank you for your time. Please call me if you think of anything else that might help Hank Tierney. Especially anyone who might have had a problem with Mulligan."

She agreed, and Avery gave the woman a hug. "Thank you, Delia. Things may not have gone well at the Mulligans, but I know you tried to help me and my brother. I owe you for that."

Guilt streaked Delia's face as she hugged Avery in return. "I'm sorry about Hank. I really am."

Avery nodded, although tears filled her eyes as she pulled away.

"One more thing," Jaxon said. "Tell me the names of the other children who lived with the Mulligans."

Delia looked startled for a moment. "I'm not sure I could release that information even if I had it. But I left all those files in the social services office."

"Think about it and maybe you'll remember a name," Jaxon said. "One of them might be willing to come forward and testify about the abuse to help Hank." He pinned her with a dark look. "After all, you owe Avery and Hank that much."

AVERY STARED OUT the window at the passing scenery, Delia's ashen face flashing in her mind. Jaxon's last comment had upset the woman. But if she were upset, maybe she could help.

The bare trees looked as desolate as she felt. Hank had been in jail over half of his life and had missed the changing of the seasons, missed birthdays and holidays and building a career for himself.

She wanted him to breathe fresh air, to get a second chance at life and to spend his next birthday eating birthday cake and opening presents.

A noise sounded, and children raced onto the playground, laughing and talking. They looked so happy and carefree, just innocent kids skipping rope and playing children's games.

She and Hank had never been innocent. And neither one of them had a family.

Hank because he was incarcerated.

Her because she'd locked herself in a mental prison of her own. Shut herself off from trusting or loving a man because Mulligan had robbed her of her innocence.

She would show that bitter, mean old man that he wouldn't take anything else from her. She would get Hank out.

Then she would work on herself. Learn to trust again.

"Are you okay?" Jaxon asked as they drove away from the school.

Avery nodded. "Delia seemed sincere."

Jaxon clenched his jaw. "Maybe. But she should have pushed Hank's attorney to explore the abuse angle in Hank's defense."

Avery rubbed the scar around her wrist. "That's my fault. I should have spoken up and confided in her."

"If she was good at her job, she would have picked up on it," Jaxon said. "And she should have researched the family and made certain the home was safe and secure before leaving you there."

Avery couldn't argue with that. But she sensed Delia carried guilt around with her already regarding that mistake.

Jaxon maneuvered through traffic until he reached the body shop on the edge of town. Several rusted, broken-down cars sat on cinder blocks, a fenced-in area held a mountain of old tires and other car parts and pieces, ranging from new fenders to motors, were scattered across the junkyard.

"What are we doing here?" Avery asked.

"Casey, my contact at the social service office, sent me a list of children who lived with the Mulligans prior to you and your brother. One of the boys, Shane Fowler, runs this place."

Avery's heart pounded. "You think if we get some of the others to speak up, it might help Hank."

Jaxon frowned and adjusted his hat as he reached for the

door handle. "It might. It'll certainly establish a pattern of abuse, which could be argued in a self-defense plea."

Hope fluttered in Avery's chest. Mulligan had abused her and Hank.

Which meant they most likely weren't the first. And they probably wouldn't have been the last if someone hadn't stopped the old man by ending his life.

THE JUNKYARD LOOKED like a sad place where old cars had gone to die. Jaxon had worked at one when he was a teenager, though, and he understood the value of recycling, of reusing good parts in another vehicle to save the owner the cost of expensive repairs.

He also couldn't fault any guy from making an honest living, and being an auto mechanic or specializing in body repairs took skills.

Ironically, though, Mulligan had worked at a garage years ago.

Jaxon took Avery's elbow as they walked across the yard to the office. Hubcaps, tires and an assortment of axels were scattered in organized piles near the trailer. He knocked but no one answered, so he opened the door and peeked inside.

"No one is here."

Avery touched his arm. "I see someone over there."

She pointed to a row lined with hoods, and Jaxon headed that way. "Mr. Fowler?"

A stocky man wearing a plaid shirt and overalls looked up, adjusted his hat to shade his eyes and frowned. His arms were tatted up, a jagged scar discolored his left cheek and his hands looked battered and bruised. "Yeah?"

Jaxon flashed his badge, identified himself and introduced Avery.

"Am I in some sort of trouble with the law?" Fowler coughed into his hand. "I mean, I pay my taxes and all. And I run a legitimate business."

The man's paranoia made Jaxon question whether or not he might be doing something illegal. But Jaxon wasn't interested in petty crimes.

"No, sir," Jaxon said. "We came to talk to you about Wade Mulligan. You lived with him when you were a kid, didn't you?"

Fowler's eyes sharpened. "Yeah. But that was a lifetime ago."

Avery cleared her throat. "Shane, I'm Hank Tierney's sister, Avery. We also lived with the Mulligans."

"Aw, hell," the man muttered. "I shoulda recognized you from the news. They been talking about your brother's execution all week. Showed a picture of you when you was little."

Avery's mouth twitched. "That's because the date is approaching. I'm trying to stop him from being put to death."

Fowler wiped his greasy hands on a rag he pulled from his back pocket. "What's that got to do with me?"

"Both Hank and Avery were abused by Mr. Mulligan." Jaxon watched for a reaction, but Fowler didn't seem surprised. "How was the family when you lived with the Mulligans?"

The man backed up, his posture defensive. "Like I said, it was a long damn time ago."

"But you remember whether or not he hit you," Jaxon said.

Fowler ran a hand across the scar on his face. "So what if he did? I was a smart mouth back then."

"Were there any girls living in the home when you lived there?" Jaxon asked.

Fear flickered in Fowler's gray eyes. "Yeah, a couple."

"Did Wade Mulligan ever go in their room at night?"

Fowler rubbed his hands on the grease rag again, looking into the black smears as if they might offer him a way out.

"I was just a kid back then," he said. "I didn't know what he was doing was wrong."

Avery sucked in a sharp breath. "So he did molest the girls?"

Fowler looked up at her, guilt registering a second before he jerked his head to stare across his junkyard. "I didn't see nothing, but I heard 'em crying at night. I went to the door once, but he beat me and told me to stay out of grown-up business."

"So you stayed quiet?" Jaxon said, unable to hide the disgust in his tone.

Fowler gestured toward his scarred cheek. "Monster sliced my face that night. Said the next time he'd put that knife in my gut. What the hell was I supposed to do?"

"You could have told someone," Avery said angrily. "You could have called 911 or let the social worker know. If you had, you might have saved those girls and me and my brother."

AVERY WAS TREMBLING so badly she thought she was going to have to sit down. Anger at this man ballooned inside her. If he'd turned in Mulligan, she and Hank would have been spared.

Their entire life had been destroyed by the events that had happened in that house. Events that could have been prevented.

"I'm sorry," Fowler said, his voice almost childlike now. "I was scared. I...know I shoulda said something."

"Classic abuse," Jaxon said. "Who were the girls who were there when you were?"

Fowler leaned against the fence, wiping sweat from his neck with his hand. "Priscilla Janice and Renee Feldon."

"Do you know where either of them are now?"

"Priscilla OD'd on heroin a few years back. Don't know

where Renee is. Last I heard she was turning tricks on the streets."

"When was that?" Jaxon asked.

"About ten years ago."

Avery clenched her hands together. One girl had over-dosed while another resorted to hooking. No doubt both their problems had been caused by Wade Mulligan's abuse.

"If we get a stay for Hank Tierney, would you be willing to testify to the abuse?" Jaxon asked.

Fowler looked down at his shoes. "I don't know. I'm not sorry the bastard's dead, but I ain't proud that he used me for a punching bag."

"Please," Avery said. "Wade Mulligan deserved to die, but my brother didn't kill him."

Jaxon cleared his throat. "You want your self-respect back? Then stand up to him."

"But he's dead," Fowler said.

"My brother isn't," Avery said quietly.

The man looked up at her, his scar reddening in the sun-light. "All right, I'll do it."

They thanked him, then walked back to the car in silence. Avery flipped on the radio to distract herself from the bit-terness eating at her as Jaxon drove from the parking lot.

But a special newscast was airing. "This late-breaking story in. Hank Tierney, whose execution is scheduled just a few days away, was stabbed today in a prison fight. Guards were moving him from his cell block when a fire erupted in a neighboring cell. Before they realized what was happen-ing, two inmates attacked Tierney."

Avery choked on a sob while she waited to hear if her brother was still alive.

Chapter Ten

"Tierney was taken to the infirmary, where he was treated and received thirteen stitches in his abdomen," the reporter continued. "Investigators are looking into the attack, and Tierney has been moved to isolation for his protection."

Avery clutched her middle, pain knifing through her. "I have to go see him."

"I doubt they'll allow that," Jaxon said. "But I can call and make sure he's all right."

"Will you?"

"Of course." He was beginning to think he'd do anything she asked. He retrieved his cell phone and punched the number for the prison. "Yes, this is Sergeant Jaxon Ward. I need to speak to the warden."

A pause, and then Jaxon spoke again.

"I'm calling to check on Hank Tierney."

Silence from Jaxon while he listened to the warden, then a heavy sigh. "All right, alert me if there are any more problems."

Avery tugged at his arm as he hung up. "Well, how is he?"

"No major organs were damaged. He's going to be all right."

His comment didn't soothe her worries. "Why would someone attack Hank?"

Jaxon squared his shoulders. "Prison fights are almost a daily occurrence, Avery. You can't read too much into this."

Avery's anger rose. "The timing has to mean something. Somebody wants Hank dead." She clutched Jaxon's arm, the wheels turning in her head. "Do you think it's because we're asking questions?"

Jaxon's hands tightened around the steering wheel. "That's possible, but it might not be related to us. Hank probably made enemies on the inside."

"But why try to kill him when he's scheduled to die?" Emotions clogged Avery's throat. "The only answer that makes sense is that someone doesn't want him to be cleared."

Jaxon cut his eyes toward her, his expression dark. "Try not to jump to conclusions, Avery."

"How can I not?" Hysteria clawed at her. "First I receive a threatening call and now Hank is attacked."

Jaxon cupped her face between his hands. "Look at me, Avery. Hank is going to be all right. And I'm not going to let anyone hurt you."

She blinked to stem the tears, but she was terrified for Hank and for herself.

Maybe Hank had survived this time, but what if someone came after him again?

UNABLE TO STAND to see Avery suffering, Jaxon pulled her into his arms and rubbed her back. "I'm sorry, Avery. You don't deserve this."

"Maybe I do," she said in a low voice. "If I hadn't told the police I saw Hank stabbing Wade, maybe the lawyers would have gotten him off."

"It's not your fault," Jaxon said. "There was too much evidence against Hank anyway. Even without his confession, his prints on the knife and the number of stab wounds would have earned him a conviction." She relaxed against him for a moment, and he stroked her hair. The sweet scent of her fruity shampoo suffused him, stirring emotions and desires he didn't want to feel.

She was strong and resilient, but she had deserved to have adults who loved her and took care of her, not ones who mistreated her and made her feel ashamed.

Answering her questions about the attack on her brother wasn't simple, either. It was very possible that Hank was assaulted because they were trying to free him.

There were protestors both for and against his execution. The story had been splattered across the news for the past two weeks. And if one of the other kids who'd lived with Mulligan had killed him, that person wouldn't want Hank exonerated and the finger pointed at him or her.

"But Hank's been through so much," she said. "I hate to think about him being in solitary confinement."

"It's for his protection," Jaxon said. "Now, there's another foster child who lived with the Mulligans that we need to question."

Avery sighed against him and lifted her head. Her eyes were luminous with pain and something else indefinable. Maybe surprise that she'd allowed herself to lean on him.

She inhaled sharply, visibly pulling herself together. "Who is it?"

Jaxon released her, instantly missing the feel of her in his arms. "Lois Thacker, the girl you remembered. She's a cop."

Avery's eyes flickered with a spark of hope. "Let's go."

Jaxon started the engine and swung the vehicle back onto the road. Avery turned to look out the window while he drove toward Laredo.

AVERY CLOSED HER eyes during the ride and fell asleep, her mind heavy with fear for Hank and the pressing time restraints of getting him released.

But her nightmares returned to another night at the Mulligans....

It was dark inside, the rain pinging off the tin roof. Joleen was passed out on the couch, and Wade had just come in. He saw there was no food on the table and bellowed, then threw the cast-iron skillet across the room. It hit the wall with a bang, then dropped to the floor with a thunderous sound.

"Come on, Avery." Hank grabbed her hand and they ran outside. Rain soaked them, but they didn't stop running until they reached the old shed. Hank slid open the door and ushered her inside.

"We'll hide behind that cabinet." They crawled behind the cabinet, pulling an old blanket over them to hide in case Wade came looking.

A few minutes later, the door screeched open. Then Wade yelled their names. A cigarette lighter flicked, the glow of it bursting into the shed.

She buried her head against her brother, and he covered her with himself as they waited in the dark....

Avery jerked awake as the car stopped, trembling as she recalled what had happened next. In a fit of rage, Wade had thrown tools and junk across the shed.

But he hadn't found them.

They'd spent the night there that evening, cowering and hiding and cold.

Hank had saved her.

She had to save him now.

When she looked up, Jaxon was watching her. "Bad dream?"

Embarrassed, she looked down at her hands. At the scar that was always there, reminding her of where she'd come from. Not that she needed it.

Her scars ran deep.

"Memories."

His dark gaze settled over her, and he reached out and covered her hand with his. She started to pull away, but he touched the scar with one finger, and she watched him trace it.

"We'll get the truth, Avery. I promise."

She wanted to curl her hand in his as she had done with Hank's when she was small. Wanted to bury herself against him and hold on to him forever.

But she had to stand on her own.

JAXON AND AVERY stopped at the receptionist desk, where he introduced himself and Avery and asked to speak to Lois Thacker. He'd already looked her up and learned she was a beat cop and covered a section of town known for hookers, addicts and the homeless.

"She and her partner, Bain Whitefeather, are on patrol now."

"Can you call her and ask her to meet us?" Jaxon said.

The woman nodded, made the call, then hung up. "She said to meet her at the Cactus Coffee Shop."

"Thanks." He and Avery walked back outside to his SUV, and he plugged the name of the coffee shop into his GPS. Fifteen minutes later, they parked in front of the small corner café with the big cactus in front. A patrol car sat next to the sign, a Native American cop inside on the radio.

When they entered, he spotted a female in uniform already seated with coffee in a booth. She was probably in her mid-thirties, with dirty blond hair, a sharp angled face and short wide hands. She was slightly overweight, wore no makeup and her curly hair was cropped short.

"Do you want something?" he asked Avery.

"Just plain coffee."

He ordered them each a cup, and then they walked over to Lois. He flashed his badge and identified himself.

Avery extended her hand. "I'm Avery Tierney. Thank you for meeting us, Lois."

The cop's gray eyes flickered with recognition. "You're Hank Tierney's sister?"

Avery nodded, her body tense. "His execution is coming up, and I'm trying to stop it."

"Hmm. Interesting." Lois rubbed her hand over the baton at her waist. "I thought he did it. In fact, I was tempted to send him a thank-you note. Can't believe they convicted him in the first place."

"I agree," Avery said.

Jaxon adjusted his Stetson. "We now have reason to believe he didn't murder Mulligan, that his confession was false."

Lois pursed her thick lips. "False? Only time that happens is when a suspect is coerced or covering for someone else." Her gaze latched on to Avery. "That it? He covered for you?"

"Yes, because he thought I stabbed Wade Mulligan, but I didn't."

"We think that someone else came into the house that night and killed Mulligan," Jaxon explained. "So we're talking to everyone associated with the Mulligan family."

"The old lady hated him," Lois admitted. "But she was scared to death of him, too. I can't imagine her having the guts to stab him." She shrugged. "Although from what I've seen on the streets, you never know about people. She could have had it planned and sneaked in and offed him."

"How long did you live with the Mulligans?" Jaxon asked.

Lois scowled and then took a swig of her coffee. "About a year. I was thirteen at the time."

Jaxon's pulse spiked. "Thirteen. Were any other kids there when you lived in the house?"

Anger tightened the lines on Lois's face. "Yeah. A little girl named Dotty."

"What happened when you were at the house?" Jaxon asked.

Lois clenched the coffee cup so tightly coffee spilled over. "Joleen drank a lot, passed out almost every night."

Avery cleared her throat. "And Wade?"

Lois looked up at Avery, pain mingling with rage. "He used to come in my room. Used me. Hit me. Did whatever he wanted while Joleen lay passed out in the other room."

"Did you ever tell anyone?" he asked.

She rubbed a hand down her coffee cup. "Not at first. I tried to fight him off, but I was a scrawny thing back then. Didn't do any good."

"So he continued?" Avery said.

Lois nodded. "But one night when he was done with me, I heard him going into Dotty's room." Her voice warbled. "She was seven. The tiniest little thing you ever saw. Scared of the dark and dogs and everything else in the world."

Silence stretched between them, the reality needling Jaxon. "What happened that night?"

"I grabbed the baseball bat, ran in there and hit the bastard with it. Knocked him upside the head till he got off Dotty."

Pain wrenched Avery's face, making Jaxon want to hold her again. But they had to finish this interview.

"Next day the old man sent me away. But I was scared for Dotty and told the social worker what happened."

Avery gasped softly "You told on him?"

Lois nodded, her eyes grave with dark memories. "Heard they took Dotty to another house. I thought they might lock the old man up, but they didn't." She tapped her badge. "That's when I decided to become a cop. Try to clean garbage off the streets."

"Do you know what happened to Dotty?" Jaxon asked.

Lois propped her head on one hand for a moment, then gave a clipped nod. "Used my connections here at the department about a year ago and found out that she died in an alley. Pimp beat her to death."

Avery gasped. "That's horrible."

"What's bad is that I tried to help Dotty by telling, and

it didn't do a damn bit of good. Two months after I was taken away, I heard they were putting kids back with the Mulligans."

"Who was the social worker?" Jaxon asked.

"Some lady named Erma Brant."

"She never should have placed other kids there," Avery whispered.

Jaxon nodded agreement as he studied Lois. She'd been abused by the old man, caught him abusing another younger girl, then been removed from the home. She must have been furious when she learned more children were being put in that situation.

Had she been angry enough to sneak back to the Mulligans' and kill Wade, then escape without anyone knowing she was there?

Chapter Eleven

Jaxon studied Lois. She was tough, strong, had been a fighter. And she was smart.

Smart enough to have planned revenge on Mulligan?

"Lois, where were you the night Mulligan was murdered?"

Lois's sharp gaze flew to Jaxon, her jaw twitching. "Damn. You think I killed the old man?"

Jaxon shrugged. "If Hank didn't, it stands to reason that one of the other kids who'd been abused by him did."

Lois ran a finger along the rim of her cup. "I suppose I can see why you'd think that." She scribbled down a number and a name. "The night he died, I was at a group home. The house parent's name was Henrietta."

"Does she still live there?" Jaxon asked.

"Yeah, I had to see a juvy there about a month ago. Place hasn't changed a bit. Old and run-down, but Henrietta was decent. If it wasn't for her, I might have wound up on the streets."

Avery shifted in her chair. "Can you think of anyone else who would have wanted Wade dead? Another kid who was placed there?"

"Hell, probably all of them."

True, Jaxon thought. "Anyone specific?"

The cop finished her coffee and crumpled the cup in her

hands. "There was one other boy and his sister who lived with the Mulligans before me. I heard Mulligan used to beat the boy, and later, that his sister got pregnant."

Suspicions mounted in Jaxon's mind. "What happened?"

"Mulligan forced the girl to get an abortion. I think she wound up having a breakdown or something."

"Did Erma Brant place them there, as well?"

Lois nodded. "If you ask me, that woman should have had to serve time herself."

THIRTY MINUTES LATER, Avery and Jaxon located BJ Wilson at a rehab facility on the east side of town. The way the rustic building was set back on farmland and surrounded by trees made it look like a wilderness retreat.

A barn looked as if it held horses, and another area appeared to be used for farming. Part of the therapy for the residents?

From Jaxon's phone call, he'd learned BJ was a heroin addict and had been caught stealing from his employer.

He'd spent two years in prison, but upon release, he immediately hit the streets for drugs. According to his probation officer, he'd managed to get BJ in rehab instead of sending him back to prison, but he wasn't hopeful the guy would last.

"I feel sorry for him," Avery said as they entered the rehab clinic. "No doubt his past put him here."

"Choices put him here," Jaxon said in a brusque tone. "A lot of people experience trauma in their lives. Not everyone turns to drugs or violence to deal with it."

"But he never had a chance."

Jaxon shrugged. "You went through hell, but you didn't turn to drugs or violence."

Avery's heart swelled at the admiration in his tone. Then again, he was giving her too much credit. She might not be an addict or a criminal, but she was scarred.

She'd never had a relationship with a man in her life. Never gotten close to anyone.

A receptionist greeted them and showed them to the director's office. On both sides of the hall were rooms that resembled classrooms, and a medical office sat on the corner of the corridor. Another door led to an outside garden area, complete with a recreational area that included seating, card tables, an area for arts and crafts activities and a path that looked as if it led to the creek.

The director, Cam Sanders, was a middle-aged woman with wavy red hair and a kind smile but sad eyes.

Jaxon introduced himself and Avery and explained that he needed to talk to BJ.

"How is he doing?" Avery asked.

"He's been here three weeks and finally settling in. But I'm not sure he'll make it out on the streets by himself. He needs supervision and structure and doesn't seem to be able to manage that on his own."

She steepled her hands on the desk. "What is it you want to talk to him about?"

Avery glanced at Jaxon, and he indicated for her to take the lead.

"My brother is Hank Tierney." She paused, giving Ms. Sanders time to process her statement. Recognition quickly dawned.

"I see. What do you and your brother have to do with BJ?"

"We lived in the same foster home, not at the same time, but BJ knew the man my brother was accused of killing."

"Other than dredging up painful memories, what do you think you'll accomplish by talking to BJ?"

Jaxon shifted. "We're building a case to show that Wade Mulligan was abusive to the children under his care."

The director buttoned her suit coat. "But Hank Tierney

confessed, and proving Mulligan was abusive only confirms his motive."

"Yes, but it also opens the door to others with motive, which could be enough to cast reasonable doubt on Hank," Jaxon pointed out.

Irritation flashed in the woman's eyes. "So you came here to ask BJ if he killed Mulligan?"

Avery's stomach clenched. "No. We just want to know what happened with him and his sister."

Ms. Sanders stood. "I don't know if that's a good idea. The counselor working with him said his traumatic past contributed to his addiction problems."

"My brother's life depends on us learning the truth," Avery argued.

Jaxon crossed his arms. "Isn't facing the truth imperative for a patient's recovery?"

Ms. Sanders worried her bottom lip with her teeth, fidgeting as if she were debating the issue. "Let me speak to BJ's counselor. If he agrees, I'll let you talk to him."

"Thank you," Avery and Jaxon both murmured at once.

The woman's heels clicked as she crossed the room and left. Jaxon paced to the window and looked out. The skies looked gloomy and gray, winter taking its toll as wind swirled dead grass and tumbleweed across the parking lot.

A second later, the director returned. "All right. Dr. Kemp says you can speak with BJ, but only in his presence."

They followed the woman down a hall past several private rooms to a sunroom off the back that overlooked the creek.

A thin man in his late thirties wearing jeans and a flannel shirt sat in a straight chair at a small table set up with checkers. He looked antsy and nervous and kept tapping one of the checkers against the board.

Another man, more distinguished looking, graying at his temples, sat across from him. Obviously the therapist. He angled himself toward them as they approached.

Ms. Sanders introduced them, and Dr. Kemp gestured for them to join him and BJ around the checkers table. The doctor addressed BJ. "BJ, Jaxon Ward is a Texas Ranger, and Avery's brother, Hank, is in prison for murdering Wade Mulligan."

BJ rocked himself back and forth, his eyes twitching as if he had a nervous tic.

"You… Hank killed him. That's good," BJ said.

Avery sucked in a deep breath. "Wade Mulligan deserved to die, didn't he, BJ?"

BJ clawed at his arms. "Yeah, he was a monster."

"Did he hurt you and your sister?" Jaxon asked.

BJ clawed harder, drawing Avery's gaze to his track marks. "Yeah, he was mean. He used to beat me. And what he did to Imogene… I should have killed him."

Avery's heart pounded, but Dr. Kemp gave her a warning look.

"Did she tell anyone what he did?" Jaxon asked.

Emotions clouded BJ's face, his eyes twitching again. "No, she was ashamed. But she cried all the time and then she got pregnant."

"I'm so sorry for what he did," Avery said. "I know how she felt, how you felt, because Wade Mulligan did the same thing to me and my brother."

"He got you pregnant?" BJ asked.

Avery quickly shook her head. "No, but he came into my room at night. I used to cry all the time, too. And I was glad when he died."

"Me, too." BJ stood and bounced from one foot to the other. "I wanted to kill him. I should have. Especially after he made Imogene get rid of the baby." His voice cracked. "That destroyed her. She didn't want to be pregnant, but she hated what he made her do. And then she got so depressed she cut her wrists with a kitchen knife."

Avery's breath grew pained as she imagined the scene.

"Did you see her do that?" she asked softly.

BJ stopped bouncing and sank into his chair again, then looked at the doctor.

"Go on, BJ, you're doing fine," Dr. Kemp encouraged.

BJ wiped at his eyes. "No, but I found her. She climbed in the bathtub. She wasn't naked or anything. She was just in there in her clothes, and she cut her wrists and there was blood everywhere." He sniffed and rubbed his nose on his sleeve. "I guess she got in the tub 'cause she knew he'd be mad if she made a mess on the floor."

Tears burned the backs of Avery's eyelids. If Imogene had attempted suicide in that house, why had the social worker placed her and Hank there afterward?

JAXON GRITTED HIS teeth at the injustice of the entire situation. People hadn't been doing their jobs, or else so many kids wouldn't have been hurt by Mulligan.

He wanted to have a chat with Erma Brant.

But he forced his voice to be calm when he addressed BJ. "What happened after the suicide attempt?"

BJ looked to the doctor as if asking permission to finish, and Dr. Kemp gave him an encouraging nod. "They took her to a hospital," BJ said. "And from there to a juvenile facility. They tried to put me in a group home, but after the Mulligans, I wasn't going to stay, so I ran away."

"Where did you go?" Avery asked.

"I lived on the streets." BJ shrugged as if that had been nothing. "It was better than getting beat every day and watching your sister get molested."

"Where's your sister now?" Avery asked.

BJ became agitated again and clawed at his arms once more. "In a hospital. They say she went crazy. Half the time, she doesn't even know me anymore."

His voice choked, and Dr. Kemp stood and rubbed BJ's shoulders. "You did good, BJ. I know it's painful, but remember what we said about healing. Talking about it can help."

"How?" he cried. "It doesn't change a damn thing. Imogene's still locked up in that crazy house." He flung his hand across the checkers and sent them scattering across the floor. "And look at me. I'm nothing but a junkie."

"You're stronger than you think," Dr. Kemp said. "You're working hard in therapy and on your way to recovery."

Jaxon sensed it was time to leave, but he had to ask one more question. "Where were you the night Mulligan was killed, BJ?"

Dr. Kemp pivoted, eyes blazing with anger.

BJ looked stunned for a moment as if he didn't understand the question.

"That's enough," Dr. Kemp said. "We're finished."

Jaxon watched BJ sink into the chair and begin rocking himself again. "Do you remember, BJ?"

BJ's eyes looked tormented as he lifted his head. "I told you, on the streets. Probably passed out in a ditch somewhere."

Dr. Kemp gestured toward the door. "I said, it's time to go."

Jaxon gave him a clipped nod, then placed his hand at the back of Avery's waist. "Thank you for talking to us, BJ."

Avery didn't speak as they walked out to the car, but once they shut the door, she sagged against the seat. "I feel so bad for him and his sister."

Jaxon nodded. "So do I. But remember, Avery. If Hank didn't kill Mulligan, someone else did."

Her eyes widened. "You think BJ might have?"

He shrugged and started the engine. "Both he and Imogene had motive. And he has no alibi."

Avery fiddled with her jacket. "You're right. He could have been high, killed Wade and not even remembered it."

Jaxon clenched the steering wheel with a white-knuckled

grip. "True. And it'll be hard to prove, although his story could cast doubt on Hank's guilt." He pulled out of the parking lot. "There's one more thing. BJ said his sister tried to kill herself with a kitchen knife. Mulligan was also stabbed with a kitchen knife."

"That's right," Avery said. "Hank admitted he took a knife from the kitchen earlier that day."

"According to the trial transcript, the prosecutor argued that act implied the murder was premeditated."

"He took it to defend himself and me," Avery interjected.

"I understand that," Jaxon said. "And I don't blame Hank. I wouldn't blame BJ or Imogene or Lois Thacker, either, if they'd killed Mulligan. I just don't understand why the defense attorney didn't bring all this up at the trial."

"Because of the confession," Avery admitted, her voice heavy.

"It was still shoddy police work and defense work," Jaxon said. "Let's talk to Imogene and see if she can add anything to BJ's story. Then we'll pay Hank's original attorney a visit. And we're going to talk to Erma Brant."

"I have some questions for her," Avery said darkly.

He spun the vehicle toward the local psychiatric hospital. If Imogene were as unstable as BJ implied, they might not learn anything.

Then again, with every person who confirmed that Mulligan was an abuser and rapist, they added another suspect to the growing list.

Suspects that might lead them to the real killer. Or at least to a new trial that could save Hank's life.

"AVERY TIERNEY IS working with a Texas Ranger to get her brother exonerated."

"But Hank stabbed Mulligan a dozen times."

"True. But the Ranger says he only confessed to save his sister because he thought she killed Mulligan."

That statement could blow the original case to hell.

No…it was the pathetic attempt of a death row inmate to save himself at the last minute, nothing more.

But if a Ranger was asking questions and got a new trial, police would be looking for the real killer.

That would be dangerous.

Hell, Hank Tierney had been violent and had stabbed his foster father multiple times. That was the damn truth.

Whether or not he'd delivered the deadly blow didn't matter, did it?

Hank was violent. He would have hurt someone else. Probably *would* have killed someone if he hadn't been stopped.

Getting him off the streets had been the best thing for everyone, hadn't it?

Chapter Twelve

Avery had been surprised the rehab facility wasn't drab and depressing. Instead the sunroom and outside facilities were cheery and relaxing.

But the mental hospital radiated a different feel. The building was housed behind a gate, as if it were a prison. The building was old and weathered, the land dry and parched. Jaxon phoned ahead to ask permission to visit Imogene, and was given an okay, although the nurse in charge warned him that Imogene would probably be unresponsive.

Inside, the hospital walls were painted a dull green, the floors were faded gray and everything from the dingy chairs in the waiting room to the cafeteria they passed desperately need a face-lift.

The doctor in charge of Imogene's care, a fiftysome-thing bohemian-looking lady, met them in her office. "I'm Dr. Pirkle. I understand the reason you're here, but I'm not sure Imogene will be helpful."

"Just let us talk to her for a minute," Jaxon said. "It's important."

The woman's sharp eyes darted sideways to Avery. "Her mental state is fragile. She's making strides, but she suffered a psychotic break, is bipolar and struggles with depression. She doesn't need a setback."

"We don't want to hurt her," Avery said. "You can be

present when we talk to her. And the moment you sense we might be upsetting her, we'll leave."

Dr. Pirkle stood, her brows knitted. "All right. Follow me."

She led them to a room across from another nurse's station. Dr. Pirkle knocked gently on the door and opened it.

Avery's heart hammered at the sight of the frail-looking blonde sitting by the window staring outside. She was so thin that Avery wondered if she ever ate, her skin so pale she obviously didn't get out in the sun much.

She didn't look at them as they crossed the room, but kept her hands buried in the folds of the blanket on her lap. Unlike her brother, whose anxiety had displayed itself by perpetual motion, Imogene was so still she might have been a stone statue.

Dr. Pirkle laid a hand on Imogene's shoulder and knelt in front of her. "Imogene, you have some visitors." She introduced them, but Imogene didn't show a reaction.

The doctor stood and gestured for them to begin.

"Why don't you try talking to her?" Jaxon suggested to Avery.

Emotion thickened her throat as she pulled a chair from the corner and situated it beside Imogene. When she sat down, she offered Imogene a smile.

"Imogene, I'm Avery," she said softly. "We just talked to your brother, BJ."

Her eyelids fluttered, and she slowly turned her head to look at her. Avery's chest constricted at the flat, dead look in the young woman's eyes.

"He's all right," Avery said. "He loves you and misses you, Imogene."

Imogene's lip quivered slightly.

"He's sorry that you're having a hard time and wants you to get better."

Imogene's breath quickened slightly.

"I know what happened to you," Avery said softly. "Because I lived in the house with Wade and Joleen Mulligan."

Tension stretched in the silence, Imogene's breath becoming unsteady.

"Mr. Mulligan hurt me, too," Avery said. "And my brother, Hank, he used to beat him like he did your brother."

Imogene's hands dug deeper into the blanket.

"One night after Mr. Mulligan came into my room, he ended up dead. The police thought my brother killed him. You may have heard the story."

Imogene looked into Avery's eyes, her only acknowledgment.

"But they were wrong. Hank did stab Wade, but Wade was already dead." She paused, searching for a reaction.

An odd, eerie smile slowly formed on Imogene's face.

"We believe someone else sneaked into the house that night. Someone who took a kitchen knife and stabbed Wade before my brother came into the room."

"You and your brother had reason to hate Mulligan," Jaxon said. "He forced you to have an abortion. Your brother ran away and started doing drugs."

"Do you think it's possible that he broke into the house and killed Wade?" Avery asked.

Dr. Pirkle's soft gasp of disapproval echoed between them.

"I did it," Imogene said, shocking them all. "I wanted him dead."

Her eyes suddenly looked wild, excited, crazed. She lifted her hands above her head, positioning them as if she were holding a knife, and brought it down in a stabbing motion. "I hated him and wanted him dead. I stabbed him in the chest, over and over and over." Her voice rose, her breath raspy as she continued the motion. "He shouted out in pain, but this time I was the one making him cry. He begged me to stop, begged me to let him go, but I didn't." She shook her head back and forth, lost in the moment. "I stabbed him again. Blood spurted everywhere. All over his chest and face, all over my hands." She looked down and touched her shirt. "All over my blouse. I had a white blouse on that day, but then it was red. But it looked pretty that way. Pretty with his blood on it because that meant he was dead, and he couldn't ever touch me again."

She drove her hands down one more time, twisting them around and around as if she were burying the knife inside Wade Mulligan's body. "And then he stopped crying. Stopped breathing. It was so beautiful."

Another silence fell over the room as they digested what she'd said.

"So you killed Wade Mulligan?" Jaxon finally asked.

Dr. Pirkle cleared her throat. "That's enough."

Imogene closed her eyes and made a soft mewling sound. "I killed him. Then BJ killed him again. Then we dragged his body outside and dug a hole and buried him in it. I threw dirt on his face and laughed and laughed and laughed as we spread it over him. Then BJ pried open his mouth and dumped more dirt inside it so he couldn't ever yell or say vile things again." She started to hum beneath her breath. "We covered him all over so we'd never see those mean eyes again, never see them again…."

Avery's stomach knotted.

Had Imogene or her brother really stabbed Wade, or was she simply delusional?

JAXON AND AVERY waited in the hallway for Dr. Pirkle as she spoke to Imogene. When she emerged from the room, anger slashed her features.

"I can't believe you came here to implicate Imogene in a crime to exonerate your brother, Miss Tierney." She slanted Jaxon a harsh look. "And you, Sergeant Ward, you know that anything Imogene said in her condition is not going to stand up in court."

"I'm aware of that," Jaxon said. "But if Imogene did kill Mulligan, or if her brother did, and you know the truth, you should tell us."

"Anything I've learned through my patient's private therapy sessions is privileged and you know that, too."

Avery sighed next to him, and Jaxon wanted to pull her up against him, but he refrained. "Yes, of course. Although if Imogene killed Wade, you could use an insanity defense. And Hank would get the freedom he deserves."

"She didn't kill him," Dr. Pirkle said. "Although she certainly sounded venomous in there, her story was just that— a story. A fantasy. In her delusions, she has imagined doing what she didn't have the courage to do back then."

"You mean she blames herself?" Avery asked.

Dr. Pirkle shrugged. "Most victims experience some sort of self-blame, think they deserved the abuse and ask themselves why they didn't do things differently." Her stare pierced Avery. "I'm sure you understand that feeling."

Jaxon's jaw tightened, but Avery simply nodded.

"More than you know." She lifted her chin. "That's one reason I'm determined to free my brother. He wouldn't have lied about killing Wade if he hadn't been protecting me."

Dr. Pirkle squeezed Avery's hand in hers. "I'm truly sorry for how you've suffered, for how your brother suffered. After hearing Imogene's story, I believe that man deserved what he got. But I don't see how I can help you any further."

Jaxon wanted to be angry with the doctor, but he understood her position. Hell, Imogene was an emotionally unstable woman and needed protection.

But he hadn't learned anything new here, and he needed something that would make a judge grant a stay for Hank.

He thanked Dr. Pirkle, and he and Avery walked down the hall, the silence thick with anxiety.

His phone buzzed, and he checked the text. The forensic examiner from the lab.

Stop by. I need to show you something I saw on Mulligan's autopsy report.

Jaxon texted that he'd be right there, then gestured for Avery to get in the SUV.

"We're going to the lab," Jaxon said. "Our analyst finally reviewed Mulligan's autopsy."

Avery leaned against the back of the seat, a troubled look on her face. "Imogene is a wreck and her brother an addict. I'm not sure they can help us.'

"Two more lives completely destroyed by Wade Mulligan," Jaxon muttered.

"I know. Which makes me wonder why the social worker placed me and Hank with the family. I can't believe nobody picked up on the problems in that house. Especially after Lois and Dotty."

"SOMEONE SHOULD HAVE stopped him," Jaxon agreed. "We're going to talk to Erma Brant after we see this autopsy and find out just what she was thinking."

Avery twisted her hands together. "How does she live with herself?"

"Good question. Ask her that when we see her."

"I intend to."

Dark clouds hovered above, threatening rain, late-afternoon shadows slanting across the road. It took almost an hour to reach the county lab, which was housed in an old brick building, set away from the road about a mile from the warehouse district.

They bypassed several offices and labs where workers were processing evidence collected from various cases, running DNA tests and analyzing photographs.

Jaxon knocked on the door to Dr. Jeremy Riggins's office. The doctor yelled for him to come in, and Avery followed him inside. Jaxon made the introductions, and Dr. Riggins led them over to his workstation.

"I studied the autopsy report," Dr. Riggins said. "Wade Mulligan definitely bled out from a stab wound that penetrated his aorta."

That was nothing new.

"You said you found something else?" Jaxon asked.

Dr. Riggins glanced at Avery. "Maybe you should step out, Miss Tierney. What I'm going to show you is pretty graphic."

Avery folded her arms. "Go ahead. I'll be fine."

Dr. Riggins glanced at Jaxon for confirmation, and Jaxon gestured for him to continue.

He indicated a whiteboard on the wall, then flipped it over on the stand to reveal numerous photographs of Wade Mulligan's body in various states—clothed, bloody and dead, on the floor of the bedroom where he'd been murdered, and others of him naked on the autopsy table.

Jaxon pointed to the pictures. "There are the photographs the ME took of Mulligan when he got him on the table."

Jaxon noted the gashes on the man's chest, and glanced at Avery to see if she was okay. Her face had paled slightly, her lips pinched.

Dr. Riggins pointed to several of the stab wounds. "If you look at the angle of these, they all slant the same direction, indicating that they were done by a right-handed person."

Which made sense. Hank was right-handed. He pointed to the numerous small stab wounds. "Those were the wounds Hank inflicted."

"But look here." Dr. Riggins used a pointer to highlight another stab wound, this one slightly different. "It's not only deeper and wider but slants the opposite direction."

Jaxon's heart hammered. "That one was made by someone other than Hank. By someone left-handed."

Dr. Riggins pushed his glasses up his nose with a smile. "Exactly."

Avery made a low sound in her throat. "What are you saying?"

Adrenaline rushed through Jaxon. This was what they needed, some concrete evidence to support the theory that there had been another perpetrator.

"It means that a second person stabbed Wade," Jaxon said.

"Not only that," Dr. Riggins said as he pointed to the wound again, "but this wound was the fatal one. It sliced through the aorta. Mulligan probably died within seconds."

Jaxon gritted his teeth. This should be good news.

Except that Avery was left-handed.

AVERY MENTALLY DIGESTED the implications of the ME's report. "That means Hank was telling the truth."

"It could mean a second person actually killed Mulligan," Jaxon said quietly.

Avery glanced at her hands, her eyes widening. "My God, I'm left-handed."

She staggered back against the table. "Hank thought I stabbed Wade. And I...don't remember what happened that night." Fear clogged her throat. "What if I did do it?"

Regret flashed in Jaxon's eyes. "Avery, don't jump to conclusions. You were just a child."

Avery rubbed the scar on her wrist. "I didn't want to remember." Her breath caught. "But then I thought Hank was guilty. I didn't see any reason to relive it." Maybe she should try harder now.

If she could recall the details of that night, if she'd witnessed the murder, she might be able to identify the killer.

"Ms. Tierney," Dr. Riggins said. "The wound made by the left hand was the fatal one and much deeper than the other wounds, which appear more superficial. It tore through muscle and tissue. But I doubt a nine-year-old girl would have that kind of strength."

Relief filled Avery. "If you show this to a judge, he'll have to stop the execution and grant a new investigation."

Jaxon scrubbed a hand over the back of his neck. "I wish it was that simple. But the prosecutor can easily argue that Hank used his left hand at some point. Maybe he grabbed the knife with his left hand at first because he was holding Mulligan down with his right, or he dropped it at some point and then retrieved it with his other hand."

Avery's hopes wilted.

"Don't get too discouraged, Avery," Jaxon said. "This is a start. But we need more." He turned back to the forensic specialist. "Is there anything else you can tell us from the body?"

Dr. Riggins studied the photographs intently. He pointed to a cut on the man's right wrist. "The only defensive wound Mulligan sustained is that cut. Which suggests that he raised his arm in an attempt to deflect the blow from the left-handed attacker."

"So that wound, which was the killing blow, was delivered first," Jaxon said.

Avery's hope stirred to life again. "That confirms Hank's story, that Mulligan was dead when he stabbed him."

Dr. Riggins pulled a hand down his chin. "Based on angle and depth of the wounds, I would testify that there were two different attackers."

"But we still need proof that someone else was there," Jaxon pointed out.

Avery's head began to pound. "Maybe it's time I work

on recovering my memory. If I saw the killer and can identify him, or her, then I can free my brother."

JAXON FELT THE fear emanating from Avery as he drove her back to her house.

She'd blocked out the traumatic events of that night because they were so horrible. Reliving them would be a nightmare come true.

But would it help her heal?

And how could she go on if she continued to be plagued with guilt over Hank's incarceration? Worse, how would she live with herself if she learned she had killed Mulligan?

He pulled down the road leading to Avery's but slowed as he approached, a bad feeling in his gut.

Avery suddenly sat up straighter and gasped as they parked.

Jaxon's pulse hammered when he saw the words painted on the front door.

"An eye for an eye. Hank Tierney should die."

Chapter Thirteen

Avery stumbled from the SUV, shock rolling through her. "Who did this?"

She turned to Jaxon, hands on her hips. "Who cares enough about Hank and a murder he supposedly committed twenty years ago to torment me?"

"The person who really killed Mulligan," Jaxon said matter-of-factly.

Fear shot through Avery, and she pivoted to search the street, then the woods behind her house.

Jaxon also visually searched the perimeter as they approached the front door. "There's another possibility. There are always lunatics who follow death row cases. One of them could have paid you a visit because he knows you're trying to stop the execution. You'd be surprised at the fanatics who protest against the death penalty while others lobby for it. Some of them even write prisoners and offer conjugal visits and marriage proposals."

"But the warden said that Hank hadn't had any visitors, not until I asked to see him."

Jaxon snapped his fingers as if a thought just occurred to him. "I'll call the warden and ask if Hank received any suspicious mail. It's possible the killer wrote him."

Avery started to touch the wording on the door, but Jaxon caught her hand. "Don't. I want a crime team to process this place. Maybe whoever left that message also left a fingerprint."

He stepped aside to call the crime team.

Although her first instinct was to run inside, grab cleaning supplies and erase the ugly message, Avery stepped back from the door, knowing Jaxon was right.

Memories of her teenage years bombarded her. The other teens teasing her, calling her a murderer's daughter. A murderer's sister.

Making jokes about when she would go ballistic and start her own killing spree.

One day a group had painted the word *killer* all over her locker.

After that, others had taunted her with the name. They said she had bad blood. That she'd end up in jail just like her father and brother.

Once she'd even considered getting a gun and firing it at the next person who tortured her with ugly words.

She'd even sneaked out of the group home that night and met a guy on the streets in a dark alley, one who'd promised her a Saturday-night special.

But she'd seen another little girl that night. A tiny little thing walking with her mother. They were holding hands singing some silly song about a frog. They'd looked so normal.

Her heart had ached. She'd never had normal.

Heaven help her, but she'd wanted normal. Wanted a family and someone to love her.

A light had flickered in her head—if she shot someone, she'd never have that life. She'd become exactly what the others kids called her. A killer. She'd prove that she had bad blood. And she'd end up in prison like her father and brother.

So she'd turned around and walked down the street, following the woman and child. She'd stood in the shadows and watched them enter the Humane Society. A few minutes later, they came out with a scruffy-looking dog.

The little girl and mother had laughed and giggled as the puppy licked the child's face and nuzzled up to her.

After they left, Avery had walked into the Humane Society and strolled through, looking at the lost and abandoned animals. She knew just how they felt and wanted to take them all home that day.

But the group home didn't allow pets, so she'd offered to volunteer at the adoption center.

"Avery, are you all right?"

She looked up at him as he pocketed the phone. So much had happened in the two days since she'd met him.

Hank could still die.

A strangled sob escaped her, and she spun around to avoid letting him see her cry.

"What if I did do it?"

"Aw, Avery, I don't think you did."

Then he slid his arms around her from behind. Unable to help herself, she leaned into him, turned around and buried herself in his arms.

JAXON STROKED AVERY'S back, her warm body heating his own. He only meant to comfort her, but her fingers trailed across his chest, and his lungs squeezed for air.

She felt so sweet and hot at the same time, and the feeling stirred protective instincts that made him want to alleviate all the pain in her life. She also aroused a passionate need inside him that made him want to carry her to bed and make love to her until dawn.

Make love?

Hell. What was wrong with him? Avery was a…a woman who'd been victimized. Who needed his professional help.

She lifted her head and looked up at him with those

sensual, lonely eyes, and his heart tripped, robbing all rational thoughts from his head.

He pressed a hand to her cheek, ordering himself to pull away. They were in the middle of a crime scene.

But her eyes fluttered, and she emitted a soft purr that ripped away his resolve, and he lowered his head. He hesitated, his lips an inch from her mouth, and searched her face.

The flare of need in her expression triggered his own, and he was lost.

He closed his lips over hers, his heart hammering wildly as she kissed him in return. She threaded her hands in his hair, digging her fingers deeper as she pulled him closer.

He forced himself to be gentle when he wanted to swing her up, take her inside and prove to her that men could be gentle and loving at the same time.

Heat exploded between them, her breath rasping against his neck as he ended the kiss. But she cradled his face between her hands and looked at him again. Heat flared as she traced one finger over his mouth.

He sucked in a breath, allowing her to take her time, to memorize his lips the way he wanted to memorize every inch of her.

But his cell phone buzzed on his hip, and he stilled. What the hell was he doing?

He eased away from her, aware that their breathing sounded raspy in the silence.

"Avery?"

Her eyes were swimming with desire and other emotions he didn't understand.

"I shouldn't have done that."

A small smile tugged at her lips. "I wanted it."

That admission made him want to kiss her again. But his phone buzzed once more, and the sound of an engine broke the spell.

He stepped back and answered his phone as he went to meet the crime team. Damn, it was his director on the phone.

"Ward, I need an update," the director said in a demanding tone.

Jaxon grimaced. The last thing his boss wanted was to know that he'd kissed Avery Tierney. And that he believed Hank was innocent. "I've been talking to people involved in the original investigation to verify stories."

"What the hell does that mean?"

That I think you made a mistake. But he needed concrete proof before he confronted him.

He lowered his voice so Avery wouldn't hear. "You wanted me to make sure the conviction wasn't overturned, so I'm reviewing the case. If it's solid, there's nothing to worry about." There, that was a roundabout answer.

The director heaved a breath. "All right. Just talk to D.A. William Snyderman. He was the assistant D.A. back then. He'll confirm that we ran the investigation by the book."

He was also friends with the director. Now Jaxon understood even more his boss's determination to keep the execution on track. Both his and the D.A.'s reputations depended on it.

"I plan to," Jaxon said. "But I have to go now."

Three crime team workers exited the van, and he pocketed his phone and introduced himself. Avery was standing by his SUV, her arms wrapped around her waist as she stared at the ugly taunt on her door.

Lieutenant Carl Dothan introduced him to the other two crime investigators—Samantha Franks and Wynn Pollock. "What happened?" Dothan asked.

Jaxon explained about Avery's connection to Hank Tierney. "Someone vandalized the outside of the house and painted that threat on Ms. Tierney's door."

"How's the inside of the house?" Franks asked.

Self-disgust ripped through Jaxon. He hadn't even checked. He'd been too busy kissing Avery.

"I haven't been inside, didn't want to contaminate anything out here." Sounded feasible. "I called you to start processing the outside and canvass the neighbors to see if they witnessed anything." He gestured toward the house. "I'll search the inside now."

"You didn't think whoever did this might still be around?" Dothan asked.

Jaxon's gut tightened. "There was no sign of that, no car or anyone on foot when we arrived. Ms. Tierney was understandably upset, so I called you. She received a disturbing phone call earlier and is pretty shaken up."

Lieutenant Dothan gave a clipped nod, then turned to Franks and Pollock. "Franks, canvass the neighborhood. Pollock, start with the photographs, and I'll search the yard and drive for forensics."

They dispersed, and Jaxon walked back to Avery. "Stay here. I'm going to search the inside of the house and see if whoever did this broke in."

Something he should have done already. But he'd been too distracted by Avery.

Dammit, if he messed up, it might mean the difference between making a valid case to save Hank and not.

He couldn't let himself be sidetracked again.

"Stay here," Jaxon told Avery.

She shook her head. "Let me go with you. I'll be able to tell if anything is missing or if someone's been inside."

His gaze locked with hers for a tense second. Other emotions flickered there as well—regret that he'd kissed her?

She didn't regret it, though.

Avery had never been kissed. Not by a man.

She thought she never would be, that she wouldn't be able to be intimate.

But she felt safe in Jaxon's arms. Safe in his kiss.

She wanted more.

Emotions mingled with desire, stirring relief and need at the same time. Maybe she could be normal after all.

Maybe she could even have a relationship and a family of her own someday.

"Stay behind me," Jaxon ordered. "Is there a back door we can go in while CSI processes the front door?"

She nodded, trembling slightly as they walked to the back entrance of the house. She scanned the backyard and woods beyond, but everything seemed quiet. Still. The wind had even died down, yet the darkness hovering over the yard gave her an eerie feeling.

She climbed the two steps to the screened back porch, peering inside at the rustic table and chairs. Nothing looked out of place or as if anyone had been inside.

"Let me," Jaxon said when she reached for the doorknob.

She stepped aside, her body tingling as his hard chest brushed hers. He jiggled the door, and it screeched open. Jaxon arched a brow at her, and she tensed.

"It was locked."

He gestured for her to stay behind him, then inched inside. The back door stood ajar, causing fear to course up her spine.

Jaxon pulled his gun and held it at the ready, then tiptoed toward the door. He eased inside, looking left and right. Avery peered over his shoulder, staying close to him as they entered.

The kitchen looked untouched, as did the den and connected dining area.

Jaxon swung his gun toward the stairs. "Upstairs?" he said in a low voice.

"Two bedrooms. First one is mine, second is a guest room."

Jaxon slowly inched his way up, Avery on his heels. He

paused on every other step to listen for sounds of an intruder, but the only sound Avery heard was their breathing and the slow hum of the heater.

The curtains fluttered in her room, jerking her attention to her bed.

Nausea gripped her stomach as she realized someone had been inside.

Pictures of Wade Mulligan's mutilated dead body were scattered across her bed.

But the picture in the middle was the one that made her cringe.

It was a photograph of her with a knife stuck in the middle.

JAXON RELEASED A string of expletives. Dammit, Avery didn't deserve this.

He glanced over his shoulder at her and saw her sway slightly. Worried, he slid an arm around her waist. "I'm here, Avery. It's going to be all right."

"Surely one of the neighbors saw something."

"Hopefully so." He took her hand and guided her back to the stairs. "Don't touch anything. Maybe this creep left a print and we can nail him."

AVERY TIERNEY HAD found her presents. The fear on her face had been priceless and meant that scare tactics might work on her.

Although that Texas Ranger was a problem.

But processing the scene would take time.

Time away from looking into Hank Tierney's case.

Time was all that was necessary. If the Ranger and Avery didn't find the truth, Hank Tierney would die.

Then there would be no reason to reopen the case, and Avery and the Ranger would have to stop asking questions.

Chapter Fourteen

Jaxon ushered Avery outside and encouraged her to sit in the SUV and wait. He strode over to Lieutenant Dothan and explained that they needed to process the interior of the house.

"I'll do it myself," Dothan said.

"Thanks. I'm going to take Avery somewhere safe for the night. Let me know what you find."

Dothan agreed, and Jaxon joined Avery. When he cranked the engine, Avery frowned. "Where are we going?"

He had to get her away from her house. Knowing her room had been violated had to be unsettling for her, especially that damn picture of her with the knife in it. That was a blatant threat. "To my place. The crime team will call me with their findings."

"Your place?" Avery asked in a soft rasp.

Damn. The earlier kiss taunted him. He hadn't thought how his suggestion might sound. "I just want you to be safe tonight." He forced his eyes on the road. "Don't worry, Avery. You'll have your own room."

"I wasn't worried," she said softly.

His gaze cut to hers. The husky sound in her voice matched the simmering desire in those eyes.

Dammit, he was in trouble.

Heat speared him, but he forced his attention back to the road. He'd already screwed up by kissing her earlier instead of searching the house before he called CSI. Hell, what if the intruder had been there when they arrived?

He could have caught him in the act.

Although it was doubtful that he'd been present. Not that he couldn't have sneaked out the back and disappeared into the woods....

"Uh, Jaxon," Avery said as they drove into town. "I don't have clothes or a toothbrush with me."

He hadn't considered that. "Not a problem. I'll stop and let you pick up whatever you need."

He veered into the parking lot of the discount store and parked. "I'll call the prison warden and ask him to collect Hank's mail while you run inside."

"Can I see Hank again?" Avery asked.

"I'll ask."

She thanked him, then jumped out and hurried into the store.

Jaxon punched the number for the warden, keeping an eye on the door of the store in case someone had followed Avery.

"We typically examine the mail when it's delivered, although sometimes that takes time and we fall behind," the warden said. "I don't recall anything suspicious. Just the typical hate mail along with the sympathizers for his cause. A couple of offers for conjugal visits. Another group wanting to rally to save him."

"Just box it all up. I need to study the correspondence."

The warden agreed, and Jaxon hung up. If Mulligan's killer hadn't trashed Avery's house, then someone else had.

Maybe he'd find a clue as to his or her identity in those letters.

Or…it was possible that the killer felt remorse over Hank's upcoming execution.

Enough so that he or she might have contacted Hank?

AVERY STRUGGLED TO shake off her nerves as she stepped on the front porch of Jaxon's ranch house. The sprawling land with horses roaming free and cattle grazing was a picture of beauty. It reminded her of old Western movies about families working together and riding and…loving each other.

Like a real family.

"This is beautiful," Avery said. "You live here alone?"

Jaxon nodded. "Yeah, I bought it a while back. I need to hire some help, though. With me gone working cases, I can't manage it by myself."

Nerves fluttered in her stomach. Being in his home felt…intimate.

But he'd only brought her here because she'd been threatened.

He probably brought women here all the time. Maybe not from his cases, but a man like Jaxon probably had a half dozen lovers waiting for him to call. She was probably interfering with a hot, sexy night with one of them this evening.

He opened the door and ushered her inside. "Make yourself at home, Avery. It's not fancy, but it's comfortable."

Avery admired the rustic pine floors, the masculine furniture and the fireplace. It looked perfect. Like a home where a man lived.

A painting of several wild mustangs graced the wall above the couch, while another one of the famous Cherokee Crossing where the Native Americans and settlers had met to build a town hall together hung above an oak table.

"I don't have much food in the house," he admitted in a voice laced with regret. "But I can fix us omelets."

"That's fine," Avery said, a tingle spreading up her back at the idea of Jaxon cooking for her.

He's just doing his job, she reminded herself.

Except that kiss had been sensual. Not just Jaxon doing his job. At least she didn't think it was.

It felt more like Jaxon being the sexy protector. As if for a moment, Jaxon had wanted her.

But he'd pulled back and hadn't pushed her. Which made her respect him even more. Some men would have taken advantage.

But not Jaxon.

"There's a hall bathroom here," he said. Then he showed her to the bedroom. "This is my room, but you can sleep in here tonight. There's a full bath that joins the room if you want to wash up while I throw together some food."

She glanced at the log-cabin quilt on the sleigh bed and once again felt as if she'd come home. "Thanks, I think I will." Just seeing those ugly pictures made her feel dirty all over.

He returned to the living room, grabbed the bag of items she'd bought at the discount store and set them in the room. She grabbed the bag and ducked into the bathroom.

One glance in the mirror and she grimaced. Her hair was a wreck, what little makeup she'd put on this morning was long gone and her eyes looked…frightened.

Was she frightened of Jaxon? Or simply scared of the way he made her feel?

She flipped on the shower water and cranked it up, then peeled off her clothes. Her nipples budded to stiff peaks, her body trembling as she remembered Jaxon's lips on hers. God help her, but she wanted to feel them on her mouth again.

She closed her eyes as the hot water sluiced over her, and she imagined the door sliding open and Jaxon stepping inside with her. She could almost feel his big hands running over her shoulders, down her arms, then touching her waist as he drew her closer. She leaned her head back, her body tingling as she imagined his lips on her neck, his tongue teasing her earlobe.

Naked body against naked body…

She jerked her eyes open, so hot she could hardly breathe.

What in the world was happening to her? She never fantasized about being with a man....

Disturbed by her train of thought, especially in light of the fact that she needed Jaxon to help clear Hank, she flipped the water to cold, rinsed off, then climbed out and dried off. She slipped on the pajamas she'd bought to sleep in, then brushed through her damp hair.

Jaxon was not interested in her. He had simply been comforting her because she'd been a trembling mess earlier. He would have done the same for any woman who'd been in need.

She was just so inexperienced that she'd read more into it.

She absolutely had to get control of herself and focus on finding Hank's killer.

For heaven's sake, he could be put to death by the end of the week.

And that would be her fault.

Reality sobered her, and she opened the door. Steam oozed from the bathroom, and her breath caught at the sight of Jaxon by the bed.

"I put clean sheets on for you," he said.

Her gaze met his, her earlier fantasy taunting her. She wanted to ask him to join her in bed, to beg him to touch her all over and kiss her again.

His gaze raked over her, heat simmering between them.

Instead of coming toward her, though, he backed toward the kitchen. "The food is ready."

Disappointment snaked through her. But freeing Hank was more important than her own needs, so she followed him into the kitchen.

JAXON CLEANED UP the dishes after their meal and was grateful when Avery retired to the bedroom. Having her in his kitchen, in his house, his shower and now his bedroom was wreaking havoc on his common sense.

It also felt intimate, something he hadn't shared with a woman in… Something he'd never shared with a woman. He liked his bachelor status, his nights of sex, but his mornings without a woman to push him for more.

Oddly the thought of waking up beside Avery didn't panic him.

It should, dammit.

He knew he wouldn't sleep much tonight, not with Avery in his bed. Not unless he joined her, and that wasn't going to happen.

Determined to focus on work, he spread out the files on the Tierney case and studied them once more. He scribbled Mulligan's name at the top of a legal pad, then Hank and Avery's names below.

As much as he hated to admit it, Avery was still a suspect. She was left-handed, and even though she had only been nine, fear could trigger an adrenaline rush that could have given her the strength to stab Mulligan.

If she had killed him, it would also explain why she'd blocked out the traumatic memory. And an attorney could plead self-defense.

But how would Avery handle knowing that she was the reason her brother had been behind bars for twenty years?

She already harbored too much guilt.

He rubbed a hand over his chin. Hell, did he honestly believe Avery had killed her foster father?

He scribbled the names of the D.A. and public defender who'd handled the case, knowing he needed to talk to them.

Next he listed the social workers—Delia Hanover and Erma Brant.

Delia had claimed not to know about the abuse. What about Erma?

He would speak to her next.

Below those names he wrote a list of the foster children they knew about.

Shane Fowler—body shop owner—claimed to know of the abuse.

Lois Thacker—now a cop—knew of abuse. Had the right temperament? But right-handed.

Lenny Ames—committed suicide.

Dotty—dead.

Imogene Wilson—in a psychiatric hospital—confessed to murder, but delusional.

Imogene's brother, BJ—drug addict who hated Mulligan—no solid alibi.

Any one of the fosters had motive.

He remembered the autopsy and realized he needed to find out which one of them had been left-handed.

Other than Avery.

AVERY CURLED INTO Jaxon's bed, the day's events traipsing through her mind. She and Jaxon had made headway toward proving Hank's innocence. At least the autopsy might help.

But time was running out.

She tossed and turned, but finally buried her head into the pillow. Although Jaxon had changed the bedding, his strong masculine scent permeated the room. She closed her eyes and imagined his big muscular arms enveloping her, and her breathing steadied.

Jaxon was in the next room. He would protect her.

She was safe for tonight.

Tomorrow they would find a way to clear her brother.

Slowly she drifted to sleep, but the nightmare came again....

She was back at the Mulligans' old house, curled in her bed, the covers tugged up to her neck. Joleen was gone, and Wade had come in, blustering again.

He didn't like the dinner she'd cooked for him and Hank. She'd made tomato soup and grilled-cheese sandwiches, and he wanted meat.

She clenched her teddy bear, checked to make sure the stick was still under the bed, closed her eyes and finally fell asleep, praying he'd leave her alone tonight. But some time later, the door burst open, jarring her. Then Hank's voice.

"Leave her alone," Hank shouted.

The fists came next. Hank was fighting Wade, but Wade was dragging him across the hall back to his room.

Rain pattered on the tin roof. Suddenly the wind swirled through the house. She looked over and saw the curtains flapping against the windowsill.

Then a voice whispered, "It'll be all right."

A woman's voice... But whose?

Footsteps sounded and fear clawed at her chest. He was coming into her bedroom again.

She screamed, and then everything went dark....

Some time later, Hank's shout jolted her from the darkness. He was beside the bed, pulling something from her hands. She clenched it tighter, but he pried her fingers loose.

"Give it to me, sis," he said in a low voice. "It's okay now."

Her fingers loosened. The room swirled, colors dancing in front of her eyes. Red, then black. Blood. Everywhere.

She looked down and saw blood on her hands.

Then Hank knelt over Wade. Wade was on the floor, not moving. More blood. Hank raised the knife and jabbed it into the man's chest.

She screamed again, a scream that echoed off the cold walls....

"Avery!" The door burst open, and she jerked awake. Her heart was racing, her body trembling. For a moment, she was so lost in the nightmare that she was disoriented. She didn't know where she was.

Didn't realize who the man was in the doorway.

Mulligan... He'd come back to get her.

She cried out as he strode to the bed. The mattress sagged; then he reached for her, and she swung her fists at him.

She had to get away....

JAXON BRACED HIMSELF as he drew Avery against him, but she beat at him with her fists, her scream punctuating the air as she tried to push him away.

Dammit, she was in the throes of a nightmare.

Or...a memory.

He murmured soft words, trying to soothe her. "Avery, wake up, it's me, Jaxon."

Sweat rolled down his neck. Her scream had sent a streak of cold terror through him. He'd run to the bedroom in a panic, fearing the worst. Someone was trying to kill her. Someone who'd followed them here and broken in.

Her cries echoed in the room, a haunting sound that made his blood go cold.

He cradled her closer. Avery was safe. At least physically.

"It's over, I've got you," he whispered. "You're safe, Avery. He can't hurt you anymore."

Except that dead man was still hurting her because he couldn't tell them who'd killed him.

Avery stilled, her breath rasping out as she opened her eyes. She blinked several times, obviously trying to focus.

"It's me—Jaxon," he said huskily. "I'm here, Avery."

She clutched his chest, her eyes pained as she looked into his eyes. "There was someone else there that night," she said in a raspy voice.

"What?"

"I remembered," she said. "The window, it was open. I felt the wind blowing in, saw the curtains flapping."

Jaxon's pulse kicked up. "You saw someone?"

She pushed a tangled strand of hair from her damp cheek. "No, but I heard a voice. She told me it was going to be okay."

"She?"

Avery nodded. "Yes, it was a woman's voice. She... comforted me. Then...everything went black."

"Did you recognize the voice. Was it Joleen? Maybe Imogene?"

Confusion clouded her face again, and another sob tore from her throat. "I don't know. It was just a whisper."

Pain wrenched Avery's eyes, and she released him and stared at her hands. "But...when the darkness lifted, I looked down. Hank was there, telling me it would be all right. He was taking something from my hands."

She trembled more violently. "I had the knife in my hands, the bloody knife." Her tormented gaze met his. "God, Jaxon...I think I might have killed Wade."

Chapter Fifteen

Jaxon stroked Avery's back, hating the fear in her voice.

"What if I did it?" Tears streaked from her big eyes. "Maybe Hank was right. I stabbed him, and then Hank took the knife from me and cleaned it off so no one would know." Her voice cracked. "He stabbed Wade to cover up for me, and I let him."

Jaxon's chest tightened. That version fit—the reason police had found no other prints than Hank's was that he'd wiped them off to erase Avery's.

"I have to come forward, to confess," she said, her voice panicked.

Jaxon gripped her arms and forced her to look at him. "Stop it, Avery. If it had happened like that, you were only a child and blocked out the memory to protect your mind until you were ready to deal with it."

"Well, I'm not a child anymore. I can free Hank."

Jaxon shook his head. "It wouldn't work. At this point, no one would believe you. They'd think you were just making it up to save Hank."

"But if Hank and I both tell the same story—"

"Do you really think your brother will agree to that?"

She wiped at her eyes. "I'll convince him to."

"I'm sorry, Avery. No judge would buy it." He hesitated. "Besides, I don't believe that you killed Mulligan."

"Why not?" Avery cried. "He was attacking me. I could have brought a kitchen knife to bed with me earlier."

"Did you?" he asked.

She looked down at his hands where they held her, confusion marring her face. "I...I'm not sure. But I could have. I was afraid. I knew he'd come in because Joleen was gone for the night."

Jaxon gently tilted her chin up. "Avery, do you remember taking a knife from the kitchen?"

Her face crumpled, and she shook her head. "No, but that doesn't mean I didn't do it."

He stroked her hair back from her cheek. "You said something about the window being open. Did you leave it open at night?"

She jerked her gaze toward him, seemingly surprised by the question. "No. I always wanted it closed. I was scared a monster might get in."

Of course, there was one already in the house.

"And you said you heard a woman's voice?"

"Yes. She whispered that it would be all right."

"Was the voice Joleen's?"

"I don't know. It was really low and I didn't see her face."

AVERY HAD DOUBTED everything about that horrible night. But she hadn't imagined that woman's voice.

Someone else had been in the house that night.

That woman could have killed Wade.

"What do you think she meant? That everything would be all right? Were you crying? Was Wade in the room at the time?"

Avery closed her eyes, desperate to sort through the memory. "I don't remember. Just that I was hiding under the covers, and she touched my arm and squeezed it, then whispered to me."

"Did you hear any other noise? Did Wade come in the room when she was there, or was he already dead?"

Her head throbbed from trying to recall the details. "I... don't know. Everything is so jumbled. I...I remember hearing footsteps, and then...I felt the cold air from the window."

"What did you do then?"

Avery massaged the scar on her wrist. "I was hiding in the bed, and I waited until it was quiet. Then I looked down and saw the knife. It was all bloody...."

"What happened next?"

"I...think I blacked out for another minute. The next thing I remember is Hank taking the knife from me. Then he was standing over Wade's body. He raised the knife and drove it down into him. Then I screamed. And he...he stabbed him over and over again."

Jaxon rubbed her arms. "Who called the police? Did you phone them?"

She blinked hard, a headache pulsing behind her eyes. Finally she shook her head. "No. I...just remember crying and seeing Hank with that knife. Then suddenly the police burst in and everyone was yelling. Then some female officer wrapped me in a blanket, and I saw lights from the police car swirling in the dark and an ambulance, and a big policeman dragged Hank toward his car."

Her body shook with emotions as another flood of tears rained down her face. They had ripped Hank from her life that day, and she'd thought she lost him forever.

And she *would* lose him if she didn't find a way to stop the execution.

So who was the woman she'd heard whispering to her that night?

LATER AT THE PRISON, Jaxon explained to the warden his reasons for requesting Hank's mail. "Someone has been threatening Ms. Tierney. There might be a clue as to who it is in the correspondence. Can you think of anyone specific that's written to him? Someone suspicious?"

"To tell you the truth," the warden said, "we haven't had time to sort through it all. The past six months, after that reporter wrote the story on death row and mentioned Tierney, we've been flooded with mail. So have the prisoners awaiting execution."

"Let me have the mail. I'll look through it, then have the FBI lab analyze it. We have specialists who can detect patterns, threats, look at handwriting analysis, even search for underlying meanings in messages."

"Fine, take them. We've got our hands full here."

Avery cleared her throat. "I want to see my brother again."

The warden graced her with a sympathetic look. "Of course."

He led them into the hallway and arranged for them to visit in a private room as he'd done before. "Have you found any evidence to exonerate Hank?"

Jaxon clenched his jaw. "We're still working on it."

Avery had lapsed into a worried silence, and remained quiet as the guard escorted them to a visitors' room.

Hands clenched, Avery slid into the chair in front of the table, but her gaze was glued to her scar. She was obviously pushing herself to recall the details of that night.

The door squeaked open, and Hank shuffled in, chained and handcuffed again. Avery looked up at him with such a deep sadness that a knot formed inside Jaxon's belly.

Would she survive if they didn't save her brother?

AVERY SWALLOWED HARD to keep from bursting into tears. Hank's face looked bruised and battered, his arms scraped, and he was limping as if he was in pain.

Even worse, despair darkened his eyes.

Metal clanged as he dropped into the chair. "You came back? Why?"

Avery flinched at the distrust in his voice. But she deserved it. "I told you I was going to get you free, and we're working on it." She gestured toward Jaxon. "We've been questioning everyone we can think of who might know what happened that night."

A faint spark of hope flickered in his eyes for a second, then disappeared. "But you still don't know who killed Mulligan."

Avery laid her hand over his. He stiffened, and looked at her hand as if it felt foreign to be touched.

At least gently. He'd been beaten on for years. That was obvious.

"No," Jaxon said. "But we questioned some of the other foster children placed with the Mulligans, and they confirmed Mulligan's abusive behavior. Their testimony will work in your favor."

A muscle twitched in Hank's forehead. "But it won't get me off?"

Avery had to offer him some hope. "It proves others had motive, so we can argue reasonable doubt."

Hank balled his hands into fists, but Avery didn't let go of his hand.

"But none of those other fosters were at the house," Hank said, his voice deflated.

Avery took a deep breath. "I think someone was," she said. "I remembered something, Hank. I woke up and the window was open in my room."

Hank narrowed his eyes. "So?"

"I always kept it shut, remember? I was scared of the monsters in the woods."

"The only monster was Mulligan," Hank muttered.

She rubbed her finger over his knuckle. "True. But I remembered something else. I heard a woman's voice."

Hank went very still. "A woman? Who?"

"I don't know yet." Avery's lungs strained for air as panic threatened. "But I distinctly remember hearing her voice. I was hiding under the covers, and she touched my arm and murmured that everything was going to be all right."

Hank stared at their hands again, emotions rippling across his face. "How does that help us?"

Jaxon's dark eyes promised nothing, making Avery want to cry again. "If Avery remembers that a woman was there, we'll find her. She could have come in and killed Mulligan. Avery was in shock from witnessing the murder and picked up the knife. Then you thought she'd killed him, so you wiped off the prints in an attempt to cover for her."

"You didn't see her because she climbed out my window," Avery said. "I remember it being open and the wind blowing."

Hank dropped his head forward, his voice a self-deprecating murmur. "So I wiped off the only evidence that could potentially clear me."

Pain wrapped itself around Avery and wouldn't let go. Hank was right.

Between the two of them, they had let the real killer go free.

JAXON STUDIED HANK. He had been hardened by prison. Hell, he'd been hardened by life long before he was locked in a cell.

He'd been abused and was filled with rage that night, but maybe he remembered more than he'd revealed. Some detail that could help Jaxon crack the case.

"Hank, what about you? What do you recall from that night?"

Hank's eyes flared with suspicion. "You think I did it?"

"No," Jaxon said, realizing how much he meant it. "And I'm trying to help you and your sister." In spite of the fact that his boss would be more than pissed. "So cut the bull and tell us everything that happened that night."

"I already have." Hank's voice sounded raw with worry. "When the old lady left, I knew Mulligan would go in Avery's room that night, so I took a knife from the kitchen and hid it in the bed. Later, when I heard him going toward her room, I tried to stop him. But he hit me and tied me to the bed." He paused, his breath raspy. "A few minutes later, I heard Avery screaming and I was furious. I twisted and turned until I got hold of the knife and cut myself free." He ran a hand over his shaved head. "When I went in and saw Avery with that bloody knife in her hands and Mulligan lying there dead, I freaked out. I figured she'd killed him, so I took the knife from her and wiped it clean and then I stabbed him."

Jaxon's pulse clamored. "You said you had a knife in your bedroom. But Avery had another knife and you took it and used it to stab Mulligan." He paused. "What happened to the first knife?"

Hank pinched the bridge of his nose. "I don't know. I think I had it when I went in the room, but maybe I dropped it somewhere."

A tense silence stretched for a full minute. "I'm going to ask the D.A. and your defense attorney," Jaxon said. "It should have shown up in the crime scene photos."

Hank made a low sound in his throat. "Even if you find the other knife, won't the lawyers argue that Avery had it with her?"

"That's possible," Jaxon said. "But I don't like the fact that there was no mention of it at the trial. That makes me wonder why."

Avery squeezed her brother's hand. "Hang in there, Hank."

His defeated look tore at Jaxon. Hank Tierney didn't expect anyone to believe him or help him.

"One more question," Jaxon said. "Hank, do you know who called the police? Was it you or Avery?"

Hank shook his head, his eyes flat again. "No. I didn't call them. And Avery was too upset. She couldn't stop crying."

Jaxon swallowed a curse. That was another question for the D.A. and defense attorney. Had a neighbor phoned it in? And how did the neighbor know unless he or she had seen something? The houses were too far apart for one of them to have heard Avery crying.

Unless the caller had been inside the house....

Which meant the killer might have called 911 after he or she left.

LEAVING HANK IN prison ripped at Avery's nerves.

She and Jaxon had to find this mystery woman.

He drove to a set of office buildings not too far from the prison. "Wright Pullman was your brother's defense attorney," he said to Avery. "Do you remember him?"

Avery searched her memory banks. An image of a young man in a suit at the courthouse with Hank flashed back. "Vaguely."

"Did he question you?" Jaxon asked as they walked up to Pullman's office door.

"I honestly don't remember," Avery said. "I was pretty out of it back then. I just remember begging them not to take Hank away."

Hank had been her only safety net.

Jaxon spoke to a receptionist, who asked them to wait in the front room. Avery noted the office furniture was cheap, the paintings generic, the carpet low-grade.

"I did a little research on Pullman," Jaxon said when the receptionist disappeared into the back. "He's nothing more than a glorified ambulance chaser."

The receptionist returned. "Mr. Pullman will see you now."

Avery followed Jaxon into the man's office, her gaze surveying Wright Pullman. He was older now, in his forties probably, with a bad comb-over, wire-rimmed glasses and a beard. His suit looked as cheap as his office furniture.

Jaxon quickly made introductions and explained the reason for their visit.

Pullman toyed with a pen on his desk. "I figured someone would show up asking questions. Always happens with a death row case."

"Do you remember my brother?" Avery asked.

"Hard to forget." The lawyer's chair squeaked as he shifted. "He was one of my first cases. I was just a public defender back then, swamped with cases that nobody wanted." He crossed his legs. "But that one stuck out in my mind."

"Why is that?" Jaxon asked.

"'Cause the kid was only fourteen. But it was obvious he was guilty. He admitted to stabbing Mulligan a dozen times." He shot Avery a look of regret. "I know you're probably grasping for some way to save him now, but no one coerced that confession from him. And he was dangerous. Hell, he scared me. I've never seen a kid with so much rage."

Avery planted her hands on his desk and leaned forward. "Yes, he was full of rage because Wade Mulligan was molesting me. Did you know that when you went to court?"

The man's freckled skin paled. "Look, I did everything I could. I tried to cut a deal with the assistant D.A. who prosecuted the case, but he refused. He was a cocky bastard who wanted to make a name for himself, and that case got a lot of press."

Avery shivered at the memory of reporters dogging her.

"The A.D.A. used the shock factor of those photos of the multiple stab wounds to convince the jury that Tierney killed Mulligan in cold blood, and that he was a danger to society."

"How about arguing that there were extenuating circumstances?" Jaxon asked. "That Hank was defending himself and his sister from abuse?"

"I...didn't know," Pullman said in a low voice.

"Because you didn't do your job," Jaxon snapped. "You readily accepted the kid's confession at face value. If you'd talked to the social workers and other foster kids placed with the Mulligans as I have, you would have realized that Hank was protecting Avery that night."

Pullman's thin lips darted into a frown. "Listen here, I did do my job. But I was young, overworked, and the A.D.A. was determined to make an example out of Tierney."

"Do you remember photographs of the crime scene?" Jaxon asked.

Pullman's eyes narrowed. "What are you getting at?"

"Hank Tierney claims he had a knife in his room with him. That Mulligan tied him up as he did most nights so he could molest Avery."

Pullman's Adam's apple bobbed.

"He cut himself free, then went in to save Avery. But he claims Mulligan was already dead. That he thought Avery killed the old man, so he took a bloody knife from her hand, wiped it off, then stabbed Mulligan to cover for her."

Pullman fiddled with his suit jacket again. "You believe that story?"

"Yes," Avery said. "I remember a little more now. The window in my bedroom was open, and I heard a woman's voice. I think someone else was there."

Pullman looked confused. But he stood, went to a filing cabinet and removed a file. He flipped through it, then spread the crime scene pictures across his desk.

Avery had seen them before, but the gruesome sight of Mulligan's chest bleeding from the stabbing still turned her stomach.

Pullman tapped a finger on one of the pictures, then

shoved the report in front of Jaxon. "There was no second knife there, and no mention of it in the report."

Avery glanced at Jaxon, questions nagging at her. "Then someone took it."

"Or if police found it, they doctored the report," Jaxon suggested.

"You'd have to ask the officer who filed the report about that," Pullman said.

"Who called the police that night?" Jaxon asked.

Pullman scanned one of the pages. "All it says here is that a woman phoned 911 saying there was a disturbance at the house. When the police arrived, they found Mulligan dead with Hank standing over the body holding the bloody knife in his hand."

"Did anyone try to find out the identity of the female caller?" Jaxon asked.

Pullman shook his head. "Didn't seem important at the time."

Avery's heart raced. "Not important? What if that woman was in the house? She could have been the woman I heard in my room that night."

Jaxon snatched the report to look at it again. "Hell, Pullman, that was your case, your reasonable doubt. She could have killed the damn man herself, then called 911."

"I THOUGHT THAT Texas Ranger was supposed to keep things on track for the execution."

"He is."

"Well, hell, that's not what he's doing. He's trying to prove Tierney is innocent."

He muttered a string of expletives. "What?"

"Tierney's sister sucked him into believing her brother was all noble, some kind of hero protecting his little sister. And if he finds out about the second knife…"

"The second knife wasn't in the crime photos," he pointed out.

"No. But he's still digging." A heavy sigh escaped. "And he wants to know who called in the murder. He's going to try to make it look like the caller murdered Mulligan."

Dammit to hell and back. "What about my name?"

"I erased it from the police report just as you asked."

"Good. I don't want this cluster coming back to haunt me." Or screw up his career.

He'd worked too hard to build his reputation to go down now for putting away a punk like Hank Tierney.

Chapter Sixteen

Jaxon skimmed the police report again before he drove away from Pullman's office.

"Do you see anything else that can help Hank?" Avery asked.

Jaxon shrugged. "The officer who signed this report was named O'Malley. I'm going to call him and ask him some questions. But first, let's talk to the D.A."

Hope lit her eyes for a fraction of a second, making Jaxon want to promise her they'd save her brother.

But he didn't know if he could keep that promise.

As he drove, Avery seemed lost in thought, her emotion at having seen Hank obviously taking a toll.

He had a bad feeling about Pullman and the police report. Something wasn't right.

Either the second knife hadn't been found, or someone had removed it from the scene and intentionally covered up the fact that it had ever been there.

The only person who would do that was the real killer— or someone connected to him or her.

He parked, and together he and Avery walked up to the courthouse. They went through security, and then he escorted her to the D.A.'s office.

The man's reputation for being a cutthroat prosecutor was legendary in south Texas. From his first case as the assistant

D.A. when he'd tried Hank, William Snyderman had established himself as a winner who showed no sympathy for the criminals he put behind bars.

Jaxon knocked on the man's door and pushed it open when Snyderman called for him to come in.

Unlike Pullman, who looked shady, Snyderman was distinguished with close-cropped hair, gray at the temples, and a smile showcasing his confidence. He wore a designer suit, a red power tie and a black onyx signet ring encrusted with his initials in gold.

"I've been expecting to see you," Snyderman said as he extended his hand in greeting.

Of course, Director Landers would have relayed that he'd asked Jaxon to oversee the case.

Snyderman offered Avery a smile and his hand. "I'm sorry about your brother, Miss Tierney."

Avery bit down on her lip as she shook his hand. "I remember you," she said. "You're the reason my brother is on death row."

Snyderman squared his shoulders, a sharp glint in his eye. "Your brother is on death row because he murdered a man."

"What if he didn't?" Avery countered. "What if he's innocent and you convicted the wrong person?"

Snyderman's jaw hardened. "You don't really believe that, do you, Miss Tierney?"

"Yes, I do," Avery said, standing her ground. "And I'm going to prove it."

Snyderman started to speak, but Jaxon threw a hand up to keep them from arguing. Snyderman's tongue was like a viper, and Jaxon didn't want Avery to get stung.

"I have a few details I'd like for you to clarify," Jaxon said.

Steel-gray eyes cut to Jaxon for a second before he gestured for them to sit down. Jaxon had seen his ironclad control in court, and watched as Snyderman adopted his lawyer persona.

"What details?" Snyderman asked.

Jaxon explained that Avery remembered the voice of a woman from that night, and that the window had been opened, indicating a third party might have come into the house and left. "Coupled with the fact that the call to 911 came from a female, it's possible it was the same person, and that that woman killed Mulligan."

"You really are grasping, aren't you?" Snyderman asked. "Have you seen the crime photos? There's a picture of Hank with blood all over him, his hand clenching the murder weapon."

"That's also a problem," Jaxon said. "You see, Hank admitted he took a kitchen knife with him to bed, and he used it to escape after Mulligan tied him up. He heard the man going into Avery's room and ran in to save her. There, he found her holding a knife. She was in shock, so he wiped it down and then stabbed Mulligan to cover up for her."

Snyderman leaned back in his seat, hands steepled as he studied Jaxon then Avery. "That's quite a story."

"It's true," Avery said.

Snyderman's eyebrow shot up. "If I remember correctly, a second knife wasn't found at the crime scene."

Jaxon rubbed a hand over his chin. "That's one thing that's bothering me," he said. "If there was a second knife, it would prove that another person had been in that house that night."

"Not necessarily," Snyderman said, always the devil's advocate. "You could argue that both Hank and Avery took knives earlier." He angled his head toward Avery. "It might even suggest that you two planned the murder together."

Avery shot up from her seat, eyes glinting with fury. "We

didn't plan anything," she said. "Wade Mulligan beat Hank and molested me."

"There is your motive," Snyderman said, voice oozing confidence.

Avery crossed her arms. "Yes, we had motive, but so did other kids who'd lived there. One of them could have sneaked in that night and stabbed Wade."

"With you in the room?" Snyderman's voice screamed with disbelief. "And if that's the case, why wouldn't you have told the police that, Miss Tierney? If you believed your brother was innocent, why did you testify that he stabbed Mulligan?"

"I was just a child," Avery said in a tortured whisper. "I was frightened, and…traumatized by that night."

Jaxon fisted his hands by his sides. Snyderman was pointing out the obvious holes in their theory, the same way a judge or another attorney would.

But the bastard was wrong. He had to be.

Jaxon cleared his throat, adopting his own authoritative air. "Miss Tierney is not on trial, Snyderman. She was only nine at the time and in shock. You know from experience that children often repress traumatic memories, but years later when they reach adulthood, those memories resurface."

Snyderman sighed warily. "That may be true, but you've shown me nothing to make me believe that Hank Tierney was wrongly convicted."

Jaxon hated to admit it, but the D.A. was right. He had a decent theory but no concrete evidence, not even a specific suspect. Just conjecture.

He still didn't like the man's attitude toward Avery, though. "Just for a moment, consider the possibility that our theory is correct," Jaxon said. "If a third party, say this woman who called in the murder, sneaked in and killed Mulligan, she's gotten away all these years. Avery's scream must have prompted her to run, and the woman dropped the knife. The ME also confirmed that the actual fatal wound was made by a left-handed person, not a right-handed one. Hank Tierney is right-handed."

For the first time since they'd entered, unease flashed on Snyderman's face. But not for long. "A right-handed person could have used his left hand to inflict that wound to confuse police."

"Hank was fourteen, emotional, in a rage. I hardly think he had the presence of mind to make a decision like that."

Snyderman steepled his hands again. "But it's possible. He could have planned it while he was tied up in his room. Or hell, for days, for that matter."

Jaxon narrowed his eyes. "Did the police find ropes in Hank's bedroom? They should have, and the defense attorney should have made the argument of abuse."

Snyderman looked down at his hands. "I don't recall."

Jaxon didn't remember seeing them in the report or photos, either.

"But if there were ropes," Snyderman continued, "the police could have assumed Hank planned to use them to tie up Mulligan."

The man had an answer for everything.

Jaxon leaned forward, his gaze penetrating Snyderman. "You know, I believe the police did a shoddy job of processing this case. I know the defense attorney didn't do his job. And now I'm wondering if you didn't do yours, either."

Snyderman leaned forward as well, meeting Jaxon's gaze head-on, his eyes cold. "What are you implying, Sergeant Ward?"

Jaxon gritted his teeth. He could be about to kiss his career goodbye. But Avery was counting on him, and Hank Tierney might lose his life for doing nothing but protecting his little sister.

Jaxon couldn't live with that.

"I understand you built your reputation on this conviction," Jaxon said, forging ahead in spite of the warning in the D.A.'s eyes. "But maybe you, the police and the defense attorney were a little too eager to close this case."

Anger seared Snyderman's expression. "You're implying that the police removed evidence? That I acted with impropriety?"

"I don't know," Jaxon said. "But I'm going to talk to the officer who wrote that initial report. O'Malley, I think it was."

Snyderman grunted. "O'Malley died five years ago."

Damn, but Snyderman almost looked smug about the man's death.

And with O'Malley dead, how would they learn if someone had found that second knife?

He didn't like the other question nagging at him. Director Landers had made his career on this case, as well. Had he hidden or covered up evidence that could have cast doubt on Hank's guilt, maybe even exonerated him?

AVERY WAS SHAKING with anger and frustration as they left the D.A.'s office.

Just the sound of Snyderman's harsh voice had triggered memories of sitting in court twenty years ago. Of watching the faces of the jurors as he'd ranted about Hank's violent tendencies, about the number of times he'd stabbed Mulligan.

Then he'd plastered pictures of the bloody scene in her bedroom the night of the murder on a screen, and the women and men watching had gasped and whispered in shock.

The psychologist who'd treated her after the murder had tried to shield her from the sight of the photos, but she'd seen them anyway.

"Are you okay?" Jaxon asked.

No, she wasn't okay. How could she be? Time was running out, and she knew her brother was innocent but couldn't prove it.

"It's my fault. If I'd told the social worker about what Wade was doing, maybe she would have removed us from the home and none of this would ever have happened."

Jaxon cradled her hand in his. "We're not giving up yet, Avery. Let's talk to that social worker and see if she can shed some light on the situation."

She gripped his hand, taking comfort in the warmth of his fingers as he enclosed her smaller hand in his.

Thirty minutes later, they parked at Erma Brant's house, a small wooden-framed structure on a street lined with similar older homes.

"You worked with Delia," Jaxon said as they walked up the sidewalk to the door. "Did you ever meet Erma Brant?"

"I don't think so," Avery said. "But Hank and I did go through a couple of other social workers before Delia was assigned to us."

Jaxon knocked, and she glanced at the withered flowers and peeling paint on the house. The screens were torn, and the house needed a new roof.

Seconds later, a thin woman wearing a housedress and bedroom shoes opened the door. She squinted up at them over bifocals. "Yeah?"

"Mrs. Brant?" Jaxon said. "My name is Sergeant Jaxon Ward with the Texas Rangers. Can we talk to you for a minute?"

"You want Erma," the woman said in a high-pitched voice.

"Yes," Jaxon said.

"That's my sister. Come on in, she's in the kitchen."

They followed her through a cluttered foyer piled high with laundry, knickknacks and dozens of magazines, then found Erma Brant sitting in a wheelchair at a round oak table.

"Erma, it's one of them Texas Rangers," the sister shouted.

She made a sign with her hand to indicate Erma was hard of hearing.

Erma looked at Jaxon with a scowl, then glanced at Avery. "My God, you're Hank Tierney's sister, aren't you?"

Avery nodded. "You remember me?"

Erma's lip quivered as she took a sip of tea. "Didn't really know you and your brother, but I saw your pictures in the news. They've been showing it again, what with the execution coming up."

"That's the reason we're here," Jaxon said. "Erma, there's some new information that's come to light, and we need your help. We now know that Wade Mulligan was abusing Hank and Avery."

Avery watched for shock on the woman's face, but her expression went flat. "Who are you?"

"Avery Tierney," Avery said.

Erma suddenly looked confused and glanced at her sister. "What are they doing here? Where's Mama?"

The sister rushed over and patted Erma's back, then gave Avery and Jaxon a wary look. "I'm sorry, I should have warned you. Erma has some memory problems."

"Alzheimer's?" Jaxon asked.

The sister nodded. "Started about ten years ago. She has good days and bad days. Sometimes she remembers details of things that happened years ago but can't remember my name or her own."

"Get these people some tea," Erma said. "I should have made my shortcakes."

Despair tugged at Avery. How could Erma help them if her memories were faulty?

Jaxon slipped into the chair across from Erma. "Erma, you were telling us that you saw the story about Wade Mulligan being murdered on the news."

Erma's eyes widened. "Yes, that was horrible. They say those kids that lived with him killed him."

Avery tensed. "Did you know that Wade was hurting the little girl and boy?"

Erma's hand trembled so hard the teacup rattled against the saucer. "I got Imogene out of there."

"You did?" Avery asked. But not before she'd been totally traumatized.

Jaxon lowered his voice. "Did you report the abuse to the police?"

Erma set down the teacup. "I told one of them. He said he talked to the couple, but they claimed the kids were lying."

Erma stood and walked to the window, then picked up a doll in the corner and began to rock it in her arms. "Shh, baby, don't cry," Erma whispered. "Mama's right here."

Avery glanced at Jaxon and saw the frustration on his face. They were losing Erma again.

"I'm sorry," the sister said. "When she shuts down, she shuts down."

Erma sank into the rocking chair and began to hum and stroke the doll as if it were a child.

Jaxon addressed the sister. "Did Erma ever talk to you about the Mulligans or the Tierney arrest?"

"No, not really. Although she was upset about all the children placed with the Mulligans. She said she felt sorry for them." Erma's sister fiddled with the collar of her blouse. "When she reported Imogene's abuse and the police didn't do anything, she said she was going to quit work, that she couldn't do her job anymore."

"So she left social work?" Jaxon asked.

Erma's sister nodded. "Said she was going to leave a note in the files for the person who filled her position, a note telling them not to put any more children in the Mulligan house."

Avery froze. Had Erma left a note in the file? If so, why hadn't Delia mentioned it?

And what if Erma had discovered that she and Hank had been placed with the Mulligans against her advice?

She looked at the frail, unstable woman in front of her. She was confused now. But she was whispering to the baby doll that everything would be all right.

Just as the woman had whispered to Avery the night of the murder.

Dear God, had Erma come to check on her and Hank? Had Erma sneaked in and whispered to her that everything would be all right?

She'd been burned out on the job. She was upset with the police for not believing her, for not stopping Mulligan.

What if she'd been angry enough to kill Mulligan so he couldn't abuse any more children?

JAXON LISTENED TO Avery's theory as they drove back to her house.

"I need to talk to Delia again," Jaxon said. "Find out why she said she didn't see the note Erma left in the files requesting that the Mulligans not be used as a foster family again."

Avery grabbed one of the boxes holding her brother's mail and carried it to the house. He snagged the other two boxes and followed her.

But his phone buzzed as she started to open the door. He checked the number.

Director Landers. Probably going to fire his butt.

"Let me take this," he said, then stepped to the edge of the porch.

Avery went inside and closed the door, and he saw a light flip on. He punched the director's number, bracing himself.

A second later, Avery's scream pierced the air.

Jaxon's heart clenched as he shoved his phone in his pocket, reached for his gun and rushed to the door.

Chapter Seventeen

Avery swung her elbow backward and jabbed her attacker in the stomach. He tightened his grip.

"Be still," the man growled. "I'm not going to hurt you."

Old fears crawled inside her, memories of Mulligan's attacks, and she screamed and stomped on his foot as hard as she could, using self-defense moves she'd learned in a class at the gym. He bellowed again, then shoved her toward the chair in the living room.

She fell into it, hands reaching out to catch her from bouncing off and hitting the floor.

"Damn, Avery, I'm here to help!"

Avery froze, the man's rough voice resurrecting some distant memory from the past. Gasping for a breath, she pushed up from the chair with her hands and turned to face him.

Dark shadows hovered around his silhouette, but she could tell he was big. Over six feet. Broad shouldered.

And he was clutching his belly and breathing hard.

"Freeze—police!" Jaxon shouted as he crept up behind her attacker.

Avery's lungs strained for air as she cried out.

The man spun around and kicked Jaxon's gun from his hand, sending it sailing across the floor.

Avery struggled to see the intruder's face, but suddenly Jaxon lunged onto the man's back.

Avery clenched the chair edge as Jaxon knocked him to the floor. Jaxon jumped him and tried to jerk his arms behind him, but the man shoved him, then rolled over and slammed his fist into Jaxon's jaw.

Jaxon grunted and punched him in the stomach, and they traded blows, rolling across her floor as they fought.

"Get off me!" the man shouted.

"You son of a bitch, you're not going to hurt Avery," Jaxon growled.

"I'm not trying to," the man yelled.

Avery's heart pounded, but she turned on the lamp by the chair. A soft light washed over the room, and she stared in shock at the man lying on the floor with Jaxon straddling him.

"Jaxon, stop," she whispered.

He swung his gaze up toward her, his eyes feral. "What?"

Avery stood on shaky legs, walked over and looked down at the man. It had been over twenty years since she'd seen him.

His face was weathered, wrinkled, and age spots dotted his bald head.

But she would never forget his face or those twisted eyes.

"Avery?" Jaxon said.

"Tell him to let me go," the man growled.

Jaxon jerked the man by the collar.

"It's okay, Jaxon," Avery said. "You can release him. He's Roth Tierney, my father."

JAXON SHOT THE man below him a sinister look. He could feel Avery trembling beside him. "You're Avery's father?"

The bald man grunted a yes.

Jaxon cursed. "Then why the hell did you break in and attack her?"

"I just wanted to talk to her." He gestured at Jaxon's hands, which were still planted firmly on the man's chest where he was sitting on him to hold him down. "Now let me up."

Jaxon glanced at Avery and saw the bewilderment and hurt on her face, firing his anger even more. "Just don't touch her again," he warned.

The beefy man's eyebrows shot up, but Jaxon ignored them. As far as he knew, Avery's old man hadn't been part of her life in years. And he was the reason she and her brother had ended up in foster care in the first place.

But he yanked the man by his collar, then climbed off him and moved to stand beside Avery. He planted his feet firmly in place, arms folded, daring the man to approach her.

No one was ever going to hurt Avery again.

Avery's raspy breathing punctuated the silence as her father stood. Time had been rough on him. His hands were scarred, a prison tattoo wound across his wrist, his teeth were crooked and yellowed, his hair was gone and he had a paunch.

"What are you doing here, Dad?" Avery asked in a frosty tone.

He brushed off his jeans with his hands. "We need to talk."

Jaxon cleared his throat and pointed to the sofa. While Tierney walked over and took a seat, he retrieved his gun and stowed it in his holster. Avery claimed the club chair in front of the fireplace, but Jaxon remained standing.

His instincts were on full alert.

"I thought you were still in prison," Avery said.

Tierney shook his head. "I've been out awhile."

"How long?" Jaxon asked.

Tierney knotted his scarred hands on his thighs. "Since right before Hank went to jail."

Shock flashed on Avery's face. "What?"

Tierney studied her for a long moment, then glanced at

Jaxon, the air thick with tension. "I've been out," he said. "Well, in and out a few times over the past twenty years."

Avery's look flattened. "What do you want? If it's money, I don't have any."

"I don't want money," he said. "I came to help you."

Jaxon scrutinized him. "How do you plan to do that?"

Tierney hissed between his teeth. "Look, Avery, I know you and Hank got sent to foster care 'cause of me, 'cause I killed that man. I screwed up."

"You tore our family life apart," Avery said bitterly.

"I know," Tierney said. "And when I got out on parole, I came looking for you and Hank. I found out you were at the Mulligans and I went there and watched you get on the school bus, watched you and Hank outside."

Jaxon wondered where this was going.

"You watched us?" Avery asked, her voice laced with unease.

"Yeah." Tierney dropped his head forward and studied his blunt nails. "I saw what he was doing to you," he mumbled. "I knew it was my fault. I…wanted to stop him."

Disbelief registered on Avery's face.

"What did you do?" Jaxon asked.

Tierney raised his head and looked at Avery, then at Jaxon. A vein throbbed in his forehead. "I broke in the damn house and stabbed the creep."

Jaxon narrowed his eyes. "You killed Mulligan?"

Tierney nodded, then held out his hands, wrists pressed together in surrender. "You can arrest me now, Sergeant Ward."

Avery's head was reeling from seeing her father again. And here he was, after being absent from her life for twenty years, turning himself in for Wade Mulligan's murder?

She didn't know what to believe….

Jaxon wrangled a pair of handcuffs from his jacket pocket

and snapped them around her father's wrists. She wasn't sure what he was thinking, if he believed her father, but he looked more than happy to handcuff him.

Mixed emotions pummeled Avery. She wanted to free Hank more than anything. Her father's arrest might make that possible. She certainly didn't have any emotional attachment to the man. "If you killed Wade Mulligan, why didn't you come forward sooner? Why did you let Hank go to prison for life?"

Tierney's nostrils flared. "Because the stupid boy confessed, and stabbed Mulligan a bunch of times. I…thought maybe he inherited my bad genes, and that he needed to do a little juvy time to straighten him up." A hefty amount of regret darkened his face. "I never thought he'd be convicted."

"But he was convicted and is going to be put to death this week," Avery cried, heart sick that her father would stand by and let Hank suffer. "For heaven's sake, Hank confessed because he thought I killed Wade Mulligan. He was only protecting me."

Shock registered on her father's eyes. Then a string of curse words exploded.

"How could you do that to us?" Avery whispered in a raw voice. "I lost everything that day, and so did Hank."

He grunted. "I figured he'd do a little time and then they'd let him out. I never expected him to get the death sentence."

"But when they gave it to him, why didn't you come forward then? Why wait until a few days before the execution?"

"I know it was wrong, but I'm here now." Emotions glittered in her father's eyes, maybe true remorse; then he tightened his jaw and faced Jaxon. "You can take me in now, Sergeant Ward. I'll confess to everything, and then you can get my son free."

JAXON WASN'T CONVINCED Tierney was guilty. His appearance at this late date seemed too…coincidental. Any lawyer would argue that he'd only come forward to save his son from dying.

Then again, if Jaxon could use his confession to get a stay, it would give him more time to investigate and unearth the truth.

Anguish filled Avery's eyes. Damn. He wanted to sweep her in his arms and comfort her. But Tierney shoved up from the chair, his expression hard as he gestured toward the door.

"Let's go, Sergeant. Sooner we get this over with, sooner you can get my boy out of prison."

Jaxon's dark gaze met the man's, searching for the truth.

He needed to learn more about Tierney's prison behavior. What other crimes he might have committed since he said he'd been released.

And why had he been released?

Hell, if he were lying and taking the blame for his son, it was probably the first noble thing he'd ever done in his life.

And Jaxon didn't intend to stop him. Avery and Hank deserved help, and it was about time their loser old man stepped up.

"Mr. Tierney, you are under arrest for the murder of Wade Mulligan. You have the right to remain silent…" He read Tierney his Miranda rights as he escorted him outside to his SUV.

Avery followed him, her arms wrapped around herself, her breathing choppy.

"Stay here and lock the doors," he said. "I'll call you."

She shook her head. "No. I'm going with you."

Jaxon ground his teeth, but the determined look on Avery's face warned him not to argue. Hell, how could he blame her?

She hadn't seen her father in two decades, and now he'd confessed to the murder that had sent her brother to death row. If it were his family, he'd insist on being present to see what happened.

"Wait on me, Jaxon. Let me lock up and grab my coat."

He gave her a clipped nod. "I'll be right here."

Her eyes softened as if she realized he meant that on more than one level.

And he did. Hell, he wanted to erase the pain in those damn gorgeous eyes of hers, and make her smile.

But tonight was bound to be rough. And they had their work cut out for them to convince a judge to postpone the execution.

Worry knitted her brow as if she realized the same thing, then she ran back toward the house.

Jaxon shoved Tierney into the backseat, then leaned across him to buckle his seat belt. "You'd better not be messing with Avery," he said in a lethal voice. "You've hurt her enough already."

Tierney lifted his head, his bald head pulsing red with anger. For a brief second, his gaze connected with Jaxon's, though, and Tierney's eyes flashed with understanding.

"I'm not here to hurt her," he said in an equally low, lethal tone. "For the first time in my life, I'm trying to do the right thing."

Whether he meant he was telling the truth about the murder or just trying to save his children, Jaxon didn't know.

He didn't care.

He climbed into the front, waited until Avery joined him, then started the engine and drove toward the jail.

Traffic was minimal as he passed through Cherokee Crossing. Most of the residents had settled in for the night, although the cantina was hopping with live music and the diner was still full with the late night supper crowd.

Avery twisted her hands in her lap, obviously grappling with emotions. Her father sat ramrod straight, staring out the window with a resigned look on his face. He'd been down this road before.

Prison was nothing new. Hell, sometimes lifers were released and didn't know what to do with themselves.

The system didn't prepare them for life on the outside. And society wasn't exactly jumping to employ ex-cons. Without a family member or friend providing support and a place to live, they wound up frustrated and failing.

Some even resorted to petty crimes to violate parole so they could go back to jail and have three square meals a day and a place to sleep.

Avery tugged her shawl around her as they got out, and he opened Tierney's door and escorted him inside. Deputy Kimball looked up from the front desk with a frown.

"Deputy, this is Roth Tierney, Hank Tierney's father. He just confessed to the murder of Wade Mulligan."

Jaxon's phone buzzed, and he checked the caller ID. Dammit—Director Landers.

"Book him and put him in an interrogation room. I need to answer this call. Then we'll take his statement."

Deputy Kimball grabbed Tierney's arm and led him through a set of swinging doors. Avery sank into the chair across from the deputy's desk, her face ashen.

Jaxon stepped outside for a moment and punched the director's number.

"What the hell is going on?" Director Landers bellowed. "Snyderman called and said you're trying to prove Hank Tierney is innocent."

Jaxon swallowed hard. "I reviewed all the evidence, and I had questions. But there is a problem, Director."

The director's hiss punctuated the air. "What?"

"Hank Tierney's father showed up and confessed that he killed Wade Mulligan."

The director spewed a dozen curse words. "You'd better put a lid on this right now, Ward. If Tierney's conviction is questioned, it could cast doubt on every case Snyderman and I worked for the past twenty years."

He didn't need another reminder.

But could he drop the case without knowing the truth?

Jaxon glanced through the window and saw Avery tracing that scar around her wrist, and he knew the answer.

He'd risk his job, his life, everything to save her from any more pain. And he would find the truth no matter what happened to him afterward.

Chapter Eighteen

Avery twined her hands together as she settled on the bench in the front room of the sheriff's office, her thoughts jumbled. She felt just as nervous as she had when she was called to the principal's office as a child.

Or worse—the way she had the day she sat outside the courtroom with that psychologist waiting to learn her brother's fate.

That day had ended in disaster and had shredded what was left of her trust in people. And in the system.

Would this day end as badly?

She mentally replayed the conversation with her father at her house, but anxiety needled her.

Had her father really broken in and killed Wade Mulligan?

If so, how had he gotten in without her seeing him?

She distinctly remembered hearing a woman's voice whisper to her that everything would be all right. Not a man's.

Although she had been afraid of Mulligan and had hidden under the covers, had repressed memories of most of that night. Maybe her father had been there.

If he'd broken into her room, she would have been frightened by him. She hadn't seen him since she was four years old, when he'd been incarcerated. She probably wouldn't have even recognized him.

And a big man climbing in her bedroom window in the dark would have terrified her.

She closed her eyes, desperately pressing her brain to recall more details....

The window screeched open, the wind was blowing, she was cold, so cold she was shaking. She heard his footsteps, heard Wade grumbling about Joleen being gone, smelled cigarette smoke and whiskey...

Knew he was coming for her.

Her skin crawled, and nausea rolled through her. Then she heard Hank yelling at Wade...heard Wade's fist slamming into Hank. Hank's grunt of pain. But Hank wasn't giving up.

He was strong and tried to take care of her. But Wade was big and mean, and he always got what he wanted.

She clenched the sheets, wishing she had some way to fight off Wade. She should have put Hank's baseball bat under her bed. Maybe she'd get it tomorrow. But that wouldn't help her tonight.

Hank shouted at Wade, but he must have tied him up because Wade's footsteps thundered in the hall. Then he burst through her door.

She squinted through the dark and saw his big shadow. Smelled him again.

She thought she was going to be sick. Then he moved toward her....

She screamed but...then everything went dark. Muffled sounds followed. Someone moving. A low voice. A grunt.

A thump. Wade falling?

She was shaking all over. Heard a moan. Wade...

A whisper brushed near her ear. "It'll be all right now...."

A woman's voice. Not her father's.

Then a hand touched her. Soft. Gentle.

The wind swirled cold air through the room. She tugged the quilt down and saw red, red everywhere. Blood...

Wade was on the floor, not moving. She had to get to Hank. She vaulted from the bed and ran toward Wade, had to get past him.

But just as she made it to him, his hand snaked out and grabbed her ankle. She froze, looked down and screamed at the blood on his chest. His eyes were wide, whites bulging, blood oozing from his mouth.

He jerked her foot and tried to drag her to the floor. Terrified, she spotted the knife and she reached for it....

The door to the front office opened, and Avery jerked her eyes open. Jaxon stood in the doorway, his expression guarded.

She started to say something, but what more could she tell him? She still believed a woman had been in her room. She didn't remember her father at all....

But she did remember picking up that knife.

Only it was bloody, and Wade was injured before she picked it up. Meaning she hadn't killed him.

Relief surged through her at that realization, although she still didn't know the truth.

Because if her memory of that woman was real, the woman killed Wade, not her father.

JAXON STRODE INTO the sheriff's office, knowing he might be about to kiss his career goodbye. But the truth—and Avery—meant more to him than the job.

Odd—he'd never felt that way before. Had never thought he would.

But he couldn't abandon his integrity. If he did, he'd completely lose himself.

"Where did you go?" Avery asked.

"I had a phone call. I'll take your father's statement now."

Avery nodded, although he couldn't help thinking she looked like a confused, lost child sitting on that bench.

"Can I come with you?"

Jaxon shook his head. "An attorney could argue that your presence affected your father's statement."

"I see. All right."

"Do you want some coffee or something while you wait?"

She shook her head. "Thanks, though."

She was so polite and humble it aroused tender feelings inside him.

No one had ever taken care of her.

He wanted to change that.

A dangerous place to be, Ward.

Forcing himself back in professional mode, he strode through the double doors to the back and found Deputy Kimball guarding the door to the interrogation room.

"You want me in there?" the deputy asked.

Jaxon hesitated. He didn't, but it would probably be best to have confirmation that he'd handled the interrogation by the book. He didn't intend for the confession to get thrown out on a technicality. "You have cameras?"

The deputy shook his head. "No, but I have a recorder."

"Good. Set it up."

Jaxon opened the door, bracing himself in case Tierney had suddenly changed his story, but the big man looked calm, resigned. Determined. He was staring at his blunt nails again, his handcuffed hands splayed on the table.

"We're going to tape this interrogation," Jaxon said as Deputy Kimball set up the tape recorder. "All right with you, Tierney?"

His cold eyes stabbed Jaxon. "I figured you would."

"All right, then." Jaxon gave a brief introduction for the taping purposes. "This is Sergeant Jaxon Ward, Texas Ranger. Also present is Deputy Kimball from the Cherokee

Crossing Sheriff's Department. We are here to interview Mr. Roth Tierney."

He recited the date and time. "Now, Mr. Tierney, tell us exactly what happened the night Wade Mulligan was murdered."

Tierney heaved a big breath. "When I got outta prison, I looked up the kids. But when I tried to see them, the social workers told me no. And my probation officer warned me not to go near them."

Jaxon frowned. "Why?"

"He said I needed to prove myself first. Get a job. A decent place to live." He worked his mouth from side to side. "Like going through the proper channels ever worked for me or did my kids any good."

Jaxon resisted a comment. "Go on."

"I found out Hank and Avery were living at the Mulligans', and I drove by the house." He rubbed a hand over his eyes. "I just wanted to see them, make sure they were okay."

"*Did* you see them?"

Tierney nodded. "Just glimpses. I watched them get on the bus to go to school. Walk to the store. I…couldn't believe how big my boy was, but I could tell he had an attitude. He looked like I did at that age. Full of rage."

"And Avery?"

The man chewed the inside of his cheek for a minute. "I never seen anything prettier in my life. Reminded me of her mama before she got messed up on drugs and ran off."

Jaxon bit back a retort. "Did you talk to her?"

Tierney shook his head. "I figured she hated me. I know they told her what I done, and figured I needed to clean up first. But—" he hesitated "—I knew something was wrong. She looked so sad, and she had bruises on her legs."

Jaxon grimaced. "What did you do then?"

"I was still trying to do the right thing, didn't figure I'd do the kids any good if I ended up back in prison. But

I couldn't get those bruises out of my mind, so that night I drove by again. I parked in front of the house. Then I heard screaming." He made a low sound in his throat. "I couldn't let that bastard hurt her anymore, so I went up to the window and looked in. That's when I saw Mulligan sneaking into Avery's room." His cheeks reddened with anger, and he balled his hands into fists. "I ain't no fool. I did time. I knew what that SOB was doing to my little girl." He banged his fists on the table. "I had to stop him. So I sneaked in the window and killed him."

Jaxon waited for him to elaborate, but Tierney leaned back in the chair as if he were finished.

Dammit, Jaxon had to do his job and ask for more details.

Police received false confessions all the time. Mentally unstable folks, delusional ones, or some just wanting to take credit for a crime for attention.

Others did so to cover for someone else.

The key to discerning whether or not the confession was real lay in the details.

Police usually omitted facts from the news to help them later weed out the phonies and pinpoint the right perpetrator.

"How did you kill him?" Jaxon asked.

Tierney heaved a breath. "I stabbed him."

"Did you have a knife with you?"

Tierney hesitated. "No. I grabbed a kitchen knife when I went inside and used it."

Jaxon studied him. Tierney could have learned that from the news report. "Where exactly did you stab him?"

Tierney's mouth twitched with anger. "In the chest, where else? I wanted to kill the jerk."

"How many times did you stab him?" Jaxon asked.

For a moment, Tierney looked away, as if he didn't intend to answer.

"How many times?" Jaxon asked.

"Once. Went straight through the heart. Learned that in prison. Fastest way to kill someone is to aim for a main artery."

"Then what did you do?"

The man's mouth twitched again. "I threw the knife down. Avery was on the bed screaming and I panicked. I didn't want to get caught, so I rushed outside. I figured Hank would call the police and they'd think there was an intruder, and then Avery and Hank would go back to social services. Then I might get them back."

"But that didn't happen," Jaxon said, stating the obvious.

Tierney shook his head. "Hell, no, Hank had to go in and stab the bastard a bunch of times, then tell everyone he killed Mulligan."

Disgust ate at Jaxon. "Why didn't you come forward and admit the truth then?"

Tierney locked eyes with him. "I seen the meanness in my boy's eyes. I figured he needed some cooling-off time. I never thought they'd sentence him to death row."

Jaxon crossed his arms. "But they did, and you've had plenty of time to confess before now."

Tierney's cuffs clanged against the table. "Truth is, I went on a bender after that night. Lasted a few weeks. Then I wound up back in prison for violating parole. By then, the trial was over and Hank had been sent away."

Jaxon still didn't know if Tierney was telling the truth. But if his confession cast doubt on Hank, he could use it.

So he shoved a pad in front of the man. "Write down everything you just told me."

Tierney grabbed the pen, then picked up the pad Jaxon had laid on the table and began to write.

A knot seized Jaxon's belly. The stab wound to the aorta had been made by a man holding a knife with his left hand.

Tierney was right-handed.

BY THE TIME Jaxon emerged from the back, Avery thought she was going to pull her hair out. She'd already bitten her fingernails down to the nubs.

She stood, anxious to hear what he had to say, but his expression was unreadable.

"Deputy Kimball is securing your father in a cell for the night," Jaxon said. "I need to make a couple of calls, and then I'll drive you back to your house."

Jaxon stepped outside again, and she paced, wondering if she should ask to see her father. But bitterness swelled inside her. What could she possibly have to say to him?

Thanks for finally coming forward? Thanks for trying to save me twenty years ago?

Thanks for letting Hank rot in a cell when you could have spoken up years ago and my brother might have had a life?

Jaxon returned a moment later, his mouth set. "I left a message with my director and the judge explaining the turn of events."

"What happens next?" Avery asked.

"We'll contact the governor to grant a stay for Hank."

Hope jolted through Avery. Was it really going to happen?

Would they free her brother? Would she and Hank finally get a chance to be a family again?

Chapter Nineteen

"Thank you, Jaxon."

A tense heartbeat passed before he acknowledged her words. "Let's go."

She glanced at the door leading to the back rooms, but old hurts and shame mushroomed inside her, overriding her need to see her father. If he'd really loved her, he would have stuck around that night and made sure she and Hank were safe.

He should have been there for both of them at the trial, as well.

But he'd abandoned them and caused them to suffer for most of their life. How could she possibly forgive him for that?

Jaxon seemed distracted as he drove her back to her house. When they arrived, he parked and followed her up to the door.

"Thanks for tonight," Avery said.

"I'm coming in."

"But my father is locked up."

"He may have killed Mulligan, but he didn't leave you threats or paint nasty words on your house."

Avery's stomach clenched. She'd forgotten about the vandalism.

"I still think the key to the threats may be in the mail Hank received at the prison."

"We can look over everything tonight."

"I'll do it while you go to bed," Jaxon said. "You've got to be exhausted, Avery."

It had been a traumatic day. But for the first time in years, she had hope that her brother might be released, and that she might have some kind of family again.

All thanks to Jaxon.

"I'm sure you're tired, too," she said softly. "Maybe we can look at those letters tomorrow."

Jaxon shook his head. "No, I want to review them tonight."

She reached up to touch him, but he stepped away. "Go to bed, Avery."

Hurt stabbed her. Before when he'd kissed her, she'd thought he might have felt something.

But she'd obviously imagined the attraction because she had no experience with men.

So she retreated to the bathroom to get ready for bed alone.

WORRY STILL NAGGED at Jaxon as he watched Avery head into the bedroom. Convincing the judge that Tierney's confession hadn't been fabricated because of a last-ditch attempt to overturn Hank's conviction was going to be damn hard.

He didn't want to burst Avery's bubble that he might not be able to pull it off.

Especially if he pointed out that her father was right-handed, and they believed the real killer had inflicted the wound with his left hand.

Dammit, if only they had prints to match or some other piece of concrete evidence to point to the real murderer.

He made a makeshift desk on Avery's kitchen table, then took the first box of Hank's mail and began to sort through it.

He skimmed through each letter, noting the tone, and

divided them into categories—sympathetic letters stating views against the inhumane treatment of prisoners and the death sentence, personal letters from women who'd read Hank's story or seen his picture and wanted to meet him. Others offered conjugal visits and the occasional marriage proposal. Some pro–death penalty people claimed that an eye for an eye was the appropriate punishment. Religious zealots also promised to pray for his soul to be saved so he could enter Heaven.

The past few weeks Hank's mail had increased exponentially due to the publicity about the upcoming execution. He quickly read through the people's reactions and comments.

But one letter caught his attention, and made him pause. He read it a second time, trying to discern the underlying meaning—if there was one.

Dear Hank,

I'm so sorry that you spent your life in prison, and have prayed for you every day for the past twenty years. You were a lost, angry boy, and you had reason to be angry.

I wish I could change the outcome of that night for you. But I know you hated Wade Mulligan, and he deserved to die for what he did to you and your sister.

Mistakes were made back then. The Mulligans never should have been allowed to have children in their home. I'm so sorry that you and Avery were hurt by them.

At least Wade's death saved other children from suffering the way you did.

I pray for your soul, and for forgiveness for my own.

Jaxon exhaled. There was no signature. But it certainly sounded as if the writer had known the situation in that house.

As if he or she felt guilty.

The verbiage also sounded like that of a woman.

Avery claimed she'd heard a woman's voice that night, a woman assuring her everything would be all right now.

He studied the names of all the females associated with the case.

Joleen could have killed her husband, except he didn't think she had the courage. And she certainly hadn't appeared to harbor guilt over anything, not enough to write an apology note for it.

Imogene Wilson had ranted that she'd killed Mulligan, but her mind was so fractured that her testimony wouldn't stand up in court. She also wouldn't have had the mental capacity to write Hank and apologize, either.

The same went for Erma Brant. At one time she might have had the presence of mind to kill Mulligan and regret the way it turned out for Hank. But this letter had been postmarked in the past six months. Erma had been suffering from dementia for years.

Lois Thacker, now a police officer, had been honest about the Mulligans' abuse, but she seemed too hardened to write a heartfelt letter like this. Of course, he hadn't spoken with her for long. As a cop, she would know how to cover herself and avoid suspicion.

He skimmed his notes again. Delia Hanover had been nice, worked with children and was sincerely sorry for Hank and Avery. But at the time, she was young and new on the job, and claimed she hadn't known about the abuse. He couldn't imagine her killing anyone, much less being devious enough to cover up a crime.

Who else?

A noise jarred him, and he stood and walked to the back porch door to look out. The wind whirled, snapping trees and sending tumbleweed across Avery's backyard. Shadows flickered in the woods, making him tense.

But he studied the thicket of trees and didn't see any movement.

The noise sounded again, and he walked back to the hall, then realized the sound was coming from Avery's bedroom.

His heart squeezed. What if someone had climbed through the back window?

He gripped the gun in his holster and peered into her room.

Moonlight streaked the walls and floor, a sliver of golden light dappling Avery's bed where she lay thrashing against the covers.

Another nightmare.

Hell. As much as he wanted to end this ordeal for her tomorrow, he still wasn't certain they had Mulligan's real killer in custody.

He started to close the door and leave her, but she cried out again, and his heart wrenched.

Maybe he didn't have all the answers tonight. But he could offer her some comfort.

Unable to resist, he eased inside and walked toward her bed. When he reached the side, she startled and opened her eyes.

"Avery?"

Seconds stretched, causing his heart to hammer.

Then she reached out her hand and beckoned him to come to her.

AVERY BLINKED JAXON into focus. His dark features were almost lost in the shadows, but she couldn't confuse his raw masculine scent with anyone else. Strength and courage emanated from him as he reached his hand out and took hers.

"You were having another nightmare," Jaxon said as he lowered himself onto the mattress beside her. He removed his holster and laid it and his weapon on the nightstand.

Her cheeks heated with embarrassment, but he was so

close that she breathed in his essence, and all embarrassment faded.

She was just a woman here, and he was a man. The dark room, moonlight and his quiet breathing seemed so intimate that she lost her inhibitions.

She'd never trusted anyone before, but she trusted Jaxon with her brother's life. With her life.

With her heart…maybe not. But close enough that she wanted to feel him next to her.

"Jaxon," she whispered. "Lie down with me. Hold me."

Wariness echoed in the next breath he took. "That's not a good idea, Avery."

Need and desire rippled through her. The fact that he was trying to be polite only made her want him more.

"Why not?" She reached up and tugged at his shirt collar. "I don't want to be alone."

He closed his eyes, his body tensing, but she ran a hand down his chest, then drew slow circles on his abdomen. He sucked in a sharp breath, then caught her hand in his.

"You're playing with fire, Avery."

A smile curved her mouth. She'd never been one to play games, to flirt. She didn't even know how.

But for once in her life she wanted to feel a man next to her. To touch him.

To be with him.

Instinctively she knew that Jaxon would never hurt her.

She licked her lips, hoping he wouldn't reject her as she lifted her finger and traced it along his lower lip. "I want to be with you, Jaxon."

He hissed between clenched teeth. "I'm trying to be noble, Avery. The last thing I want to do is take advantage of you."

She raised her head and flicked her tongue along his lips where her finger had just been. "You are noble. That's one reason I want you," she said in a husky whisper. "I need you."

A low groan rumbled from his throat, and then he slid his hands beneath her head and brought his mouth to hers. "Stop me anytime," he murmured.

"I won't," she said softly.

He lifted his head and looked into her eyes. His were dark with passion and hunger, but there was something else there. Control. A fierce determination that she believe him.

"I mean it," he said against her ear. "Anytime—"

"Shh." She kissed him tenderly. "I trust you." She threaded her fingers deep into his thick dark hair. "Please make love to me, Jaxon."

Emotions flashed on his face. Then he moaned again and claimed her mouth with his.

JAXON HAD FOUGHT his desire as long as he possibly could. Avery's soft plea turned him inside out. He wanted nothing more than to please her and chase away her bad dreams.

He gently traced his tongue along her mouth, tentatively at first, his body hardening as she parted her lips and invited him inside. Need drove him to deepen the kiss, and their tongues tangled in a sweet erotic dance unlike anything he'd ever experienced.

She moved against him, her hands pulling him closer, heat erupting between them as he stroked her hair away from her face. Her breath rushed out, her chest rising, breasts brushing his chest.

Her fingers slowly moved down to his back, clutching him, and he kissed her, then traced his tongue along the soft shell of her ear. She curled up against him, her hands growing urgent as she tugged at his shirt.

She was wearing a tank top and pajama pants, her nipples tightening below the thin material and making him ache for a taste.

She reached for his buttons and began unfastening them, their tongues dancing again as he helped her remove his shirt. She ran her hands over his bare chest, raking her fingers through the soft mat of dark hair on his torso.

"It feels good to touch you," she whispered.

A heady sensation shot through her, setting him on fire as her hand slid lower to his belt.

But he caught her hand and looked into her eyes again. "Avery?"

Pure feminine sex oozed from her eyes as she smiled. "You're going to force me to beg, Jaxon?"

The flirtatious tone to her voice made a laugh rumble from his chest. He'd wanted to pleasure her tonight, and she was smiling. There was so much more he could give her....

"I would never force you to do anything," he said, serious now.

"I know. Make me forget the past, Jaxon. Show me what it's like to be loved."

His gaze locked with hers. He was honored to have her trust. Heart pounding with the need to have her, he cradled her face between his hands again and kissed her once more, teasing her with frantic strokes until she moaned and lifted her hips into his.

His sex swelled and throbbed to be inside her.

Hungry to taste her, he slowly traced her nipples with his fingers through the thin tank, then kissed and suckled her neck, inching down to tease her nipples. She murmured a low sound in her throat and clutched his arms, silently asking for more.

Determined to please her, he lifted her tank, and she helped him peel it over her head. Her bare breasts were larger than he'd imagined, her nipples dark and stiff, enticing him to take them into his mouth.

He traced one with his fingertip while he closed his lips over the other. She cried out his name and ran her foot up his calf, teasing him. He laved both breasts, then inch by inch skimmed her pajama pants down her legs. The pair of see-through lacy white panties surprised him.

Her breath rasped out as he eased her legs apart and kissed her through the thin lace.

"Jaxon?"

"Let me have you," he whispered hoarsely.

She threw her head back and moaned as he tugged her panties down with his teeth, then teased her femininity with his tongue before he tasted her sweetness.

Chapter Twenty

Avery tingled all over from Jaxon's erotic ministrations. He lifted her hips and planted his tongue inside her, and she clenched the sheets, mind-numbing sensations spiraling through her.

He stroked her until she cried out his name and begged him to join his body with hers. Slowly he rose above her, rolled on a condom, then framed her face with his hands.

"Are you sure, Avery?"

"I've never been more certain of anything in my life."

Heat flared in his eyes as he nudged her legs apart and stroked her with his thick erection. She was moist and achy, her body begging for more, and she opened to him, welcoming him inside her as he gently entered her.

He paused, his arms shaking as he exerted control, giving her time to adjust to the feel of him. Hunger and passion drove her to pull his hips closer, and she moved against him in an urgent cry for him to go deeper.

Spurned by her encouragement, he moved his hips in a circular motion, thrusting deeper, inching out, then thrusting again. Erotic sensations shot through her, and soon they were tangled in each other's arms, bodies gliding against each other, kisses and tongues colliding as their lovemaking became more frantic.

Another orgasm began to build, the incessant throbbing

for more causing her to whisper his name, and he lifted her hips and filled her, his body jerking with his own release as her orgasm claimed her.

"I never knew it could be so beautiful," she whispered.

"Me, neither," he admitted gruffly.

They lay entwined, breathing unsteady, the heat between them rippling through her in the aftermath of their lovemaking. Who knew that touches and kisses could be so gentle and passionate? That they could feel so good, not hurtful?

That she would want Jaxon the way she had? The way she still wanted him?

Jaxon eased himself off her, then slid from bed and went into the bathroom. She suddenly felt bereft.

But he returned a moment later, slipped back into bed and pulled her into his arms.

"I'm glad you came back," she whispered.

His breath brushed her cheek. "I shouldn't have gotten in bed with you in the first place."

She shushed him, then cradled his face between her hands and kissed him. "You didn't enjoy it?"

"That's not what I meant." He nipped at her neck, then gently eased a strand of hair from her cheek. "You're beautiful, Avery. No matter what happens, don't forget that."

She stilled in his arms for a moment, wondering what he meant. Was he already pulling away?

Trying to warn her not to expect anything more from him?

Or warn her that he didn't think Hank would be freed?

He traced one finger down the slope of her breast, and she banished thoughts of Hank and her father and the investigation, and Wade Mulligan.

From this moment on, she would remember how it felt to have Jaxon's hands touching her, and no one else's.

Her heart stuttered, and she ran a hand over his hard chest, titillating sensations spiraling through her as he sucked in a sharp breath. The desire that heated his eyes emboldened her, and she crawled on top of him and kissed him again, naked skin against naked skin.

Then words were forgotten as they made love again. This time when her release spiraled through her, she bit back words of love, knowing Jaxon wouldn't want to hear them.

JAXON LEFT AVERY sleeping the next morning and showered, self-recriminations beating at him.

He hadn't made love to a woman in a while. Actually, he didn't know if he'd ever made love. He'd had sex before, but love was never involved. Neither was tenderness or the desperate kind of need he felt with Avery.

He'd certainly never slept all night with his partner, nor held her and loved her again and again.

He still wanted her.

Damn, emotional entanglements were dangerous. Avery might appear strong, but she'd been hurt badly before, and she was fragile.

Thankfully he kept a change of clothes in a duffel bag in his SUV in case he got stuck overnight on a case, and he dressed, then strapped on his gun and brewed a pot of coffee.

His phone buzzed, indicating a text, and he checked it. The director and the D.A. were going to meet him at the jail.

He started to scribble a note to Avery, but she appeared, her face flushed from their lovemaking, her eyes glittering with the memories.

His body hardened. In spite of his reservations, he wanted her again.

"I have to go to the sheriff's office," he said instead. "I'm meeting the D.A. and director of the FBI there."

Avery tightened the belt to her robe and poured herself a cup of coffee, although her hand trembled slightly. "I'll go with you."

"No." The word came out harsher than he'd intended, so

he tried to soften his reaction. "Stay here and shower. Rest. I'll call you when the meeting's over and let you know what happens."

"But this is about my brother," Avery said.

He didn't want to hurt her or disappoint her. And this meeting might not go well. "Please let me do my job and handle it."

Avery blew on her coffee. "All right. But promise you'll call me as soon as you can."

"I promise." He gestured toward the door. "Just keep the doors locked."

Avery nodded, and he put his mug in the dishwasher and headed out the door before he did something foolish like take her back to bed and admit that he loved her.

Dread for the upcoming meeting balled in his belly as he drove toward the jail. The director and the D.A. would be furious that Hank Tierney's father had come forward with a confession.

And could he present Tierney's confession to the judge knowing that it might not be legitimate?

Avery's face flashed in his mind, followed by Hank's tortured look. If he didn't, Hank might be put to death. And that would kill Avery.

But was he crossing the line by placing her feelings before the letter of the law?

AVERY CARRIED HER coffee to the table and saw the piles of letters Jaxon had sorted through. It took only a few minutes to understand the categories he'd organized them into.

She squinted to decipher his handwriting. He'd made several notes on a legal pad regarding the investigation and people they'd questioned.

Another letter lay separate from the pile, drawing her attention, and she picked it up and read it.

Dear Hank,

I'm so sorry that you spent your life in prison, and have prayed for you every day for the past twenty years. You were a lost, angry boy, and you had reason to be angry.

I wish I could change the outcome of that night for you. But I know you hated Wade Mulligan, and he deserved to die for what he did to you and your sister.

Mistakes were made back then. The Mulligans never should have been allowed to take children into their home. And I'm so sorry that you and Avery were hurt by them.

At least Wade's death saved other children from suffering the way you did.

I pray for your soul and for forgiveness for my own.

Avery's chest tightened. That letter…sounded like an apology. As if the person writing it knew that Hank was innocent.

Because the letter had been written by the real killer?

Not by her father, either. The handwriting was too feminine.

She glanced at the pad again. Jaxon had made a list of all the females they'd spoken with regarding Mulligan.

Two of the fosters, Imogene and Lois. The two social workers, Erma Brant and Delia Hanover.

Dear God, had one of them killed Wade?

And if so, what did Jaxon intend to do about her father?

Confusion and worry clawed at her, and she hurried to get dressed. Ten minutes later, she grabbed her purse and jacket and raced out the door.

Her father's confession taunted her as she barreled down the drive and onto the street leading into town. Had Jaxon decided the confession was bogus? That the woman in the letter killed Wade?

Was that the reason he hadn't wanted her to go with him today?

Pain wrenched her heart. She'd trusted Jaxon. Had given him her body and her heart. Did he have any feelings toward her?

She spun into the parking lot and climbed out, her nerves raw as she went inside. Jaxon's SUV was there, along with a black sedan.

But the front office was empty. Anxious, she opened the double doors to the back, pausing at the sound of loud voices.

Jaxon's. Then another man's.

She eased closer to the door, prepared to knock, but the man's words stopped her.

"Listen here, Ward, you were supposed to come here and make sure Hank Tierney's conviction wasn't questioned, not drum up another suspect that could make all of us who worked that case look like fools. And—" the man's voice rose "—I told you that if this case gets overturned, it'll mean every single case D.A. Snyderman or I worked will come under scrutiny. We're talking about hundreds of cases over the years."

Avery's chest constricted with hurt. Jaxon had come to Cherokee Crossing to make sure Hank was executed, not to find the truth.

But he'd pretended he wanted to help her. He'd lied to her and used her and…slept with her when he was working against her the entire time.

JAXON CHOKED BACK his anger. If he wanted to make a point with the director and D.A. Snyderman, he had to present a logical explanation.

"I understand your concerns," he said. "But as a lawman, I can't ignore the facts or that Hank recanted his confession."

"That boy was dangerous and deserved to go to jail," Snyderman said. "You saw how brutal he was in his attack."

"Hank Tierney was enraged because he was trying to protect his sister," Jaxon said through gritted teeth. "Tierney's lawyer should have used that in his defense. He should have called the social workers, other foster kids and teachers to testify that the children in that house were in danger."

"He got a defense," Snyderman said. "And all of us did our jobs back then."

The door swung open, and Jaxon jerked around to see Avery standing in the doorway glaring at all of them. "Did you do your jobs or did you railroad a frightened fourteen-year-old boy into prison?"

Jaxon opened his mouth to apologize, but Snyderman spoke up. "No one railroaded him into anything, Miss Tierney. Your brother confessed. He had the murder weapon in his hand and there were no other prints on it."

"Because he wiped them off to protect me!" Avery shouted.

Snyderman and the director exchanged concerned, nervous looks.

"You have no proof that your brother didn't kill Mulligan," Director Landers said.

Avery shot Jaxon a look of pure hatred. She'd obviously heard their conversation through the door and thought he'd betrayed her.

"What about my father's confession?" Avery asked.

Director Landers crossed his arms. "That will never hold up in court."

"It's obvious he's lying as a last attempt to save your brother," Snyderman said.

Avery turned to Jaxon. "Is that what you think, Sergeant Ward?"

The fact that she'd used his title and last name indicated

how upset she was. Dammit, he was caught between a rock and a hard place.

"Do you?" Avery cried.

Jaxon heaved a breath. He wanted to lie and protect her. He wanted to free her brother.

But his integrity won out. "I don't know," he said honestly. "You and I discussed the autopsy. The fatal wound was inflicted by a left-handed person."

Avery's brows rose, but resignation settled on her face. "And my father is right-handed."

He nodded.

"I'm left-handed," Avery said with a tilt to her chin. She faced Snyderman and the director. "I had the knife in my hand, and I had motive." She held out her arms. "Arrest me and set my brother free."

"Avery, stop it," Jaxon said. "Making a false confession is serious. I'm trying to unearth the truth once and for all."

"You're all trying to bury my brother." Tears glittered in Avery's eyes. "And that's not right."

Jaxon moved toward her, but she stepped back, her hand flying up in a warning for him not to touch her.

Then she turned and ran from the room. Jaxon started after her, but the director stepped in front of him. "Let her go, Ward. We're not finished here."

Jaxon stared at the director, his anger mounting. No, they weren't finished.

But he couldn't drop the case without finding the truth. He'd already lost Avery.

And he might lose his job.

But a man's life was at stake.

He would make sure justice was served, no matter who it hurt or what it cost him.

TEARS FLOODED AVERY's eyes as she ran from the jail. She couldn't believe what a fool she'd been. That she'd trusted

Jaxon and opened herself up to him when he'd been working against her these past few days.

Although he had at least interviewed different people regarding the murder. That list of females on his pad at home flashed in her mind.

Which of those women were left-handed?

Not Joleen. Besides, she was too big a coward to have killed Wade.

And she definitely wasn't the kind of person to harbor enough guilt to write a heartfelt letter to Hank in prison.

Imogene was another possibility—but she was too unstable to testify about anything. The same with Erma.

Lois was a cop and could have been tough enough to kill Wade, even when she was young. She also could have decided to pay penance by becoming an officer who locked up others, like Wade.

Frustration made the tears come harder. Who else?

Delia Hanover, the woman who'd placed her and Hank in the home. She seemed nice, calm, caring. She worked with children now.

Avery struggled to recall if she was left- or right-handed and couldn't remember.

But Erma had said she'd written a note to the social worker who'd replaced her, advising her not to put children with the Mulligans.

Had Delia lied? Had she seen that note?

If so, why had she placed them in that house? Had she simply made a mistake?

What if there were foster children she and Jaxon had missed? Another female who'd been abused by Mulligan?

Delia would have access to those records. Avery started the car and sped toward the school. It was early morning and buses were just starting to run.

Maybe she could catch Delia before school started.

She punched the number for the school into her phone

and waited while it rang. When the receptionist answered, she asked for Delia.

"I'm sorry, but she called in sick today," the woman said.

"This is urgent. Can you tell me where she lives?"

"I'm sorry, but I'm not supposed to give out that information."

Avery thanked her and hung up, then pulled to the side of the road and did an internet search to find the woman's name. She found her address in seconds, and veered into a neighborhood of small wooden ranch homes.

Delia's car sat in the drive. Breathing out in relief, she parked and rushed up to the door. She knocked, praying Delia would have some answers that would help Hank. Another suspect.

The door opened and Delia appeared, her face ashen, her eyes dark.

"Delia, can we talk?"

Delia nodded and opened the door.

Then Avery saw the gun in the woman's hands.

Chapter Twenty-One

Jaxon berated himself for not handling the situation with Avery and his boss better.

Truthfully, Director Landers's attitude from the beginning had disturbed him.

"You know that Tierney's story has holes in it," Director Landers pointed out. "If he killed Mulligan, one of the kids would have seen him."

"He could have sneaked out before Hank came in the room," Jaxon said.

"But you said the fatal wound was made by a left-handed person," Snyderman said.

True. Jaxon's phone buzzed. The lab. "Let me take this."

He stepped aside and answered the call. "Sergeant Ward."

"This is Lieutenant Dothan. When we processed Ms. Tierney's house, I lifted some prints. I don't know if it means anything, but the print matched one we had in the system."

Jaxon clenched the phone tighter. "Whose was it?"

"A woman named Delia Hanover. She's a social worker—"

"I know who she is," Jaxon said, his chest tightening.

"Then it's not important?"

"It might be." Why would Delia's print be at Avery's house? Unless she had been the one to vandalize the place....

"Where did you find the print? What room?"

"The bedroom."

Jaxon's pulse hammered. "Thanks." He ended the call, his pulse spiking.

Director Landers cleared his throat. "Ward, this confession of Tierney's won't stand up."

Jaxon whirled on him. "You've wanted to bury this investigation to protect your career all along."

"I told you that reopening it would bring every case Snyderman and I worked into question."

Jaxon glared at both of the men. "What about the truth? The lab just called and said that a print was found at Avery's house when it was vandalized. That print belonged to the social worker who placed Avery and Hank in the Mulligan house." He folded his arms. "Someone tried to scare her away from investigating. I think that person was Delia Hanover."

Snyderman's face went pale, and he sank into the chair and scrubbed a hand down his chin. "Dear Lord."

A vein throbbed in Director Landers's forehead. "Why would she do that?"

"You know who she is, then?" Jaxon asked.

His boss scowled. "What difference does it make? Hank Tierney was convicted. He stabbed Mulligan numerous times. He was dangerous and we removed him from the streets."

"He was a fourteen-year-old boy who tried to save his little sister from being raped repeatedly by the man who was supposed to be taking care of him!" Jaxon bellowed.

Snyderman looked up at him grimly. "Hank Tierney was full of rage."

"He should have been," Jaxon said in a dark voice. "He was the only one protecting his sister."

"Delia tried," Director Landers said.

Jaxon swung his head back to his boss. "So you knew her?"

Director Landers looked shell-shocked for a moment as if he didn't realize he'd spoken.

"I...met her at the trial."

Snyderman cursed. "Give it up, Landers," he murmured. "It's time to tell the truth. Hank Tierney doesn't deserve to die, not if Mulligan was raping his sister."

"He was," Jaxon said.

"Tierney's lawyer should have done his homework," Snyderman said. "He should have brought up the abuse. But he was just a young punk overloaded with cases. And Hank's confession pretty much made the case."

"Because no one wanted to dig any deeper into the ugliness of the system," Jaxon muttered.

"That wasn't it," Director Landers said, his voice tinged with anger. "We were all young and ambitious and we wanted to do the right thing."

"The right thing would have been to find the truth, not lock up an innocent kid for trying to save his sister from a damned pedophile."

Snyderman grunted. "We thought Hank Tierney was dangerous," he said in a low voice.

Jaxon arched a brow. "But you knew he didn't kill Mulligan?"

A tense silence stretched between them; then Jaxon pounded his fist on the table. "Tell the truth once and for all, dammit. What happened?"

"Delia..." Director Landers began. "She was young, enthusiastic. It was her first job. She really cared about helping kids."

"Then you knew her personally, not just from the trial?"

Landers dropped his head into his hand with a groan. "Yes, we were dating," he admitted. "A few weeks after Delia placed the Tierney kids with the Mulligans, she found a note from the previous social worker."

"Erma Brant said she left a note advising against placing any more children with the Mulligans."

Director Landers gave a clipped nod. "Somehow the

note got lost. When Delia found it, she freaked out. She was terrified."

"Hadn't she been to the Mulligans' for a follow-up visit?" Jaxon asked.

Landers shook his head. "She was swamped with cases, and hadn't had time. But that night…she drove over." He sank into the chair and drummed his fingers on the table.

Jaxon tapped his foot impatiently. "Go on."

"When she arrived, she heard Avery screaming. Hank and Mulligan were going at it. She looked in the window and saw the old man tying Hank to the bed."

Jaxon swallowed back his disgust.

"What happened next?"

Director Landers sighed. "You have to understand. She didn't go over there to hurt Mulligan or kill him. But when she saw him go into Avery's room and realized what he was doing, she blamed herself. She panicked, grabbed a kitchen knife and ran in to stop him. He turned to fight her, and she stabbed him in self-defense."

"Then she whispered to Avery that everything would be all right," Jaxon said.

Landers nodded gravely.

"But instead of calling the police and explaining, she ran," Jaxon concluded, mentally putting together the pieces. "And when Hank freed himself, he went in and saw Avery. She was traumatized from witnessing the crime, had picked up the knife and crawled back in bed. He thought she stabbed Mulligan, so he took the knife from Avery, wiped her prints off, effectively wiping off Delia's, then stabbed Mulligan repeatedly. The police rushed in, and he confessed to cover for Avery."

Landers nodded again, his expression torn. Snyderman remained silent, a muscle ticking in his jaw.

"Delia was the one who called the police?" Jaxon asked.

"Yes," Landers said. "At that point, she didn't know

what Hank had done. She just wanted to get the kids someplace safe."

"But she allowed Hank to take the fall."

"She was scared. She called me and we talked," Director Landers explained.

Jaxon turned to the D.A. "They consulted you?"

"Yes," he admitted. "Delia didn't know what to do. She was going to turn herself in."

"But when we saw the crime pictures, the dozen stab wounds made by Hank, we realized he was dangerous," Landers added. "We thought it was best for Delia to continue helping other kids and for Hank to be locked away."

As much as he hated to admit it, Jaxon understood their logic. But they had destroyed a kid's life. "Hank Tierney may have needed psychological help, but he was a teenager, and he deserved a chance," Jaxon said. "You ruined not just his life, but Avery's, as well."

"It was an impossible situation," Director Landers said.

Jaxon didn't intend to let him off the hook. "I understand you had client privilege," he said to the D.A. "But, Director Landers, you were sworn to uphold the law. Locking an innocent kid in jail was not the answer. Even worse, you knew there were extenuating circumstances, and you did nothing to help Hank's defense. And Joleen Mulligan should have been prosecuted herself."

"I know," Director Landers said. "There's not a day that's gone by that I haven't debated whether or not I did the right thing. But when I saw the rage inside that boy and those stab wounds, I honestly thought it was a matter of time before he killed someone else. And Delia… She would never have survived prison."

"That wasn't your decision to make." Jaxon had to make this right. "The fact that all of you were willing to allow an innocent man to die to save your reputations is despicable." He reached for his phone.

He had to call a judge.

Then Avery.

Better yet, he wanted to give the director a chance to do the honorable thing. He gestured toward the phone. "Call the judge and tell the truth, Landers. If you don't turn yourself in, I'll arrest you myself."

Director Landers wiped at a bead of sweat trickling down his face. Snyderman nodded for Landers to make the call.

Jaxon stepped aside and punched Avery's number. She'd been upset when she'd left. Hopefully she'd driven straight home.

But Delia had been at her house before. What if she returned?

Fear needled him as he waited for Avery to answer. When she didn't, panic seized him, and he jogged outside to his SUV. If Delia suspected they were close to discovering the truth and that they might expose her, she might be desperate.

He had to find Avery.

AVERY STARED AT Delia Hanover in shock. "What are you doing, Delia?"

"You couldn't stop, couldn't let it alone, could you?" Delia cried.

"You were the one who threatened me over reopening the case." Confusion swirled in Avery's head. She was still reeling from learning that Jaxon had been working against her. And now Delia was holding a gun on her....

The woman's hand shook as she waved Avery to come in. "I tried to help you," Delia whispered. "I tried so hard, but I messed up."

Avery inhaled a deep breath. She had to stall. Figure out a way to convince Delia to drop the gun.

But Delia shoved the barrel into her ribs and pushed her into the den. Desperate for an escape, Avery glanced around the room. Basic furniture. A table loaded with folders. French doors leading to a patio…

A suitcase also stood by those doors, as if Delia had planned a trip.

If Delia planned to kill her and escape, Avery at least wanted answers.

"Why didn't you want me to reopen Hank's case?" Avery asked, although she had a bad feeling that she knew.

"I'm sorry about Hank, more than you'll ever know, Avery." Tears moistened Delia's troubled eyes. "I never meant for him to be arrested. It just…happened."

"What do you mean, it just happened?"

"I came over to see how you and Hank were doing, but then I heard you screaming and crying and saw Hank and Mulligan fighting. Then I watched him tie Hank to the bed."

Avery bit her lip as the memory washed over her. "You were the woman I heard that night. The one that whispered to me."

Delia nodded, a tear trickling down her cheek. "When I saw what he was doing, I panicked. I didn't know, not before then. I swear I didn't. But earlier that day, I found a note Erma Brant left."

"You should have removed us from the family then," Avery said sharply.

Delia began to pace, waving the gun with one hand and pulling at her hair with the other. "That's what I intended to do. That night, I drove over, planning to take you both away myself. But I saw Mulligan going in your room and you screamed, and I panicked. I grabbed a knife to protect myself, but when I tried to stop Mulligan, he came at me. He grabbed me and we fought, and I had the knife and…I stabbed him."

Avery could easily imagine the scenario she described. "You saved me," she whispered. "You cared enough to come and protect me," she said. "So why did you let Hank go to prison? You could have pleaded self-defense."

Delia's eyes flickered with wild panic as if she were re-living the night herself. "I was scared. It was my first job, and I wanted to make it work, wanted to help others. And my father… He's a judge. He warned me not to go into social work, said I wasn't cut out for it. I knew if I was arrested, it would not only ruin my career, but his, as well."

"You were worried about your career!" Avery said, her voice shrill. "What about my life? What about Hank's? He was just a kid and you stole his life from him."

A sob escaped Delia. "I didn't think he'd go to prison," she cried. "But when I saw how many times he stabbed Mulligan, I thought it was too late for Hank, that he was like his father, and he'd be better off locked away. I thought you'd be safer that way."

"Safer?" Avery cried. "Hank confessed to protect me. He's the only one who ever loved me, and because of me, and you—" she jabbed her finger in the air at Delia "—he's about to die."

Delia looked frantic, desperate. She paused by the window and rubbed her hand over her face, swiping at the tears. "I'm sorry, Avery. I'm so sorry. But—"

"There is no but," Avery said. "You can't let Hank die, Delia." She softened her voice, desperate to appeal to the woman's morals. "You're not a bad person. I know that. You care about the kids you help, just like you cared about us back then. A judge will understand that."

Delia shook her head back and forth, sobbing. "No, they won't. And my father… He'll hate me."

She raised the gun, and Avery held her breath, terrified Delia was going to shoot her.

But the woman turned the gun on herself and placed the barrel at her temple.

Chapter Twenty-Two

Jaxon checked the time as he drove from the jail. Delia would probably be at school. He punched the number for the office. "This is Texas Ranger Sergeant Ward. Is Delia Hanover at school today?"

"I'm afraid not. She called in sick."

"Where does she live?"

"I'm not supposed to give out that information."

"This is a police emergency. Lives may depend on it. Now give me her address."

The woman coughed nervously, then stuttered the address.

Jaxon recognized the street. Not far from the school.

He pressed the accelerator and sped down the road, rounding the curve on two wheels. Tires screeched, his adrenaline pumping as he neared the street. He veered right, slowing as he approached her house and saw Avery's car parked in front. He parked on the curb, slid from the vehicle and hurried toward the house, scanning the perimeter.

Early-morning sunlight slanted off the dry grass. The car in the neighboring driveway fired up its engine and the driver backed out, probably heading to work. A young mother across the street hustled her brood into a minivan. A jogger ran by with his chocolate Lab.

Everything looked normal and quiet. Just another day in Cherokee Crossing.

But instincts warned him that Delia Hanover might have figured out he and Avery were close to the truth, and that she was scared.

Her secret had been safely hidden for twenty years. She wouldn't want the truth to be exposed now.

He paused to listen as he reached the front door, but everything seemed quiet. Still, he pulled his gun at the ready, then stepped to the side and peered through the front window.

His chest clenched. Avery was standing within inches of Delia, while Delia clutched a gun in her hand.

He jumped back from the window so Delia wouldn't see him, then crept around the back of the house to sneak inside and surprise her from the rear.

But just as he reached the door, a gunshot blasted the air.

AVERY DIVED ON top of Delia, desperately trying to knock the gun from her hand. It went off, the bullet exploding in the ceiling, plaster raining down.

"Let me go!" Delia cried.

"You're not going to kill yourself," Avery shouted. "You're going to tell the truth and help free Hank."

Delia still had hold of the gun, and Avery struggled to pry it from her fingers. They rolled sideways, and she clawed at Delia's hand, trying to pin the woman down with her body.

But Delia was strong and used her weight to buck Avery off her. Avery fell to the floor, grasping for Delia's hand.

But Delia raised the gun again and kicked at Avery to keep her away.

Suddenly a crash sounded, and footsteps pounded.

Delia startled, and Avery crawled toward her to grab the gun. But Delia lifted her hand again, the gun wavering as she struggled to stand.

"Don't move, Delia. Put the weapon down!"

Jaxon burst into the room, his weapon aimed at Delia.

Delia cried out in surprise, and Avery scrambled backward away from the woman.

"Put it down," Jaxon ordered.

"I can't go to jail," Delia cried. "I can't…"

Jaxon cut his eyes toward Avery as if to ask if she was okay, and she gave him a quick nod.

"We'll explain what happened that night," Avery said in a low voice. "You defended yourself."

"But I let Hank be wrongly convicted," Delia cried. "I… should have told."

"Yes, you should have," Jaxon barked. "But it's not too late to do the right thing, Delia."

Delia was sobbing openly now, her hand shaking, the gun wavering toward Jaxon.

Feelings of betrayed splintered through Avery. Jaxon had kept his reason for investigating the case a secret to protect his boss.

But she didn't want him to die.

JAXON KEPT HIS hand steady as Delia backed up against the wall. "Delia, you don't want to shoot me or Avery. When you killed Mulligan, it was self-defense. You were trying to save two children from a monster. A judge and jury will sympathize with that." He lowered his voice. "But killing us is not the same thing. It's murder."

"I don't want to hurt either of you," Delia said, choking on more tears. "I just want this to be over."

"It will be when you lower the gun," Jaxon said. "We'll talk to the judge and explain."

But Delia shook her head back and forth, the panic on her face sending a chill through Jaxon.

"You've done good things for other children since that day," he said, grasping for a way to stop her from further self-destruction.

Delia blinked, her hand bobbing up and down. "But

it doesn't make up for that night." She glanced at Avery, sorrow wrenching her face. "I'm so sorry about Hank."

Then she swung the gun up toward her head.

Avery screamed, "No!"

Jaxon fired a shot at the floor beside Delia. She startled at the sound, and he lunged toward her and knocked the weapon from her hand.

The gun skittered to the floor, and he kicked it away. Then Delia doubled over into a knot on the floor and began to wail.

He glanced at Avery. "Are you okay?"

She nodded, although tears were streaming down her face, as well.

Delia was a pitiful mess, but she'd also tried to kill herself and taken Avery at gunpoint, so he yanked his handcuffs from his pocket, knelt and cuffed her.

She didn't fight him. Instead she crumbled, sobbing uncontrollably as he removed his phone and punched Deputy Kimball's number. "I'm bringing Delia Hanover in for the murder of Wade Mulligan. Ask a judge to meet us at the jail."

He went to Avery to help her up, but she waved his hands off and stood. Her breath was unsteady, pain still radiating from her eyes. "Can we get Hank out now?"

"That's the reason I asked the judge to meet us. He'll need to contact the governor and stop the execution. There will be a formal hearing, of course, and then hopefully Hank will be released."

A smile of relief curved Avery's mouth, but the sadness in her eyes remained.

She thought he'd betrayed her by withholding the truth about his initial reason for coming to Cherokee Crossing from her.

That secret had torn them apart and destroyed her trust in him.

And he didn't know how to win it back.

AVERY FELT NUMB as Jaxon escorted a sobbing Delia out to his SUV.

She followed them, her heart aching for Delia, yet she couldn't prevent the anger eating at her. Delia had deprived her brother of a life on the outside.

He was thirty-four now, not old, yet when he was freed, he'd have to start all over. He'd finished his GED in prison, but had no college or technical training. No job waiting or home or family.

Still, she couldn't wait to tell him that he was really going to be free.

Jaxon shut the back door, closing Delia in. She buried her head in her hands, doubling over as she cried.

"I'll call you when things are settled," Jaxon said.

"No, I'll follow you to the jail. I want to be there when Hank gets free."

"It won't happen today," Jaxon said. "It'll take time to set up the hearing."

"I know, but I want to see him," Avery said. "I have to let him know what's happened."

Jaxon hesitated. "Avery, go home and let me handle the arrangements. There's a lot to do. We have to book Delia, and I need to talk to the judge. And I haven't had time to tell you, but apparently Director Landers, my boss, knew what Delia did. He was a rookie back then, and he and Delia were dating. She told him what happened, but he covered it up. They both thought Hank was dangerous."

"That doesn't make it right."

"No, it doesn't," Jaxon said. "But we're going to."

His conviction warmed her. It must have been hard for him to admit that his boss had crossed the line. "Will you call and see if I can visit Hank and fill him in?"

Jaxon studied her for a long moment. "Of course. Hank deserves to know tonight."

His gaze locked with hers, and Avery's heart ached. Jaxon was the first man she'd ever really trusted.

And he'd let her down.

But in the end, he'd come through for her, and for her brother.

"I'm sorry about the director," he said, his jaw hard. "I didn't know, Avery. I swear I didn't."

She swallowed hard. She believed him. But her heart and her emotions were in shambles.

A sad look passed over his face; then he climbed into the SUV and started the engine.

Delia was still sobbing as he drove away.

Avery ignored the pang of sympathy tugging at her, jumped in her car and headed toward the prison.

Hank had waited twenty years for vindication.

She didn't want him to have to wait another minute.

AVERY LET HERSELF into her house, disappointment dogging her. She hadn't been able to see Hank.

Jaxon had phoned, but a brutal stabbing by another inmate had resulted in two dead guards and another dead inmate, and the prison was on twenty-four-hour lockdown.

Hank would have to go to bed tonight without knowing that he was going to be freed. She just prayed nothing happened to him until he was released.

But just to be on the safe side, she had phoned Ms. Ellis, the lawyer who'd initially been interested in Hank's case. The lawyer promised to contact Jaxon and to represent Hank in court. Avery's trust in the system was still shaky, and Avery felt better knowing she and Hank had another professional on their side.

Avery hesitated as she entered, remembering the pictures Delia had cut up and left on her bed. Remembering the words she'd written and that threatening phone call.

Delia had obviously been terrified of the truth being exposed.

Shaken by the day's events, she showered and pulled on her pajamas, then poured herself a glass of wine and padded outside to her screened porch. She settled in the swing, pushing it back and forth with her foot as she sipped the wine.

Outside the wind tossed dead leaves around, and the trees swayed, the woods dark and desolate looking. She'd been afraid of the dark half her life.

She'd been afraid of so many things.

Afraid of getting close to anyone. Of letting a man touch her.

Just as she was afraid of owning her house. Of having a pet. It hurt too much to lose them.

Jaxon had changed all that. And he hadn't abandoned the case, even though his boss had turned out to be dirty.

She closed her eyes and remembered his fingers roving over her body, his tongue touching her intimate places, his body coupling with hers, and heat suffused her.

She had practically begged Jaxon to make love to her.

And he had been gentle. Loving.

He'd even promised to stop if she'd wanted him to.

How could she blame him for having sex with her when she'd wanted him so badly?

When she still did?

A lonely feeling washed over her as she studied the night sky.

Jaxon had never mentioned love or wanting a relationship. When the case was dismissed and Hank was set free, she would need to help Hank get on his feet and figure out what to do with his life. With his second chance.

Jaxon would move on to another case.

And she would have to let him.

Chapter Twenty-Three

"Hank Tierney, you are hereby exonerated of the murder conviction against you for the death of Wade Mulligan." The judge angled himself toward Hank. "It is a travesty that it took so long for justice to be served, but you do realize the part you played in impeding the investigation?"

Hank sat stoically, his face etched in disbelief. "Yes, sir."

"That said, the court apologizes for the injustice done to you by the system and the failure of your attorney at the time to provide an adequate defense. In addition, the officer in charge of the investigation has admitted to omitting key evidence in the crime and faces charges himself.

"In the light of new evidence, you are free to go."

He pounded the gavel, and everyone except Hank stood. He was still sitting in shock by Jaxon and Ms. Ellis, who patted him on the back. "Congratulations, Hank, you've been exonerated. Your name is clear now. And I'll see what I can do about obtaining monetary restitution."

Avery jumped up and hurried around to her brother. "Hank, did you hear, you're free?"

Her brother slowly looked up at her, tears pooling in his eyes. "For real?"

"Yes, for real," Avery said with a nervous laugh. "I tried to see you last night at the prison to give you a heads-up, but the prison was on lockdown and they wouldn't let me visit."

Hank looked at Jaxon, then the lawyer, then her. "Delia, our social worker, killed that bastard Mulligan?"

"Yes." Avery drew him into a hug. "It's over, Hank. It's finally over and you can go home."

"I don't believe it," Hank mumbled.

She pulled away, and Jaxon extended his hand to Hank. "Believe it, Hank. It was too long in coming, but justice finally prevailed."

And not a minute too soon. Two more days and Hank would have been put to death.

A smile started on Hank's face, and he shook Jaxon's hand. But his frown returned when he faced Avery. "You said I can go home. But I don't have a home or a job or anywhere to go."

Avery's heart swelled. "Yes, you do—you're coming home with me. I'm even thinking of buying my little house."

He looked at her with such relief that she hugged him again. "I know it'll take time, brother, but we'll work it out. The important thing is that you were exonerated. You're not only free, but your name has been cleared."

Not that it would replace the twenty years he'd lost.

Hank turned to Jaxon with a sheepish look. "Thank you, Sergeant Ward. I never trusted a cop before, but I appreciate what you did."

Avery's gaze met Jaxon's, but he simply shrugged. "I was just doing my job."

So that was it, Avery thought. He had just been doing his job. Nothing personal.

She should be so detached.

Her father appeared then, cutting off any further exchange. He looked old and weathered, but he had tried to do the right thing for Hank at his own expense.

Maybe it was time for forgiveness.

"Thank you, Dad," Avery said. "Hank and I appreciate what you did for him."

Hank rubbed a hand over his shaved head, his expression torn. "Yeah, thanks. I…never would have expected you to do something like that."

Their father gave a self-deprecating laugh. "To tell you the truth, neither did I. But when I saw the news and thought about you dying when it was my fault you and your sister ended up with that family, I had to do something."

Hank hesitated, but shook his father's hand. Avery bit her lip to keep from crying.

Maybe she could put her family back together again.

The thought gave her hope, but Jaxon turned and headed out the door, and a dull ache rippled through her.

Only Jaxon wouldn't be part of her future.

THE PAST TWENTY-FOUR hours had been hell. Jaxon hated that he'd been forced to make the director turn himself in. Everyone in the Texas Ranger Division was upset, and Landers was right—already the hounds were surfacing to question his other arrests.

Snyderman received sanctions, but the moment Landers had confided in him, hiring Snyderman as his attorney, client privilege kicked in.

Delia's father had shown up, irate, and accused Jaxon of framing Delia, but the woman had confessed.

Now he watched Avery leave with her brother and father, grateful at last that she could have the family she deserved.

But as he walked outside to his vehicle, a sense of loss engulfed him. And when he made it to his ranch, the place he loved, the vast wide-open spaces and sprawling land suddenly looked empty and lonely.

Just like Avery, he'd guarded his heart all his life. Had allowed himself only a physical connection with a woman. Had focused on his job.

Because catching killers was a lot less scary than sharing your heart.

He climbed out, his boots crunching as he walked across the pasture to the barn. He hadn't spent much time here lately. Things were looking run-down.

He needed help.

An idea struck him, and he returned to his SUV and headed back toward town.

Avery might not forgive him for Director Landers, but maybe he could make amends by offering her brother a job on his ranch.

It wouldn't be easy for Hank to acclimate back into society. And if Hank didn't want the job, that was fine.

But Jaxon wanted to give the man a second chance.

Then maybe Avery would give him a second chance, as well.

AVERY HAD JUST walked outside to plant some bulbs when Jaxon pulled up. She'd left Hank inside with Ms. Ellis—Lisa—giving them some privacy. Apparently something had sparked between them when they met, and Avery thought her brother might just have a lover in his future.

But the moment Avery saw Jaxon, nerves fluttered in her stomach. What if something had gone wrong and he was here to take Hank back to prison?

When he climbed from the driver's side, tingles of desire danced down her spine, and she drank in his strong masculine presence.

She'd never met a man like him. She'd certainly never meet another.

"Jaxon," she said, grappling for words. "Is everything all right? The judge. Hank—"

"Everything is fine. Don't worry, your brother is free and clear."

Relief made her sag against the shovel she was holding.

"You're planting flowers?" Jaxon asked.

She nodded. "Hank has missed the seasons," she said. "I want him to see the tulips come to life in the spring."

"Nice."

For a moment, they stood looking at each other, an awkward silence lingering between them. Finally he tipped his Stetson.

"I stopped by because of Hank. Him and your father."

Avery's stomach knotted again. "Why? What's wrong?"

"Nothing." He threaded his fingers through his hair, then settled his hat back in place. "When you were at the ranch, I told you I'm busy, gone on cases, and need some help working the horses, repairing fences. If your father and brother want a job and don't mind hard work, I could use them on the spread."

Avery leaned the shovel against the side of the house. "You're serious, Jaxon?"

"Yes."

"That would be perfect. I know Hank would like to work outdoors." She hesitated. "But are you sure you want to take my father on? He is an ex-con."

"He redeemed himself at the end," Jaxon said. "Everyone deserves a second chance."

Love bloomed in Avery's chest. Was he asking for one? "You are an amazing man, Jaxon."

He shrugged. "It's the least I can do."

"You've already done enough. My goodness, you tracked down Delia and saved Hank."

"When I pulled up at the house and heard gunfire last night, I thought I'd lost you," Jaxon said in a gruff voice.

Avery licked her lips, touched. "I jumped Delia to keep her from committing suicide."

"That's even more admirable," Jaxon said. "Especially considering the fact that she was responsible for Hank's incarceration and partially responsible for your abuse by leaving you in that devil's home."

Avery softened at his possessive tone.

"I know it was difficult for you," she said in a low murmur. "That you were in a tough spot with your boss."

Jaxon shrugged, his rugged face set in a frown. But his eyes locked with hers, and something heady flickered there. Need? Desire? Passion?

"You did it for me, didn't you?" Avery whispered.

"Partly. And partly for your brother." His voice cracked, and he reached for her. Circled his arms around her wrist and drew her to him. "But I did it mostly because it was the right thing to do. I couldn't have lived with myself if I'd covered up the truth."

"Well, whatever your reason, I appreciate it." She thumbed a strand of his dark hair from his forehead, and her finger tingled. She wanted to touch him all over again.

His eyes flared with hunger. "I'm not here for your thanks."

She smiled at the glint in his eyes. "Why are you here, then?"

A heartbeat passed. His thick arousal pressed against her belly. Her heart drummed so loud she could hear it roaring in her ears.

She ached to have him closer.

"I came for this." He whispered her name in a husky tone that made her shiver all over, then pressed his lips to hers. Erotic sensations mingled with emotions, nearly overpowering her, and she kissed him back, tangling her tongue with his in a frenzy of wild abandon.

When he finally pulled away, they were both breathless, but he held her close and nuzzled her neck with his lips. "I love you, Avery."

Avery's heart fluttered. All her hopes and dreams had been stirred to life the past few days with Jaxon.

Could she dare believe that they would come true?

With this man, maybe she could.

She was tired of running and being scared.

He seemed to be searching her face, and she realized that he was scared, too. Maybe nervous that she didn't return his feelings.

Empowered by that thought, she looped her arms around his neck, then brushed herself against him in a slow seductive move. "I love you, too, Jaxon. I never thought I could... love any man. But I love you with all my heart."

He teased her lips apart with his tongue. "Good. 'Cause I don't want to be alone anymore. And that ranch is awful lonely without you."

"Really?" she said in a teasing voice.

"I can still smell you on my sheets." He rubbed his forehead against hers. "And my shower is big enough for two."

"I noticed."

"You're going to buy this house, though?"

She shrugged. "I just wanted to finally have a permanent home. Maybe get a dog."

A smile twitched at his eyes. "A ranch is a great place for a dog."

"I bet it is."

Passion glazed his eyes. "I want you in my bed, Avery. But that's not all." His voice broke. "I want you to be my wife."

Her heart soared as he swung her up in his arms and carried her to his SUV. Ten minutes later, they parked at his ranch.

She climbed out, breathing in the pure beauty of the land and the man—and the fact that he wanted to share his life with her.

He swept her up in his arms again, kissed her with all the fervor of a lover desperate for more, then carried her inside to bed.

They made love all through the night, whispering promises that they would be together the rest of their lives.

Promises she knew that the man in her arms would keep.

* * * * *

"I'm not going anywhere. I'm a man of my word."

She met his gaze. "Somehow I knew that."

"No matter how long it takes, I'm not leaving you." Austin knew even as he made the promise that there would be hell to pay with his family. She started to turn away.

"One more thing," he said. "Did your sister have a key to this house?"

"No." Realization dawned on her expression. She shivered.

"Then there is nothing to worry about," he said. "Try to get some sleep."

"You, too."

He knew that wouldn't be easy. An electricity seemed to spark in the air between them. They'd been through so much together already. He didn't dare imagine what tomorrow would bring.

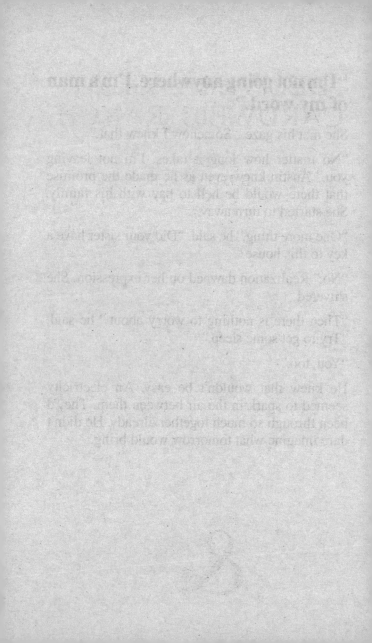

DELIVERANCE AT CARDWELL RANCH

BY
B.J. DANIELS

Published in Great Britain 2014
by Mills & Boon, an imprint of Harlequin (UK) Limited,
Eton House, 18-24 Paradise Road, Richmond, Surrey, TW9 1SR

© 2014 Barbara Heinlein

ISBN: 978-0-263-91378-1

46-1214

New York Times bestselling author **B.J. Daniels** wrote her first book after a career as an award-winning newspaper journalist and author of thirty-seven published short stories. That first book, *Odd Man Out*, received a four-and-a-half-star review from *RT Book Reviews* and went on to be nominated for Best Intrigue that year. Since then, she has won numerous awards, including a career achievement award for romantic suspense and many nominations and awards for best book.

Daniels lives in Montana with her husband, Parker, and two springer spaniels, Spot and Jem. When she isn't writing, she snowboards, camps, boats and plays tennis. Daniels is a member of Mystery Writers of America, Sisters in Crime, International Thriller Writers, Kiss of Death and Romance Writers of America.

To contact her, write to B.J. Daniels, PO Box 1173, Malta, MT 59538, USA, or e-mail her at bjdaniels@mtintouch. net. Check out her website, www.bjdaniels.com.

Chapter One

Snow fell in a wall of white, giving Austin Cardwell only glimpses of the winding highway in front of him. He'd already slowed to a crawl as visibility worsened. Now on the radio, he heard that Highway 191 through the Gallatin Canyon—the very one he was on—was closed to all but emergency traffic.

"One-ninety-one from West Yellowstone to Bozeman is closed due to several accidents including a semi rollover that has blocked the highway near Big Sky. Another accident near West Yellowstone has also caused problems there. Travelers are advised to wait out the storm."

Great, Austin thought with a curse. *Wait out the storm where?* He hadn't seen any place to even pull over for miles let alone a gas station or café. He had no choice but to keep going. This was just what this Texas boy needed, he told himself with a curse. He'd be lucky if he reached Cardwell Ranch tonight.

The storm appeared to be getting worse. He couldn't see more than a few yards in front of the rented SUV's hood. Earlier he'd gotten a glimpse of the Gallatin River to his left. On his right were steep rock walls as the two-lane highway cut through the canyon. There was nothing but dark, snow-capped pine trees, steep mountain cliffs and the frozen river and snow-slick highway.

"Welcome to the frozen north," he said under his breath as he fought to see the road ahead—and stay on it. He blamed his brothers—not for the storm, but for his even being here. They had insisted he come to Montana for the grand opening of the first Texas Boys Barbecue joint in Montana. They had postponed the grand opening until he was well enough to come.

Although the opening was to be January 1, his cousin Dana had pleaded with him to spend Christmas at the ranch.

You need to be here, Austin, she'd said. *I promise you won't be sorry.*

He growled under his breath now. He hadn't been back to Montana since his parents divorced and his mother took him and his brothers to Texas to live. He'd been too young to remember much. But he'd found he couldn't say no to Dana. He'd heard too many good things about her from his brothers.

Also, what choice did he have after missing his brother Tag's wedding last July?

As he slowed for another tight curve, a gust of wind shook the rented SUV. Snow whirled past his windshield. For an instant, he couldn't see anything. Worse, he felt as if he was going too fast for the curve. But he was afraid to touch his brakes—the one thing his brother Tag had warned him not to do.

Don't do anything quickly, Tag had told him. *And whatever you do, don't hit your brakes. You'll end up in the ditch.*

He caught something in his headlights. It took him a moment to realize what he was seeing before his heart took off at a gallop.

A car was upside down in the middle of the highway, its headlights shooting out through the falling snow toward the river, the taillights a dim red against the steep canyon wall. The overturned car had the highway completely blocked.

word, he drove, the taillights dim red against the deep
cut of the river. The overturned car had the highway completely blocked.

Chapter Two

Austin hit his brakes even though he doubted he stood
a chance in hell of stopping. The SUV began to slide
sideways toward the overturned car. He spun the wheel,
realizing he'd done it too wildly when he began to slide
toward the river. As he turned the wheel yet again, the
SUV slid toward the canyon wall—and the overturned
car.

He was within only a few feet of the car on the road,
when his front tires went off the road into the narrow
snow-filled ditch between him and the granite canyon
wall. The deep snow seemed to grab the SUV and pull
it in deeper.

Austin braced himself as snow rushed up over the
hood, burying the windshield as the front of the SUV
sunk. The ditch and the snow in it were much deeper than
he'd thought. He closed his eyes and braced himself for
when the SUV hit the steep rock canyon wall.

To his surprise, the SUV came to a sudden stop before
it hit the sheer rock face.

He sat for a moment, too shaken to move. Then he remembered the car he'd seen upside down in the middle of
the road. What if someone was hurt? He tried his door,
but the snow was packed around it. Reaching across the
seat, he tried the passenger side. Same problem.

As he sat back, he glanced in the rearview mirror. The rear of the SUV sat higher, the back wheels still partially up on the edge of the highway. He could see out a little of the back window where the snow hadn't blown up on it and realized his only exit would be the hatchback.

He hit the hatchback release then climbed over the seat. In the back, he dug through the clothing he'd brought on the advice of his now "Montana" brother and pulled out the flashlight, along with the winter coat and boots he'd brought. Hurrying, he pulled them on and climbed out through the back into the blinding snowstorm, anxious to see if he could be of any help to the passengers in the wrecked vehicle.

He'd waded through deep snow for a few steps before his feet almost slipped out from under him on the icy highway. No wonder there had been accidents and the highway had closed to all but emergency traffic. The pavement under the falling snow was covered with glare ice. He was amazed he hadn't gone off the road sooner.

Moving cautiously toward the overturned car, he snapped on his flashlight and shone it inside the vehicle, afraid of what he would find.

The driver's seat was empty. So was the passenger seat. The driver's air bag had activated then deflated. In the backseat, though, he saw something that made his pulse jump. A car seat was still strapped in. No baby, though.

He shined the light on the headliner, stopping when he spotted what looked like a woman's purse. Next to it was an empty baby bottle and a smear of blood.

"Hello?" he called out, terrified for the occupants of the car. The night, blanketed by the falling snow, felt too quiet. He was used to Texas traffic and the noise of big-city Houston.

No answer. He had no idea how long ago the accident had happened. Wouldn't the driver have had the good sense to stay nearby? Then again, maybe another vehicle had come from the other side of the highway and rescued the driver and baby. Strange, though, to just leave the car like this without trying to flag the accident.

"Hello?" He listened. He'd never heard such cold silence. It had a spooky quality that made him jumpy. Add to that this car being upside down in the middle of the highway. What if another vehicle came along right now going too fast to stop?

Walking around the car, he found the driver's side door hanging open and bent down to look inside. More blood on the headliner. His heart began to pound even as he told himself someone must have rescued the driver and baby. At least he hoped that was what had happened. But his instincts told him different. While in the barbecue business with his brothers, he worked as a deputy sheriff in a small town outside Houston.

He reached for his cell phone. No service. As he started to straighten, a hard, cold object struck him in the back of the head. Austin Cardwell staggered from the blow and grabbed the car frame to keep from going down. The second blow caught him in the back.

He swung around to ward off another blow.

To his shock, he came face-to-face with a woman wielding a tire iron. But it was the crazed expression on her bloody face that turned his own blood to ice.

Chapter Three

Austin's head swam for a moment as he watched the woman raise the tire iron again. He'd disarmed his fair share of drunks and drugged-up attackers. Now he only took special jobs on a part-time basis, usually the investigative jobs no one else wanted.

Even with his head and back aching from the earlier blows, he reacted instinctively from years of dealing with criminals. He stepped to the side as the woman brought the tire iron down a third time. It connected with the car frame, the sound ringing out an instant before he locked an arm around her neck. With his other hand, he broke her grip on the weapon. It dropped to the ground, disappearing in the falling snow as he dragged her back against him, lifting her off her feet.

Though she was small framed, she proved to be much stronger than he'd expected. She fought as if her life depended on it.

"Settle down," he ordered, his breath coming out as fog in the cold mountain air. "I'm trying to help you."

His words had little effect. He was forced to capture both her wrists in his hands to keep her from striking him as he brought her around to face him.

"Listen to me," he said, putting his face close to hers. "I'm a deputy sheriff from Texas. I'm trying to help you."

She stared at him through the falling snow as if un-comprehending, and he wondered if the injury on her forehead, along with the trauma of the car accident, could be the problem.

"You hit your head when you wrecked your car—"

"It's not my car." She said the words through chatter-ing teeth and he realized that she appeared to be on the verge of hypothermia—something else that could explain her strange behavior.

"Okay, it's not your car. Where is the owner?"

She glanced past him, a terrified expression coming over her face.

"Did you have your baby with you?" he asked.

"I don't have a baby."

The car seat in the back of the vehicle and the baby bottle lying on the headliner next to her purse would in-dicate otherwise. He hoped, though, that she was tell-ing the truth. He couldn't bear the thought that the baby had come out of the car seat and was somewhere out in the snow.

He listened for a moment. He hadn't heard a baby cry-ing when he'd gotten out of the SUV's hatchback. Nor had he heard one since. The falling snow blanketed ev-erything, though, with that eerie stillness. But he had to assume even if there had been a baby, it wasn't still alive.

He considered what to do. His SUV wasn't coming out of that ditch without a tow truck hooked to it and her car certainly wasn't going anywhere.

"What's your name?" he asked her. She was shak-ing harder now. He had to get her to someplace warm. Neither of their vehicles was an option. If another vehi-cle came down this highway from either direction, there was too much of a chance they would be hit. He recalled glimpsing an old boarded-up cabin back up the highway. It wasn't that far. "What's your name?" he asked again.

She looked confused and on the verge of passing out on him. He feared if she did, he wouldn't be able to carry her back to the cabin he'd seen. When he realized he wasn't going to be able to get any information out of her, he reached back into the overturned car and snagged the strap of her purse.

The moment he let go of one of her arms, she tried to run away again and began kicking and clawing at him when he reached for her. He restrained her again, more easily this time because she was losing her motor skills due to the cold.

"We have to get you to shelter. I'm not going to hurt you. Do you understand me?" Any other time, he would have put out some sort of warning sign in case another driver came along. But he couldn't let go of this woman for fear she would attack him again or worse, take off into the storm.

He had to get her to the cabin as quickly as possible. He wasn't sure how badly she was hurt—just that blood was still streaming down her face from the contusion on her forehead. Loss of blood or a concussion could be the cause for her odd behavior. He'd have to restrain her and come back to flag the wreck.

Fortunately, the road was now closed to all but emergency traffic. He figured the first vehicle to come upon the wreck would be highway patrol or possibly a snow-plow driver.

Feeling he had no choice but to get her out of this storm, Austin grabbed his duffel out of the back of the SUV and started to lock it, still holding on to the woman. For the first time, he took a good look at her.

She wore designer jeans, dress boots, a sweater and no

coat. He realized he hadn't seen a winter coat in the car or any snow boots. In her state of mind, she could have removed her coat and left it out in the snow.

Taking off his down coat, he put it on her even though she fought him. He put on the lighter-weight jacket he'd been wearing earlier when he'd gone off the road.

In his duffel bag, he found a pair of mittens he'd invested in before the trip and put them on her gloveless hands, then dug out a baseball cap, the only hat he had. He put it on her head of dark curly hair. The brown eyes staring out at him were wide with fear and confusion.

"You're going to have to walk for a ways," he said to her. She gave him a blank look. But while she appeared more subdued, he wasn't going to trust it. "The cabin I saw from the road isn't far."

It wasn't a long walk. The woman came along without a struggle. But she still seemed terrified of something. She kept looking behind her as they walked as if she feared someone was out there in the storm and would be coming after her. He could feel her body trembling through the grip he had on her arm.

Walking through the falling snow, down the middle of the deserted highway, felt surreal. The quiet, the empty highway, the two of them, strangers, at least one of them in some sort of trouble. It felt as if the world had come to an end and they were the last two people alive.

As they neared where he'd seen the cabin, he hoped his eyes hadn't been deceiving him since he'd only gotten a glimpse through the falling snow. He quickly saw that it was probably only a summer cabin, if that. It didn't look as if it had been used in years. Tiny and rustic, it was set back in a narrow ravine off the highway. The windows had wooden shutters on them and the front door was secured with a padlock.

They slogged through the deep snow up the ravine to the cabin as flakes whirled around them. Austin couldn't remember ever being this cold. The woman had to be freezing since she'd been out in the cold longer than he had and her sweater had to be soaked beneath his coat.

Leading her around to the back, he found a shutter-less window next to the door. Putting his elbow through the old, thin glass, he reached inside and unlocked the door. As he shoved it open, a gust of cold, musty air rushed out.

The woman balked for a moment before he pulled her inside. The room was small, and had apparently once been a porch but was now a storage area. He was relieved to see a stack of dry split wood piled by the door leading into the cabin proper.

Opening the next door, he stepped in, dragging the woman after him. It was pitch-black inside. He dropped his duffel bag and her purse, removed the flashlight from his coat pocket and shone it around the room. An old rock fireplace, the front sooty from years of fires, stood against one wall. A menagerie of ancient furniture formed a half circle around it.

Through a door, he saw one bedroom with a double bed. In another, there were two bunk beds. The bathroom was apparently an outhouse out back. The kitchen was so small he almost missed it.

"We won't have water or any lavatory facilities, but we'll make do since we will have heat as soon as I get a fire going." He looked at her, debating what to do. She couldn't go far inside the small cabin, but she could find a weapon easy enough. He wasn't going to chance it since his head still hurt like hell from the tire iron she'd used to try to cave in his skull. His back was sore, but that was all, fortunately.

Because of his work as a deputy sheriff, he always

carried a gun and handcuffs. He put the duffel bag down on the table, unzipped it and pulled out the handcuffs.

The woman tried to pull free of him at the sight of them.

"Listen," he said gently. "I'm only going to handcuff one of your wrists just to restrain you. I can't trust that you won't hurt me or yourself if I don't." He said all of it apologetically.

Something in his voice must have assured her because she let him lead her over to a chair in front of the fireplace. He snapped one cuff on her right wrist and the other to the frame of the heaviest chair.

She looked around the small cabin, her gaze going to the back door. The terror in her eyes made the hair on the back of his neck spike. He'd once had a girlfriend whose cat used to suddenly look at a doorway as if there were something unearthly standing in it. Austin had the same creepy feeling now and feared that this woman was as haunted as that darned cat.

With the dried wood from the back porch and some matches he found in the kitchen, he got a fire going. Just the sound of the wood crackling and the glow of the flames seemed to instantly warm the room.

He found a pan in the kitchen and, filling it with snow from outside, brought it in and placed it in front of the fire. It wasn't long before he could dampen one end of a dish towel from the kitchen.

"I'm going to wash the blood off your face so I can see how badly you've been hurt, all right?"

She held still as he gently applied the wet towel. The bleeding had stopped over her eye, but it was a nasty gash. It took some searching before he found a first aid kit in one of the bedrooms and bandaged the cut as best he could.

"Are you hurt anywhere else?"

She shook her head.

"Okay," he said with a nod. His head still ached, but the tire iron hadn't broken the skin—only because he had a thick head of dark hair like all of the Cardwells—and a hard head to boot.

The cabin was getting warmer, but he still found an old quilt and wrapped it around her. She had stopped shaking at least. Unfortunately, she still looked confused and scared. He was pretty sure she had a concussion. But there was little he could do. He still had no cell phone coverage. Not that anyone could get to them with the wrecks and the roads the way they were.

Picking up her purse, he sat down in a chair near her. He noticed her watching him closely as he dumped the contents out on the marred wood coffee table. Coins tinkled out, several spilling onto the floor. As he picked them up, he realized several interesting things about what was—and wasn't—in her purse.

There was a whole lot of makeup for someone who didn't have any on. There was also no cell phone. But there *was* a baby's pacifier.

He looked up at her and realized he'd made a rooky mistake. He hadn't searched her. He'd just assumed she didn't have a weapon like a gun or knife because she'd used a tire iron back on the highway.

Getting up, he went over to her and checked her pockets. No cell phone. But he did find a set of car keys. He frowned. That was odd since he remembered that the keys had still been in the wrecked car. The engine had died, but the lights were still on.

So what were these keys for? They appeared to have at least one key for a vehicle and another like the kind used for house doors.

"Are these your keys?" he asked, but after staring at them for a moment, she frowned and looked away.

Maybe she had been telling the truth about the car not being hers.

Sitting back down, he opened her wallet. Three singles, a five—and less than a dollar in change. Not much money for a woman on the road. Not much money dressed like she was either. Also, there were no credit cards.

But there was a driver's license. He pulled it out and looked at the photo. The woman's dark hair in the snapshot was shorter and curlier, but she had the same intense brown eyes. There was enough of a resemblance that he would assume this woman was Rebecca Stewart. According to the ID, she was married, lived in Helena, Montana, and was an organ donor.

"It says here that your name is Rebecca Stewart."

"That's not my purse." She frowned at the bag as if she'd never seen it before.

"Then what was it doing in the car you were driving?"

She shook her head, looking more confused and scared.

"If you're not Rebecca Stewart, then who are you?"

He saw her lower lip quiver. One large tear rolled down her cheek. "I don't know." When she went to wipe her tears with her free hand, he saw the diamond watch.

Reaching over, he caught her wrist. She tried to pull away, but he was much stronger than she was, and more determined. Even at a glance, he could see that the watch was expensive.

"Where did you get this?" he asked, hating that he sounded so suspicious. But the woman had a car and a purse she swore weren't hers. It wasn't that much of a leap to think that the watch probably wasn't hers either.

She stared at the watch on her wrist as if she'd never

seen it before. The gold band was encrusted with diamonds. Pulling it off her wrist, he turned the watch over. Just as he'd suspected, it was engraved:

To Gillian with all my love.

"Is your name Gillian?"

She remembered *something,* he saw it in her eyes.

"So your name *is* Gillian?"

She didn't answer, but now she looked more afraid than she had before.

Austin sighed. He wasn't going to get anything out of this woman. For all he knew, she could be lying about everything. But then again, the fear was real. It was almost palpable.

He had a sudden thought. "Why did you attack me on the highway?"

"I…I don't know."

A chill ran the length of his spine. He thought of how she'd kept looking back at the car as they walked to the cabin. She had thought someone was after her. "Was there someone else in the car when it rolled over?"

Her eyes widened in alarm. "In the trunk."

He gawked at her. *"There was someone in the trunk?"*

She looked confused again, and even more frightened. "No." Tears filled her eyes. "I don't know."

"Too bad you didn't mention that when we were down there," he grumbled under his breath. He couldn't take the chance that she was telling the truth. Why someone would be in the trunk was another concern, especially if she was telling the truth about the car, the purse and apparently the baby not being hers.

He had to go back down anyway and try to put up some kind of flags to warn possible other motorists. He just hated the idea of going back out into the storm. But if there was even a chance someone was in the trunk…

Austin stared at her and reminded himself that this was probably a figment of her imagination. A delusion from the knock on her head. But given the way things weren't adding up, he had to check.

"Don't leave me here," she cried as he headed for the door, her voice filled with terror.

"What are you so afraid of?" he asked, stepping back to her.

She swallowed, her gaze locked with his, and then she slowly shook her head and closed her eyes. "I don't know."

Austin swore under his breath. He didn't like leaving her alone, but he had no choice. He checked to make sure the handcuff attached to the chair would hold in case she tried to go somewhere. He thought it might be just like her, in her state of mind, to get loose and take off back out into the blizzard.

"Don't try to leave, okay? I'll be back shortly. I promise."

She didn't answer, didn't even open her eyes. Grabbing his coat, he hurried out the back door and down the steep slope to the highway. The snow lightened the dark enough that he didn't have to use his flashlight. It was still falling in huge lacy flakes that stuck to his clothing as he hurried down the highway. He wished he'd at least taken his heavier coat from her before he'd left.

His SUV was covered with snow and barely visible. He walked past it to the overturned car, trying to make sense of all this. Someone in the trunk? He mentally kicked himself for worrying about some crazy thing a delusional woman had said.

The car was exactly as he'd left it, although the lights were starting to dim, the battery no doubt running down. He thought about turning them off, but if a car came along, the driver would have a better chance of seeing it with the lights on.

He went around to the driver's side. The door was still open, just as he'd left it. He turned on the flashlight from his pocket and searched around for the latch on the trunk, hoping he wouldn't have to use the key, which was still in the ignition.

Maybe it was the deputy sheriff in him, but he had a bad feeling this car might be the scene of a crime and whoever's fingerprints were on the key might be important.

He found the latch. The trunk made a soft *thunk* and fell open.

Austin didn't know what he expected to find when he walked around to the back of the car and bent down to look in. A body? Or a woman and her baby?

What had fallen out, though, was only a suitcase.

He stared at it for a moment, then knelt down and unzipped it enough to see what was inside. Clothes. Women's clothing. No dead bodies. Nothing to be terrified of that he could see.

The bag, though, had been packed quickly, the clothes apparently just thrown in. That in itself was interesting. Nor did the clothing look expensive—unlike the diamond wristwatch the woman was wearing.

Checking the luggage tag on the bag, he saw that it was in the same name as the driver's license he'd found in her purse. Rebecca Stewart. So if Rebecca Stewart wasn't the woman in the cabin, then where was she? And where was the baby who went with the car seat?

He rezipped the bag and hoisted it up from the snow. Was the woman going to deny that this was her suitcase? He reminded himself that she'd thought there was *someone* in the trunk. The woman obviously wasn't in her right mind.

He shone the flashlight into the trunk. His pulse quickened. Blood. He removed a glove to touch a finger to it. Dried. What the hell? There wasn't much, but enough to cause even more concern.

Putting his glove back on, he closed the trunk and picked up the suitcase. He stopped at his rented SUV to look for something to flag the wreck, hurrying because he was worried about the woman, worried what he would find when he got back to the cabin. He was digging in the back of the SUV, when a set of headlights suddenly flashed over him.

He turned. Out of the storm came the flashing lights of a Montana highway patrol car.

Chapter Four

"Let me get this straight," the patrolman said as they stood in the waiting room at the hospital. "You handcuffed her to a chair to protect her from herself?"

"Some of it was definitely for my own protection, as well. She appeared confused and scared. I couldn't trust that she wouldn't go for a more efficient weapon than a tire iron."

The patrolman finished writing and closed his notebook. "Unless you want to press assault charges…that should cover it."

Austin shook his head. "How is she?"

"The doctor is giving her liquids and keeping her for observation until we can reach her husband."

"Her husband?" Austin thought of the hurriedly packed suitcase and recalled that she hadn't been wearing a wedding ring.

"We tracked him down through the car registration."

"So she *is* Rebecca Stewart? Her memory has returned?"

"Not yet. But I'm sure her husband will be able to clear things up." The patrolman stood. "I have your number if we need to reach you."

Austin stood, as well. He was clearly being dismissed and yet something kept him from turning and walking away. "She seemed…terrified when I found her. Did she say where she was headed before the crash?"

"She still seems fuzzy on that part. But she is in good hands now." The highway patrolman turned as the doctor came down the hallway and joined them. "Mr. Cardwell is worried about your patient. I assured him she is out of danger," the patrolman said.

The doctor nodded and introduced himself to Austin. "If it makes you feel better, there is little doubt you saved her life."

He couldn't help but be relieved. "Then she remembers what happened?"

"She's still confused. That's fairly common in a case like hers."

The doctor didn't say, but Austin assumed she had a concussion. Austin couldn't explain why, but he needed to see her before he left. The highway patrolman had said they'd found her husband by way of the registration in the car, but she'd been so sure that wasn't her car.

Nor had the highway patrolman been concerned about the baby car seat or the blood in the trunk.

"Apparently the baby is with the father," the patrolman had told him. "As for the blood in the trunk, there was so little I'm sure there is an explanation her husband can provide."

So why couldn't Austin let it go? "I'd like to see her before I leave."

"I suppose it would be fine," the doctor said. "Her husband is expected at any time."

Austin hurried down the hallway to the room the doctor had only exited moments before, anxious to see her before her husband arrived. He pushed on the door slowly and peered in, half fearing that she might not want to see him.

He wasn't sure what he expected as he stepped into the room. He'd had a short sleepless night at a local motel. He had regretted not taking a straight flight to Bozeman this morning instead of flying into Idaho Falls the day before. Even as he thought it through, he reminded himself that the woman would have died last night if he hadn't come along when he did.

Austin told himself he'd been at the right place at the right time. So why couldn't he just let this go?

As the door closed behind him, she sat up in bed abruptly, pulling the covers up to her chin.

Her brown eyes were wide with fear. He was struck by how small she looked. Her unruly mane of curly dark hair billowed out around her pale face, making her look all the more vulnerable.

"My name's Austin. Austin Cardwell. We met late last night after I came upon your car upside down in the middle of Highway 191." He touched the wound on the back of his head where she'd nailed him. "You remember hitting me?"

She looked horrified at the thought, verifying what he already suspected. She didn't remember.

"Can you tell me your name?" He'd hoped that she would be more coherent this morning, but as he watched her face, it was clear she didn't know who she was any more than she had last night.

She seemed to search for an answer. He saw the moment when she realized she couldn't remember anything—even who she was. Panic filled her expression. She looked toward the door behind him as if she might bolt for it.

"Don't worry," he said quickly. "The doctor said memory loss is pretty common in your condition."

"My *condition?*"

"From the bump on your head, you hit it pretty hard in the accident." He pointed to a spot on his own temple. She raised her hand to touch the same spot on her temple and winced.

"I don't remember an accident." She had pulled her arms out from under the covers. He noticed the bruises on her upper arms. They were half-moon shaped, like fingerprints—as if someone had gripped her hard. There was also a cut on her arm that he didn't think had happened during her car accident.

She saw him staring at her arms. When she looked down and saw the bruises, she quickly put her arms under the covers again. If anything, she looked more frightened than she had earlier.

"You don't remember losing control of your car?"

She shook her head.

"I don't know if this helps, but the registration and proof of insurance I found in your car, along with the driver's license I found in the purse, says your name is Rebecca Stewart," he said, watching to see if there was any recognition in her expression.

"That isn't my name. I would know my own name when I heard it, wouldn't I?"

Maybe. Maybe not. "You were wearing a watch…"

"The doctor said they put it in the safe until I was ready to leave the hospital."

"It was engraved with: 'To Gillian with all my love.'" He saw that the words didn't ring any bells. "Are you Gillian?"

She looked again at the door, her expression one of panic.

"Don't worry. It will all come back to you," he said, trying to calm her even though he knew there might always be blanks that she could never fill in if he was right

and she had a concussion. He wished there was something he could say to comfort her. She looked so frightened. "Fortunately a highway patrolman came along
when he did last night."

"Patrolman?" Her words wavered and she looked
even more terrified, making him wonder if he might
be right and that she'd stolen the car, the purse and the
watch. She'd said none of it belonged to her. Maybe she
was telling the truth.

But why was she driving someone else's car? If so,
where was the car's owner and her baby? This woman's fear of the law seemed to indicate that something
was very off here. What if this woman wasn't who they
thought she was?

"Where am I?" she asked, glancing around the hospital room.

"Didn't the doctor tell you? You're in the hospital."

"I meant, where am I…?" She waved a hand to en-
compass more than the room.

"Oh," he said and frowned. "Bozeman." When that
didn't seem to register, he added, "Montana."

One eyebrow shot up. *"Montana?"*

It crossed his mind that a woman who lived in Helena, Montana, wouldn't be confused about what state
she was in. Nor would she be surprised to find herself
still in that state.

He reminded himself that the knock on her head could
have messed up some of the wiring. Or maybe she'd been
that way before.

Her gaze came back to him. She was studying him
intently, sizing him up. He wondered what she saw and
couldn't help but think of his former girlfriend, Tanya,
and the argument they'd had just before he'd left Texas.

"Haven't you ever wanted more?" Tanya hadn't looked

at him. She'd been busy throwing her things into a large trash bag. When she'd moved in with him, she'd moved in gradually, bringing her belongings in piecemeal.

"I'm only going to be gone a week," he'd said, watching her clean out the drawers in his apartment, wondering if this was it. She'd threatened to leave him enough times, but she never had. Maybe this was the time.

He had been trying to figure out how he felt about that when she'd suddenly turned toward him.

"Did you hear what I said?"

Obviously not. *"What?"*

"This business with your brothers..." She did her eye roll. He really hated it when she did that and she knew it. *"If it isn't something to do with* Texas Boys Barbecue*..."*

He could have pointed out that the barbecue joint she was referring to was a multimillion-dollar business, with more than a dozen locations across Texas, and it paid for this apartment.

But he'd had a feeling that wasn't really what this particular argument was about, so he'd said, *"Your point?"* even though he'd already known it.

"You're too busy for a relationship. At least that is your excuse."

"You knew I was busy before you moved in."

"Ever ask yourself why your work is more important than your love life?" She hadn't given him time to respond. *"You want to know what I think? I think Austin Cardwell goes through life saving people because he's afraid of letting himself fall in love."*

He wasn't afraid. He just hadn't fallen in love the way Tanya had wanted him to. *"Glad we got that figured out,"* he'd said.

Tanya had flared with anger. *"That's all you have to say?"*

And he'd made it worse by shrugging, something he knew *she* hated. He hadn't had the time or patience for this kind of talk at that moment. *"Maybe we should talk about this when I get back from Montana."*

She'd shaken her head in obvious disgust. *"That is so like you. Put things off and maybe the situation will right itself. You missed your own brother's wedding and you don't really care if they open a barbecue restaurant in Montana or not. But instead of being honest, you ignore the problem and hope it goes away until finally they force you to come to Montana. For once, I would love to see you just take a stand. Make a decision. Do something."*

"I missed my brother's wedding because I was on a case. One that almost got me killed, you might remember."

Tears welled in her eyes. *"I remember. I stayed by your bedside for three days."*

He sighed and raked a hand through his hair. *"What I do is important."*

"More important than me." She'd stood, hands on hips, waiting.

He'd known what she wanted. A commitment. The problem was, he wasn't ready. And right then, he'd known he would never be with Tanya.

"This is probably for the best," he'd said, motioning to the bulging trash bag.

Tears flowing, she'd nodded. *"Don't bother to call me if and when you get back."* With that, she had grabbed up the bag and stormed to the door, stopping only long enough to hurl his apartment key at his head.

"Where are my clothes?"

Austin blinked, confused for a moment, he'd been so lost in his thoughts. He focused on the woman in the hospital bed. "You can't leave. Your husband is on his way."

Panic filled her expression. She tried to get out of the bed. As he moved to her bedside to stop her, he heard the door open behind him.

Chapter Five

Austin turned to see a large stocky man come into the room, followed by the doctor.

"Mrs. Stewart," the doctor said as he approached her bed. "Your husband is here."

The stocky man stopped a few feet into the room and stood frowning. For a moment, Austin thought there had been a mistake and that the man didn't recognize the woman.

But the man wasn't looking at his wife. He was frowning at Austin. As if the doctor's words finally jarred him into motion, the man strode to the other side of the bed and quickly took his wife's hand as he bent to kiss her forehead. "I was so worried about you."

Austin watched the woman's expression. She looked terrified, her gaze locking with his in a plea for help.

"Excuse me," Austin said as he stepped forward. He had no idea what he planned to say, let alone do. But something was wrong here.

"I beg your pardon?" said the alleged husband, turning to look at Austin before swinging his gaze to the doctor with a *who the hell is this?* expression.

"This is the man who saved your wife's life," the doctor said and introduced Austin before getting a page that he was needed elsewhere. He excused himself and hurried out, leaving the three of them alone.

"I'm sorry, I didn't catch your name," Austin said.

"Marc. Marc Stewart."

Stewart, Austin thought, remembering the name on the driver's license in the purse he'd found in the car. "And this woman's name is Rebecca Stewart?" he asked the husband.

"That's right," Marc Stewart answered in a way that dared Austin to challenge him.

As he looked to the woman in the bed, Austin noticed that she gave an almost imperceptible shake of her head. "I'm sorry, but how do we know you're her husband?"

"Are you serious?" the man demanded, glaring across the bed at him.

"She doesn't seem to recognize you," he said, even though what he'd noticed was that the woman seemed terrified of the man.

Marc Stewart gave him the once-over, clearly upset. "She's had a *concussion.*"

"Old habits are hard to break," Austin said as he displayed his badge and ID to the alleged Marc Stewart. "You wouldn't mind me asking for some identification from you, would you?"

The man looked as if he might have a coronary. At least he'd come to the right place, Austin thought, as the alleged Marc Stewart angrily pulled out his wallet and showed Austin his license.

Marc Andrew Stewart, Austin read. "There was a car seat in the back of the vehicle she was driving. Where is the baby?"

"With my mother." A blood vessel in the man's cheek began to throb. "Look Deputy…Cardwell, is it? I appreciate that you supposedly saved my wife's life, but it's time for you to butt out."

Austin told himself he should back off, but the fear in the woman's eyes wouldn't let him. "She doesn't seem to know you and she isn't wearing a wedding ring." He didn't add that the woman seemed terrified and had bruises on her upper arms where someone had gotten rough with her. Not to mention the fact that when he'd told her that her husband was on his way, she'd panicked and tried to leave. Concussion or not, something was wrong with all this.

"I think you should leave," the man said.

"If you really are her husband, it shouldn't be hard for you to prove it," Austin said, holding his ground—well, at least until Marc Stewart had hospital security throw him out, which wouldn't be long, from the look on the man's face. The woman in the bed still hadn't uttered a word.

For a moment, Marc Stewart looked as if he was about to tell him to go to hell. But instead, he dug into his pocket angrily and produced a plain gold band that caught the light as he reached for the woman's left hand.

"My wife left it by the sink yesterday," Marc Stewart said by way of explanation. "She always takes it off when she does the dishes. Sometimes she forgets to put it back on."

Austin thought, given the bruises on the woman's upper arms, that she had probably thrown the ring at him as she took off yesterday.

When she still didn't move to take the ring, the man snatched up her hand lying beside her on the bed and slipped the ring on her finger.

Austin watched her look down at the ring. He saw recognition fill her expression just before she began to cry. Even from where he stood, he could see that the ring, while a little loose, fit close enough. Just as the photo ID in Rebecca Stewart's purse looked enough like the woman on the bed. He told himself there was nothing more he could do. Clearly she was afraid of this man. But unless she spoke up…

"I guess I'll leave you with your husband, unless there is something I should know?" Austin asked her.

"Tell the man, Rebecca," Marc Stewart snapped. "Am I your husband?" He bent down to kiss her cheek. Austin saw him whisper something in her ear.

She closed her eyes, tears leaking from beneath dark lashes.

"We had a little argument and she took off and apparently almost got herself killed," Marc said. "We both said and did things we regret, isn't that right, Rebecca? Tell the man, sweetheart."

Her eyes opened slowly. She took a ragged breath and wiped away the tears with the backs of her hands, the way a little kid would.

"Is that all there is to this?" Austin asked, watching her face. Across from him, he could see Marc gritting his teeth in fury at this interference in his life.

She nodded her head slowly, her gaze going from her husband to Austin. "Thank you, but he's right. It was just a foolish disagreement. I will be fine now."

FEELING LIKE A fool for getting involved in a domestic dispute, Austin headed for Cardwell Ranch. Last night, a wrecker company had pulled his rental SUV out of the ditch and brought it to the motel where he was staying. Fortunately, his skid into the ditch hadn't done any damage.

Highway 191 was now open, the road sanded. As he drove, Austin got his first real look at the Gallatin

Canyon or "the canyon" as his cousin Dana called it. From the mouth just south of Gallatin Gateway, fifty miles of winding road trailed the river in a deep cut through the mountains, almost all the way to West Yellowstone.

The drive along the Gallatin River was indeed breathtaking—a snaking strip of highway followed the Blue Ribbon trout stream up over the Continental Divide. This time of year, the Gallatin ran crystal clear under a thick cover of aquamarine ice. Dark, thick snowcapped pines grew at its edge, against a backdrop of the granite cliffs and towering pine-clad mountains.

Austin concentrated on his driving so he didn't end up in a snowbank again. Piles of deep snow had been plowed up on each side of the road, making the highway seem even narrower, but at least traffic was light. He had to admit, it was beautiful. The sun glistening off the new snow was almost blinding in its brilliance. Overhead, a cloudless robin's-egg-blue sky seemed vast and clearer than any air he'd ever breathed. The canyon looked like something out of a winter fairy tale.

Just before Big Sky, the canyon widened a little. He spotted a few older cabins, nothing like all the new construction he'd seen down by the mouth of the canyon. Tag had told him that the canyon had been mostly cattle and dude ranches, a few summer cabins and homes—that was, until Big Sky resort and the small town that followed at the foot of Lone Mountain.

Luxury houses had sprouted up all around the resort. Fortunately, some of the original cabins still remained and the majority of the canyon was national forest so it would always remain undeveloped. The "canyon" had remained its own little community, according to Tag.

Austin figured Tag had gotten most of his information

from their cousin Dana. This was the only home she'd known and, like her stubborn relations, she apparently had no intention of ever leaving it.

While admiring the scenery on the drive, he did his best not to think about Rebecca Stewart and her husband. When he'd left her hospital room, he'd felt her gaze on him and turned at the door to look back. He'd seen her take off the ring her husband had put on her finger and grip it in her fist so tightly that her knuckles were white.

Trouble in paradise, he thought as he reached Big Sky, *and none of my business.* As a deputy sheriff, he'd dealt with his share of domestic disputes. Every law enforcement officer knew how dangerous they were. The best thing was to stay out of the middle of them since he'd seen both husbands and wives turn on the outsider stepping in to try to keep the peace.

Cardwell Ranch was only a few miles farther up the highway from Big Sky. But on impulse, he swung onto the road to Big Sky's Meadow Village, where he suspected he would find the marshal's department.

His cousin Dana's husband, Marshal Hud Savage, waved him into his office and shook his hand. "We missed you at the wedding." The wedding, of course, had been his brother Tag's, to Lily McCabe, on July 4. He knew he would never live it down.

"I was hoping to get up for it, but I was on a case..." He hated that he'd missed his own brother's wedding, but hoped at least Hud, being a lawman, would understand.

"That's right. Deputy sheriff, is it?"

"Part-time, yes. I take on special cases."

"As I recall, there were extenuating circumstances. You were wounded. You're fine now?"

He nodded. He didn't want to talk about the case that

had almost gotten him killed. Nor did he want to admit that he might not still be physically a hundred percent.

"Well, have a seat," Hud said as he settled behind his desk. "And tell me what I can do for you. I suspect this isn't an extended family visit."

Austin nodded and, removing his hat, sat down, comfortable at once with the marshal. "You might have heard that I got into an accident last night. My rental SUV went into the ditch."

"I did know about that. I'm glad you weren't hurt. We couldn't assist because we had our hands full down here with a semi rollover."

"I was lucky I only ended up in the ditch. What made me hit my brakes was that I came upon a vehicle upside down in the middle of the highway last night."

Austin filled him in on the woman and everything that had happened up to leaving her about thirty minutes ago at the hospital in Bozeman.

"Sounds like she and her husband were having some marital issues," the marshal said.

Austin nodded. "The trouble is I think it's more than that. She had bruises on her arms."

"Couldn't the bruises have been caused by the accident?"

"No, these were definitely finger impressions. More than that, she seemed scared of her husband. Actually, she told me she wasn't Rebecca Stewart, which would mean this man wasn't her husband." He saw skepticism in the marshal's expression and admitted he would have felt the same way if someone had come to him with this story.

"Look," Austin said. "It's probably nothing, but I just have this gut feeling…"

Hud nodded, as if he understood gut feelings. "What would you like me to do?"

"First, could you run the name Marc Stewart. They're apparently from Helena."

"If it will relieve your mind, I'd be happy to." The marshal moved to his computer and began to peck at the keys. A moment later, he said, "No arrests or warrants. None on Rebecca Stewart either. Other than that…"

Austin nodded.

Hud studied him. "There's obviously something that's still worrying you."

He couldn't narrow it down to just one thing. It was the small things like the older-model car Rebecca had been driving, the baby seat in the back, the woman's adamant denial that she was Rebecca Stewart, the look of fear on her face when he'd told her that her husband was on his way to the hospital, the way she'd cried when he'd put that ring back on her finger.

Then there was that expensive diamond watch. *To Gillian with all my love.*

He mentioned all of this to the marshal and added, "I guess what's really bothering me is the inconsistencies. Also she just doesn't seem like the kind of woman who would leave her husband—let alone her baby—right before Christmas, no matter what the argument might have been about. This woman is a fighter. She wouldn't have left her son with a man who had just gotten physical with her."

Hud raised a brow as he leaned back in his chair. "You sure you didn't get a little too emotionally involved?"

He laughed. "Not hardly. Haven't you heard? I'm the Cardwell brother who never gets emotionally involved in anything. Just ask my brothers, or my former girlfriend, for that matter." He hesitated even though common sense told him to let it go. "There's no chance you're going into Bozeman today, is there?"

Hud smiled. "I'll stop by the hospital and give you a call after I talk to her and her husband."

"Thanks. It really would relieve my mind." Glancing at his watch, he saw he was late for a meeting with his brothers.

He swore as he hurried outside, climbed behind the wheel of his rental SUV and drove toward the small strip shopping mall in Meadow Village, all the time worrying about the woman he'd left in the hospital.

THE BUILDING WAS wood framed with stone across the front. It looked nothing like a Texas barbecue joint. As Austin climbed out of the SUV and walked through the snow toward the end unit with the Texas Boys Barbecue sign out front, he thought of their first barbecue joint.

It had been in an old small house. They'd done the barbecuing out back and packed diners in every afternoon and evening at mismatched tables and chairs to eat on paper plates. Just the smell of the wonderfully smoked meats brought people in. He and his brothers didn't even have to advertise. Their barbecue had kept people coming back for more.

Austin missed those days, sitting out back having a cold beer after the night was over and counting their money and laughing at what a fluke it had been. They'd grown up barbecuing so it hadn't felt like work at all.

As he pushed open the door to the building his brothers had bought, he saw by the way it was laid out that the space had started out as another restaurant. Whatever had been here, though, had been replaced with the Texas Boys Barbecue decor, a mix of rustic wood and galvanized aluminum. The fabric of the cushy red booths was the same as that on the chairs, and red-checked tablecloths covered the tables. The walls were covered with old photos of Texas family barbecues—just like in their other restaurants.

Through the pass-through he could see a gleaming kitchen at the back. Hearing his brothers—Tag, Jackson, Laramie and Hayes—visiting back there, he walked in that direction.

"Well, what do you think?" Tag asked excitedly.

Austin shrugged. "It looks fine."

"The equipment is all new," Jackson said. "We had to add a few things, but other than that, the remodel was mostly cosmetic."

Austin nodded. "What happened to the restaurant that was here?"

"It didn't serve the best barbecue in Texas," Tag said.

"We'd hoped for a little more enthusiasm," Laramie said.

"Sorry."

"What about the space?" Hayes asked.

"Looks good to me." He saw them share a glance at each other before they laughed and, almost in unison, said, "Same ol' Austin."

He didn't take offense. It was actually good to see his brothers. There was no mistaking they were related either since they'd all inherited the Cardwell dark good looks. A curse and a blessing. When they were teens they used to argue over who was the ugliest. He smiled at the memory.

"Okay, we're opening a Texas Boys Barbecue in Big Sky," he said to them. "So buy me some lunch. I'm starved."

They went to a small sandwich shop in the shadow of Lone Mountain in what was called Mountain Village. As hungry as he was, Austin still had trouble getting down even half of a sandwich and a bowl of soup.

During lunch, his brothers talked enthusiastically

about the January 1 opening. They planned two grand openings, one on January 1 and another on July 4, since Big Sky had two distinct tourist seasons.

Apparently the entire canyon was excited about the Cardwell brothers' brand of barbecue. His brothers Tag, Hayes and Jackson now had all made their homes in Montana. Only he and Laramie still lived in Texas, but Laramie would be flying back up for the grand opening whenever that schedule was confirmed. None of them asked if Austin would be coming back for that one. They knew him too well.

Austin only half listened, too anxious for a call from the marshal. When his cell phone finally did ring, he quickly excused himself and went out to the closed-in deck. It was freezing out here, but he didn't want his brothers to hear. He could actually see his breath. He'd never admit it, but he couldn't imagine why they would want to live here, as cold and nasty as winter was. Sure, it was beautiful, but he'd take Texas and the heat any day.

"I just left her hospital room," the marshal said without preamble the moment Austin answered.

"So what do you think?"

"Apparently she has some loss of memory because of the concussion she suffered, according to her husband, which could explain some of your misgivings."

"Did you see the bruises on her arms?"

The marshal sighed. "I did. Her husband said they'd had a disagreement before she took off. He said he'd grabbed her a little too hard, trying to keep her from leaving, afraid in her state what might happen to her. As it was, she ended up in a car wreck."

"What does she say?"

"She doesn't seem to recall the twenty-four hours

before ending up upside down in her car in the middle of the highway—and even that is fuzzy."

"You think she's lying?" Austin asked, hearing something in the marshal's voice.

Hud took his time in answering. "I think she might remember more than she's letting on. I had some misgivings as well until Marc Stewart showed me a photograph of the four of them on his cell phone."

"*Four* of them?"

"Rebecca and her sister, a woman named Gillian Cooper, Marc and the baby. In the photo, the woman in the hospital is holding the baby and Marc is standing next to her, his arm around her and her sister."

Austin sighed. Gillian Cooper. Her sister. That could explain the watch. Maybe her sister had lent it to her. Or even given it to her.

"The doctor is releasing her tomorrow. I asked her if she wanted to return home with her husband."

Austin figured he already knew the answer. "She said yes."

"I also asked him to step out of the room. I then asked her if she was afraid of him. She said she wasn't."

So that was that, Austin thought. "Thanks for going by the hospital for me."

"You realize there is nothing we can do if she doesn't want to leave him," Hud said.

Austin knew that from experience, even though he'd never understood why a woman stayed in an abusive marriage. Disconnecting, he went back into the restaurant, where his brothers were debating promotion for the new restaurant. He was in no mood for this.

"I really should get going," he said, not that he really had anywhere to go, though he'd agreed to stay until the opening.

Christmas was only a few days away, he realized. Normally, he didn't do much for Christmas. Since he didn't have his own family, he always volunteered to work.

"Where are you going?" Tag asked.

"I've got some Christmas shopping to do." That, at least, was true.

"Dana is planning for us all to be together on Christmas," Tag said as if he needed reminding. "She has all kinds of plans."

Jackson laughed. "She wants us all to try skiing or snowboarding."

"There's a sledding party planned on Christmas Eve behind the house on the ranch and, of course, ice skating on an inlet of the Gallatin River," Hayes said with a laugh when he saw Austin's expression. "You really have to experience a Montana Christmas."

He tried to smile. Anything to make up for missing the wedding so everyone would quit bringing it up. "I can't wait."

They all laughed since they knew he was lying. He wasn't ready for a Montana Christmas. He'd already been freezing his butt off and figured he'd more than experienced Montana after crashing in a ditch and almost getting killed by a woman with a tire iron. However, never let it be said he was a Scrooge. He'd go Christmas shopping. He would be merry and bright. It was only for a few days.

"You know what your problem is, Austin?" his brother Jackson said as they walked out to their vehicles.

Austin shook his head although he knew what was coming. He'd already had this discussion with Tanya in Houston.

"You can't commit to anything," Jackson said. "When we decided to open more Texas Boys Barbecues in Texas—"

"Yes, I've been told I have a problem with commitment," he interrupted as he looked toward Lone Mountain. The peak was almost completely obscured by the falling snow. Huge lacy flakes drifted down around them. Texas barbecue in Montana? He'd thought his brothers had surely lost their minds when they had suggested it. Now he was all the more convinced.

But they'd been right about the other restaurants they'd opened across Texas. He wasn't going to stand in their way now. But he also couldn't get all that excited about it.

"Can you at least commit to this promotion schedule we have mapped out?" Hayes asked.

"Do what you think is best," he said, opening the SUV door. "I'll go along with whatever y'all decide." His brothers didn't look thrilled with his answer. "Isn't that what you wanted me to say?"

"We were hoping for some enthusiasm, *something,*" Jackson said and frowned. "You seem to have lost interest in the business."

"It's not that." It wasn't. It was his *life*. At thirty-two, he was successful, a healthy, wealthy American male who could do anything he wanted. Most men his age would have given anything to be in his boots.

"He needs a woman," Tag said and grinned.

"That's *all* I need," Austin said sarcastically under his breath and thought of Rebecca and the way she'd reacted to her husband. What kind of woman left her husband and child just before Christmas?

A terrified one, he thought. "I have to go."

"Where did you say you were going?" Hayes asked before Austin could close his SUV door.

"There's something I need to do."

"I told you he needed a woman," Tag joked.

"Dana is in Bozeman running errands, but she said to

tell you that dinner is at her house tonight," Jackson said before Austin could escape.

All the way to the hospital in Bozeman, all Austin could think about was the woman he'd rescued last night. Rescued? And then turned her over to a man who terrified her.

Austin thought of that awful old expression: she'd made her bed and now she had to lie in it.

Like hell, he thought.

Chapter Six

When he reached the hospital, Austin was told at the nurses' station that Mrs. Stewart had checked out already. His heart began to pound harder at the news, all his instincts telling him he had been right to come back here.

"I thought the doctor wasn't going to release her until tomorrow?"

"Her husband talked to him and asked if she was well enough to be released. He was anxious to get her home before Christmas."

Austin just bet he was. "He was planning to take her straight home from the hospital?" he asked and quickly added, "I have her purse." He'd forgotten all about putting it into his duffel bag last night as the highway patrolman helped the woman down to his waiting patrol car.

"Oh, you must be the man who found her after the accident," the nurse said, instantly warming toward him. "Let me see. I know her husband stayed at a local motel last night. I believe they were going to go there first so she could rest for a while before they left for Helena."

"Her husband got in last night?" Austin asked in surprise. Helena was three hours away on Interstate 90.

"He arrived in the wee hours of the morning. When he came by the hospital to see his wife, he thought he'd be able to take her home then." She smiled at how anxious the husband had apparently been. "He left the name of the motel where he would stay if there was any change in her condition," the nurse said. "Here it is. The Pine Rest. I can call and see if they are still there."

"No, that's all right. I'll run by the motel." He realized Rebecca Stewart wouldn't have been allowed to walk out of the hospital. One of the nurses would have taken her down to the car by wheelchair. "You don't happen to know what Mr. Stewart was driving, do you?" She remembered the large black Suburban because it had looked brand-new.

The Pine Rest Motel sat on the east end of town on a hill. Austin spotted Marc Stewart's Suburban at once. Austin had to wonder why Marc's "wife" had been driving an older model car.

That didn't surprise him as much as the lack of a baby car seat in the back of the Suburban. Marc had had the vehicle for almost a month according to the sticker in the back window. The lack of a car seat was just another one of those questions that nagged at him. Like the fact that Marc Stewart had gotten his wife out of the hospital early just to bring her to a motel in town. That made no sense unless he'd brought her there to threaten her. That Austin could believe.

The black Suburban was parked in front of motel unit number seven—the last unit at the small motel.

Austin didn't go anywhere without his weapon. But he knew better than to go into the motel armed—let alone without a plan. He tended to wing things, following his instincts. It had gotten him this far. But it had also nearly gotten him killed last summer. He had both the physical and mental scars to prove it.

Glancing at the purse lying on the seat next to him, he wondered if all this wasn't an overreaction on his part.

Maybe it had only been an argument between husband and wife that had gotten out of control. Maybe once Rebecca Stewart's memory returned, she wouldn't be afraid of her husband.

Maybe.

He picked up the purse. It was imitation leather, a knockoff of a famous designer's. He pulled out the wallet and went through it again, this time noticing the discount coupons for diapers and groceries.

He studied the woman in the photo a second time. It wasn't a great snapshot of her, but then most driver's license mug shots weren't. Montana only required a driver to get a license every eight years so this photo was almost seven years old.

If it hadn't been for the slight resemblance... He put everything back into the purse, opened the car door and stepped out into the falling snow.

Every cop knew not to get in the middle of a domestic dispute. This wasn't like him, he thought as he walked through the storm to the door of unit number seven and knocked.

At his knock, Austin heard a scurrying sound. He knocked again. A few moments later, Marc Stewart opened the door a crack.

He frowned when he saw Austin. "Yes?"

"I'm Austin Cardwell—"

"I know who you are." Behind the man, Austin heard a sound.

"I forgot to give Rebecca her purse," he said.

Marc reached for it.

All his training told him to just hand the man the damned purse and walk away. It wasn't like him to butt into someone else's business—let alone a married couple's, even if they had some obvious problems—when he wasn't asked.

"If you don't mind, I'd like to give it to her myself," he heard himself say. Behind the man, Austin caught a rustling sound.

"Look," Marc Stewart said from between gritted teeth. "I appreciate that you found…my wife and kept her safe until I could get here, but your job is done, cowboy. So you need to back the hell off."

Rebecca suddenly appeared at the man's side. "Excuse my husband. He's just upset." She met Austin's gaze. He tried to read it, afraid she was desperately trying to tell him something. "But Marc's right. We're fine now. It was very thoughtful of you to bring my purse, though."

"Yes, thoughtful," Marc said sarcastically and shot his wife a warning look. "You shouldn't be up," he snapped.

She was pale and a little unsteady on her feet, but she had a determined look on her face. Behind her, he saw her open suitcase—the same one he'd found in the overturned car's trunk. The scene looked like any other married couple's motel room.

Even before Marc spoke, Austin realized they were about to pack up and leave.

"We were just heading out," Marc said.

"I won't keep you, then," Austin said, still holding the purse. Rebecca Stewart looked weak as she leaned into the door frame. He feared her husband had gotten her out of the hospital too soon. But that, too, was none of his business. "I didn't want you leaving without your purse."

"Great," Marc said and turned to close her suitcase. "We have a long drive ahead of us, so if you'll excuse us…" Austin stepped aside to let him pass with the suitcase. "You should tell him our good news," he called over his shoulder.

"Good news?" Austin asked, studying the woman in the doorway. He realized that even though her suitcase had been open, she was still wearing the same clothing she'd had on last night. That realization gave him a start since there was a spot of blood on her sweater from her head injury the night before.

"We're pregnant again," Marc called from the side of the Suburban, where he was loading the suitcase.

Austin was watching her face. She suddenly went paler. He thought for a moment that she might faint.

"Marc, don't—" The words came out like a plea.

"Andrew Marc, our son, is going to have a baby sister," Marc said as if he hadn't heard her or was ignoring her. "Isn't that right, Rebecca? I think we'll call her Becky."

Austin met her gaze. "Congratulations." He couldn't have felt more like a fool as he handed her the purse.

She took it with trembling fingers, her eyes filling with tears. "Thank you for bringing my purse all this way." Her fingers kneaded the cheap fabric of the bag. He saw she was again wearing the wedding band that her husband had put on her finger at the hospital. That alone should have told him how things were.

"No problem. Good luck." He meant it since he knew in his heart she was going to need it. He started to step away when she suddenly grabbed his arm.

"Wait, I think this must be your coat," she said and turned back into the room.

"That's okay, you should keep it," he said.

She returned a few moments later with the coat.

"Seriously, keep it. You need it more than I do."

"Take the damned coat," Marc called to him before slamming the Suburban door.

Austin shook his head at her. "Keep it. Please," he said quietly.

Tears filled her eyes. "Thank you." She quickly reached for his hand and pressed what felt like a scrap of paper into his palm. "For everything." She then quickly pulled down her shirtsleeve, which had ridden up. He only got a glimpse of the fresh red mark around her wrist.

Austin sensed Marc behind him as he helped her into his coat. It swallowed her, but the December day was cold, another snowstorm threatening.

"Well, if we've all wished each other enough luck, it's time to hit the road," Marc said, joining them. "Hormones." He sounded disgusted as he looked at his wife. "The woman is in tears half the time." He put one arm around her roughly and reached into his pocket with the other. "Forgive my manners," he said, pulling out a crinkled twenty. "Here, this is for your trouble."

Austin stared down at the twenty.

Marc thrust the money at him. "Take it." There was an underlying threatening sound in his voice. The man's blue eyes were ice-cold.

"Please," Rebecca said. Austin still couldn't think of her as this man's wife. There was pleading in her voice, in her gaze.

"Thanks," he said as he took the money. "You really didn't have to, though."

Marc chuckled at that.

"Have a nice trip, then. Drive carefully." Austin turned and walked toward his rental SUV.

Behind him, he heard Marc say, "Get in the car."

When he turned back, she was pulling herself up into the large rig. He climbed into his own vehicle, but waited until the Suburban drove away. He caught only a glimpse of her wan face in the side window as they left. Her brown eyes were wide with more than tears. The woman seemed even more terrified.

His heart was already pounding like a war drum. That red mark around her right wrist. All his instincts told him that this was more than a bossy husband.

He tossed down the twenty and, reaching in his pocket, took out the scrap of paper she'd pressed into his palm. It appeared to be a corner of a page torn from a motel Bible. There were only four words, written in a hurried scrawl with an eyeliner pencil: "Help me. No law."

Chapter Seven

Austin looked down the main street where the black Suburban had gone. If Marc Stewart was headed for Helena,
he was going the wrong way.

He hesitated only a moment before he started the engine, backed up and turned onto the street.

Bozeman was one of those Western towns that had
continued to grow—unlike a lot of Montana towns. In
part, its popularity was because of its vibrant and busy
downtown as well as being the home of Montana State
University.

Austin cursed the traffic that had him stopped at every
light while the black Suburban kept getting farther away.
What he couldn't understand was why Marc Stewart was
headed southwest if he was anxious to get his wife home.
Maybe they were going out for breakfast first.

He caught another stoplight and swore. The Suburban
was way ahead and unfortunately a lot of people in Bozeman drove large rigs, which made it nearly impossible to
keep the vehicle in sight. He was getting more nervous by
the moment. All his instincts told him the woman hadn't
been delusional. She was in trouble.

From the beginning, she'd said the car wasn't hers,
the purse wasn't hers and that her name wasn't Rebecca
Stewart. What if she had been telling the truth?

It was that thought that had him hitting the gas the moment the light changed. Determined not to have to stop at the next one, he sped through the yellow light and kept going. He sped through another yellow light, barely making it. But ahead, he could see the Suburban. It was headed southwest out of town.

That alone proved something, didn't it?

But what? That Marc Stewart had lied about wanting to get his wife home to Helena as quickly as possible. What else might he be lying about? The pregnancy?

Austin used the hands-free system in the SUV to put in a call to the doctor at the hospital who'd handled the case. He knew he couldn't ask outright about the patient's condition. But…

Dr. Mayfield came on the line.

"Doctor, it's Austin Cardwell. I'm the man who found Rebecca Stewart—"

"Yes, I remember you, Mr. Cardwell. What can I do for you?"

"I ended up with Mrs. Stewart's purse after last night's emergency." He was counting on the doctor not knowing he'd already stopped by the hospital earlier. "I wanted to drop it by if Mrs. Stewart is up to it."

"I'm sorry, but her husband checked her out earlier today."

"I noticed she has prenatal vitamins in her purse when I was looking for her identification."

A few beats of silence stretched out a little too long. "Mr. Cardwell, I'm not sure what Mrs. Stewart told you, but I'm not at liberty to discuss her condition."

"Understood." He'd heard the surprise in the silence before the doctor had spoken. "Oh, one more thing. I just wanted to be sure she got her watch before she left the hospital. She was worried about it."

"Just a moment." The doctor left the line. When he came back, he said, "Yes, her husband picked it up for her."

Her husband picked up the watch with the name Gillian on it?

"Thank you, Doctor." He disconnected. Ahead, he could see the black Suburban still headed west on Highway 191. Marc had lied about her being pregnant, but why?

Austin thought about calling Marshal Hud Savage, but what would he tell him? That Marc Stewart was a liar. That wasn't illegal. Even if he told the marshal about the note the woman had passed him or about the diamond watch with the wrong name on it, Austin doubted Hud would be able to do more than he already had. Not to mention Rebecca had specified, *No law.*

Her name isn't Rebecca, just as she'd said, he realized with a jolt.

It's Gillian. Gillian Cooper. Rebecca's sister? The thought hit him like a sledgehammer. That was the only thing she had reacted to last night other than the man who was pretending to be her husband. It was the name on the expensive watch. It was proof—

Austin groaned as he realized it proved nothing. If she was Rebecca, she could have a reason for wearing her sister's watch. He thought of a woman he knew who wore her brother's St. Christopher medal. Her brother had died of cancer a few years before.

So maybe there was no mystery to the watch. But the woman in that black Suburban was in trouble. She'd asked for his help. Even if she was Rebecca and Marc Stewart was her husband, she was terrified of him. Terrified enough to leave her child and run.

That was the part that just didn't add up. Maybe Marc

wouldn't let her take the child. All this speculation was giving him a headache.

Austin saw the four-way stop ahead. The black Suburban was in the left-hand turn lane. Marc Stewart was turning south—back up the Gallatin Canyon where Austin had found her the night before. So where was he going if not taking her home?

Instead of taking the highway south, though, the Suburban pulled into the gas station at the corner. Austin slowed, hanging back as far as he could as he saw Marc pull up to a gas pump and get out. The woman climbed out as well, said something to Marc and then went inside.

Austin saw his chance and pulled behind the station. He knew he didn't have much time since he wasn't sure why the woman had gone into the convenience store. If he was right, the man would be watching her, afraid to let her out of his sight. All he could hope was that the Suburban's gas tank was running low. He knew from experience that it took a long while to fill one.

Once inside the store, he looked around for the woman, anxious to find her since this might be his only chance to talk to her. There were several women in the store. None was the one he'd rescued last night.

It had only taken a few minutes for him to park. Surely she hadn't already gone back out to her vehicle. He glanced toward the Suburban from behind a tall rack of chips. Its front seats were both empty. Marc was still pumping gas into the tank, his gaze on the front of the store. The glare on the glass seemed to keep him from seeing inside. The woman was in here. Austin could think of only one other place she might be.

He found the restrooms down a short hallway. As she came out of the ladies' room, she saw him and froze.

Eyes wide with fear, she looked as if she might turn and run. Except there was nowhere to run. He was blocking her way out.

He rushed to her. "Talk to me. Tell me who you are and what is going on."

She shook her head, glancing past him as if terrified Marc Stewart would appear at any moment.

"You gave me the note. You obviously are in trouble. Let me help you."

"I'm sorry. I shouldn't have involved you," she said. "Please forget I did. You can't help me." She tried to step past him, but he grabbed her arm. She flinched.

"He hurt you again, didn't he?"

"You don't understand. He has my sister."

"Your *sister*?"

Tears welled in her eyes. "Rebecca. If I don't go with him—" Her eyes widened in alarm again and he realized a buzzer had announced that someone had entered the store. Fortunately he and the woman couldn't be seen where they were standing, though. At least not yet.

"Your name is Gillian, isn't it? The watch—"

"Where are your restrooms?" he heard Marc ask the clerk.

Gillian gripped his arm, her fingers digging into his flesh. "If you tell anyone, he'll kill her."

There wasn't time to reassure her. "Where's he taking you?"

"A cabin in Island Park."

"Here, take this. If you get a chance, call me." He pressed one of his business cards into her palm and then pushed into the men's restroom an instant before he heard Marc's voice outside the door.

"It took you long enough," Marc snapped. "Come on."

Austin waited until he was sure they were gone before

he opened the door and headed for his SUV. He had no idea what Island Park was or how to get there. All he knew was that he had no choice but to go after her.

Chapter Eight

As Gillian climbed into the Suburban, she could feel Marc watching her, his eyes narrowed.

"It took you long enough in there," he said, studying her. "You didn't try to make any calls while you were in there, did you?" he asked, his voice low. She knew how close he was to hitting her when his voice got like that.

"How would I have made a call? You have my cell phone, I have no money and, in case you haven't noticed, there aren't pay phones around anymore."

He narrowed his eyes in warning. She knew she was treading on thin ice with him, but kowtowing to him only seemed to make him more violent.

Marc was still staring at her as if searching for even a hint of a lie. "I figure if anyone could find a way, it would be you. I've learned the hard way what you're capable of, sister-in-law. Let's not forget that you've managed to get some local marshal sniffing around—not to mention a deputy from *Texas*."

"I told you that wasn't my doing. The deputy was merely worried about me." She looked away, wishing he would start the engine. He was looking for any excuse to hurt her again.

"*Worried about you?* That Texas cowboy took a shine to you after you told him you weren't my wife. You take a shine to him, too? The patrolman said the cowboy had you in some cabin handcuffed to a chair. He have his way with you?"

"You disgust me," she said and turned to look out the side window. A pickup had pulled up behind them, the driver now waiting for the gas pump.

"Gave you his coat. How gallant is that?" he said, his voice a sneer. "You must have done something to keep him coming back."

She wished he would just start the engine. "You know I didn't know what I was saying. I have a concussion. Or don't you believe that either?" She turned to face him, knowing it was a daring thing to do. He was just looking for an excuse. He hated everything about her and her sister.

"Right, your head injury from an accident that would never have happened if you hadn't—"

"Been running for my life?"

His face twisted into a mask of fury. "You—"

She braced herself for the smack she knew was coming. The only thing that saved her was the driver behind them honking loudly.

Marc swore and flipped the man off, but started the engine and pulled away from the pump and onto the highway headed south toward West Yellowstone.

Gillian breathed a small sigh of relief. All she'd done was buy herself a little time. She'd be lucky if Marc didn't kill her. Right now, she was more worried about what he'd already done to Rebecca.

"What are you looking at?" Marc snapped.

"Nothing," she said as she turned toward him.

"You were looking in your side mirror." He hurriedly checked his rearview. "Is that cowboy following us?"

She realized her mistake. "What cowboy?"

"Don't give me that what cowboy bull. You know damned well. That *Texas* cowboy. Did you see him back there?"

"In the ladies' room?" She scoffed at his paranoia. "I was only looking out the window." It was a lie and she feared he knew it.

He kept watching behind them as he drove. "If you said something to him back at the motel—"

"You were there. You know I didn't say anything. Why did you say Rebecca was pregnant with a baby girl?" She held her breath for his answer.

Marc let out a snort. "I figured it would just get the guy off my back once he thought you were pregnant." He chuckled as if pleased with himself and seemed to relax a little, although he kept watching his mirror.

She hated that she'd involved Austin Cardwell in all this, but she'd been so desperate… Now she prayed that if he really was following them, that he didn't let Marc see him. There was no telling what Marc would do.

"What did you tell him last night?"

Gillian didn't need to ask whom he was talking about. "I didn't even know who I was last night, so how was I going to tell him anything?"

"That was convenient. But you recognized *me* when you saw me, didn't you?"

She'd been so confused, so terrified and yet she hadn't known of what or whom. But once Marc had come into her hospital room, she'd remembered, even before he'd whispered in her ear, "I'll kill your sister if you don't go along with what I say."

It had all come back in a wave of misery that threatened to overwhelm her. When Marc had slipped her sister's wedding band onto her finger… She hadn't been able to hold back the tears. She'd made matching rings for her sister and Marc when they'd married. Marc had lost his almost at once, but Rebecca… She felt a sob try to work its way up out of her chest. If Marc was carrying Rebecca's wedding ring in his pocket, was she even still alive?

AUSTIN STAYED BACK, letting the black Suburban disappear down Highway 191 toward Big Sky, while he called Hud.

"I need a favor," he said. "Does Marc Stewart own a cabin in a place called Island Park?"

Silence, then, "I'm sure you have a good reason to ask."

"I do."

"Want to tell me what's going on?"

"I wish I could."

"I hope you know what you're doing," the marshal said.

Austin hoped so, as well.

More silence, then the steady clack of computer keys.

"Funny you should ask," Hud said when he came back on the line. "Marc Stewart has been paying taxes on a place in Island Park."

Austin leaned back, relieved, as he drove out of the valley and into the canyon. The traffic wasn't bad compared to Houston. Most every vehicle, other than semis, had a full ski rack on top. The roads had become more packed with snow, but at least he had some idea now where Marc Stewart might be heading.

"Where and what is Island Park?"

Hud rattled off an address that didn't sound like any he'd ever heard. "How do I find this place?" he asked frowning. "It doesn't sound like a street address in a town."

"Finding it could be tricky. Island Park is a thirty-three-mile-long town just over the Montana border from

West Yellowstone. Basically, it follows the highway. The so-called town is no more than five hundred feet wide in places. They call it the longest main street in the world."

"Seriously?"

Austin was used to tiny Texas towns or sprawling urban cities.

"Owners of the lodges along the highway incorporated back in 1947 to circumvent Idaho's liquor laws, which prohibited the sale of liquor outside city limits."

"So how do I find this cabin?"

"In the middle of winter? I'd suggest by snowmobile unless it is right off a plowed road, which will be doubtful. Have you ever driven a snowmobile?"

"No, but I'll manage." He'd deal with all that once he knew where to look for the cabin.

"I don't know Island Park at all so I can't help you beyond the address I gave you. I should warn you that you're really on your own once you cross the border into Idaho. I would imagine any help you might need from law enforcement would have to come out of Ashton, a good fifty miles to the south. Where you're headed is very isolated, with cabins back in heavily wooded areas. They get a lot of snow over there."

"Great." He'd already known that he was on his own. But now it was clear there would be no backup should he get himself in a bind. He almost laughed at that. He couldn't be in a worse situation right now, headed into country he didn't know and into a possible violent domestic dispute between Marc Stewart and his real wife.

"I suppose you won't be able to join us for dinner tonight?"

Austin had forgotten about dinner. "I'll try my best, but if things go south with this…"

"Not to worry. Dana is used to having a marshal for

a husband. Just watch your back. And keep in touch," Hud said.

Austin didn't see the black Suburban again on the drive through the canyon. When the road finally opened up, he found himself on what apparently was called Fir Ridge. Off to his left was a small cemetery in the aspens and pines. Then the highway dropped down into a wooded area before crossing the Madison River Bridge and entering the small tourist town of West Yellowstone.

Had Marc stopped here to get Gillian something to eat? Buy gas? Or was he just anxious to get to wherever he was going?

Austin had no way of knowing. He only knew that he couldn't cross paths with him if he hoped to keep Gillian alive. All his training told him to bring the law into this now. Going in like the Lone Ranger was always a bad idea—especially when you weren't sure what you were getting into.

And yet, he couldn't make himself do it. Gillian did not want the law involved. She was terrified of Marc Stewart, and with her sister in danger, Austin couldn't chance that calling in law enforcement would push Marc into killing not only her, but also her sister, as well.

Not that he wasn't worried about getting her killed himself. If only he'd had more time with Gillian at the convenience store. There was so much he needed to know. Such as where was Rebecca's young son, Andrew Marc? Was he really with his grandmother? Or was that, too, a lie?

West Yellowstone was a tourist town of gas stations, curio shops, motels and cafés. Austin took the first turn out and headed for the Idaho border. He still hadn't seen the black Suburban. He could only hope that Gillian was right about where Marc was taking her.

Last night, Gillian had been driving her sister's car. He suspected the registration, the purse, the baby car seat, even the suitcase in the back belonged to her sister, Rebecca.

From the way the clothes had been thrown into the suitcase, he was assuming Rebecca had tried to leave her husband. So how had Gillian ended up in her sister's car?

He had many more questions than he had answers. No wonder he felt anxious. Even if he hadn't been shot and almost died just months ago when a case had gone wrong, he would have been leery of walking into this mess. No law officer in his right mind wanted to go in blind.

His cell phone rang. He snatched it up with the crazy thought that somehow Gillian Cooper had gotten away from Marc and was now calling.

"Where the hell are you?" his brother Tag demanded. "You did remember that we're supposed to have dinner with Dana, didn't you?"

Austin swore under his breath. "Something has come up."

"*Something?* Like something came up and you couldn't make my wedding?"

"Do we have to go through this again? I'm sorry. If it wasn't important—"

"More important obviously than your family."

"Tag, I'll explain everything when I get back. I'm sure you can go ahead with…" He realized his brother had hung up on him.

NOT THAT HE could blame his brother. He disconnected, feeling like a heel. He had a bad habit of letting down the people he cared about. He blamed his job, but the truth was he felt more comfortable as a deputy than he did in any other relationship.

"Maybe I'm like my dad," he'd said to his mother when she'd asked him why of the five brothers, he was the one who was often at odds with the others. *"Look how great Dad is with his sons,"* he'd pointed out.

His parents had divorced years ago when Austin was still in diapers. His mother had taken her five boys to live in Texas while their father had stayed in Big Sky. Austin had hardly seen his father over the years. He knew that his brothers had now reconciled with him, but Austin didn't see that happening as far as he was concerned. He wouldn't be in Montana long enough, and the way things were going...

It amazed him that his mother always stood up for the man she'd divorced, the man who had fathered her boys. *"I won't have you talk about your father like that,"* his mother had said the last time they discussed it. *"Harlan and I did the best we could."*

Austin had softened his words. *"You did great, Mom. But let's face it, I could be more like Harlan Cardwell than even you want to admit."*

"Tell me, is there anything you care about, Austin?" she'd asked, looking disappointed in him.

"I care about my family, my friends, my town, my state."

"But not enough to make your own brother's wedding."

"I was on a case."

"And there was no one else who could handle it?"

"I needed to see it through. I might not be great at relationships, but I'm damned good at my job."

"Watch your language," she'd reprimanded. *"A job won't keep you warm at night, son. Someday you're going to realize that these relationships you treat so trivially*

are more important than anything else in life. I thought almost losing your life might have taught you something."

As he dropped over the Idaho border headed for Island Park, he thought no one would ever understand him since he didn't even understand himself. He just knew that right now Gillian Cooper needed him more than his brothers or cousin Dana did. Just as the woman he'd tried to save in Texas had needed him more than Tag had needed another attendant at his wedding.

He'd failed his family as well as that woman in Texas, though, and it had almost cost him his life. He couldn't fail this one.

"You look like hell."

Gillian didn't bother to react to Marc's snide comment as they drove into West Yellowstone. He wanted to argue with her, to have an excuse to hit her. His anger was palpable in the interior of the Suburban. She'd outwitted him—at least for a while before she'd lost control of Rebecca's car and crashed.

Her head ached and she felt sick to her stomach. How much of it was from the accident? The doctor had discussed her staying another night, but Marc had told her that her sister would be dead if she did. She wasn't sure if her ailments were from her concussion solely or not. She'd often felt sick to her stomach when she thought of the man her sister had married.

"I'll get you something to eat," Marc said. "I don't want you dying on me. At least not yet." He pulled into a drive-through. "What do you want?"

She wasn't hungry, but she knew she needed to eat. She would need all her strength once they reached the cabin.

Marc didn't give her a chance to answer, though. "Give

us four burgers, a couple of large fries and two big colas."
As he dug his wallet out, she felt him looking at her.
"You're just lucky you didn't kill yourself last night. As
it is, you owe me for a car."

Just like Marc to make it about the money.

"I'm sure my insurance will pay for it," she said drily.
"If I get to make the claim."

He snorted as he pulled up to the next window and
paid. A few moments later, he handed her a large bag of
greasy smelling food.

Just the odor alone made her stomach turn. She
thought she might throw up. "I need to go to the bathroom." The business card Austin Cardwell had given her
was hidden in her jeans pocket. She knew she should have
thrown it away back at the convenience store, but Marc
hadn't given her a chance.

He shook his head. "You just went back at Four Cor-
ners."

"I have to go again." She had to get rid of the business
card. If Marc found it on her—

She regretted telling Austin where they were headed.
Not only had she put him in danger and possibly made
things even worse, but she wasn't sure he would be able
to find the cabin anyway. She'd stolen glances in the side
mirror and hadn't seen his SUV. He was a deputy sheriff
in Texas. What if he contacted law enforcement here?

No, she couldn't see him doing that. Just as she couldn't
see him giving up. He was back there somewhere. He'd
saved her life last night. But she wasn't so sure he could
pull it off again. Worse, she couldn't bear the thought that
she might get him killed.

If she could get to a phone, she could call the number on the card and plead with him not to get involved.
Even as she thought it, she knew he wouldn't be able to

turn back now. She'd seen how determined he was at the hospital and later at the motel room. Her heart went out to him. Why couldn't her sister have married someone like Austin Cardwell?

"You'll just have to hold it," Marc was saying. "Hand me one of the burgers and some fries," he said as he drove onto the highway again.

She dug in the bag and handed him a sandwich. The last thing she wanted was food, but she made herself gag down one of the burgers and a little of the cola. Marc ended up devouring everything else. She prayed her sister was still alive, but in truth she feared what was waiting for her at the cabin.

As they drove up over the mountain and dropped down into Idaho, she stared out the window at the tall banks of plowed snow on each side of the road. Island Park was famous for its snow—close to nine feet of it in an average winter. And where there was snow...

Three snowmobiles buzzed by like angry bees on the trail beside the highway and sped off, the colorful sleds catching the sunlight.

She stole a glance in the side mirror. The highway behind them was empty. Her stomach roiled at the thought that Austin was ahead of them because of their food stop, that he might be waiting at the cabin, not realizing just how dangerous Marc was.

Gillian closed her eyes, fighting tears. She'd been so afraid for her sister she'd been desperate when she'd asked for his help. If only she could undo what she'd done. The man had saved her life last night and this was how she repaid him, by getting him involved in this?

There was no saving any of them, she thought as more snowmobiles zoomed past, kicking up snow crystals into the bright blue winter sky. It wasn't until they passed a cabin with a brightly decorated tree in the front yard that she remembered with a start that Christmas was only a few days away.

Chapter Nine

Not long after the Idaho border, the terrain closed in with pines and more towering snowbanks. Austin started seeing snowmobilers everywhere he looked. They buzzed past on brightly colored machines, the drivers clad in heavy-duty cold-weather gear and helmets, which hid their faces behind the black plastic.

Even inside the SUV, he could hear the roar of the machines as they sped by—all going faster on the snow track next to him than he was on the snow-slick highway.

Just as Hud had told him, he began to see cabins stuck back in the pines. He would need directions. He figured he was also going to need a snowmobile, just as Hud had suggested, if the cabin was far off the road.

When he reached the Henry's Fork of the Snake River, he pulled into a place alongside the highway called Pond's Lodge. The temperature seemed to be dropping, and tiny snowflakes hung around him as if suspended in the air as he got out of the SUV. He shivered, amazed that people lived this far north.

Inside, he asked for a map of the area.

"You'll want a snowmobile map, too," the older woman behind the counter said.

He thought she might be right as he stepped back outside. Snow had begun falling in huge lacy flakes. He wasn't all that anxious to get out in it on a snowmobile for the first time. But after a quick perusal of the map, he knew a snowmobile was his best bet.

As the marshal had told him he would, he could see the problem of finding the cabin—especially in winter. He figured a lot of the dwellings would be boarded up this time of year. Some even inaccessible.

He had to assume that Marc Stewart's family cabin would be open—but possibly not the road to it. What few actual roads there were seemed to be banked in deep snow. Clearly most everyone traveled by snowmobile. He could hear them buzzing around among the trees in a haze of gray smoke.

Back in his rented SUV, he drove down to a small out-of-the-way snowmobile rental. The moment he walked in the door, he caught the scent of a two-stroke engine and the high whine of several others as two snowmobiles roared out of the back of the shop. Even the music playing loudly from overhead speakers behind the counter couldn't drown them out. Beneath the speakers, a man in his late twenties with dozens of tattoos and piercings glanced up. The name stitched on his shirt read "Awesome."

"My man!" he called. "Looking for the ultimate machine, right? Are we talking steep and deep action or outrageous hill banging to do some high marking today?"

The man could have been speaking Greek. "Sorry, I just need one that runs."

Awesome laughed. "If it's boondocking you're looking for, chutes, ridges, big bowls, I got just the baby for you." He shoved a map at him. "We have an endless supply of cornices to jump, untouched powder and more coming down, mountainsides just waiting for you to put some fresh tracks on them."

"Do you have one for flat ground?"

Awesome looked a little disappointed. "You seriously want to pass up Two Top, Mount Jefferson and Lion's Head?"

He seriously did. "I see on your brochure that you have GPS tours. It says here I can pinpoint an area I want to go to with the specific coordinates and you can get me there?"

"I can." Awesome didn't seem all that enthusiastic about it, though. "We have about a thousand miles of backwoods trails."

"Great. Here is where I need to go. You have a machine that can get me there?"

He looked at the map, his enthusiasm waning even faster. "This address isn't far from here. I suppose you need gear? Helmet, boots, bibs, coat and gloves? They're an extra twenty. I can put you in a machine that will run you a hundred a day."

"How fast do these things go," Austin asked as one sped by in a blur.

"The fastest? A hundred and sixty miles an hour. The ones we have? You can clock in at a hundred."

Austin had no desire to clock in at a hundred. Even the price tag shocked him. The one sitting on the showroom floor was on sale for fourteen thousand dollars and everyone around here seemed to have one. He figured Marc Stewart would have at least one of the fastest snowmobiles around. He tagged the guy as someone who had done his share of high marking. "What is high marking, by the way?"

Awesome laughed and pointed at a poster on the wall. "You try to make the highest mark on the side of a mountain." On the poster, the rider had made it all the way up under an overhanging wall of snow."

"It looks dangerous."

Awesome shrugged. "Only if you get caught in an avalanche."

Austin didn't have to worry about avalanches, but what he was doing was definitely dangerous. Gillian was terrified for her sister. Austin wouldn't be trying to find them if he didn't believe she had good reason for concern.

But he was smart enough to know that a man like Marc Stewart, when trapped, might do something stupid like kill an off-duty state deputy sheriff who was sticking his nose where it didn't belong.

GILLIAN LOOKED OUT through the snow-filled pines as Marc drove. She couldn't see the cabin from the road. She'd been here once before, but it had been in summer. The cabin sat on Island Park Reservoir just off Centennial Loop Trail. While old, it was charming and picturesque. At least that's what she'd thought that summer she and her sister had spent a week here without Marc.

That had been before Rebecca and Marc had married, back when her sister had been happy and foolishly naive about the man she'd fallen in love with.

Gillian hugged herself as she remembered her sister's text message just days before.

On way to your house. I've left Marc.

She'd tried her sister's number, but the call went straight to voice mail. She'd texted back. Are you and Andy all right?

No answer. Helena was a good two hours away from Gillian's home in Big Sky. Even the way her sister drove, Rebecca wouldn't have arrived until after dark. Gillian had paced, checking the window anxiously and asking herself, "What would Marc do?" She feared the answer.

It was night by the time she finally saw her sister's

car pull up out front. Relieved to tears, she'd run outside without even a coat on. But it hadn't been Rebecca in the car.

By the time she'd realized it was Marc alone and furious, it was too late. He'd grabbed her and thrown her into the trunk. She'd fought him, but he'd been so much stronger and he'd taken her by surprise. He'd slammed the trunk lid and the next thing she'd known the car was moving.

"Did you really forget your name?" Marc asked, dragging her out of her thoughts. He sounded amused at the idea. "Sometimes I'd like to forget my name. Hell, I'd like to forget my life."

She didn't tell him that pieces of memory had her even more confused. She'd remembered there was someone in the trunk of the car she'd been driving, but she hadn't remembered it was her.

When Austin had returned to the cabin with the patrolman, he'd told her that the only thing he'd found in the trunk of the car was a suitcase. She'd been more confused.

It wasn't until she'd laid eyes on her alleged *husband* that she'd remembered Marc forcing her into the trunk. When he'd stopped at a convenience mart in the canyon, she'd shoved her way out by kicking aside the backseat.

She hadn't known where they were when she'd crawled out. He'd left the car running because of the freezing cold night. Not knowing where she was, she'd just taken off driving, afraid that he would get a ride or steal a car and come after her.

The next thing she remembered was waking up in a hospital with vague memories of the night before and a tall Texas cowboy.

"I'm curious. Where was it you thought you were

going?" Marc asked. He sounded casual enough, but she could hear the underlying fury behind his words.

"I have no idea." She'd been running scared. All she'd been able to think about was getting to a phone so she could call the police. Her cell phone had been in her pocket when she'd rushed out of her house, but Marc had taken it.

"You should have waited and run me down with the car." Marc glanced over at her. "Short of killing me, you should have known you wouldn't get away."

She shuddered at the thought, but knew he was right. She had managed to get away from him, but not long enough to help herself or her sister. Maybe that had been a godsend. He'd told her at the hospital that if they didn't get back to her sister soon, she would be dead.

Gillian hadn't known then where he'd left Rebecca. But she'd believed him. He'd had her sister's wedding band in his pocket. It wasn't until Marc headed out of Bozeman that she'd figured out where he was taking her.

Now Marc slowed the Suburban as he turned down a narrow road with high snowbanks on each side. He drove only a short distance, though, before the road ended in a huge pile of snow. She glanced around as he pulled into a wide spot where the snow had been plowed to make a parking area. Other vehicles were parked there, most of them with snowmobile trailers.

"Here." He tossed her a pair of gloves. A snowmobile buzzed past, kicking up a cloud of snow. "If you want to see your sister alive, you will do what I say. Try to make another run for it—"

"I get it." As angry and out of control as he was, she feared what kind of shape her sister was in. Marc had told Austin that their son, Andrew Marc, was with his grandmother. That had been a lie since Marc's parents were both dead and he had no other family that she knew of.

So where was Andy? Was he with his mother at the cabin? She didn't dare hope that they were both safe.

Marc backed up to where he'd left his snowmobile trailer. Both machines were on it, Gillian noticed, and any hope she'd had that her sister might have escaped evaporated at the sight of them. Even if Rebecca was able to leave the cabin, she had no way to get out. The snow would be too deep. One step off the snowmobile and she would be up to her thigh in snow. As she glanced in the direction of the cabin, Gillian could see the fresh tracks that Marc had made in and back out again from the cabin on the deep snow. Neither trip had packed down the trail enough to walk on.

Marc cut the engine. She could hear the whine of snowmobiles in the distance, then an eerie quiet fell over the Suburban.

"Come on," he said as he reached behind the seat for his coat. "Your sister is waiting."

Was she? Gillian could only pray it was true as she pulled on the coat Austin had given her and climbed out into the falling snow. Even as she breathed in the frosty air, she prayed they hadn't arrived too late. Marc had told her last night that if Rebecca was dead, it was her fault for taking off in the car and causing him even more problems.

The only thing that made her climb onto the back of the snowmobile behind her brother-in-law was the thought of her sister and nephew. Whatever was going on, Marc had brought her here for a reason. She couldn't imagine what. But if she could save Rebecca and Andy...

Even as she thought it, Gillian wondered how she would do that against a man like Marc Stewart.

AUSTIN WAS PLEASED to find that driving a snowmobile wasn't much different from driving a dirt bike. Actually, it was easier because you didn't have to worry as much about balance. You could just sit down, hit the throttle and go.

With the GPS in his pocket, along with a map of the area, and his weapon strapped on beneath his coat, he headed for Marc Stewart's cabin. The area was a web of narrow snow-filled roads that wove through the dense pines. From what he could gather, the Stewart cabin was on the reservoir.

He followed Box Canyon Trail until it connected with another trail at Elk Creek. Then he took Centennial Loop Trail.

He passed trees with names on boards tacked to them. Dozens of names indicating dozens of cabins back in the woods. But he had a feeling that the Stewart cabin wasn't near a lot of others or at least not near an occupied cabin.

Snowmobiles sped past, throwing up new snow, leaving behind blue exhaust. It was snowing harder by the time he reached the spot on the GPS where he was supposed to turn.

He slowed. The tree next to the road had only four signs nailed on it. Three of them were Stewart's. Off to his right, Austin saw a half dozen vehicles parked at what appeared to be the entrance to another trailhead that went off in the opposite direction from the Stewart family cabins.

The black Suburban was parked in front of a snowmobile trailer with one machine on it. There were fresh snow tracks around the spot where a second one must have recently been unloaded.

Austin double-checked the GPS. It appeared the cabin

at the address the marshal had given him was a half mile down a narrow road.

As he turned toward the road, he saw that there were several sets of snowmobile tracks, but only one in the new snow—and it wasn't very old based on how little of the falling snow had filled it.

Marc and Gillian weren't that far ahead of him.

Chapter Ten

The road Austin had taken this far was packed down from vehicles driving on it. But the one that went back into the cabins hadn't been plowed since winter had begun so the snow was a good five or six feet deep.

Austin had to get a run at it, throttling up the snowmobile to barrel up the slope onto the snow.

Fortunately, the snowmobile ahead of him had packed down the new snow so once he got up on top of it, the track was fairly smooth. Still, visibility was bad with the falling snow and the dense trees. He couldn't see anything ahead but the track he was on. According to the map, the road went past the Stewart cabins for another quarter mile before it ended beside the lake.

His plan was to go past the cabin where the snowmobile had gone, then work his way back. As loud as the snowmobile motor was, it would be heard by anyone inside the cabin. His only hope for a surprise visit would be if those inside thought he was merely some snowmobiler riding around.

A corner of a log cabin suddenly appeared from out of the falling snow. Austin caught glimpses of more weathered dark log structures as he continued on past. The shingled roofs seemed to squat under the layers of snow, the smaller cabins practically disappearing in the drifts.

No smoke curled out of any of the rock chimneys. In fact as he passed, he saw no signs of life at all. Wooden shutters covered all the windows. No light came from within.

He would have thought that the cabins were empty, still closed up waiting for spring—if not for the distinct new snowmobile track that cut off from the road he was on and headed directly for the larger of the three cabins.

Austin kept the throttle down, the whine of his snowmobile cutting through the cold silence of the forest as he zoomed past the cabins huddled in the pines and snow. He stole only a couple of glances, trying hard not to look in their direction for fear of who might be looking back.

MARC PULLED AROUND the back of the cabin and shut off the snowmobile engine.

Gillian could barely hear over the thunder of her heart. Her legs felt weak as she slipped off the back of the machine and looked toward the door of the cabin. The place was big and rambling, dated in a way that she'd found quaint the first time her sister had invited her here.

"Isn't this place something?" Rebecca had said, clearly proud of what she called Stewart Hall.

The main cabin reminded Gillian of the summer lodges she'd seen on television. All of it told of another time: the log and antler decor, furniture with Western print fabric, the bookshelves filled with thick tomes and board games, and the wide screened-in front porch with its wicker rockers that looked out over a marble-smooth green lake surrounded by towering pines.

"It is *picturesque,"* Gillian had said, not mentioning that it smelled a little musty. *"How often does Marc's family get up here?"*

"There isn't much family left. Just Marc and me."

Rebecca's hand had gone to her stomach. Her eyes brightened. *"That's why he wanted to start our family as soon as possible."*

"You're pregnant?*"* Her sister and Marc had only been married a few months at that time. But Gillian had seen how happy her sister was. *"Congratulations,"* she'd said and hugged Rebecca tightly as she remembered how she'd tried to talk her out of marrying Marc and her sister had accused her of being jealous.

Now as she watched Marc pocket the snowmobile key, she wished she'd fought harder. Even when they were only dating, Gillian had seen a selfishness in Marc, a need to always be the center of attention, a need to have everything his way. He was a poor sport, too, often leaving games in anger. They'd been small things that Rebecca had ignored, saying no man was perfect.

Gillian wished she had fought harder. Maybe she could have saved Rebecca from a lot of pain. But then there would be no baby. No little Andy...

"You know what you have to do," Marc said as he reached in another pocket for the key to the door.

She nodded.

"Do I have to remind you what happens if you don't?" he asked.

Gillian looked into his eyes. It was like looking into the fires of hell. "No," she said. "You were quite clear back at the motel."

AUSTIN RODE FARTHER up the road until he could see another cabin in the distance. He found a spot to turn the snowmobile around. The one thing he hadn't considered was how hard it would be to hike back to the Stewart cabins.

The moment he stepped off the machine, his leg sunk

to his thighs in the soft snow. His only hope was to walk in the snowmobile track—not that he didn't sink a good foot with each step.

He checked his gun and extra ammunition and then headed down the track. The falling snow made him feel as if he were in a snow globe. Had he not been following the snowmobile track, he might have become disoriented and gotten lost in what seemed an endless forest of snow-covered trees that all looked the same.

An eerie quiet had fallen around him, broken only by the sound of his own breathing. He was breathing harder than he should have been he realized. It had been months now since he'd been shot. That had been down on the Mexico border with heat and cactus and the scent of dust in the air, nothing like this. And yet, he had that same feeling that he was walking into something he wouldn't be walking back out of—and all because of a woman.

A bird suddenly cried out from a nearby tree. Austin started. He couldn't remember ever feeling more alone. When he finally picked up the irritating buzz of snowmobiles in the distance, he was thankful for a reminder of other life. The snow had an insulating effect that rattled his nerves with its cold silence. That and the memory of lying in the Texas dust, dying.

It seemed he'd been wrong. He hadn't put it behind him, he realized with a self-deprecating chuckle. And now here he was again. Only this time, he didn't know the area, let alone what was waiting for him inside that cabin, and he wasn't even a deputy doing his job.

The structure appeared out of the falling snow. He realized he couldn't stay on the track. But when he stepped off into the deep snow, he found himself laboring to move. It was worse under the trees, where it formed deep wells. If you got too close… He stepped into one and dropped, finding himself instantly buried. He fought his way to the surface like a swimmer and finally was able to climb out. The snow had chilled him. He'd never been in snow, let alone anything this deep and cold.

But his biggest concern was what awaited him ahead. He had no idea what he was going to do when he reached the main cabin. He needed to know what was going on inside. Unfortunately, with the shutters on all the windows, he wasn't sure how to accomplish that.

As he neared the side, he saw an old wooden ladder hanging on an outbuilding and had an idea. It was a crazy one, but any idea seemed good right now. The snow was deep enough where it had drifted in on this side of the cabin that it ran from the roof to the ground. If he could lay the ladder against the snowdrift, it was possible he could climb up onto the roof. The chimney stuck up out of the snow only a few feet. With luck, he might be able to hear something.

The snowmobile that had made the recent tracks to the cabin was parked out back—just as he'd suspected. Steam was still coming off the engine, indicating that whoever had ridden it hadn't been at the cabin long.

Austin took the ladder and, working his way through the snow, leaned it against the house and began to climb.

IT WAS LIKE a tomb inside the cabin with the shutters closed and no lights or heat on. Gillian stood in the large living room waiting for Marc to turn on a lamp. When he did, she blinked, blinded for a moment.

In that instant, she saw the cabin the way it had been the first time she'd seen it. The Native American rugs, the pottery and the old paintings and photographs on the walls. The vintage furniture and the gleam of the wood floors.

She'd felt back then that she'd been transported to another time, one that felt grander. One she wished she'd had as a child. She'd envied Marc his childhood here on this lake. How she'd longed to have been the little girl who curled up in the hammock out on the porch and read books on a long, hot summer day while her little sister played with dolls kept in one of the old trunks.

If only they could have been two little girls who swam in the lake and learned to water-ski behind the boat with her two loving parents. And lay in bed at night listening to the adults, the lodge alive with laughter and summer people.

For just an instant, Gillian had heard the happy clink of crystal from that other time. Then Marc stepped on a piece of broken glass that splintered under his snowmobile boot with the sound of a shot. He kicked it away and Gillian saw the room how it was now, cold, dark and as broken as the lonely only child Marc Stewart had been.

Most of the lighter-weight furniture now looked like kindling. Anything that could be broken was. Jigsaw pieces of ceramic vases, lamps and knickknacks littered the floor, along with the glass from the picture frames.

The room attested to the extent of Marc Stewart's rage—not that Gillian needed a reminder.

She looked toward the large old farmhouse-style kitchen. The floor was deep in broken dishes and thrown cutlery.

Past it down the hall, she saw drops of blood on the worn wood floor.

"Where's my sister? Rebecca!" Her voice came out too high. It sounded weak and scared and without hope. *"Rebecca?"*

"She's not up here," Marc said as he kicked aside what was left of a spindle rocking chair.

The weight of the fear on her chest made it hard to even say the words. *"Where is she?"*

"Down there." He pointed toward the old root cellar door off the kitchen.

Gillian felt her heart drop like a stone. She couldn't get her legs to move. Just as she couldn't get her lungs to fill. "You left her down there all this time?"

"We would have been here sooner if it wasn't for you." Marc looked as if he wanted to hit her, as if it took everything in him not to break her as he had everything else in this cabin. "Are you coming?"

Austin climbed across the roof to the chimney. The snow silenced his footfalls, but also threatened to slide in an avalanche that would take him with it should he misstep. He knelt next to the chimney to listen just as he heard Gillian call out her sister's name.

He waited for an answer.

He heard none.

"Can't you bring her up here?" Austin heard the fear in Gillian's voice. Bring her up? Was there a basement under the cabin? He didn't think so. A root cellar possibly? Then he felt his skin crawl as he remembered a root cellar one of his friends had found at an old abandoned house. He was instantly reminded of the musky smell, the cobwebs, the dust-coated canning jars with unidentifiable contents and the scurry of the rats as they'd opened the door.

"I thought you understood that we were doing this my way," Marc said, his tone as threatening as the smack that followed his words and Gillian's small cry of pain. "Come on."

Austin heard what sounded like the crunch of boot heels over gravel, then nothing for a few moments.

Chapter Eleven

Gillian peered down the steep wooden stairs into the dim darkness and felt her stomach roil. Only one small light burned in a black corner of the root cellar. The musty, damp smell hit her first.

"Rebecca?" she called and felt Marc shove her hard between her shoulder blades. She would have tumbled headlong down the stairs if she hadn't grabbed the door frame.

"Move," Marc snapped behind her.

Gillian thought she heard a muffled sound down in the blackness, but it could have been pack rats. What if Marc had lied? What if Rebecca was dead? Then the only reason Marc had come after her and brought her back here was to kill her, too.

She took one step, then another. There was no railing so she clung to the rough rock wall that ran down one side of the stairs. With each step, she expected Marc to push her again. All her instincts told her this was a trap. She wouldn't have been surprised to hear him slam and lock the door at the top of the steps behind her. Leaving her to die down here would be the kind of cruel thing he would do.

To her surprise, she heard the steps behind her groan with his weight as he followed her down. It gave her little relief, though. The moment she reached the bottom, she turned on him. "Where is she? Marc, where is my sister?"

Gillian heard another moan and turned in the direction the sound had come from. Something moved deep in the darkest part of the root cellar. "Oh, God, what have you done to her?"

Marc pushed her aside. An instant later, a bare overhead bulb turned on blinding her. Gillian blinked, shielding her eyes from the glare as she tried to see—all the time terrified of what Marc had done to her sister.

In the far reaches of the root cellar, Gillian saw her. Rebecca was shackled to a chair. He'd left her water and a bucket along with at least a little food. But there was dried blood on her face and clothes. Her face was also bruised and raw, but her eyes were open.

What Gillian saw in her sister's eyes, though, sent her heart plummeting. Regret when she saw her sister, but when her gaze turned to her husband, it was nothing but defiance. Gillian tried to swallow, but her mouth felt as if filled with cotton balls.

"You're her last hope, big sister," Marc said as he looked from his wife to her. "Get her to tell you what she did with my ledger, my money and my son…" He met her gaze. "Or I will kill her and then I will beat it out of you since I know she tells you everything."

Not everything, Gillian thought. She swallowed again, her throat working. "I already told you that I don't know."

He nodded, his facial features distorted under the harsh glare of the single bulb hanging over his head. How could such a handsome man look so evil…?

"Either you get it out of her or I will beat her until her last scream." He handed her a key to the lock on the shackles.

Gillian moved to her sister, falling on her knees in

front of her. She worked to free her, her hands shaking so hard she had trouble with the lock. "She needs water and food and help out of this chair." She turned to glare back at him. "It's too cold and damp down here. I think she is already suffering from hypothermia. She's going to die before you can kill her."

He took a step toward her. "Who the hell do you think you are, telling me what I *have* to do?"

It took all of her courage to stand up to him knowing the kind of man he was. But if she and Rebecca had any chance, they had to get out of this root cellar.

"If she dies, then what she knows dies with her," Gillian said quickly. "I told you. I don't know. She didn't tell me because she knows I'm not as strong as she is. I would tell you."

He seemed to mull that over for a moment, his gaze going to his wife. Marc looked livid. He raised his hand and Gillian tried not to cower from his fist.

To her surprise, he didn't strike her. "Fine," he said with a curse.

Rebecca didn't move, didn't seem to breathe. If it weren't for the movement of her eyes, Gillian would have sworn she was already dead.

"I hope you don't think you're going to get away again," Marc said, meeting her gaze. "I have nothing to lose and I'm sick of both of you."

AUSTIN HEARD THE sound of footfalls and murmured voices. He froze, listening, and was relieved when he heard Gillian's voice. He hadn't been able to hear anything for a while.

"We need to get her warm." Her voice was louder. So were the footfalls. They'd come up from the root cellar.

He also heard another sound, a slow shuffling, almost dragging, gait.

"Maybe you could build a fire or turn on the furnace."

Marc swore at Gillian's suggestion. The footfalls stopped abruptly. Gillian let out a small cry. Austin cringed in anger, knowing that Marc had hit her.

"Enough wasting time," Marc snapped.

"You want her to talk? Then give me a chance. But first we need to warm her up. Can you get some quilts from the bedroom?"

Marc swore loudly, but Austin heard what sounded like him storming away into another room. "Move and I'll—" he said over his shoulder.

"I'm not going to move," Gillian snapped. "My sister can barely stand, let alone run away. I'm going to put her in the living room in front of the fireplace. Maybe you could build a fire?"

Austin didn't catch what Marc said. He could guess, though. Marc was an abusive SOB. But Austin still had no idea why he'd brought Gillian and her sister here, nor where the child was. From what he had surmised, Marc thought Gillian could get her sister to talk, but talk about what?

Austin decided it didn't matter. Marc had forced Gillian to come here against her will. He had abused her and her sister and had apparently held Rebecca captive here. It was time to put a stop to this.

Working his way back off the roof, he walked around to where Marc had left the snowmobile. All Austin's instincts warned him not to go busting in. He couldn't chance what Marc would do.

He moved carefully back the way he'd come until he was at the far side of the cabin complex. He found an old door with a single lock and waited until he heard the sound of several snowmobiles nearby. Hoping they would drown out the noise, he busted the lock and carefully shoved open the door.

GILLIAN HELPED HER SISTER into a straight-backed chair from the dining room and gently wiped her sister's face with the hem of her sweater. "Oh, Becky."

Rebecca's gaze locked with hers, her voice a hoarse whisper. "I thought I could do this without getting you involved."

Marc returned with the quilts and dropped them next to the chair.

"We're going to need a fire," Gillian said, not looking at him as she rubbed life back into her sister's hands and arms.

After a moment, she glanced over her shoulder to see what Marc was doing. He was busy building a fire in the rock fireplace using some of the furniture he'd destroyed. He struck a match to the wadded up newspaper under the stack of wood. The paper caught fire. The dried old wood of the furniture burst into flames and began to crackle warmly.

"She needs something to drink. Is there any water in the kitchen?"

"What do you think?" Marc snapped. "It's winter. Everything is shut off."

"Maybe you could melt some snow." She motioned with her head for him to go as if the two of them were in collaboration. The thought made her sick.

He glanced from her to her sister and back again. "Don't do anything stupid," he said as he walked into the kitchen and came back out with a pot in one hand.

Marc had both women in an old cabin in the woods, far enough from the rest of the world that they would never be found if he killed them and buried them in the root cellar. So what was the stupid thing he thought she might do?

He gave her a warning look anyway and left, going out the back door where he'd left the snowmobile. She let go of her sister's arms and to her surprise Rebecca fell over in the chair, catching herself before she fell on the littered floor.

Gillian helped her sit up straighter, shocked at how weak her sister was and terrified she wasn't going to survive this.

Marc came back in, shot them a look, but said nothing as he headed for the kitchen with the cooking pot full of fresh snow. She heard him turn on the stove. She could feel time slipping through her fingers.

"Becky, what's going on?" she whispered. "What is this about some ledger of Marc's? And where is Andy?"

Her sister shook her head in answer as she glanced toward the kitchen, where Marc was cussing and banging around.

"Tell him what he wants to know—otherwise he is going to kill you," Gillian pleaded.

"So sorry to get you—" her sister said from between cracked and cut lips.

"Becky—"

"Remember when we were kids and that big old tree blew over?"

Gillian stared at her. Had her brain been injured as a result of Marc's beating? Gillian's heartbreak rose in a sob from her throat as she looked at what that bastard had done to her sister.

Rebecca suddenly gripped her arm, digging in her fingernails. "Tell me you remember," her sister said.

"I remember."

Her sister's eyes filled with tears. "Love you." She licked her lips, her words coming out hoarse and hurried. "Save Andy. Make Marc pay." Pain filled her sister's eyes. "Can't save me."

"Stop talking like that. I'm not leaving here without you."

Her sister smiled, even though her lips were cut and bleeding, and then shook her head. "Get away. Run. He'll hurt you." She stopped talking at the sound of heavy footfalls headed back in their direction.

Gillian stared at her sister. "What are you going to do?" she whispered frantically. She could feel Marc closing the distance.

"Get ready to run," her sister said under her breath as Marc's shadow fell over them.

"What's all the whispering about?" Marc demanded as he handed Gillian a cup of melted snow.

She held it up to her sister's swollen lips. Her gaze met Rebecca's in a pleading gesture. Her sister was talking crazy. Worse, she seemed about to do something that could get them both killed.

Without warning, her sister knocked the cup out of her hand. It hit the floor, spilling the water as it rolled across the floor.

"You stupid—" Marc shoved Gillian out of the way. She fell backward and hit the floor hard. From where she was sprawled, she saw him pull his gun and crouch down in front of Rebecca. He put the end of the barrel against his wife's forehead. "Last chance, Rebecca."

With horror, Gillian saw Becky's expression—and what she had picked up from the floor and hidden in her hand. "No!" she screamed as her sister swung her arm toward Marc's face. The shard of sharp broken glass clutched in her fingers momentarily flashed as it caught the dim light.

Blood sprouted across Marc's cheek and neck as Rebecca raked the glass down his face. He bucked back and then shoved the barrel of the gun toward Rebecca's head as Gillian scrambled to her feet and launched herself at him.

The sound of the gunshot boomed, drowning out Gillian's scream as she careened into him, knocking them both to the floor.

THE DOORKNOB TURNED in Austin's hand as he heard the scream. He charged into the cabin, running toward the echoing sound of the scream and the gunshot, his heart hammering in his chest.

His lungs ached with the freezing-cold musty smell of the cabin. He had his gun drawn, his senses on alert, as he burst into the room and tried to take in everything at once. He saw it all in those few crucial seconds. The large wrecked living room; the small glowing fire crackling in the huge stone fireplace; snowy, melting footprints on the worn wood floor; and three people—all on the floor.

"Drop the gun!" Austin ordered as he saw Gillian and Marc struggling for the weapon. The other figure—Rebecca Stewart, he assumed—lay in a pool of blood next to them.

There was no way he could get a clear shot. He rushed forward an instant before the sound of the second gunshot ripped through the room. The bullet whistled past him. Marc wrestled the gun from Gillian and scrambled to his feet, dragging her up with him as a shield, the barrel of his gun against her temple.

"You drop *your* gun or so help me I will put a bullet

in her head," Marc said, sounding in pain. Austin saw that he was bleeding from a cut down his cheek and neck.

"You can't get away," Austin said his weapon aimed at Marc's head.

Marc chuckled at that as he lifted Gillian off her feet and backed toward the door where he'd left his snowmobile. "Drop your gun or I swear I will kill her!" Marc bellowed. His eyes were wide, blood streaming down his face, but the gun in his hand was steady and sure.

"The police are on their way. Let her go!" Austin doubted the bluff would work and it was too risky to try a shot since Marc was making himself as small a target as possible behind Gillian.

Marc kept backing toward the door. His snowmobile was just outside. If he could manage to get to it… Austin couldn't stand the thought of the man getting away, but his first priority had to be the safety of the women. Austin knew Marc wouldn't try to take Gillian with him. He needed to get away quickly. If he could make him let her go… He wouldn't be surprised, though, if at the last moment Marc put a bullet in her head.

Gillian was crying, the look on her face one of horror more than terror. She was looking at her sister crumpled on the floor in front of the fireplace. Rebecca wasn't moving.

Marc dragged Gillian another step back. He would have to let Gillian go to open the door. Austin waited as the seconds ticked by.

As Marc reached behind him to open the door, Austin knew he would have only an instant to take his shot. Moving fast, Marc shoved Gillian away, turned the gun and fired as Austin dove to the side for cover—and took his own shot.

He heard a howl of pain and then a loud crash, looking

in time to see Marc grab a large old wooden hutch by the door and pull it down after him. The hutch crashed down on its side, blocking the door as Marc made his escape.

Austin raced toward the door but couldn't see Marc or the snowmobile to get off a shot. As he started to scramble over the downed hutch, he heard the engine, smelled the smoke as the man roared away.

Behind him, Gillian, sobbing hysterically, pushed herself up from the littered floor and rushed to her sister.

His need to go after Marc blinded him for a moment. He'd wounded Marc, but it hadn't been enough to stop him. He couldn't bear the thought of Marc getting away after what he'd done. He swore under his breath. But as badly as he wanted the man, he couldn't leave Gillian and her sister to chase after him.

"Help her," she pleaded from where she was kneeling on the floor. "My sister—"

He holstered his gun and knelt down next to Rebecca to feel for a pulse. "She's alive." Just barely. He checked his phone. Still no service.

"Go for help. I'll stay here with her," Gillian said. "Go."

Chapter Twelve

Marc couldn't believe this. He was bleeding like a stuck pig. Reaching the road and his Suburban, he stumbled off the snowmobile and lurched toward his vehicle. He couldn't tell how badly he was wounded, but his movements felt too slow, which he figured indicated that he was losing blood fast.

He thumbed the key fob, opened the Suburban's door and pulled himself inside. The last thing he wanted to do was take the time to check his wounds for fear the cowboy would be coming after him, but something told him if he didn't stop the bleeding, he was a dead man either way.

The Texas deputy had said he'd already called the cops. Marc couldn't risk that the man was telling the truth. His hand shook as he turned the rearview mirror toward him and first inspected the cut.

"Son of a bitch!" He couldn't believe what Rebecca had done to him. The cut ran from just under his eye, down his cheek to under his chin and into his throat. He took off his gloves and pressed one to the spot that seemed to be bleeding the most.

After a few moments, the bleeding slowed—at least on his face. He could feel blood running down his side, chilling him as it soaked into his clothing. He became aware of the pain. His shoulder felt as if it were on fire. Unzipping his coat, then unbuttoning his shirt, he inspected the damage.

Again, he'd been lucky. The bullet had only grazed his shoulder. He stuck the other glove on the wound and zipped his coat back up. He would have to get more clothes. He couldn't wear a coat drenched in blood with a bullet hole in it—especially given the way his face looked.

He swore again, furious with Rebecca but even more furious with himself. She'd purposely pushed him so he would pull the trigger. Now he was no closer to finding his ledger and his money—or his son—than he had been at first.

Starting the Suburban, he pulled away. He would have to ditch this rig and pick up another. That was the least of his problems. He knew someone who could stitch up his wounds and get him another vehicle.

But now he was a man on the run from the law.

GILLIAN WAS CRADLING her sister's head in her arms when Austin returned with local law enforcement. Rebecca was breathing, but she hadn't regained consciousness. Gillian had wanted to go in the ambulance with her sister, but the officer had needed her to answer questions about what had happened.

"I'll take you to the Bozeman hospital to see your sister," Austin said when the interrogation had finally ended and they were allowed to go.

Gillian was still shaken and worried about her sister as she climbed into Austin's SUV. The officers who'd questioned them had taken them to a local station to talk. She'd been grateful to get out of the cold cabin.

"We have to make sure Marc doesn't get to Becky," she said as Austin pulled onto Highway 191, headed north.

"That isn't going to happen. There will be a guard outside her room at the hospital, not that I suspect Marc will try to see her. There is a BOLO out on your brother-in-law. He can't get far in that large black Suburban. Also, he's wounded and needs medical attention. Law enforcement has thrown a net over the area. When he shows his face, they will arrest him."

She glanced at the Texas cowboy. "You don't know Marc. He has access to other vehicles. He's resourceful. He'll slip through the net. He has nothing to lose at this point. He will be even more dangerous."

"You don't have any idea where your brother-in-law might go?"

She shook her head, then winced in pain. "The man is crazy. Who knows what he'll do now."

"Whatever information he was trying to get out of your sister…he didn't get it, right?"

"No," she said, her eyes filling with tears. "Apparently Rebecca would rather die than tell him."

"I'm trying to understand all of this. Marc Stewart brought you to the cabin to make your sister talk, right? He thought she would tell you. Did she?"

Gillian wiped her tears. "No. Rebecca knew the moment I saw what he'd done to her that I would have told him anything he wanted to know. She didn't tell me *anything*. I didn't know about any ledger or about Andy being gone until Marc told me. I'm just praying she regains consciousness soon and tells us where we can find Andy. My nephew is only ten months old…."

"Maybe Marc will turn himself in given that he's wounded and now wanted by the law."

She scoffed at that. "I highly doubt that since whatever is in this ledger Rebecca took would apparently put

Marc behind bars for years. He'd never go down without a fight."

"A lot of criminals say that—until it comes time to die and then they find they prefer to turn state's evidence," Austin said. "Your sister never even hinted what Marc might be up to?"

"No. I knew they were having trouble. I couldn't understand why she stayed with the man. He was domineering and tight with the money, and treated Rebecca as if she was his property. But I never dreamed something like this would happen. When Rebecca texted me that she had left Marc, I was shocked since there had been no warning."

AUSTIN GLANCED OVER at her as he drove. Gillian looked numb. Her face was still pale, her eyes red from crying. He hated to ask, but he needed to know what they were up against. "Would you mind telling me how all this began?"

She sat up a little straighter, drawing on some inner strength that impressed him. He knew given what she'd been through, she must be exhausted let alone physically injured and emotionally spent.

"I had no idea what was going on. Rebecca and Andy had been at my house just a week before and everything seemed to be fine. Then I got the text. When I saw her car pull up to my house last night, I ran out thinking it was her."

He listened to her explain that instead of it being her sister in the car, it had been Marc. She told him how Marc had thrown her into the trunk and she'd escaped partway down the canyon.

"So there *had* been someone in the trunk," he said. It all made sense now. Even as confused as she'd been after her car accident, she'd recalled someone in the trunk.

"I wasn't thinking clearly when I took off. I just knew I had to get away from Marc and find my sister."

"You did everything you could to save her without any thought to your own life," Austin said. "This is on Marc, not you. But there is one thing I don't understand. Why did your sister choose now to leave him? I mean, had something happened between them?"

Gillian sighed. "I don't know. All I can figure is that Rebecca got her hands on Marc's business ledger, saw what was inside and realized she was married to a criminal—as well as an abuser. Apparently there was a reference to all the money Marc had stashed in the ledger and that's why she went to the Island Park cabin and he followed her there." She shook her head. "I don't know what she was thinking. How could she not know what Marc would do?"

"It sounds as if she was just trying to keep her son safe from him," Austin said. "She was also trying to protect you by not telling you anything." He felt Gillian's gaze on him.

"I'm sorry I dragged you into this."

"We're past that. As I told you before, I'm a deputy sheriff down in Texas. I'm glad I can help."

"I wish you could help, but I have no idea where my sister hid her son, let alone this ledger that Marc is losing his mind over. Marc will only be worse now. He's dangerous and desperate. I'm afraid of what he will do—especially if he finds his son."

Austin hated the truth he heard in her words. He'd known men like Marc Stewart. "Which is another reason I don't want to let you out of my sight. It won't make any difference if he believes your sister told you anything or not. He'll blame you."

"He already does for involving you in this. I'm so sorry. But I can't ask you—"

"I'm in this with you," he said, reaching over to take her hand. He gave it a squeeze and let go.

Gillian met his gaze. Her eyes shimmered with tears. "If you hadn't shown up when you did…" She looked away. He could tell she was fighting tears, worried about her sister and her nephew, and maybe finally realizing how close she had come to dying back there. "I have to find Andy and this notebook, ledger, whatever it is, before Marc does. If he finds it first, he'll skip the country with Andy. I know him. I wouldn't be surprised if he doesn't have a new identity all set up."

MARC AVOIDED LOOKING in the mirror as he drove. His friend had fixed him up. But when he saw his bandaged face in the mirror, it made him furious all over again. And when he was furious, he couldn't think straight.

He'd just assumed that Rebecca would cave at some point and tell him what he wanted to know. Frankly, he'd never thought her a strong woman. Boy, had she proven him wrong, he thought as he silently cursed her to hell. If she had just told him what he wanted to know all this would be over by now. She might even still be alive. Or not. But at least he would have made her death look like an accident.

Word was going to get out about Rebecca's murder. His DNA would be found at the scene. Not to mention he'd shot at a Texas deputy. Gillian would swear he'd kidnapped her… How had things gotten so out of hand? He had a target on his back now. Even with an old pickup and a change of identity, he couldn't risk getting stopped even for a broken taillight—not with this bandage down the side of his face.

His cell phone rang. "What?"

"You don't have to bite off my head."

Marc rolled his eyes, but bit his tongue. He needed his friend's help. "Sorry, Leo. What did you find out?"

"They took your wife to the hospital in Bozeman. I couldn't get any information, though, on her condition."

Rebecca was *alive*?

"As for your sister-in-law? She and some cowboy left together after spending a whole lot of time talking to the cops. I suspect they're headed to Bozeman and the hospital. You want me to keep following them?"

"The man with her? He's a sheriff's deputy from Texas. He'll know if he is being followed, so no. I'll call you if I need you."

He disconnected, not sure what to do next. When his cell rang, he thought it was Leo again. Instead it was his…so-called partner. In truth, Victor Ramsey ran the show and always had. Marc began to sweat instantly as he picked up.

"What the hell is going on, Marc? Why are there cops after you?"

AT THE HOSPITAL in Bozeman, Gillian was told that her sister was stable and resting. She hadn't regained consciousness, but the doctor promised he would call when she did.

Gillian tried not to let the tidal wave of relief drown out the news. Becky was alive and stable. Once she woke up, she could tell them what they needed to know. But in the meantime…

Down the hallway, she saw Austin on his cell phone and overheard the last of what he was saying as she approached. She felt awful as she realized that he'd come to Montana to see his family and Christmas was just days away…. She didn't know what she would have done without him, though, but she couldn't have him missing a family Christmas because of her.

"Hey," he said, smiling when he saw her. "Good news?"

She nodded. "Becky's still unconscious but stable. Listen, Austin, I already owe you my life and my sister's. Aside from almost getting you killed, now I'm keeping you away from your family who you came all the way to Montana to see and it's almost Christmas."

"I came up for the grand opening of our first Texas Boys Barbecue restaurant in Montana."

"Barbecue?"

He nodded at her surprise. "My brothers and I own a few barbecue joints."

"I thought you said you were a deputy sheriff?"

"I am. My brother Laramie runs the company so the rest of us can do whatever we want." He gave a shrug.

"Cardwell?" Why hadn't she realized who he was? "You're related to Dana Savage?"

"She's my cousin. She and her husband own Cardwell Ranch. My brothers came up to visit her, fell in love with Montana and all but one of them has fallen in love with more than the state and moved here."

"You can't miss this grand opening…."

"Believe me, my family can manage without me. Actually, they're used to it. I'm not good at these family events and I'm not leaving you until Marc is behind bars. You're stuck with me." He smiled. He had an amazing smile that lit up his handsome face and made his dark eyes shine.

She hadn't realized how handsome he was. Maybe because she hadn't taken the time to really look at him. "Are you trying to tell me that you're the black sheep of the family?" she asked as they took the elevator down to the hospital parking area.

He laughed at that. "And then some. I missed my brother Tag's wedding last summer. I was on a case. I'm often on a case. I'm only here now because they all ganged up on me and made me feel guilty."

"When is the grand opening?"

"The first of January. See? Nothing to worry about."

"You're that confident Marc will be caught by then?" she asked.

He turned that smile on her. "With my luck, he will and I won't have any excuse not to attend not only the grand opening but also Christmas at my cousin's house with the whole family."

"You aren't serious."

"On the contrary. I usually volunteer to work the holidays so deputies with families can spend them at home. I'm the worst Scrooge ever when it comes to Christmas. So trust me when I say my family won't be surprised I'm not there, nor will they mind all that much."

"I think you're exaggerating," she said as they reached his SUV.

He shook his head. "Nope. It's the truth. What do you suggest we do now?"

She turned to look at him. "I can't ask you—"

"You aren't asking. I already told you. I'm not leaving you alone until Marc is behind bars."

Tears filled her eyes. She bit down on her lower lip for a moment. "Thank you. I need to go to my house."

"Where is that?"

"I have a studio at Big Sky."

"A studio?"

"I'm a jeweler."

"The watch." He frowned and she could see he was wondering who'd made it for her.

"My father was the one who taught me the craft. I

lost him five years ago. Before that, my mother. I can't lose my sister."

He put an arm around her and pulled her close. "You won't. The doctor said she is stable, right? She's a strong woman and she has every reason to pull through."

Gillian nodded against his strong chest. He smelled of the outdoors, a wonderful masculine scent that reminded her how long it had been since a man had held her. She reminded herself why Austin Cardwell was here with her and stepped away from his arms.

"I need to figure out what my sister was thinking," she said as Austin opened the door to the SUV. "It was one thing to hide the ledger, but another to hide my nephew."

As he slid behind the wheel, he asked, "Those few moments you had with your sister before Marc returned, did she say anything that might have been a clue where either might be?"

"I'm not even sure she was in her right mind at the end. Marc told me she was taking some kind of pills for stress before all this happened."

Austin shook his head as he started the engine. "She got her son away from Marc and she hid a book that can possibly get her husband put away for a long time. On top of that, she wounded Marc in a way that makes him easy to spot. That doesn't sound like a woman who wasn't thinking straight."

Gillian's eyes filled with tears. "But why didn't she tell me where to find Andy and the ledger?"

"Maybe she mailed you something. Or said something that didn't make sense at the time, but will later. You've been through so much, not to mention Marc taking you out of the hospital too soon after a head injury. You say you live at Big Sky?"

"Before you get to Meadow Village. I have an apartment over my studio and shop." She rubbed her temples with her fingers.

"Headache?"

Gillian nodded. "Maybe Becky *did* send me something in the mail. If that's the case…" She turned to look at him. "Then we need to get to my house before Marc does."

THEY WERE ONLY a few miles out of Big Sky when Gillian fell into an exhausted sleep. Austin's heart went out to her. He couldn't imagine what the past forty-eight hours had been like for her. He worried about her even though she was holding up better than he would have expected. The woman was strong. Or maybe it hadn't really hit her yet.

What drove him was the thought of Marc Stewart not just getting away with kidnapping and attempted murder, but possibly finding his son and taking him out of the country. If that happened, Austin doubted either Rebecca or her sister would ever see the child again.

The man had to be stopped, and Austin was determined to do what he could to make that happen.

When Gillian woke near the outskirts of Big Sky, she looked better, definitely more determined. There was so much more he needed to know about the situation he'd found himself in and he was anxious to ask. But first they had to reach her studio. There was the chance that Marc Stewart had been there—was even still there.

Chapter Thirteen

Marc held the phone away from his ear for a moment as he considered how much to tell Victor. The first time Marc had met Victor Ramsey, he'd been amused by the man's clean-cut appearance that belied the true man underneath. That was five years ago. Victor still had one of those trustworthy faces, bright blue eyes and a winning smile. But if you looked deeper into those blue eyes, as Marc had done too many times, you would see a cold-blooded psychopath.

"What's going on, Marc?" Victor asked now as if he'd just called to catch up.

The two had met through a mutual friend, something Marc later suspected had been a setup from the start.

Want to make more money than you've ever dreamed possible? his friend had said one night after they'd consumed too much alcohol.

His answer had been, *Hell yes.* The auto body shop he'd taken over from his father was a lot of work and for average income, not to mention he hated it.

His friend, now deceased under suspicious circumstances, had made the introduction. At first Marc had been in awe of Victor, a self-made man with a lot of charm and ambition. It wasn't until he was in too deep that he'd begun to regret all of it.

"Just having a little domestic trouble," Marc answered now.

"Attempted murder is a little more than domestic trouble. I want to see you. Where are you?"

He'd been expecting this, but the last person he wanted to see him like this was Victor. "Right now isn't a great time."

"I'm staying at my place in Canyon Creek. I'll give you two hours. Don't be late. You know how I hate anyone who wastes my time." Victor hung up.

Marc swore. After Victor saw his face—and found out everything else—Marc knew he would be lucky to walk out of that meeting alive.

With a curse, he realized he had really only one choice. Get out of the country—or at least try. But it would mean leaving without his son—or settling the score with his wife, his sister-in-law and the Texas deputy who'd stuck his nose in where it didn't belong.

He would prefer to find the ledger and his son, take care of all of them and then get out of the country. Rebecca had discovered some of his money, but he had more hidden.

Unfortunately the clock was ticking and if he hoped to live long enough to do what had to be done, he would have to meet with Victor and try to talk his way out of this mess.

AUSTIN PARKED BEHIND a three-story building with a sign that read Gillian Cooper Designs. As she led the way up the back steps, Austin kept an eye out for Marc Stewart. There was no sign of his black Suburban, but Austin figured he would have gotten rid of it by now.

There were no other buildings around Gillian's. The studio and apartment sat against the mountainside with only one parking spot in back. The building was unique in design. When he asked her about it, he wasn't surprised to find out that she'd designed it herself.

As she led him into the living area, he saw that the inside was as uniquely designed as the outside with shiny bamboo floors, vaulted wood ceilings, arches and tall windows. He could see that she had more than just a talent for jewelry. The decor was a mixture of old and new, each room bright with color and texture.

Remembering how Marc had torn up the Island Park cabin, he was relieved to see that the man hadn't been in Gillian's apartment. From what he could gather, nothing had been disturbed. Maybe Marc had been wounded badly enough that he'd been forced to get medical attention before anything else. Once an emergency room doctor saw the bullet wound, the law would be called and Marc would be arrested. At least Austin could hope.

He stood in the living area, taking in the place. He found himself becoming more intrigued by Gillian Cooper as he watched her scoop up the mail that had been dropped through the old-fashioned slot in the antique front door.

"I love your house," he said, hoping he got a chance to see the jewelry she made.

"Thanks," she said as she sorted through the mail. He could tell by her disappointed expression that there was nothing from her sister. She looked up at him. "Nothing." Her voice broke as she shook her head.

"Why don't you get a hot shower and a change of clothes," he suggested.

She nodded. "There is a shower in the guest room if you…"

"Thank you." They stood like that for a moment, strangers who knew too much about each other, bound together by happenstance.

He moved first, picking up his duffel bag, which he'd brought up from the car. She pointed toward an open door as if no longer capable of speech. He'd seen it often in people who were thrown into extraordinary circumstances. They often found an inner strength that made it possible for them to do extraordinary things. But at some point that strength ebbed away, leaving them an empty shell.

The shower was hot, the water pressure strong. Austin stood under it, spent. He'd had little sleep last night and then today… He was just thankful he'd burst into the cabin when he had. He didn't want to think what would have happened otherwise. Nor did he want to think about what he'd gotten himself into and where it would end.

CLEAN AND WARM and dressed in clean jeans and a long-sleeved T-shirt, Austin went back out into the living room. Where was Marc now? Austin could only imagine. Hopefully he'd been arrested, but if that were the case, Austin would have received a call by now. The officer who'd responded to his call had promised to let him know when Marc Stewart was in custody.

Which meant Marc Stewart was still out there.

A few minutes later, Gillian emerged from the other side of the house. Her face was flushed from her shower. She wore a white fluffy sweater and leggings. Her long dark hair was still damp and framed the face of a model.

For a moment, she looked nervous, as if realizing she was now alone with a complete stranger.

"If you don't mind talking about it, could you tell me more about this ledger Marc is looking for?" he said, finding ground he knew would ease the sudden tension between them.

"I only know what Marc told me," she said as she walked to the refrigerator, opened it and held up a bottle of wine. He nodded and she poured two glasses, which they took into the living room.

Gillian curled up at one end of the couch, tucking her feet under her. Austin took a chair some distance away. He watched her take a sip of her wine and she seemed to relax a little.

"I gathered Marc wrote down some sort of illegal business dealings in a black ledger that he never let out of his sight," she said after a moment. "Marc is dyslexic so he has trouble remembering numbers, apparently. He wrote everything down. According to him, my sister drugged him and took the book."

"What do you know about your brother-in-law's business?"

"Nothing really. He owns an auto body shop, repairs cars."

"That doesn't sound like something that would force him to go to the extremes he has to recover some ledger he kept figures in."

"I'm not sure what's in it other than where he hid large amounts of money, but I gathered, from Marc's terror at the ledger landing in the wrong hands, that there is enough in it to send him to prison."

"I don't understand why she didn't take it to the police or the FBI. Marc would be in jail now and none of this would have happened."

Gillian shook her head. "Apparently she thought she could force him into giving her a divorce and custody of Andrew Marc in exchange for the ledger. She also needed money. I guess she didn't realize just how dangerous that would be."

"Or she didn't get a chance to before Marc realized the ledger was missing. He figured out she was headed for the Island Park cabin fairly quickly."

She nodded. "He'd stashed money there." She grew quiet for a moment. "Apparently she hid the ledger. I know it's not at their house. He said he tore the place apart looking for it."

"You and your sister were close. Any ideas where she could have hidden it?"

"None. Becky and I…" She hesitated, turning to glance out the side window. "We weren't that close recently. Marc thought I was a bad influence on her. I didn't want to make things worse for her but I couldn't stand being around him. He kept her on a short leash. The last time we were together before this, I begged her to leave Marc. She kept thinking he was going to change."

Austin heard the worry in her voice. "A lot of women have trouble leaving."

"I always thought my sister was smarter than that," she said as she got up to refill their glasses.

"Intelligence doesn't seem to have much to do with it." He doubted this helped at the moment. Marc Stewart was out there somewhere, wounded and still obsessed with finding not only the ledger, but also his son. Which meant Gillian wasn't safe until Marc was behind bars and maybe not even then, depending on just what Marc Stewart was involved in.

She met his gaze as she filled his glass. "You saw what Marc's like. Just out of spite, he might do something to Andy if he finds him." Her voice cracked, and for a moment, she looked as if she might break down.

Austin rose to take her in his arms. She felt small but

strong. It was he who felt vulnerable. He'd never met anyone like her, and that scared him. Not to mention the fact that Gillian felt too good in his arms.

He let go of her and she stepped away to wipe her tears.

"We'll find your nephew," he said to her back. He had no idea how, but he agreed with her. Marc was a loose cannon now. Anyone in his path was in danger. "Your sister was living in Helena? Where would she stash her son that she thought he would be safe? Marc said the boy was with his grandmother."

Gillian shook her head. "No grandparents are still alive."

"Maybe a babysitter? A friend she trusted?"

Again Gillian shook her head. "Marc didn't allow her to leave Andy with anyone, not that she had need of a babysitter because he would check on her during the day to make sure she hadn't gone anywhere."

Austin hated the picture she was painting of her sister's life. "Then how did your sister manage to not only get possession of Marc's ledger, but hide their son?"

Gillian shook her head again. "I suspect she'd been planning it for weeks, maybe even months. Rebecca did tell me when I was trying to get her to leave him that time in Helena that Marc had threatened to kill her and Andy if she did."

He guessed that Rebecca had believed her husband. But then she'd taken the ledger and thought she had leverage. "You said your sister visited a while back. Is there a chance she left you a note that you might have missed?"

Gillian shook her head and stepped to one of the windows to look out. Past her, he caught glimpses of the Gallatin River and the dense snowcapped pines. It was snowing again, huge flakes drifting down past the window. How could his brothers live in a place where it snowed like this?

"Apparently my sister found quite a bit of money that Marc kept hidden in his locked gun cabinet." She turned toward him. "It is missing, as well."

He thought of the ransacked Island Park cabin. "Your sister had gone to the cabin to get more money he had stashed there?"

She nodded. "So foolish. I guess she wanted to keep him from skipping the country and taking his money, and she thought that would work. She apparently didn't think she could keep him in jail long enough to do whatever she had planned."

He watched her look around the room as if remembering her sister's last visit. She frowned. "If Becky was well into her plan when she came to see me, why didn't she say something? Why didn't she tell me so I would know what to do now?" She sounded close to tears again.

"While she was here, where did she stay?"

"In the spare bedroom. You don't think she might have hidden the ledger in there?"

He followed her, thinking there was a remote chance at best. Still, they had to look. Like the rest of the place, it was nicely furnished in an array of colors. The wall behind the bed was exposed brick. Several pieces of artwork hung from it.

Gillian searched the room from the drawers in the bedside tables to under the mattress and even under the bed. Austin went into the bathroom and looked in the only cabinet there. No note or a ledger of any kind.

As Gillian finished, she sat down on the end of the bed. She looked pale and exhausted, like a woman who should be in the hospital.

"Are you sure you shouldn't have seen a doctor while we were at the hospital? I don't mind taking you back."

"I'm fine," she said with a sigh. "Just disappointed. I knew it was doubtful that Becky left anything. She would have been afraid I would find it and try to stop her. Rebecca never wanted to be a bother to anyone, especially me, her older sister. She hid a lot of things from me, like just how bad it was living with Marc."

"Why don't you get some rest? We can talk more in the morning and figure out what to do next."

She nodded. "I can't even think straight right now."

He reached out and took her hand to pull her up from the bed. "You still have that headache?"

She smiled at him. "It's nothing to be alarmed about. I'm fine. Really." Suddenly she froze. "Becky *did* leave something." Her voice rose with excitement. "I didn't think anything about it at the time. Since Andy had been playing with an old key ring of hers that had a dozen keys on it. She left a key on the night table beside the bed. I thought it must have come off Andy's key ring so I just tossed it in the drawer for when he came back."

She opened the drawer beside the bed and took out the key.

Austin had hoped for a safety deposit key. Instead, it appeared to be an ordinary house key. He realized that Gillian's first instinct on finding it was probably right.

"You didn't find anything else?"

She shook her head, her excitement fading. "It's probably nothing, huh?"

"Probably," he said, taking the key. "But we'll hang on to it just in case." He pocketed it as Gillian started to leave the room.

"You can have this room," she said over her shoulder.

She stopped in the doorway and turned to look back at him. "That is, if you're staying."

"As I told you, I'm not going anywhere until Marc is behind bars. I'm a man of my word, Gillian."

She met his gaze. "Somehow I knew that."

"No matter how long it takes, I'm not leaving you." Austin knew even as he made the promise that there would be hell to pay with his family. But they were used to him letting them down. She started to turn away.

"One more thing," he said. "Did your sister have a key to this house?"

"No." Realization dawned on her expression. She shivered.

"Then there is nothing to worry about," he said. "Try to get some sleep."

"You, too."

He knew that wouldn't be easy. An electricity seemed to spark in the air between them. They'd been through so much together already. He didn't dare imagine what tomorrow would bring.

She hesitated in the doorway. "If you need anything…"

"Don't worry about me." As he removed his jacket, her gaze went to the weapon in his shoulder holster. He saw her swallow before she turned away. "Sweet dreams," he said to her retreating back.

Chapter Fourteen

It had begun to snow. Large lacy flakes fell in a flurry of white as Marc pulled up to Victor's so-called cabin in the mountains overlooking Helena, Montana. The "cabin" was at least five thousand square feet of luxury including an indoor pool, a media center and a game room. At his knock, one of Victor's minions answered the door, a big man who went by only Jumbo.

"Mr. Ramsey is in the garden room." Oh, yeah, and the house had a garden room, too.

There was no garden in the glassed-in room, but there was an amazing view of the valley below and there was a bar. Victor was standing at the bar pouring himself a drink. Marc got the feeling he'd seen him drive up and had been waiting. Today he wore a velour pullover in the same blue as his eyes.

"What would you like to drink?" he asked as he motioned to one of the chairs at the bar. Victor seemed to take in his bandaged face and neck, but said nothing.

Marc took one of the chairs. "Whatever you're having."

"Wise man," Victor said with a disarming smile. "I only drink the best. Isn't that the reason you and I became friends to begin with?"

Friends? What a joke. Marc didn't need him to spell things out. "I like the best things in life like anyone else."

"But you aren't like anyone else," Victor said as he pushed what looked like three fingers of bourbon in a crystal glass over to him.

"No, I'm unique because I know you." He knew it was what the man wanted to hear, and right now he was fine with saying anything that could get him out of here. He took a gulp of the drink. It burned all the way down. As he set the glass down, he said, "Okay, I screwed up, but I'm trying to fix it."

Victor lifted a brow. "You think? And how is it you hope to do that?"

He wasn't surprised that his mess was no secret to the man. Victor had someone inside law enforcement. There was little he didn't know about.

"I didn't mean to almost kill her."

"The her you're referring to being your *wife?*"

"Who else?"

"Who else indeed. With you I never know." Victor took a sip of his drink, studying him over the rim of the glass. "Attempted murder, kidnapping, assault?" Victor leaned on the bar like one friend confiding in another. "Tell me, Marc. What's going on with you?"

He knew this tone of voice. He'd seen it used on other men who'd messed up in their little…organization. He also knew what had happened to those men. Victor was most dangerous when he was being congenial.

"The bitch drugged me and took my ledger—you know, where I kept track of the business."

Victor leaned back, his expression making it clear that his concern had shifted to himself rather than Marc's future. "By the business, you mean your automotive business."

Marc didn't answer.

"You wrote down *our* business transactions?"

"It was a lot of names and numbers, and I do better if I can write it down."

"You mean like names of our associates and their phone numbers." His voice had dropped even further.

"Yeah, that and a few transactions just so I could remember whom I'd dealt with. You have a lot of associates."

Victor looked as if he might have a coronary. "This… ledger? I'm assuming you got it back. Tell me you got it back."

"Why do you think I tried to kill her? She hid it *and* my kid. I was trying to get the information out of her…."

"That's why you involved her sister." Victor closed his eyes for a moment. He was breathing hard. Marc had never seen him lose his cool. Victor was the kind of man who didn't do his own dirty work. He prided himself on never losing control, but he seemed close right now.

"So you don't have the information and you don't know where it is," Victor said.

That about sized it up. "But I'm going to find it."

"She could have mailed it to the FBI."

Marc hadn't thought of that. Probably because he was still caught up in his old belief that Rebecca wasn't all that smart. "I don't think she'd do that."

Victor looked at him, aghast. "You don't *think* so?"

"She's just trying to use the ledger to get a divorce and custody of my kid."

"Let me guess." Victor didn't look at him. Instead, he turned his glass in his hands as if admiring the cut crystal. "You refused to give her what she wanted."

"She isn't taking my kid." The blow took him by surprise. The heavy crystal glass smashed into the side of his face, knocking him off his stool. The crystal shattered, prisms flying across the Italian rock flooring of the garden room an instant before Marc joined them.

Jumbo appeared, as if he had been waiting in the wings, expecting trouble. "You all right, Mr. Ramsey?"

Marc swore. Victor wasn't the one on the floor surrounded by glass. As he rose, he saw Victor picking glass out of his hand. Jumbo rushed around the bar to get a rag.

"No harm done. Isn't that right, Marc?" Victor said.

Blood was running down into his eye. He reached up and pulled a shard of glass from his temple.

"Get Marc a bandage to go with his other bandages, will you, Jumbo?" their boss said. "Sorry about that," he said after Jumbo had left. "I seldom lose my temper."

Marc said nothing. His head hurt like hell and this was the second time in twenty-four hours that he'd been cut. The blow had opened his other cut, and it, too, was now bleeding. First his wife had tried to kill him, now this.

Jumbo returned with a first aid kit. "Let him see to it," Victor ordered when Marc tried to take the kit from the man. It was all he could do to sit still and let an oaf like Jumbo work on him. "Here, be sure there isn't any glass in the cut first." Victor handed the man a bottle of Scotch. "Pour some of the good stuff on it."

Marc gritted his teeth as Jumbo shoved his head to the side and poured the alcohol into the wound. The Scotch ran into Rebecca's handiwork as well, sending fiery pain roaring through him. He swore, the pain so intense he thought he might black out. Jumbo patted the spot on his temple dry with surprising tenderness before carefully applying something to stop the bleeding.

"There, all better," Victor said. "Thank Jumbo. He did a great job."

"Thanks, Jumbo," Marc mumbled.

After Jumbo had cleaned up the mess and left, his boss refilled Marc's glass and got himself a new one. "Now," he said, "I don't need to tell you what needs to be done, do I?"

"No. I'm going to get the ledger." He knew better than to mention his son. Victor didn't give a crap about Andy.

The man frowned. "The sister, is she going to be a problem?"

"Naw." He tried to keep his gaze locked with Victor's, but he broke away first even though he knew it was a mistake.

"The sister isn't the only problem, is she? Who is this Texas deputy who got involved?"

Marc swore under his breath. It amazed him how Victor got his information and so quickly. He must have "associates" everywhere. The thought did nothing to make him feel better.

"I'll take care of them."

Victor shook his head. "You just get this…ledger you lost back. And what are you going to do with it?"

"Destroy it."

Victor looked pained. "Wrong, you're going to bring it to me. I'll take care of it. There are no copies, right?"

"No, I'm not a fool." From Victor's expression, it was clear he thought differently. Marc should have been relieved. What Victor was saying was that they were finished. No more money. It was over. Their relationship was terminated.

Marc searched his emotions for the relief he should have been feeling. Instead, all he could think was that he would kill them. First Rebecca. Then her sister and the cowboy. "I'll fix everything."

Victor didn't look convinced. "Just find the ledger. That's all I ask."

But Marc knew nothing in his life had ever been that simple. He downed his drink, stood up and left.

GILLIAN WENT TO her bedroom, but she doubted she would be able to sleep. Her mind was racing. She kept going over the few conversations she'd had with her sister in the months, weeks and days before all this.

What had Rebecca been thinking? Why hadn't she taken the incriminating evidence to the police? Had she really thought Marc would just agree to a divorce?

No, she thought. That's why Rebecca had hidden not only the ledger, but also her son.

As she pulled on a nightgown and climbed into bed, she was reminded that she wasn't alone in the house. That should have given her more comfort than it did. She was very…aware of Austin Cardwell. It surprised her that she could feel anything, as exhausted and distraught as she was. Mostly, she felt…off balance.

She closed her eyes, praying for the oblivion of sleep.

"I might need your help."

Gillian's eyes came open as she recalled something her sister had said. The conversation came back to her slowly.

"You know I will do anything for you."

"I don't like involving you, but if things go wrong…"

"Becky, what's going on?"

"I keep thinking about when we were kids."

"You're scaring me."

"I'm sorry. I was just being sentimental."

"Is everything okay, Becky?"

"Yes," her sister said, laughing. *"I was just remembering how much fun it was growing up. I love you, Gillian. Always remember that."*

Oh, Becky, she thought now as tears filled her eyes. Things had gone very wrong. Unfortunately, Gillian had no idea what to do about it and now she had a Texas cowboy in her spare bedroom.

She wasn't going to get a wink of sleep tonight.

MARC SCRATCHED THE back of his neck and glanced in the rearview mirror. He caught sight of a large gray SUV two cars behind him. Without slowing, he drove from Victor's toward downtown Helena. At the very last minute, he swung off the interstate and glanced back in time to see the gray SUV cross two lanes to make the exit.

He sped up, wanting to lose the tail. That damned Victor. He'd put a man on him. Marc shouldn't have been surprised. Had he been Victor, he wouldn't have trusted him either. Victor had to know that with the ledger and his testimony, his "friend" Marc could walk away from this mess a free man while Victor rotted in prison.

Not that Victor would let him live long enough for that to happen.

Swearing, he slowed down and pulled into a gas station. He saw the gray SUV go past to stop a few doors down in front of a fast-food restaurant. Getting out, he filled his tank and considered what to do next.

His throat felt dry. He would kill for a beer. The problem was stopping at just one beer. It would be too easy to get falling-down drunk. Still, he headed for one of the bars he frequented. Behind him, the gray SUV followed.

Victor's going to have me killed.

Not until I find the ledger.

The thought turned Marc's blood to ice.

But it was quickly followed by another thought.

In the meantime, Victor couldn't chance that the ledger would turn up and fall into the wrong hands. *Checkmate,* he thought with relief until he had another thought.

Unless Victor decided he could do a better job of getting the whereabouts of the book from Rebecca.

That thought echoed in his head, making his heart thump harder against his chest. Marc felt the truth of those words racing through his bloodstream. What if Victor decided to take things into his own hands?

He thought of Rebecca lying in her hospital bed. If Victor paid her one of his famous visits…

Marc reminded himself that Victor never got his own hands dirty even if he could find a way to get near Rebecca in the hospital.

What if Rebecca really had mailed the ledger to the FBI? His pulse jumped, heart hammering like a sledge in his chest. He wouldn't let himself go there. No, she'd hidden the book thinking she was smarter than he was, thinking she could force him into the divorce and take Andy from him. Stupid woman.

He tried to concentrate on what to do now. Because if she hadn't sent the book to the FBI, he had to assume she didn't know what she had in her possession. That was the good news, right?

The bad news was that no matter the outcome, he and Victor were finished. Even if he found the book and turned it over, Victor would never trust him again. Not that he could blame him. The information in that book could bring them all down. Victor would have him killed.

If he didn't find the ledger and the cops did, he was going to prison for a good part of the rest of his life. Of course that life wouldn't be long since Victor and his buddies would be in prison with him.

He still couldn't believe the mess he was in. He realized there was only one way out of this. He had to get to Rebecca before Victor did. Once she understood the consequences if she didn't turn over the ledger…he'd give her the divorce and custody. She would hand over his ledger and then when she thought she was safe, he would kidnap his kid and skip the country.

Why hadn't he thought of that in the first place? Because the woman had made him so furious. Also, he'd thought she would tell him where the ledger was with only minor persuasion.

He parked beside the bar in a dark spot away from the streetlamp and put in a call to the hospital. Rebecca was still unconscious. Swearing, he hung up.

The clock was ticking.

Inside the bar, Marc Stewart took a stool away from everyone else and ordered a beer. The bartender gave him a raised eyebrow at his bandaged face and the black eye that was almost swollen shut, but was smart enough not to comment.

The first beer went down easy. The second took a little longer. He was doing a lot of thinking. Mostly about Rebecca and how he'd underestimated her. He kept mentally kicking himself. He had to get over her betrayal and think about what to do.

"Another beer?" the bartender asked as he cleared away his second empty bottle.

Marc focused on an old moose head hanging on the wall behind the bartender that could have used a good dusting. It reminded him of something. "No, I'm good," he told the bartender. Something about the moose head still nagged at him, but his head hurt too badly to make sense of it.

He slid off the bar stool, picked up most of his change from the bar and pocketed it. But as he looked toward the door, he told himself he had to ditch the tail that he knew would be parked outside waiting.

Marc smiled to himself even though it hurt his face to do so and put in the call. It was time to take care of business.

Chapter Fifteen

Gillian thought she would never be able to sleep again. At the very least she'd expected to have horrible nightmares.

She must have fallen into a deathlike sleep. She couldn't remember anything. Now, though, it all came back in a rush, including the Texas cowboy in her spare bedroom.

What did she really know about Austin Cardwell? Nothing. Nothing except he'd saved her life twice and made her feel… She wasn't even sure how to describe it other than she felt too aware of the man.

She caught the smell of bacon cooking. *Austin?* Grabbing her robe, she opened her door to find him standing in her kitchen with a pancake flipper in his hand. He was wearing one of her aprons, which actually made her smile.

"You didn't find bacon in my refrigerator," she said.

He turned to smile back at her. "Nope. Apparently you exist on wine."

"I haven't gotten to the store in a while."

"I noticed." He flipped over what she saw were pancakes sizzling on her griddle. "Hungry?"

She started to say she wasn't. Just as she'd thought she'd never be able to sleep again, she thought the same of eating. But her stomach growled loudly at the smell of bacon and pancakes.

Austin chuckle. "I'll take that as a yes." He motioned for her to have a seat at the breakfast bar.

"I should change," she said, pulling the collar of her robe tighter.

"No need. Eat them while they're hot." He slid a tall stack of three-inch pancakes onto her plate along with two slices of bacon. "This is my mother's recipe for corn cakes. It's the Texan in me. Wait until you taste the eggs. I hope you like hot peppers."

She felt her eyes widen in surprise. "You made eggs, as well? I really can't—"

"Insult me by not trying some?"

She couldn't help but smile at him in all his eagerness. "Are you trying to fatten me up?"

"You could use a little Texas cooking—not that you aren't beautiful just as you are."

"Good catch," she said, knowing it wasn't true. She hadn't been taking good care of herself because she'd been so worried about her sister. "Thank you."

"My pleasure." He joined her, loading his plate with pancakes, bacon and eggs before putting a spoonful of the eggs onto her plate. "Just try them. Some people aren't tough enough to handle my cooking."

It sounded like a dare—just as he'd meant it to. She studied him for a moment. What would she have done without him? Died night before last in the snowstorm beside the road and no doubt yesterday in Island Park.

Austin handed her the peach jam he'd bought. "Try some of this on your pancakes. Much better than maple syrup."

"Why not?" she said, doing as he said.

"Now take a bite of the pancake and one of the egg. Sweet and hot."

She did and felt her eyes widen in alarm for a moment at the heat. But he was right. The sweet cooled it right down. "Delicious."

"Now add a bite of bacon for saltiness and you've got an Austin Cardwell Texas breakfast." He laughed as he took a bite, chewed and, closing his eyes, moaned in obvious contentment.

Gillian was caught up in his enjoyment of breakfast and her own, as well. She couldn't remember the last time she'd eaten like this and was shocked when she realized that she'd cleaned her plate.

"Well?" he said, studying her openly. "Feeling better?"

She was. Earlier when she'd awakened, she'd felt lightheaded and sick to her stomach. Now she was ready to do whatever had to be done to save her nephew, and she was pretty sure that had been Austin's plan.

"DON'T YOU DARE tell me you lost him," Victor said when he saw who was calling that morning.

"Sorry, boss. He let me think he knew he was being tailed and had accepted it."

He swore, but quickly calmed back down. He hadn't gotten where he was by losing control. True, Marc had already pushed him to the point of losing his temper. Marc Stewart had been a mistake. When he'd first met him, Marc had impressed him. He'd seemed like a man who had all his ducks in a row. That, added to the man's hunger for the finer things in life, and his charm and willingness to bend the rules, had made him a perfect associate.

Even when he'd realized the man had his flaws, he'd told himself that most men did. Unfortunately, the flaw Victor hadn't seen in Marc Stewart was about to bring them all down.

"Marc won't get far from home," Victor said. "John, I need you to watch his auto shop. Get Ray to keep an eye on the Friendly Bar over on the south side of town. It's Marc's go-to bar when things aren't going well. If either of you spot him again, stay on him. Trade off. Don't lose him again."

He hung up, hating that he hadn't put Jumbo on him. Jumbo wouldn't have lost him. Victor had realized last night after talking to Marc that he couldn't trust anyone with this, especially Marc. He'd already bungled things.

Changing into a clean sport shirt and a pair of jeans, Victor pulled on his lucky buffalo-skin boots and checked himself in the mirror. His unthreatening good looks had always served him well. He hoped they didn't let him down when he went to visit Rebecca Stewart at the hospital in Bozeman.

It was good to see some color in Gillian's face as they finished cleaning up the breakfast dishes together and she excused herself. Last night Austin had been worried he was going to have to take her back to the hospital. He was surprised she'd even been on her feet after the car wreck, the concussion and yesterday's events, not to mention Marc knocking her around before that. Her strength and endurance surprised him and filled him with admiration. If he had almost lost one of his brothers...

The thought was a punch to the gut and a wake-up call. He realized that he'd taken his four brothers for granted, assuming they would always be there.

He pulled out his cell phone and dialed his cousin Dana. He didn't want to have a long discussion with any one of his brothers. He knew it was cowardice on his part, but at the same time, he wanted to let them know he was all right and that he would try to make Christmas and the grand opening.

Actually, he didn't want to have to explain himself to anyone, even his cousin Dana. He'd hoped he would get her answering machine and he groaned inwardly when she answered on the third ring.

"Hey, Dana. It's Austin, your cousin?"

"The elusive Austin Cardwell? Hud said he met you, but I haven't had that opportunity yet."

"Sorry, but I'm afraid it could be a while yet."

She chuckled. "Hud said not to expect you for dinner until I saw the whites of your eyes."

"Your husband is one smart man."

"Yes, he is. I suppose you're calling me with a message for your brothers."

"Hud's wife is pretty sharp, as well."

She laughed. "What would you like me to tell them?"

Austin thought about that for a moment. "I'll try to make Christmas, but if I don't…"

"They're determined you will be at the grand opening. They're going to put it off until you're here. Don't see any way out for you."

"I guess it's too much to hope they'll go ahead without me if I don't show."

"Yep. Should I tell them you'll be getting back to them?"

"Tell them…I'll see them as soon as I can. You, too. If I can make Christmas, I will be there with bells on."

"Your cabin will be ready."

"Everything all right?" Gillian asked as she saw him pocket his cell phone.

"Fine. I talked to my cousin. She'll let my brothers know that I've been…detained."

She hated that he already had problems with his brothers and now she was making it worse. He followed her into the living room, the two of them sitting as they had the night before. "Are your parents still alive?"

He nodded. "Divorced. I was born in Montana, but my mother took all five of us boys to Texas when we were very young. My father stayed in Montana. Now my mother has remarried, and she and her new husband just bought a place near here where three of my brothers are living." He shrugged.

"You're lucky to have such a large family. After we lost our parents, it was just Becky and me. With her…" She fought the stark emotion that had her praying one moment and wanting to just sit down and bawl the next.

"I'm sure you already called the hospital. How is she doing?"

"There's been no change, but the doctor did say she is stable and he is hopeful. Have you ever lost anyone close to you?"

"A friend and fellow deputy." Austin hadn't gone a day in years without thinking about Mitch. "He was like a brother." He'd been even closer to Mitch than he was to his brothers. "He was killed in the line of duty. I wasn't there that day." And he'd never forgiven himself for it. He'd been away on barbecue company business.

"I'm sure it gets better," she said hopefully.

He nodded. "It does and it doesn't. You can never fill that hole in your life. Or your heart. But you put one foot in front of the other and you go on. Your sister, though, is going to come back."

"I hope you're right." She cleared her throat. "Right now I can't imagine how to go on. I'd hoped Becky had left me a letter, some kind of message…." Her voice broke.

"Tell me what you remember she said in what time you did have with her yesterday. It might help."

Shaking her head, she got up and walked to the opening into the living room. The December day glistened with fresh snow and sunshine. The bright sunlight poured through the leaded glass windows. Prisms of color sparkled in almost blinding light. She'd always loved this room because of the morning sunlight, but not even the sun's rays could warm her right now.

"Becky talked about our childhood."

"Where did you grow up?"

"In Helena. But we spent our summers at our grandfather's cabin. My sister mentioned the time the wind blew down an old pine tree in a thunderstorm. Becky and I loved thunderstorms and used to huddle together on Grandpa's porch and watch the lightning and the waves crashing on the shore." A lump formed in her throat. She couldn't lose her sister.

"Where is your grandfather's cabin?"

"Outside of Townsend on Canyon Ferry Lake."

"You think your nephew is at your grandfather's cabin?"

She shook her head. "The cabin's been boarded up for years. That's why what she said doesn't make any sense."

"Maybe she left you a message there," Austin suggested. "The only place she mentioned was the cabin, right?"

Gillian nodded.

"If your sister was in her right mind enough to hide her son and try to get Marc Stewart out of his life, then anything she said might have value. Can we get to the cabin this time of year?"

"The road should be open. They get a lot less snow up there than we do down here."

"What is the chance Marc knows about the cabin and will go there?" Austin asked.

She felt a start. "If he remembers it… I think Becky took him there once when they were dating. Since it was nothing like his family's place in Island Park, I don't think he was impressed."

"I suspect there is a reason your sister reminded you of the downed tree and your grandfather's cabin. How soon can you be ready to leave?"

Chapter Sixteen

Marc watched his side mirror as he drove toward Townsend, Montana. His mind seemed sharper this morning. His face still hurt like hell, though. He'd changed the bandage himself, shocked at the damage his wife had done and all the more determined to kill her.

Last night, he'd managed to lose his tail and find a cheap motel at the edge of town, where he'd fallen asleep the instant his head hit the pillow.

It was this morning after a shower that he'd thought of that old moose head he'd seen at the bar and remembered his wife's family's cabin. Rebecca had taken him to see it when they were dating. As far as he knew, though, Rebecca and her sister still owned the place.

She'd been all weepy and sentimental because the cabin had belonged to her grandfather who'd died. Apparently she and her sister had spent summers there with the old man. He didn't get the weepy, emotional significance of the small old place in the pines. That was probably why he'd forgotten about it. That and the fact that they'd never returned to the place.

But he was good at getting back to a place he'd only been to once. He paid attention even when someone else was driving. Given how his wife felt about the old cabin, wasn't it possible she might return there when she had something to stash?

He drove toward the lake. The sleep had helped. He felt more confident that he could pull himself out of this mess. Ahead, he saw a sign that looked familiar and began to slow. If Rebecca had hidden the ledger at the cabin—which he was betting was a real possibility—then he would know soon enough.

Marc hoped his instincts were right as he turned off the main highway and headed down the dirt road back into the mountains along the lake. It had snowed so there was a fine dusting on the road, but nothing to worry about. This area never got as much snow as those closer to the mountains.

The road was the least of his worries anyway. He thought of Gillian and the cowboy deputy. Would Gillian think of the cabin?

Swearing under his breath, he realized that if he had, then she would, too. Maybe she was already there. Maybe she already had her hands on the ledger. The thought sent his pulse into overdrive.

But as he turned onto the narrow road that led up to the cabin, he saw that there were no other tracks in the new dusting of snow. His spirits buoyed. Maybe he would just wait around and see if Gillian showed up. It was a great place to hide out, especially this time of year.

He knew her. If she thought the ledger might be hidden at the cabin, she wouldn't tell the police. She would come for it herself. This cabin meant too much to her to have the police tearing the place apart looking for the ledger and any other evidence they thought they might find.

Even if the Texas deputy was still with Gillian this morning, it would just be the two of them. Marc hoped he was right. He'd brought several guns, including a rifle. This cabin that meant so much to his wife would be the perfect place to dispose of Gillian and the cowboy.

THE CABIN WAS back in the mountains that overlooked Canyon Ferry Lake. Huge green ponderosa pines glistened in the midday sun among large rock formations. It had snowed the night before but had now melted in all but the shade of the pines.

"Turn here," Gillian said when the road became little more than a Jeep trail.

Austin noticed tracks where someone had been up the road. He figured Gillian had noticed them, too. It could have been anyone. But he was guessing it was Marc Stewart. As the structure came into view, he saw that the windows were shuttered. At first glance, it didn't appear anyone had been inside for a very long time.

But as he parked, Austin saw that the front door was open a few inches and there were fresh gouges in the wood where whoever had been here had broken in. The old cabin looked like the perfect place for a wounded fugitive to lay low for a while and heal. Even though there was no sign of a vehicle and the tracks indicated that whoever had been here had left, he wasn't taking any chances.

"Stay here," Austin said as he opened his door and pulled his weapon. Long dried pine needles covered the steps up to the worn wood of the small porch. There were footprints in the wet dirt, large, man-sized soles. Austin moved cautiously as he pushed open the door. It groaned open.

A stale, musty scent rushed out. Weapon ready, Austin stepped into the dim darkness. The cabin was small so it didn't take long to make sure it was empty. As he looked around the ransacked room, it was clear that Marc had been here. From the destruction, Austin was betting the man hadn't found what he was looking for, though.

In a small trash container in the bathroom, he found some bloody bandages. From the amount of blood, it appeared Marc had been wounded enough to warrant medical attention. But no doubt not by anyone at a hospital, where the gunshot wound would have had to be reported.

When he returned to the porch, he found Gillian sitting on the front step looking out at the lake in the distance.

"He was here, wasn't he?" she said. "Did he—"

"I don't think he found anything."

Gillian nodded.

"You don't use the cabin?" Austin asked as he looked at the amazing view.

"No. It stayed in the family, but after my grandfather died…well, it just wasn't the same."

He watched her take a deep breath of mountain air before letting it out slowly. "I haven't been here in nine years. I doubt my sister has either, but I continue to pay the taxes on it."

Austin didn't want to believe that Rebecca Stewart had just been babbling when she'd mentioned the cabin. She had to be passing on a message.

"Would you mind taking a look around and see if your sister might have left you anything inside that Marc missed? He made a mess."

She nodded and pushed to her feet. There were tears in her eyes as she entered the cabin and stopped just inside the door.

Austin gave her a moment. He tried to imagine what it must have been like to visit here when Gillian's grandfather was alive. He and his brothers would have loved this place. Even at his age, he loved the smell of the pine trees, the crunch of the dried needles beneath his boot heels, the feeling of being a boy again in a place where there were huge rocks and trees to climb, forts to build and fish to catch out of the small stream that ran beside the cabin.

At the sound of her footfalls deeper in the cabin, he went inside to find her standing in the small kitchen. "My grandfather liked to cook. He made us pancakes." She looked over at Austin. "You remind me of him."

He couldn't help being touched by that. "Thank you."

Dust motes danced in the sunlight that streamed in through the cracks of the shutters. The interior of the cabin looked as if it might have been decorated in the 1950s or early 1960s. While rustic, it was cozy from the worn quilts on the couch and chairs to the soot-covered fireplace.

"There's nothing here." She shook her head. "Becky hasn't been here. She would have left at least a glass or two in the sink and an unmade bed. Everything is just as it was the last time I was here—except for the mess Marc made searching the place."

Austin couldn't help his disappointment. He'd hoped Rebecca had mentioned the cabin for a reason. Maybe she *had* been out of her head. As much as he wanted to find this ledger that would nail Marc Stewart to the wall, his greatest fear was for the boy. With whom would a woman possibly not in her right mind have stashed her ten-month-old son?

MARC HAD WAITED after he'd searched the cabin looking for the ledger. It wasn't there. He'd looked everywhere. He'd thought that maybe if Gillian really hadn't known what her sister had done with it that she and the cowboy might show up at the cabin.

But he'd never been good at waiting. Still, even as he was leaving, he hadn't been able to shake the feeling that Rebecca *had* been there. Had she left some message that he hadn't recognized? Frankly, he'd never thought his wife as that clever. But then again, he'd been wrong about how strong she was.

Belatedly, he was realizing that he might not have really known his wife at all.

RAW WITH EMOTIONS, Gillian looked around the cabin for a moment longer before turning toward the front door to escape even more painful memories.

She stumbled down the porch steps, breathing hard. Even the pine-scented air seemed to hurt her lungs. It, too, filled her with bittersweet memories.

Behind her, she heard Austin locking up the cabin. She felt as if she was going to be sick and stumbled down to the fallen tree her sister had reminded her about. Why hadn't Becky left her a clue? She'd wanted Gillian to find the ledger, get Marc put away and take care of Andy. But how did she expect her to do that without some idea of where to start? What had Becky been thinking?

She prayed that her sister had left Andy somewhere safe until she could find him.

"Is this the tree that blew over?" Austin said behind her, startling her.

Gillian stood leaning against it. The pine was old and huge. It had fallen during a summer thunderstorm, landing on a large boulder instead of falling all the way to the ground. Because of that, it laid at a slight slant a good three to six feet off the ground. She and her sister used to walk the length of it, pretending they were high-wire art-ists. Gillian had a scar on her arm from a fall she'd taken.

She told Austin about the night the tree fell and how she and Becky had played on it, needing to share the memories, fearing they would vanish otherwise. "It made a tremendous sound when it crashed," she said, her voice breaking.

"I was thinking earlier how my brothers and I would have loved this place."

She watched Austin walk around the root end of the tree. Most of the dirt that had once clung to the roots had washed off over the years in other storms. But because of its size, when the tree had become uprooted, it had left a large hole in the earth that she and Becky used to hide in.

"Gillian."

Something in the way he said her name made her start. She looked at his expression and felt a jolt. He was star-ing down into the hole.

"I think you'd better see this."

Chapter Seventeen

Austin stood back as Gillian hurried around the tree to the exposed roots and looked down into the deep cave of a hole. "What is that?"

She made a sound, half laugh, half sob. "That's Edgar."

"Edgar?" he repeated as she clambered down into the hole. She picked up what appeared to be a taxidermy-type stuffed crow on a small wooden stand and handed it up to him before he helped her out.

The bird had seen better days, but its dark eyes still glittered eerily. She took the mounted crow from him and began to cry as she held the bird to her as if it were a baby. "Edgar Allan Poe. Becky and I made friends with Edgar when he was young and orphaned. We fed him and kept him alive and he never left. He would fly in the moment we arrived at the cabin and caw at us from the porch railing. He followed us everywhere," she said excitedly and then sobered. "One time we came up and we didn't see him. We looked around for him…and found him dead. It was our grandfather's idea to have him mounted. Edgar had always looked out for us, Grandpa said. No reason he couldn't continue doing that."

Austin thought of the odd pets he and his brothers had accumulated and lost over the years and the attachment they'd had with them. "Your grandfather was a wise man."

She nodded through her tears. "Becky and I took Edgar to our tree house so he could keep an eye out for trespassers."

"Your tree house? Is that where you left him?"

Gillian met his gaze, hers widening. "Becky put Edgar here. That's what she was trying to tell me…" She pushed to her feet. "She *did* leave a message, since the last time I saw Edgar he was still in the tree house standing guard."

"Did Marc know about it?"

Gillian frowned. "I doubt it. He didn't like the outdoors much and his family's cabin was so much nicer on the lake in Idaho. Also I'm not sure how much of the tree house is even still there. It's been years."

Austin followed Gillian into the woods. They wound through the tall thick ponderosa pines. The December day was cold but clear. Sunlight slanted in through the trees but did little to warm them. The skiff of snow that had fallen overnight still hung to the pine boughs back here, making it feel even colder.

As they walked, he watched the ground for any sign that Marc had come this way. It was hard to tell since the ground was covered with pine needles.

They had gone quite a ways when Gillian stopped abruptly. He looked past her and saw what was left of the tree house. It was now little more than a few boards tacked up between trees. The years hadn't been kind to it. What boards had remained were weathered, several hanging by a nail.

He could feel Gillian's disappointment as they moved closer, stepping over the boards that had blown down. A makeshift ladder had been tacked to a tree at the base of what was left of the tree house. Austin tested the bottom step.

"I don't think it's safe for you to go up there," Gillian said.

"Your sister must have climbed up there." But he knew Rebecca weighed a lot less than he did as he tried the second step. The board held so he began the ascent, hoping for the best. It had been years since he'd climbed a tree. He'd forgotten the exhilaration of being high above the ground.

When he reached what was left of the tree house, he poked his head through the opening and felt a start much like he had when he'd seen Edgar down in the roots of the fallen tree.

"Do you see anything?" Gillian called up.

A fabric doll with curly dark hair sat in the corner of the remaining tree house floor, its back against the tree. It had huge dark eyes much like Gillian's and it was looking right at him. As he reached for it, he felt the soft material of the doll's yellow dress and knew it hadn't been in this tree long.

Other than the doll, there was nothing else in what had once been Gillian and Rebecca's tree house. He stuck the doll inside his coat and began the careful descent to the ground.

GILLIAN SET EDGAR down next to the base of a tree, thinking about her sister. Rebecca had always liked puzzles and scavenger hunts. This was definitely feeling like a combination of both.

As Austin pulled the doll from his coat, she stared at it in surprise for only a moment before taking it and crushing it to her chest in a hug.

"The doll looks like you," Austin said.

She nodded, afraid if she spoke she would burst into tears again. Her emotions were dangerously close to the surface as it was. Being here had brought back so many memories of the summers she and Becky had spent here with their grandfather.

After a moment, she held the doll at arm's length. The dolls had been a gift from their parents, she told Austin. "Mother had a woman make them so they resembled Becky and me. We never told her, but I found them to be a little creepy and used to turn mine against the wall when I slept. I half expected the doll to be turned around watching me when I woke up. But Becky loved hers so much she even took it when she went to college." That memory caused a hitch in her chest.

"The doll has to be a clue," Austin said.

"If it is, I have no idea what that clue might be." She studied the doll. Its dress was yellow, Gillian's favorite color, so she knew it was hers. The dress had tiny white rickrack around the collar and hem and puffy sleeves. She looked under the hem, thinking Becky might have left a note. Nothing. She felt all over the doll, praying for a scrap of paper, something sewn inside the stuffing, anything that would provide her with the information she desperately needed. Nothing.

When she looked at Austin, she felt her eyes tear up again. "I have no idea what this means, if anything."

"The doll wasn't in the tree long. Since it seems likely your sister left it there, it has to mean something."

She almost laughed. "If my sister was thinking clearly she wouldn't have climbed up into that tree to put my doll there without a note or some message…"

"Your sister was terrified that Marc would find not only the ledger but their son, right?" Austin asked.

She nodded.

"I know all this seems…illogical, but I think she knew she had to use clues that only you would understand, like Edgar."

"I hope you're right," she said, smiling at this man who'd been there for her since that first horrible night in the blizzard.

"Are you leaving Edgar here?" he asked.

Gillian nodded. "Becky always said this was his favorite spot. He used to fly around, landing on limbs near the tree house, watching over us as we played. I know it sounds silly—"

"No, it doesn't. I get it."

She saw that he did and felt her heart lift a little.

"So there were two dolls?" he asked. "Where is your sister's?"

VICTOR STRAIGHTENED THE white clerical collar and checked himself in the mirror before picking up his Bible and exiting the car in the hospital parking lot.

He couldn't be sure how much security the cops had on Rebecca Stewart. He suspected it would be minimal. Most police departments were stretched thin as it was. This was Montana. Security at the hospital was seldom needed. Victor was counting on the uniform outside her room being some mall-type security cop that the hospital had brought in.

The security guard would have been given Marc Stewart's description, so the man would be on the lookout for him—not a pastor. The guard would have been on the job long enough that he would be bored and sick of hospital food.

As he walked into the lower entrance to the hospital, he saw that his "assistant" was already here sitting in one of the chairs in the lobby thumbing through a magazine.

He gave Candy only a cursory glance before he walked past the volunteer working at the desk.

While some hospitals were strict about visitors, this wasn't one of them. That's what he loved about small Montana communities. People felt safe.

He already knew the floor and room number and had asked about visiting hours, so he merely tipped his head at her and said, "Hope you're having a blessed day."

She smiled at him. "You, too, Reverend."

At the elevator, he punched in the floor number. A man and woman in lab coats hurried in. Victor gave them both a solemn nod and looked down at the Bible in his hands. Before the doors could close, a freshly manicured hand slipped between them. He caught the flash of bright red nail polish and the sweet scent of perfume.

As the doors were forced open, Candy stepped in, turning her back to the three of them.

He had told her to dress provocatively but not over the top. She'd chosen a conservative white blouse and slim navy skirt with a pair of strappy high heeled winter boots. The white blouse was unbuttoned enough that anyone looking got teasing glimpses of the tops of her full breasts. She smelled good, that, too, not overdone. Her blond hair was pulled up, a few strands curling around her pretty face.

Victor was pleased as the elevator stopped and the doors opened. They all stepped off, the man and woman in the lab coats scurrying down one hallway while he and Candy took the other. He let her get a few yards ahead before following. The way she moved reminded him of something from his childhood.

If I had a swing like that, I'd paint it red and put it in my backyard.

It was a silly thing to come to mind right now. He

worried that he was nervous and that it would tip off even the worst of security guards. So much was riding on this. If he could just get into Marc's wife's room…

At the end of the hallway, he spotted the rent-a-cop sitting in a plastic chair outside Rebecca Stewart's room.

The security guard spotted Candy and got to his feet as she approached.

Chapter Eighteen

Austin found himself watching his rearview mirror. If he was right, Rebecca Stewart had left a series of clues that only her sister could decipher. She'd used items from their past, the shared memories of sisters and things that even if she had mentioned to Marc, he wouldn't have recalled. It told Austin that she'd been terrified of her husband finding their son.

He could see that it was breaking Gillian's heart, these trips down memory lane with her sister. Had Rebecca worried that she could be dead by the time Gillian uncovered them? He figured she must have known her husband well enough that it had definitely been a consideration.

No wonder she hadn't told her sister a thing. Gillian would have done anything to save her sister and Marc would have known that. He must have realized Gillian didn't know the truth. Not that he hadn't planned to use her to try to get her sister to talk. There was no doubt in Austin's mind that, in an attempt to save her sister, Rebecca had pushed Marc and his rotten temper so he would lose control and kill her. If Gillian hadn't thrown herself at Marc when she had…

The drive north to Chinook took the rest of the day. They traveled from the Little Belt Mountains to the edge of the Rockies, before turning east across the wild prairie of Montana. It was dark by the time they reached the small Western town on what was known as the Hi-Line.

Chinook, like most of the towns along Highway 2, had sprung up with the introduction of the railroad. Both freight and passenger trains still blew their whistles as they passed through town.

A freight train rumbled past as Austin parked in front of a motor inn. Gillian had called ahead but had gotten no answer at the Baker house. Austin could tell that made her as nervous as it did him. Was it possible that as careful as Rebecca had been, Marc had been one step ahead of them?

"I can't believe Rebecca would have confided in anyone," Gillian said. "But if there is even a chance Nancy knows where Becky left Andy…"

Gillian had explained about her sister's doll on the drive north. Nancy Rexroth Baker and her sister had been roommates at college. Becky had been Nancy's maid of honor when she'd married Claude. While as far as Gillian knew the two hadn't stayed in touch when Nancy had a baby girl last year they'd named her Rebecca Jane. That's the name Nancy and Becky used to call her doll at college. Touched by this, her sister had mailed Nancy her doll.

"She told you this?" Austin had asked. "Wouldn't Marc have known?"

She shook her head. "Since my sister has apparently had this plot of hers in the works for some time, I wouldn't think so. But Marc is anything if not clever. He could have known a whole lot more than Becky suspected."

Gillian tried the Baker home number again. The line went to voice mail after four rings. "Maybe we should drive by the house."

Austin didn't think it would do much good, but he agreed. She gave him the address, which turned out to be in the older section of the town just four blocks from the motel. The houses were large with wide front porches, a lot of columns and arches.

The Baker house sat up on the side of a hill with a flight of stairs that ended at the wide white front porch. There were no lights on behind the large windows at the front, no Christmas decorations on the outside, and the drapes were drawn.

"Let's see if there is an alley," Austin said and drove around the corner. Just as he'd suspected, there was. He took it, driving down three houses before stopping in front of a garage. "I'll take a look." He hopped out to check the garage. As he peered in the window, he saw that it was empty.

It came as somewhat of a relief. As he climbed back into the SUV, he said, "It looks like they've gone somewhere for Christmas."

"Christmas." The way she said it made him think that she'd forgotten about it, just as he had, even with all the red and green lights strung around town.

He thought of his brothers all gathered in Big Sky for the holidays, no doubt wondering where he was. He quickly pushed the thought away. They should be used to him by now. Anyway, his cousin Dana would have told them he was tied up. Her husband, Hud, the marshal, would have a pretty good idea why he was tied up since he would have heard about Marc Stewart's attempted murder of his wife, the kidnapping of his sister-in-law, Gillian, and the BOLO out on Marc.

As Austin drove them back to the motel, he said, "We need to get into that house because if I'm right, then this family has your nephew and he's safe. The doll brought us this far. There has to be another clue that we're missing."

"The key," Gillian said on an excited breath. "The one I found at the house after Rebecca and Andy left. Do you still have it?"

"I'M GOING TO walk back and get into the house," Austin said after they returned to the motel. He'd gotten them adjoining rooms, no doubt so he could keep an eye on her, Gillian thought.

She was grateful for everything he'd done. But she was going with him. She came out of her room and stood in front of him, her hands on her hips. "You're not going alone."

He shook his head. "Maybe you don't understand the fine line between snooping and jail. Breaking and entering is—"

"I'm going with you."

He looked like he wanted to argue, but saw that she meant what she said. "Wear something dark and warm. It's cold out."

She was already one step ahead of him as she reached for a black fleece jacket she'd grabbed as they were leaving her apartment. Donning a hat and gloves, she turned to look at him.

He was smiling at her as if amused.

"What?" she said, suddenly feeling uncomfortable under his scrutiny. She knew it was silly. He'd seen her at her absolute worst.

"You just look so...cute," he said. "Clearly breaking the law excites you."

She smiled in spite of herself. It had been a while since a man had complimented her. Actually, way too long. But it wasn't breaking the law that excited her, she thought and felt her face heat with the thought.

The night was clear and cold, the sky ablaze with stars. She breathed in the freezing air. It stung her lungs, but made her feel more alive than she had in years. Fear drove her steps along with hope. The bird, the doll, all of it had led them here. She couldn't be wrong about this. And yet at the back of her mind, she worried that none of this made any sense because Rebecca hadn't known what she was doing.

At the dark alley, Austin slowed. It was late enough that there were lights on in the houses. Most of the drapes were open. She saw women in the kitchen cooking and families moving around inside the warm-looking homes. The scenes pulled at her, making her wish she and her sister were those women.

A few doors down, a dog barked, a door slammed and she heard someone calling, "Zoey!" The dog barked a couple more times; then the door slammed again and the alley grew quiet.

"Come on," Austin said and they started to turn down the alley.

A vehicle came around the corner, moving slowly. Gillian felt the headlights wash over them and let out a worried sound as she froze in midstep. Her first thought was Marc. Her heart began to pound even though she knew Austin had his shoulder holster on and the gun inside it was loaded.

Her moment of panic didn't subside when she saw that it was a sheriff's department vehicle.

"Austin?" she whispered, not sure what to do.

He turned to her and pulled her into his arms. Her mouth opened in surprise and the next thing she knew, he was kissing her. His mouth was warm against hers.

At first, she was too stunned to react. But after a moment, she put her arms around his neck and lost herself in the kiss.

As the headlights of the sheriff's car washed over them, the golden glow seemed to warm the night because she no longer felt cold. She let out a small helpless moan as Austin deepened the kiss, drawing her even closer.

As the sheriff's car went on past, she felt a pang of regret. Slowly, Austin drew back a little. His gaze locked with hers, and for a moment they stood like that, their quickened warm breaths coming out in white clouds.

"Sorry."

She shook her head. She wasn't sorry. She felt…light-headed, happy, as if helium filled. She thought she might drift off into the night if he let go of her.

"Are you okay?" he asked, looking worried.

She unconsciously touched the tip of her tongue to her lower lip, then bit down on it to stop herself. "Great. Never better."

That made him smile. For a moment, he stood merely smiling at her, his gaze on hers, his dark eyes as warm as a crackling fire. Then he sighed. "Let's get this over with," he said and took her gloved hand as they started up the alley.

There was only an inch of snow on the ground, but it crunched under their feet. If anyone heard them and looked out their window, she doubted they would think anything of it. They would appear to be what they were, a thirtysomething couple out walking on an early December night.

She looked over at Austin. Light from one of the yards shone on his handsome face, catching her off guard. He wasn't just handsome. He was caring and kind and capable, as well. She warned herself not to let one kiss go to her head. Of course she felt something for this man who'd saved her life twice and probably would have to again before this was over.

But her pulse was still pounding hard from the kiss. It had been the best kiss she'd ever had. Not that it meant anything.

She reminded herself that this was what Austin Cardwell did for a living. Not kiss women he was trying to save, but definitely doing whatever it took to save those same women.

She'd bet there was a long line of women he'd saved and all of them had gone giddy if he'd kissed them like that. That was a sobering thought. He could have ended up kissing all of them. Or even something more intimate.

That thought settled her down. She was behaving like a teenager on a date with the adorable quarterback of the football team. She told herself it was only because she hadn't dated all that much, especially since she'd started her business. True, she hadn't met anyone she cared to date. But she wasn't the kind of woman who fell head over heels at the drop of a kiss. Even one amazing kiss on a cold winter night.

But any woman in her place would be feeling like this, she told herself. She'd never believed that knights on white horses really existed before Austin Cardwell. It was one reason she was still single. That and she liked her independence. But mostly, it was because she'd never met a man who had ever made her even consider marriage.

Becky's marriage to Marc certainly hadn't changed her mind about men in general. She'd known Marc was domineering. She just hadn't known what the man was capable of. She doubted Becky had either.

Just the thought of her sister brought tears to her eyes. She wiped at them with her free gloved hand, determined not to break down, especially now. Austin hadn't wanted to bring her along as it was.

She needed to be strong. She concentrated on finding Andy. Becky had hidden him somewhere safe. Gillian had to believe that. What better place than with someone she could trust, like her former college roommate, Nancy Baker?

Gillian hated that she'd let Marc keep her from her sister. But the few times she'd visited he'd made her so uncomfortable that she hadn't gone back. And Marc had put Becky on a leash that didn't allow her to come up to Big Sky to visit often. It wasn't that he forbade it, he just made sure Becky was too busy to go anywhere.

Rubbing a hand over her face, she tried to concentrate on what lay ahead rather than wallowing in regret. Becky was stable. Gillian couldn't count on her regaining consciousness. It was why she had to find Andy—and that damned ledger before Marc did.

Austin slowed as they reached the back of the Baker house. She saw him look down the alley both ways before he drew her into the shadows along the side of the garage. The yard stretched before them. Huge pines grew along the sides against a tall wooden fence.

They walked toward the back of the house staying in the deep cold shadows of the pines. At the back door, Austin hesitated for a moment. She could tell he was listening. She heard voices but in the distance. Someone was calling a child into the house for dinner. Closer, that same dog barked.

Austin headed up the steps to the back door. She followed trying to be as quiet as possible. The houses weren't particularly close, but this was a small town. Neighbors kept an eye on each other's homes, especially when they knew a family was away for Christmas.

That was where the Bakers had gone, wasn't it?

Gillian took a deep breath as she saw Austin pull out the key. It was such a long shot, she realized now, that she felt silly even mentioning it. But it didn't matter if the key worked or not. She knew Austin would get them into the house. She was praying once they got in the house that they wouldn't find evidence of Marc having been there—and especially not of any kind of struggle.

She held her breath as he tried the key. It slipped right in. Austin shot her a look, then turned the key. She felt her eyes widen as the door opened.

"Rebecca left the key," she said more to herself than to Austin. She knew she sounded as disbelieving as he must have felt. Her heart lifted with the first feeling of real hope she'd felt since Marc had abducted her. "It has to mean that Nancy has my nephew, that Andy is safe."

As CANDY APPROACHED, the security guard ran a hand down the front of his uniform as if to get out any wrinkles and remind himself to suck in his stomach. He stood a little straighter as well, puffing up a bit, without even realizing he was doing it, Victor thought amused.

"May I help you?" the guard asked her.

Candy gave him one of her disarming smiles.

Victor saw that it was working like a charm. He looked into one of the rooms, before moving down the hall to Rebecca's. He could hear Candy asking for directions, explaining that her best friend had just had her third baby.

"Ten pounds, eleven ounces! I can't even imagine."

Victor smiled and gave a somber nod to the guard as he pushed open the door to Rebecca's room. He was so close, he could almost taste it.

"Just a minute," the guard said, stopping him.

"I told the family I would look in on Mrs. Stewart," Victor said.

"Did you say first floor like down by the cafeteria?" Candy asked the guard, then dropped her purse. It fell open. Coins tinkled on the floor. A lipstick rolled to the guard's feet.

The guard began to stoop down to help pick it up, but shot Victor another look before waving him in.

"I'm so sorry," Candy was saying as the door closed behind Victor. "I'm so clumsy. How did you say I get to my friend's room? I would have sworn she said it was on this floor."

Victor approached the bed. He'd met Marc's wife only once and that had been by accident. He liked to keep his business and personal lives entirely separate. But there'd been a foul-up in a shipment so he'd stopped by Marc's auto shop one night after hours. Marc had told him he would be there so he hadn't been surprised to see a light burning in the rear office.

As he'd pushed open the side door, though, he'd come face-to-face with a very pregnant and pretty dark-haired woman. She'd had a scowl on her face and he could see that she'd been crying. It hadn't taken much of a leap to know she must be Marc's wife. Or mistress.

"*Sorry,*" she'd said, sounding breathless.

He'd realized that he'd startled her. "*I'm the one who's sorry.*"

"*Are you here to see Marc?*"

"*I left my car earlier,*" Victor had ad-libbed. "*The owner said he might have it finished later tonight. I saw the light on....*"

She'd nodded, clearly no longer interested. "*He's in his office,*" she'd said and he'd moved aside to let her leave.

As the door closed behind her, Marc had come out

of his office looking sheepish. *"I didn't know she was stopping by."* He'd shrugged. *"My wife. She's pregnant and impossible. I'll be so glad when this baby is finally born. Maybe she will get off my ass."*

Victor hadn't cared about Marc's marital problems. He'd never guessed that night that Rebecca Stewart might someday try to take them all down in one fell swoop.

As he stepped to the side of the bed and looked down at the woman lying there, he could see the brutality Marc had unleashed on her. His hands balled into fists at his side. He'd known this kind of violence firsthand and had spent a lifetime trying to overcome it in himself.

"Rebecca?"

Not even the flicker of an eyelid.

"Rebecca?" he said, leaning closer. "How are you doing today?"

Still nothing. Glancing toward the door, he could hear Candy just outside the room, still monopolizing the guard's attention.

Victor pulled the syringe from his pocket. He couldn't let this woman wake up and tell the police where they could find the ledger. He uncapped the syringe and reached for the IV tube.

Rebecca's eyes flew open before he could administer the drug. She let out a sound just a moment before the alarm on the machine next to her went off.

Chapter Nineteen

Marc could feel time slipping through his fingers like water. He tried to remain calm, to think. With a start, he realized something. If Gillian knew where the ledger and Andy were, then she would go to both. Once she had the ledger in her hot little hands, she would turn it over to the cops. Victor would be on his private jet, winging his way out of the country—after he had Marc killed.

Which meant Gillian really didn't know where either item was. It was the only thing that made any sense because otherwise, by now, the ledger would be in the hands of the police.

But she would be looking for it. Was she stumbling around in the dark like he was? Or had her sister given her a hint where it was? Unlike her, he had cops after him. He felt as if he was waiting for the other shoe to drop. Once that ledger surfaced… He didn't want to think about how much worse things could get for him.

For a moment, he almost wished that Rebecca had cut his throat and he'd died right there at her feet—after he'd pulled the trigger and put the both of them out of their misery.

Marc shook himself out of those dark thoughts. If he was right and Gillian didn't have a clue where the ledger was any more than he did…well, then there was still hope. He dug out his cell phone.

When the hospital answered, he asked about Rebecca's condition.

"I'm sorry," the nurse said. "I can't give out that information."

"There must be someone I can talk to. I'm her brother. I can't fly out until later in the week. I'm afraid it will be too late."

"Let me connect you to her floor."

He waited. A male nurse came on the line. He could hear noise in the background. Something was happening. Was it Rebecca?

When he asked about his "sister's" condition, the nurse started to say he couldn't give out that information over the phone. "How about her doctor? Surely I can talk to someone there." He gave him his hard-luck pitch about not being able to get there right away.

"Perhaps you'd like to talk to the pastor who just went into her room," the nurse said.

Pastor? Marc stifled a curse. *Victor.* That son of a…

"I'm sorry, I don't see him," the nurse said. "Why don't I have the doctor call you?"

Marc slammed down the phone and let out a string of oaths. How dare Victor. Marc had told him he'd handle this. Not only that, he wanted to be the person who killed her—after he found out where she'd hidden the ledger and his son.

So was Rebecca dead? The last person Victor had paid a visit to while dressed as a pastor…well, needless to say, that person had taken a turn for the worst.

ONCE THE DOOR of the Baker house closed behind them, Austin snapped on his small penlight and handed a second one to Gillian. The silence inside the house gave him the impression that no one had been home for some time.

They were standing in the kitchen. He swung the light over the counter. Empty. Everything was immaculate. No dishes in the sink. Stepping to the refrigerator, he opened it. There was nothing but condiments. No leftovers that would spoil while the family was gone. As he closed the door, he noticed the photographs tacked to it and the children's artwork. There was no photo of Gillian's sister.

"They're gone, aren't they?" Gillian said from the doorway to the living room. "But they must have Andy. My sister wouldn't have left me the key unless..." She stopped to look at him in the dim light.

He agreed, but he knew they both wanted proof. "Let's check the kid's room upstairs." It made sense that if this family had Andy they might have left something behind to assure Gillian that her nephew was fine, or, better yet, another clue as to where Gillian could find the ledger and put Marc away for a long time.

As they moved through the living room, Gillian whispered, "No Christmas tree. No presents. They aren't coming back until after Christmas."

Or until they hear that it's safe, he thought. Had Rebecca told them she would call them when it was safe? But what if she couldn't call?

They climbed the stairs to the bedrooms. It didn't take long to find the child's room. It was bright colored with stuffed animals piled on the bed. Gillian stepped to the bed. He knew she must be looking for her sister's doll. It wasn't there.

"Do you see anything of Andy's?" he asked.

She sighed and shook her head. "His favorite toy is a plush owl, but it's not here. Then again, it wouldn't be.

He'd want it with him, especially if he wasn't with his mother." Her voice broke.

They checked the other rooms but found nothing. Going back downstairs, Austin looked more closely in the living room. Rebecca had been scared of her husband. But her clues for Gillian did make him wonder about the state of her mind. He reminded himself that she'd been terrified of Marc. The clues had to be vague, things only Gillian would understand.

They searched the house, but found nothing that would indicate that Andy Stewart had been here. Like Gillian, he kept telling himself that Rebecca had left them a key to this house. Didn't that mean that the Bakers had Andy and all were safe since there was no sign of a struggle in the house?

He'd stopped to go through a desk in the study when he heard Gillian go into the kitchen. She had looked as despondent as he felt. He'd been so sure they would find—

Gillian let out a cry. Austin rushed into the kitchen to find her standing in front of the refrigerator. Her hand was covering her mouth and her eyes were full of tears as her penlight glared off the refrigerator door.

He'd checked the kitchen first thing and hadn't seen anything. As he moved closer, she pointed at what he'd assumed had been artwork done by the daughter. What he hadn't seen was a note of any kind.

"What?" he asked, looking from Gillian to the front of the refrigerator in confusion.

She carefully plucked one of the pieces of artwork from the door. "Andy."

He looked down at the sheet of paper in her hand. It was a drawing of an owl with huge round eyes. Someone had taken a crayon to it. The owl was almost indistinguishable under the purple scribbles.

"Andy?" he repeated confused.

"I told you. He loves owls."

That seemed a leap even to him.

Gillian began to laugh. "Rebecca drew this at my house when she and Andy came up to visit. Andy's favorite color is purple."

"You're sure this is the same drawing?" he asked. He couldn't help being skeptical.

"Positive. Look at this." She pointed to a spot on the owl. The artist had drawn in feathers before they had been scribbled over. In the feathers he saw what appeared to be numbers. "It's a phone number. I'm betting it is Nancy Baker's cell phone number."

VICTOR POCKETED THE syringe as he stepped back from the hospital bed. Rebecca Stewart's eyes were open. She was staring right at him, a wild, frightened look in her dark eyes.

As a doctor and two nurses rushed in, the security guard at their heels, Victor clutched his Bible and moved aside.

"What happened?" the doctor demanded.

"Nothing," he said. "That is, I was saying a prayer over her when she suddenly opened her eyes and that alarm went off."

The doctor began barking orders to the nurses. "If you don't mind stepping out, Pastor."

"I have other patients I promised to see, but I will check back before I leave," Victor said, but the doctor was busy and didn't seem to care.

On the overhead intercom, a nurse was calling a code blue as he walked toward the door. He felt the security guard's gaze on him as he stepped aside to let a crash cart be wheeled into the room. Without looking at the man, Victor started down the hallway away from all the noise and commotion in Rebecca's hospital room.

He half expected the security guard to call after him, but when he glanced back as he ducked into the first restroom he came to he saw that the guard was more interested in what was going on in Rebecca's room.

Reaching into his pocket he put on the latex gloves, then carefully removed the syringe from his other pocket and stuffed it down into the trash. Removing the gloves, he discarded them, as well. After washing his hands, he left.

The security guard didn't look his way as Victor turned and walked down the hallway, stopping at one of the empty rooms for a moment as if visiting a patient.

The guard hadn't asked his name. No one had. As he left the empty room, he saw a nurse coming out of Rebecca's room with the crash cart. He couldn't tell by the woman's face what the outcome had been for the patient.

Nor did he dare wait to find out. Turning, he walked out of the hospital.

Chapter Twenty

Marc felt sick to his stomach. His fingers shook as he dialed the hospital. Again, he pretended to be her brother.

"I have to know her condition. I can't get a flight out because of the weather right now. Tell me I'm not going to get there too late."

"Just a moment. Let me check," the nurse finally said, relenting.

He waited, his heart pounding. As long as Rebecca was alive, he stood a chance of fixing this mess. He would do anything she wanted. He would convince her to give up the ledger to save not just her own life but his and their son's. She had no idea the kind of people who would be after her and Andy.

But if Victor had killed her... *Hell,* he thought. The cops would think he'd done it! Or paid someone to do it. What had Victor been thinking?

The answer came to him like another blow, this one more painful than the crystal tumbler. Victor planned to kill everyone who knew about the ledger and what was in it. He would take his chances that wherever Rebecca had hidden it, the incriminating book wouldn't turn up. Or if it did, the finder wouldn't have a clue what it was and wouldn't take it to the authorities. Or...it was this third option that made his pulse jump. Or…Victor was tying up loose ends before he skipped the country.

The nurse came back on the line. Marc held his breath.

"Good news. Your sister's condition has been upgraded. She had an episode earlier, but the doctor is cautiously optimistic about her complete recovery."

He tried to breathe. Victor had failed? His relief was real. "Can I talk to her?"

"I'm afraid not. The doctor wants her to rest. She is drifting in and out of consciousness. Perhaps by tomorrow…"

GILLIAN COULDN'T BEAR to wait until they returned to the motel to make the call, but Austin was anxious to get out of the house. She tried the number she'd found on Rebecca and Andy's artwork on the walk back to the motel.

The phone was answered on the second ring. "Gillian?"

"Nancy." She began to cry.

"Is everything all right?" Nancy asked, sounding as anxious as Gillian felt.

"I'm sorry, I'm just so relieved. Tell me you have Andy."

Several heartbeats of unbearable silence before Nancy said, "He's safe."

"Thank God."

"He keeps asking about his mother, though. Rebecca said she would join us before Christmas."

Gillian didn't know how to tell her. "Rebecca's in the hospital. The last I heard, she's unconscious."

"Oh, no. And Marc?"

"He's on the loose. Tell me you have Andy somewhere Marc wouldn't dream of looking."

"We do."

"A deputy sheriff from Texas is helping me try to find a ledger that will send Marc to prison. Do you know anything about it?"

"No. Rebecca only told me that Marc was dangerous and she needed Andy to be safe until she could come get him. She doesn't even know where we are. I was to tell her only when she called."

"Good. I don't need to know either. I can't tell you how relieved I am that Andy is with you and safe. But did Rebecca give you a message to pass on to me if I called?"

"She did mention that it was possible you would call."

So her sister had feared she wouldn't be able to call herself. Gillian felt sick.

"Becky said that if you called to tell you she forgives you for the birthday present you gave her when she turned fourteen and that she is overcoming her fears, just as you suggested. Does that make any sense to you?"

Gillian tried hard not to burst into uncontrollable sobs. "Yes, it does," she managed to say. "That's all?"

"That's it. Whatever is going on, it reminded me of how much your sister always loved puzzles."

"Yes. I'm just grateful that Andy is with you and safe. Give him my love."

She disconnected, still fighting tears. "Andy's safe."

"I heard. Your sister left you another clue?" he asked.

Before she could answer, she saw that she had a message. "The hospital called." She hurriedly returned the call, praying that it would be good news. *Please let Becky be all right. Please.*

"Yes," the floor nurse said when he finally came on the line. "We called you to let you know that your sister is doing much better. She has regained consciousness."

"Can I talk to her?"

"I'm sorry. The doctor gave her something for the pain. She's asleep. Maybe in the morning."

Gillian smiled through fresh tears as she disconnected. "Rebecca is better." She gulped the cold night air. "And I think I know where she hid the ledger."

MARC HUNG UP from his call to the hospital, still shocked that Victor had failed. Rebecca was alive. Didn't that mean he had a chance to reason with her? He knew it was a long shot that he could persuade Rebecca of anything at this point. But if she realized the magnitude of what she'd done, given the criminal nature of his associates, maybe she would do it for Andy's sake...

He wished he'd explained things in the first place instead of losing his temper. He thought of Victor, Mr. Cool, and began to laugh. Victor must be beside himself. He was a man who didn't like to fail.

Would he try to kill Rebecca again? Marc didn't think so. It would be too dangerous. He was surprised that Victor had decided to do the job himself. That, he realized, showed how concerned the man was about cleaning up this mess—and how little confidence Victor had in him.

I'm toast.

If he'd had any doubt that Victor wouldn't let him survive, he no longer did. Now he had only one choice. Save himself. To do that, it meant going to the feds. But without the ledger...he couldn't remember names and numbers. He'd been told he was dyslexic. But he knew that wasn't right because he'd heard dyslexics had trouble writing words and numbers correctly. He thought it had more to do with not being able to remember. He could write just fine. That's what had him in this trouble.

When Victor had asked him why he'd done something so stupid as to write everything down, Marc hadn't wanted to admit that there was anything wrong with him. He'd hired someone else to handle the details at his auto shop.

But he couldn't very well do that with the criminal side of his work, could he? He told himself it was too late to second-guess that decision. He had to get his hands on the ledger. He realized there was a second option besides turning it over to the feds. He could skip the country with it. The ledger would be his insurance against Victor dusting him.

Without the ledger, though, he had no bargaining power.

Sure he knew some things about Victor's operation, but not enough without the ledger. It contained the names and dates, names he knew the feds would love to get their hands on.

Rebecca! What did you do with that damned book?

It wasn't as if he hadn't been suspicious that she was up to something in the weeks before. He'd actually thought she might be having an affair. But he'd realized that was crazy. What would she have done with Andy? It wasn't like she had a friend to watch their son. No, he'd known it had to be something else.

He wondered if she'd taken up gambling. He didn't give her much money, but she had a way of stretching what he did... No, he'd ruled out gambling. Unless she won all the time, that didn't explain her disappearances.

He had started making a habit of calling home at different hours to check on her. She was never there. Oh, sure, she made excuses.

Andy and I were outside in the yard. I didn't hear the phone. Or she didn't have her cell phone on her. Other times she was at the park or the mall. She would say it must have been too noisy to hear her phone. He told her to put it on vibrate and stick the thing in her pocket.

"Was there something you wanted?" she'd asked.

He hadn't liked the tone of her voice. She'd seemed pretty uppity. Like a woman who knew something he didn't. He'd said, "I was just making sure you and Andy were all right. That's what husbands do."

"Really." She'd actually scoffed at that.

Not only had he resented her attitude, he'd also hated that she acted as if she was smarter than him. Or worse, that she thought for a moment that she could outwit him.

That's why he'd started writing down the mileage on her car.

He had checked it each night after that since he usually got in after she and the kid were asleep, and then he would compare it the next night. It had been a head-scratcher, though. She had never gone far, so while he'd continued to write it down, he hadn't paid any attention lately.

He fished out the scrap of paper he'd been writing it down on from his wallet and did a little math. At first he thought he'd read it wrong. She'd gone over a hundred miles four days ago. The day before she'd drugged him with his own drugs, stolen his ledger and hidden his son, she'd driven more than fifty miles that morning alone.

What the hell? Marc realized that he hadn't seen his son that day. Had she already hidden him away somewhere the day before? He tried to remember. He'd gotten home late that night. He glanced into his son's room. He hadn't actually seen the boy in his bed. It could have been the kid's pillow under the covers.

He let out a string of curses. Where had she gone? Not to her family cabin, he'd already checked it. Then where? He refused to let her outsmart him. He pulled a map of

Montana from the glove box. It was old, but it would do. Suddenly excited, he drew a circle encompassing twenty to twenty-five miles out from Helena. Rebecca thought she was so smart. He'd show her.

Chapter Twenty-One

"What do you want to do?" Laramie asked his brothers. They were all sitting around the large kitchen table at their cousin Dana Savage's house on Cardwell Ranch. They'd just finished a breakfast of flapjacks, ham, fried potatoes and eggs. Hud had motioned his wife to stay where she was as he got up to refill all of their mugs with coffee.

"I hate to put off the grand opening of the restaurant," Tag said.

"Can't it wait until Austin can be here?" Dana asked.

Jackson got up to check on the kids, who were eating at a small table in the dining room. "We might never have a grand opening if we do that."

"Jackson's right," his brother Hayes said. "We know how Austin is and now apparently he's gotten involved with some woman who's in trouble." He looked toward Hud for confirmation.

The marshal finished filling their cups and said, "He got involved in a situation where he was needed. That's all I can tell you."

"A dangerous situation?" Dana asked.

Hud didn't answer. He didn't have to. His brothers knew Austin, and Dana was married to a marshal. She knew how dangerous his line of work could be.

"This is the woman he met in the middle of the highway, right?" Laramie shook his head. "This is his M.O. He'd much rather be working than be with his family."

"I don't think that's true," Dana said in her cousin's defense. "I talked to him. He can't just abandon this woman. You should be proud that he's so dedicated. And as I recall, there are several of you who are into saving women in need." She grinned. "I believe it is why some of you are now married and others are involved in wedding planning."

There were some chuckles around the table.

Laramie sighed. "Some of us are still interested in the business that keeps us all fed, though. Fortunately," he added. "Let's go ahead with the January first grand opening. I, for one, will be glad to get back to Texas. I am freezing up here."

His brothers laughed, but agreed.

"Maybe Austin will surprise you," Dana said.

Laramie saw a look pass between Dana and her marshal husband. He was worried about Austin. Last July, Austin had been shot and had almost died trying to get some woman out of a bad situation. He just hoped this wouldn't prove to be as dangerous.

MARC WENT TO an out-of-the-way bar. He hadn't seen a tail, but that didn't mean there wasn't one again. In a quiet corner of the bar, he studied the map and tried to remember any places Rebecca might have mentioned. He had a habit of tuning her out. Now he wished he'd paid more attention.

They'd gone to a few places while they were dating, but he doubted she would be sentimental about any of them, the way things had turned out. He had never understood women, though, so maybe she would hide the ledger in one of those places because she thought it was a place he would never look.

Just trying to think like her gave him a headache. He wanted to choke the life out of the woman for putting him through this. He realized he hadn't heard from Victor demanding an update. Which he figured meant he was right about one of Victor's men tailing him again.

He'd lost the tail the first time, but maybe Victor had put someone like Jumbo on him. Jumbo was a more refined criminal, not all muscle and no brains, which made him very dangerous.

Marc folded the map and put it away. He couldn't do anything until daylight. Between songs on the jukebox, he put in another call to the hospital with his brother story. He knew he was whistling in the dark. He'd be lucky if he even got to talk to Rebecca, let alone convince her he was sorry. But it was a small hospital and he doubted the cops had done more than put security outside her room, if that, since Victor had circumvented whatever safety guards they'd taken.

Still to his amazement, he was put through to Rebecca's room.

"Hello?" she sounded weak but alive. "Hello?"

"Becky, listen," he said once he got past his initial shock. "Don't hang up. I have to tell you something."

Silence.

"Are you still there?" He hated that his voice broke and even more that she'd heard it.

"What could you possibly want, Marc?"

Humor. He bit back a nasty retort. "That book you took, it doesn't just implicate me. The people I work for... Rebecca they won't let you live if I don't get that book back."

"Don't you mean they won't let *you* live?"

"Not just me. They'll go after your sister, too." He could hear her breathing. "And Andy." His voice broke at the thought.

"You bastard, what have you gotten us all into?"

"Hey, if you had left well enough alone—"

"What is it? Drugs?"

"It doesn't matter what it is. I was only trying to make some money for Andy. I wanted him to have a better life than I had."

"Money for Andy? You are such a liar, Marc." She laughed. It was a weak laugh, but still it made his teeth hurt. "You hid that money for yourself."

And now she had a large portion of it. She'd hidden that, too, he reminded himself. He felt his blood pressure go through the roof. He still couldn't believe she'd done this to him. If he could have gotten his hands on her... He took a breath, trying to regain control, as he reminded himself that he needed her help.

"Rebecca, honey, you just didn't realize what you were getting in to. But we can fix this. I can save you and your sister and our son. These people...sweetie, I need to know what you did with the ledger. Did you mail it to the police?" Her hesitation gave him hope. "I know I reacted...badly. But, honey, I knew what would happen if that ledger got into the wrong hands. These people aren't going to stop. They will kill you. I suspect one of them has already tried. You didn't happen to see a man dressed as a pastor, did you?"

Her quick intake of breath told him she had "A blond guy, good looking. He was there to kill you."

She started to say something, but began coughing. He could hear how weak and sick she was.

"He isn't going to give up. The only way out of this is the ledger. I can save us both. Honey, I'm begging you."

"Begging me?" She sounded like she was crying. "You mean like I begged you for a divorce?"

"I'm sorry. I'll give you a divorce. I'll even give you custody of Andy. I'll give you whatever you want. Just tell me where the ledger is so I can make this right."

"I don't think so," she said, her voice stronger. "It's over, Marc. I never want to see you again. Once the police arrest you…"

He swore under his breath. "I'll get out of jail at some point, Rebecca."

"Not if I have my way." The line went dead. As dead as they were both going to be, because if he went, she was going with him one way or another.

"So she told you where we could find the ledger?" Austin asked as he and Gillian walked back to the motel. She'd grown quiet after the call. He wondered if this last clue was one she didn't want to share. Was she worried she couldn't trust him?

When she said nothing, he asked, "Is something wrong?"

She looked over at him, her dark eyes bright. "I'm glad you're here with me."

Her words touched him more than they should have. There was something about this woman… He smiled, his heart beating a little faster. "So am I," he said, taking her gloved hand.

As if the touch of her had done it, snow began to fall in thick, lacy flakes that instantly clung to their clothing.

Gillian laughed. It was a wonderful sound in the snowy night. "Andy is safe, my sister is going to be all right and Marc Stewart is going to get what's coming to him." She moved closer to him as they walked. "How do you feel about caves?"

"Caves?" he said, looking over at her in surprise.

"Assuming my sister was in her right mind, she hid the ledger in a cave." She repeated the so-called clue Nancy Baker had given her.

"And from that you've decided the ledger is in some cave?"

"Not just some cave. One up Miners Gulch near Canyon Ferry Lake. Rebecca is terrified of close places, especially caves. It's a boy's fault we ended up in one on her fourteenth birthday. I had this horrible crush on a boy named Luke Snider. He was a roughneck, wild and unruly, and adorable. I was sixteen and dreamed of the two of us on outrageous adventures. I thought I would see the world with him, live in exotic places, eat strange food and make love under a different moon every night."

They had almost reached the motel. He hated to go inside. The night had taken on a magical quality. Or maybe it was just sharing it with Gillian that made him feel that way.

"You were quite the romantic at sixteen."

She laughed. "I was, wasn't I? It didn't last any longer than my crush. Luke graduated from high school, went to work at his father's tire shop. He still works there. I bought a tire from him once." She smiled at that. "I definitely dodged a bullet with Luke."

He laughed as he let go of her hand and reached for the room key.

Gillian turned her face out toward the snow. He watched her breathe in the freezing air and let it out in a sigh. "If I'm right about this clue then my sister is getting even with me for being such a brat on her birthday that year." She seemed as reluctant as he did to leave the snow and the night behind, but stepped inside.

"I suspect caves have something to do with Luke and your sister's birthday," he said.

Gillian shook snowflakes from her coat. As she slipped out of it, he took it and hung her coat, along with his own, up to dry when she made no move to go into her adjoining room.

"I overheard Luke and his friends say they were going to these caves in the gulch. I knew they wouldn't let me go along, but if I just happened to run into them in the caves… I didn't want to go alone to look for them, and my friends could not imagine what I saw in Luke and his friends. You know how it is when you're sixteen. Just seeing him, saying hi in the hall, could make my day. I wanted him to really notice me. I figured if he saw how adventurous I was in the caves… So I told my sister I had a surprise birthday present for her."

He shook his head, smiling, remembering being sixteen and impulsive. He'd also had his share of teenage crushes. He hated to think of some of the things he'd done to impress a girl. He offered her the motel chair, anxious to hear her story, but she motioned it away and sat down on the end of his bed.

"Rebecca is claustrophobic so the last place she wanted to go was into a cave. I told her she needed to overcome her fears. Her message she left with Nancy was that she was now overcoming her fears."

"She mentioned this birthday present, so you think she put the ledger somewhere in these caves?"

"If I'm right, I know the exact spot." Gillian gave him a sad smile. "The spot where Rebecca totally freaked that day." Tears filled her eyes.

Austin reached across to take her hand. "Ah, childhood memories. I can't even begin to tell you about all the terrible things my brothers and I did to each other. It's just what siblings do."

She shook her head. "I hate that I did that to her."

"And yet, when the chips were down, she went back into those caves with you."

She smiled. "If I'm right."

His voice softened. "You've been right so far about everything."

GILLIAN FELT A lump form in her throat. Her pulse buzzed at the look in his eyes. If he kissed her again… "I should—"

"Yes," he said, letting go of her. "We should get some sleep. Sounds like we have a big day ahead of us tomorrow." He rose and stepped back, looking uncertain as if he didn't seem to know what to do with his hands.

She thought of being in his arms and how easy it would be to find herself in his bed. She told herself she was feeling like this about him because he'd saved her life, but a part of her knew it was more than that. It was… chemistry? She almost laughed at the thought. It sounded so…high school.

But she couldn't deny how powerful it had felt when he'd kissed her. Or now, the way he'd looked at her with those dark eyes. She marveled at the feeling since it was something she hadn't felt in a long time. Nor had she ever experienced anything this intense. The air around them seemed to buzz with it.

He'd felt it, too. She'd seen it in his expression. What made her laugh was that she could tell he was even more afraid of whatever was happening between them than she was.

"Something funny?" he asked.

Gillian shook her head and took a step back in the

direction of her room. She realized she loved feeling like this. It didn't matter that it couldn't last. "Thank you again for *everything*."

He smiled at that and almost looked bashful.

"Everything," she repeated and stepped through the doorway, closing the adjoining door to lean against it. Her heart was pounding, her skin tingling and there was an ache inside her that made her feel silly and happy at the unexpected longing.

Chapter Twenty-Two

Marc spent the night in a crummy old motel. He couldn't go home. Not only were the cops looking for him but also he had Victor's enforcers on his tail. Victor had failed yesterday at the hospital. That meant he'd be in an even fouler mood. Marc hoped he wouldn't have to see him for a while. Never would be even better.

He'd fallen asleep after staring at the map for hours. His face hurt like hell, not to mention his shoulder. He'd drunk a pint of whiskey he'd picked up at the bar. It hadn't helped. He thought about changing the bandage, but wasn't up to looking at the damage this morning in the mirror.

Picking up the map, he stared again at the circle he'd drawn around Helena. Maybe he should expand it. That one day, she'd driven a hundred miles. He made another circle, this one fifty miles out around the city.

Where the hell did she go? He had no idea since he couldn't conceive of a place she might think to hide the ledger. She knew him and he'd thought he'd known her. She would have had to up her game to beat him, and she would have known that.

He thought back to the days before he'd awakened still half drugged and found her note telling him how things were going to be now.

Marc started to shake his head in frustration when he recalled coming home early one day to find Andy crying and Rebecca looking…looking guilty, he thought now. She'd been standing in the kitchen.

He'd told her to shut the kid up, which she had. Then she'd disappeared into the bedroom to change her clothes. He frowned now. Why had she needed to change her clothes? At the time, he couldn't have cared less. They hardly ever had sex except when he forced the issue. He hadn't been in the mood that day or he might have followed her into the bedroom and taken advantage of the situation.

What had she been wearing that she'd had to change? His pulse jumped and he sat up straighter as he imagined her standing *before* him—before she'd changed her clothing. She was wearing the pair of canvas pants he'd bought her for hunting. She'd only worn them once when she'd tagged along. It had been early in their marriage. He'd made the trip as miserable as he could since he had been hoping she wouldn't ask to come along again.

Why would she have been wearing such heavy-duty pants? He recalled that their knees had been soiled. And Rebecca's hair had been a mess. She'd looked as if she'd been working out in the yard. But there'd been snow on the ground. Where had she been that she'd gotten what had looked like mud on the pant knees?

He realized with a start that it must have been the same day she'd put so many miles on her car.

He looked at the map again.

The no trespassing sign was large, the letters crude, but the meaning clear enough. Austin looked from it to Gillian.

The climb up the steep mountain reminded him of the

difference in altitude between Montana and Texas. Add to that a sleepless night in the motel knowing Gillian was just yards away and he found himself out of breath from the climb.

They'd wound up a trail of sorts from the creek bottom through boulders and brush to reach this dark hole in the cliff. It looked like rattlesnake country to him. He was glad it was winter and cold even though there were only patches of snow in the shade—just as there had been near her family's cabin.

It amazed him how different the weather could be within the state. "It's the mountains," Gillian had said when he'd mentioned it. "Always more snow near the higher mountains."

"This isn't a mountain?" he'd asked with a laugh as he looked out into the distance. He could see the lake, the frozen surface glinting in the winter sunlight.

"Have these caves always been posted like this?" he asked as he looked again at the sign.

"It's always been closed to the public," she said with a shrug.

Great, he thought. They would probably end up in jail. But if they found the ledger, they would at least have a bargaining chip to get out.

"Would your sister really come up here alone?" he asked. He couldn't help being skeptical. Rebecca was desperate, and desperate people often did extraordinary things. Still… "What about her son? She couldn't have brought him."

"It definitely isn't like Becky, I'll admit. She must have trusted someone with Andy, someone none of us knew about. The more I'm learning about my sister, the more secrets I realize she kept from me."

They were wasting time, but he wasn't that anxious

about going into the caves. He didn't think Gillian was either, now that they were here. The adorable young Luke Snider wasn't in there with his friends to entice her.

They'd stopped at an outdoor shop on the way and bought rope and headlamps, along with a first aid kit, hiking boots and a backpack. He'd brought water and a few energy bars. He hoped they wouldn't need anything else.

"I'm assuming you remember the way?" he asked.

Gillian nodded but not with as much enthusiasm as he would have liked. "It's been a while."

"Your sister remembered," he reminded her.

"Yes, that's assuming I'm right about her message. Also, this was probably the most traumatic thing that happened to my sister until she married Marc Stewart."

"You're not reassuring me," Austin said as he stepped into the cool shade of the overhanging rock. The cave opening was large. They climbed over several large boulders at the entrance before the cave narrowed and grew dark. They turned on their lamps. A few candy wrappers, water bottles and soda cans were littered on the path back into the cave. Apparently he and Gillian weren't the only ones who'd ignored the no trespassing sign.

They hadn't gone far before the cave narrowed even more. Gillian sat down on a rock that had been worn smooth and slithered through the hole feetfirst. He followed to find the cave opened up a little more once they were inside.

Austin could feel them going deeper into the mountain. They hadn't gone far when they came to a room of sorts. Water dripped from the rocks over their heads. The air suddenly felt much colder.

"You doing all right?" he asked, his voice echoing a little.

"It was easier when I was sixteen," she said, but gave him a smile.

"That was because you were in love and chasing some cute boy."

Their gazes met for a moment and he felt as he had last night after he'd kissed her. He tamped down the feeling, not about to explore it right now. Probably never. "We should keep moving."

She nodded and led the way through a slit in the rocks that curved back into a tunnel of sorts. They climbed deeper and deeper into the mountain.

MARC STEWART HAD shared one shameful secret with his wife. He was claustrophobic. He hated being in tight spaces. When he was a kid, a neighbor boy had locked him in a large trunk. He'd thought his heart was going to beat its way out of his chest before the idiot kid let him out.

As he parked next to the white SUV below the mountain, he'd told himself if he hadn't already been in a foul mood, this would have definitely put him in one. Even when he'd seen the gulch on the map, he hadn't wanted to believe it.

But at the back of his mind, he remembered bits and pieces of stories he'd overheard between his wife and her sister. Being trapped in some cave had been one of the worst experiences of Rebecca's life. Somehow her sister Gillian was to blame.

That he knew about the caves was no mystery. He'd grown up in Helena. Every kid knew about them. Most kids had explored them. Marc Stewart was the exception.

The last thing he didn't want to believe was that his wife had gone back into the cave where she'd experienced the "then" worst thing in her life. He could imagine she'd experienced worse things since then, him being one of them.

The moment he'd seen the rig the deputy had been driving parked next to the creek below the caves, he'd sworn, hating that his hunch had been right. As he cut the engine on the old pickup, he told himself that he didn't have to go *in* the caves. He could just sit right here and wait for them to come out with the ledger.

That made him feel a little better before he realized that once they saw another vehicle, even a strange one, parked down here, they might hide the ledger. Add to that, the cowboy was a sheriff's deputy. He would probably be armed.

No, Marc realized he was going to have to go up there. He wouldn't have to go inside, though. He could wait and ambush them when they came out.

Getting out, he locked the pickup and looked around. He didn't think he'd been followed, but he couldn't be sure. Not that it mattered. He should have the ledger in his possession within the hour.

Then what?

Turn it over to Victor? Make a deal with the feds? Or make a run with it?

He didn't kid himself. He would be damned lucky to get out of this alive.

He thought of Rebecca and felt his stomach churn as he climbed the mountain. The steepness of the slope forced him to stop a half dozen times on the way up. He was trying to hurry, but he couldn't seem to catch his breath. If he didn't get to the top before they came out…

What difference would it make if some Texas deputy shot him? Really, in the grand scheme of things, wouldn't that be better than what Victor probably had planned for him? he thought as he stopped to rest a dozen yards from the cave opening. Maybe that would be the kindest ending to all of this.

The thought spurred him on. He reached the opening and slipped behind a rock to wait. The winter sun was bright but not warm. He'd never been good at waiting. His mind mulled over his predicament until his head ached.

He glanced toward the opening. Still no sound. He couldn't wait any longer. He was going to have to go in. Why hadn't he realized the cave was the perfect place to dispose of the bodies? The last thing he wanted to do was kill them outside the cave where the deed would be discovered much quicker. But if he killed them in the cave, hell, maybe he could make it look like an accident. Drop some rocks on them or something.

Warmed by that idea, he pulled his gun and headed into the cave.

DEEP IN THE CAVE, Gillian stopped to get her bearings. Her headlamp flashed across the cold, dark rock. "It's just a little farther," she said. "I remember it being…easier, though, at sixteen."

"Everything is easier when you're sixteen and think you're in love."

She smiled at that. "Was there a girl when you were sixteen?"

"Nope. I was still into snakes, frogs and fishin'. It took me another year or two before I would give up a day fishing to chase a girl."

Gillian chuckled as they moved on, climbing and slipping over rocks, as they went deeper and deeper into the mountain. She thought of Becky and how she'd forced her to come along that day—on her birthday. A wave of guilt nearly swamped her when she thought of how scared Becky had been.

Then she was reminded that if she was right, Becky had come in here alone. Gillian smiled to herself, proud of her sister. She'd always felt that she needed to protect her. She realized that she'd never thought of Becky as being strong. As it turned out, Becky was a lot tougher than any of them had thought.

She saw the opening around the next bend. Rebecca hadn't been stuck exactly at this point in the cave. The opening was plenty wide. It was just that the trail dropped a good four feet as you slipped through the hole. Unable to see where she was going to land, Rebecca had frozen.

Gillian remembered a high shelf in the rocks. She scrambled up the side of the cave wall to run her hand over it, positive that would be where her sister had hidden the ledger. Nothing.

No, don't tell me all of this has been for nothing.

As she started to climb down, she saw it. A worn, thick notebook with a faded leather cover, the edges of the pages as discolored and weathered as the jacket. She grabbed it and almost lost her balance.

As usual, Austin was there to keep her from falling. He caught her, lifting her down. She clutched the ledger to her chest, tears of relief brimming in her eyes. Finally, they could stop Marc.

"Are you sure that's it?" he asked.

She held it out to him. He glanced at the contents for a moment from the light of his headlamp before handing it back.

"No, you hang on to it," she said.

He smiled and stuck it inside his jacket.

She started to move past him on the trail they'd just come down when he grabbed her arm. "Shh," he whispered next to her ear.

Gillian froze as she heard someone coming.

AUSTIN HEARD WHAT sounded like a boot sole scrapping across a rock as the person stumbled. He motioned for her to turn off her headlamp as he did the same.

It pitched them both into total darkness. "You don't think…?" Gillian whispered.

That Marc had followed them? He wasn't about to underestimate the man. A whole lot was riding on this ledger. Marc had already proven how far he would go to get his hands on it. Austin hoped it was only kids coming into the cave, but he wasn't taking any chances.

He touched Gillian's hand. She flinched in surprise before he took her hand and led her back a few yards in the cave. He remembered a recessed area they'd passed. If they could wedge themselves into it… Otherwise, if they stayed where they were, they would be sitting ducks.

He found the opening by brushing his free hand along the rocks. Stopping, he drew her closer and whispered, "There's a gap in the rocks where we can hide. Can you slip in there?" He led her to it, still holding her hand. As she slipped in, he moved back into the crevice with her, trying to make as little noise as possible. From there, with luck, they would be able to see who passed without being noticed—if they stayed quiet. If it was Marc, then he would have recognized Austin's rental SUV. If it was kids…or cops…

The footfalls on the rocks grew louder. Austin pulled his weapon, but kept it at his side, hidden, in case it was the authorities or kids.

It didn't sound like kids, though. It sounded like a single individual moving stealthily toward them.

A beam of light flickered off the walls of the cave. Austin pressed himself against Gillian as the light splashed over the rock next to him.

MARC FELT THE cave walls closing in on him. He swung his flashlight, the beam flickering off the close confines of the walls as he moved deeper into the cavern. He was having trouble breathing.

His chest hurt, his breathing a wheeze. He stumbled again and almost fell. When he caught himself on the rock wall, he lost his grip on the flashlight. It hit, rolled, smacked a rock and went out. For a few terrifying moments, he was plunged into blackness before it flickered back on.

He lurched to the flashlight, the beam dimmer than before. Picking it up, he stood, listening. Earlier when he'd entered the cave, he'd thought he heard noises. Now he heard nothing. Was it possible he'd taken the wrong turn? The thought made his heart pound so hard it hurt. He tried to settle down. There hadn't been a fork or even a tunnel through the rocks other than the one he was on large enough to move through. He couldn't have taken a wrong turn.

More to the point, Gillian and the cowboy were in here. He'd recognized the SUV. If only he could be patient enough to find them. What if they had heard him coming? What if it was a trap and the cowboy was waiting for him around the next corner of the cave?

He shone the light into the dark hole ahead of him. His breath came out in rasps. Suddenly, there didn't seem to be enough air. If he didn't get out of here now…

He spun around, banged his head on a low-hanging ledge of rock and almost blacked out as he tried not to run back the way he'd come. To hell with the ledger. To hell with Gillian and her cowboy. To hell with all of it. He was getting out of here.

Chapter Twenty-Three

Victor believed in playing the odds. He'd always known the day could come when this life he'd built might come falling down around him. He would have been a fool not to have made arrangements for that possibility. He was no fool. He had a jet at the airport and money put away in numerous accounts around the world, as well as passports in various names.

So what was he waiting for?

He looked around his mountain home. He'd grown fond of this house and Montana. He didn't want to leave. But there was a world out there and really little keeping him here.

So why wasn't he already gone? He didn't really believe that Marc was going to save the day, did he? Isn't that why he'd gone to Rebecca Stewart's hospital room himself? It had been foolish, but he'd hoped to get the information from her and then take care of the problem. That's what he did, take care of problems. He'd especially wanted to take care of her.

He hated that he'd made this personal. He'd always said it was just business. But a few times it had felt personal enough that he'd taken things into his own hands. Killing came easy to him when it was someone he felt had wronged him. In those instances, he'd liked to do it himself.

But he'd failed and he was stupid enough to try to kill her again.

Victor glanced at the clock on the wall. Was he going to wait until the FBI SWAT team arrived? Or was he going to get out while he could?

He pulled out his phone. "Take care of Marc."

Jumbo made a sound as if he'd been eagerly awaiting this particular order. "One thing you probably want to know, though—he's gone into a cave apparently looking for his missing ledger."

"A cave?"

"He's not alone. There's a white SUV here." He read off the plate number. It was the same one Victor's informant had given him.

"The Texas deputy and Marc's sister-in-law." Victor swore. "Where is this cave?"

Jumbo described the isolated gulch.

"Make sure none of them come out of the cave."

"What about the ledger?"

Victor considered. "If he has it on him, get it. Otherwise…"

AUSTIN HELD HIS BREATH. The footfalls had been close. He'd almost taken advantage of the few moments when the person had dropped his flashlight. But he hadn't wanted to chance it, not with Gillian deep in this cave with him.

What surprised him was when the footfalls suddenly retreated. The person sounded as if he were trying to run. What the—

"What happened?" Gillian whispered.

"I don't know." He kept listening, telling himself it

could be a trick. Why would the person turn back like that? The only occasional sound he heard was some distance away and growing dimmer by the minute.

"I think he left," he whispered. "Stay here and let me take a look."

He eased out of the crevice a little, his weapon ready. In the blackness of the cave, he felt weightless. That kind of darkness got to a person quickly. He listened, thought he heard retreating footfalls, and turned on his light for a split second. He'd half expected to hear the explosion of a gunshot, but to his surprise, he heard nothing. He turned his light back on and shone it the way they'd come. Whoever it had been had turned around and gone back.

The cave, as far as he could see, was empty.

He had no idea who it might have been.

Austin felt Gillian squeeze his arm a moment before she whispered, "Are they gone?"

"It appears so, but stay behind me," he whispered.

She turned on her headlamp and they headed back the way they'd come.

"You think someone will be able to make sense of this?" Gillian asked as she watched Austin thumb through the ledger. They'd stopped to catch their breaths and make sure they were still alone.

"Yeah, I do." He looked up at her. "This is big, much bigger than some guy who owns an auto shop."

She heard the worry in his voice. "If you're going to tell me that there are people who would kill to keep this book from surfacing—"

He smiled at her attempt at humor, but quickly sobered. "I'm afraid the people your brother-in-law associated with would make him look like a choirboy."

"So we need to get this to the authorities as quickly as

possible," she said and looked down toward the way out of the cave. "You think that was Marc earlier?"

"Maybe. Or one of his associates."

"Why did he turn around and go back?" she asked with new concern.

"Good question." He tucked the ledger back into his jacket. "When we get to the opening, if anything happens, you hightail it back into the cave and hide."

"You think he's waiting for us outside?"

"That's what I would do," Austin said.

"That day with my sister? I never did see Luke. I saw him go into the cave, but I never saw them come out. There must be another way out of the caves. But I have no idea where."

Austin seemed to take in the information. "Let's hope we don't need it."

Gillian followed him as they wound their way back the route they had come. The cave seemed colder now and definitely darker. She turned off her headlamp at Austin's suggestion to save on the battery, should they need it. She could see well enough with him ahead of her lighting the way.

But just the fact that he thought they might need that extra headlamp made it clear that he didn't think they would get out of here without trouble.

As Marc stumbled headlong out of the cave, he gulped air frantically. His whole body was shaking and instantly chilled as the December air swept across his sweat-soaked skin. He bent over, hands on his thighs, and tried to catch his breath. So intent on catching his breath, he didn't even notice Jumbo at first.

When Jumbo cleared his voice, he looked up with a

start to see the big man resting against a large boulder just outside the cave.

"Where is the ledger?" Jumbo asked.

"Inside the cave."

Jumbo lifted a heavy brow. "Why don't you have it? You were just in there."

Marc shook his head as he straightened. His gun bit into his back where he'd stuffed it in the waistband of his jeans. "My wife's sister has it." Jumbo's expression didn't change. "If you are so anxious to have it, then go into the cave and get it yourself."

Jumbo acted as if he was considering that. At the same time the thought dawned on Marc, Jumbo voiced it. "If I go in for the ledger, then what do I need you for?"

Marc's mind spun in circles. Why hadn't Jumbo just come into the cave? Something told him the big man didn't like caves any better than he did. "Good point. I guess I'd better go get it."

Jumbo smiled and stood. "Or I can simply wait until she comes out of the cave and take it from her."

Marc shook his head. "You don't want to kill her and the deputy out here where their bodies will be found too soon. Anyway, the cowboy's armed and expecting trouble. Give me a minute and I'll go back in so I can take care of them."

Jumbo's smile broadened. "You're smarter than Victor thinks you are."

He wasn't sure that was a compliment, but he didn't take the time to consider the big man's meaning. He drew his gun and fired.

AUSTIN HEARD THE gunfire outside the cave. It sounded like fireworks in the distance, but he knew it wasn't that.

"Stay here," he said to Gillian. "I'll come back for you."

She grabbed his jacket sleeve. He turned toward her, pushing back his headlamp so as not to blind her. In the ambient light, her face was etched in worry.

He drew her to him. She was trembling. "You'll be all right. I'll make sure of that."

"I'm not worried about me."

He leaned back a little to meet her eyes. "Trust me?"

She nodded. "With my life."

"I will be back." He kissed her, holding her as if he never wanted to let her go. Then he quickly broke it off. "Here." He leaned down and pulled a small pistol from his ankle holster. "All you have to do is point and shoot. Just make sure it isn't me you're shooting at."

She smiled at that. "I've shot a gun before."

"Good." He didn't want to leave her, but he hadn't heard any more shots. He had to get to the cave entrance now. "Gillian—"

"I know. Just come back."

He turned and rushed as fast as he could through the corkscrew tunnel of the cave until he could see daylight ahead. Slowing, he listened for any sound outside and heard nothing but his own breathing and the scrape of his footfalls inside the cave.

Finally, when he was almost to the cave entrance, he stopped. No sound came from outside. A trap? It was definitely a possibility. He eased his way toward the growing daylight of the world outside as he heard the roar of a vehicle engine.

He rushed forward, almost tripping over a body. The man was large. Austin didn't recognize him. It appeared he'd been shot numerous times.

Below him on the mountain, an old pickup took off in a cloud of dust and gravel. He spun around at a sound behind him to find Gillian standing in the mouth of the cave. She had the gun he'd given her in her hand.

"I thought you might need me," she said as she lowered the gun.

"MARC'S NOT DONE," Gillian said as she watched Austin try to get cell phone coverage to call the police. She realized she still had the gun he'd given her. She slipped it into her pocket without thinking. Her mind was on Marc and what he would do now. "He gave up too easily. Why didn't he wait to kill us, as well?"

"He's wounded," Austin said and swore under his breath. "There is no cell phone coverage up here."

"How do you know that?"

Austin pointed to several large drops of blood a few yards from the dead man. "Right now he's headed to a doctor. Hopefully at a hospital. This is almost over."

Gillian shook her head. "I hope you're right."

He stopped trying to get bars on his phone and looked at her. "Then where is it you think he's gone?"

"If he is headed for a hospital it's my sister's. If he thinks we have the ledger and it's over... I have to get to the hospital. Now!" She could tell that Austin thought she was overreacting. "Please. I just have this bad feeling...."

"Okay. As soon as we can get cell service I'll call the hospital and make sure there is still a guard outside your sister's room and that she is safe, and then I'll call the police."

"Thank you." She couldn't tell him how relieved she was as they hurried down the mountain. Austin seemed to think that the reason Marc had left was because of his wound. The one thing she knew for sure was that Marc wasn't done.

If he'd given up on getting the ledger, then he had something else in mind. She feared that meant her sister was in danger.

VICTOR EXITED HIS car and started across the tarmac to his plane. A bright winter sun hung on the edge of the horizon, but to him it was more like a dark cloud. Jumbo hadn't gotten back to him to tell him that all his problems had been handled up the gulch. He'd been right in not waiting to see how it all sorted itself out.

He squinted and slowed his steps as he saw a figure standing next to his plane. Jumbo?

Marc Stewart stepped out of the shadow of the plane. He had his hands in the pockets of his oversize coat. "Going somewhere?"

Victor smiled, accepting that Marc wouldn't be here if Jumbo was alive. "Taking a short trip."

Marc nodded and returned his smile. "I told you I would take care of everything."

He cocked his head. "I assume you have, then."

Anger radiated off him like heat waves. "I thought you had more faith in me. Sending Jumbo to kill me? That hurts my feelings."

Victor didn't bother to answer. He'd noticed that Marc seemed to be favoring his right side. Was it possible Jumbo had wounded him?

"I can't let you get on that plane," Marc said, his hands still in his pockets. "Not without me."

"I doubt you want to go where I'm going. Nor do I suspect you're in good enough shape to travel. I'm guessing that you're wounded and that if you don't seek medical attention—"

Marc swore. "Give me the briefcase."

Victor had almost forgotten he was carrying it. He

glanced down at the metal case in his right hand. "There's nothing in there but documents. You've forced me to buy myself the same kind of protection you would have had if you'd been able to get your ledger back."

"Jumbo said I'm smarter than you think I am. Actually that was the last thing he said. Now give me the briefcase. I know it's full of money."

Before Victor could say, "Over my dead body," Marc pulled the gun from his pocket.

He glanced toward the cockpit but saw no one. Nor was there any chance of anyone appearing to turn things around. Realizing it *would* be over his dead body, Victor relented. Marc might have killed his pilot, but Victor was more than capable of flying his own plane. A flight plan had already been filed.

All he had to do was settle up with Marc. It was just money and as they say, he couldn't take it with him if Marc pulled that trigger.

Stepping toward him, Victor said, "It's all yours. A couple million in large untraceable bills." He started to hold the case out to him. At the last minute, as if his arm had a mind of its own, he swung the heavy metal case. It was just money, true enough, but it was *his* money.

He'd never thought Marc particularly fast on his feet. Nor had he thought Marc had the killer instinct. But circumstances could change a man. In retrospect he should have considered that somehow Marc had bested Jumbo. He should have considered a lot of things.

The first bullet tore through his left shoulder just above his heart. The impact made him flinch and stagger. As the second bullet punctured his chest at heart level, Marc wrenched the briefcase out of his hand.

Victor dropped to his knees and looked up at the man as his life's blood spilled out on the small airstrip's tarmac.

"I made you," he said. "You were nothing before I took you under my wing."

"Yes, you made me into the man I am now." Marc Stewart stepped to him, placed the barrel of the gun against his forehead. "You shouldn't have told Jumbo to kill me." He pulled the trigger.

Chapter Twenty-Four

Marc stood over the dead man. He wiped sweat out of his eyes, chilled to the skin and at the same time sweating profusely from the pain and the adrenaline rush.

It made him angry that Victor had put him in this position. None of this should have happened. If Rebecca hadn't— He stopped himself before he let his thoughts take him down that old road again.

What was done was done. Jumbo was dead and so was Victor. He stared down into that boy-next-door face. Victor looked good, even dead. The man's words still hung in the air. Yes, Victor had made him. He'd turned him into a killer.

Marc had been happy enough running his own body shop. Hell, he'd been proud of himself. He'd made a decent living. He hadn't needed Victor coming into his life.

But there was no going back now. *That* Marc Stewart was dead. He was now a man *he* didn't even recognize. But he felt stronger, more confident, more in control than he ever had before. Rebecca hadn't understood his frustration, his feelings of inadequacy. He'd struck out because he hadn't felt in control.

But now…he knew who he was and what he was capable of doing. He hefted the briefcase as he walked to his pickup filled with a sense of freedom. He had more money than he could spend in a lifetime. He could just take off like Victor was planning to do. He wouldn't be flying off in a jet, but he could disappear if he wanted to.

Without his son.

That thought dug in like the bullet from Jumbo's weapon that had torn through his side.

Or he could finish what he started. He thought of Rebecca. It galled him that she might win. He thought of his son. *My son,* he said under his breath with a growl.

Then there was Gillian and the cowboy deputy. He tucked the gun back into his jacket pocket as he climbed into his truck and started the engine. Once he got bandaged up... Well, the people who had tried to bring him down had no idea who they were dealing with now.

AUSTIN PUT IN the call as soon as they neared Townsend and he was able to get cell phone coverage. As he hung up, he looked over at Gillian. "The guard is outside your sister's room. Rebecca is fine. I told the doctor we are on our way."

She nodded, but he could tell she was no less worried.

He called the police, knowing there would be hell to pay for leaving the scene. Right now his main concern was Gillian, though. He'd always followed his instincts so how could he deny hers?

The drive to Bozeman took just over an hour since he was pushing it. Gillian said little on the trip. He could see how worried she was.

When his cell phone rang, he saw it was Marshal Hud Savage, his cousin-in-law. Had Hud already heard about what had happened back up the gulch?

"I was worried about you," Hud said.

With good reason, Austin thought. "I'm fine. Gillian Cooper is with me. We have Marc Stewart's ledger. We're pulling into the hospital now so Gillian can see her sister. Rebecca has regained consciousness, the doctor said. Gillian's worried that Marc is also headed there and not for medical attention. He's wounded after killing a man neither of us recognized. I spoke with the nurse earlier and all was fine, but—"

"I'll meet you there," Hud said and hung up.

THE FIRST THING Gillian saw as they started down the hallway toward Rebecca's room was the empty chair outside her door where the guard should have been. Austin had seen it first. He took off at a sprint. She wasn't far behind him, running down the hallway toward her sister's room.

Out of the corner of her eye, she saw that there was no nurse at the nurses' station. In fact, she didn't see anyone in the hallway.

The hospital felt too quiet. Her heart dropped at the thought that they'd arrived too late.

Austin crashed through the door into the room, weapon drawn, yelling, "Call security!" to her. But it was too late for that. She'd been right behind him and was now standing next to him in the center of Rebecca's room. Even if she had called security, it would have been too late.

"I wouldn't do that if I were you," Marc Stewart said. He stood shielded by Rebecca, his gun to her temple. The security guard who'd been posted at the door lay on the floor next to a nurse. Neither was moving. "Drop your gun or I will kill her and everyone else I can in this hospital."

Austin didn't hesitate, telling Gillian that he'd realized the same thing she had. Marc Stewart was no longer just an abusive bastard. He'd become a killer.

"Now kick it to me." After Austin did as he was told,

Marc turned his attention to her. "Now, you. Lock the door."

Gillian stepped to the door and locked it before turning back to the scene unfolding before her. Rebecca was conscious, her condition obviously improved, but she still looked weak. What she didn't look was scared.

"You found the ledger in the cave, didn't you?" Marc said, although he didn't sound all that interested anymore.

"I have it right here," Austin said and started to reach inside his coat.

"I wouldn't do that if I were you," Marc warned.

She could hear voices on the other side of the door. But if she turned to unlock the door, she feared Marc would shoot her sister.

"You can have it," Austin said and took a step toward Marc. "You can make a deal with it."

Marc shook his head and motioned for him to stay back. "Too late for that. Could have saved a lot of bloodshed if I had gotten the ledger back when I asked for it." Her sister made a pained sound as Marc tightened his hold on her for emphasis. "Now a lot of people are going to die because of it. Starting with you, cowboy!" He turned the gun an instant before the shot boomed.

Gillian screamed as Austin went down. She dropped to the floor next to him. She felt something heavy in her jacket pocket thud against her side. The gun. She'd forgotten about it. She reached for Austin. He'd fallen on his side. She'd expected to find him in a pool of blood, but as she knelt next to him she saw none. She could hear him gasping for breath.

"Any last words for your sister, Rebecca?" Marc demanded over the sudden pounding on the hospital room door.

Rebecca was crying. She'd dropped to the floor at Marc's feet when he'd let go of her to fire on Austin.

"Come on, don't you want to tell her how sorry you are for what you did?" Marc demanded. "I'd like to hear it. But make it quick. We don't have much time left."

Seeing that Marc's attention was on his wife, Gillian started to stick her hand in her pocket for the gun. In that instant, she saw Marc's thick leather ledger lying next to Austin, a bullet lodged somewhere in the pages. Austin's hand snaked up and took the gun from her.

"Stand up, Gillian," Marc ordered. "Rebecca, I want you to see this." He reached down to take a handful of his wife's hair and pulled her to her feet. As he did, Rebecca grabbed Austin's weapon up from the floor where he'd kicked it. She pressed the barrel into Marc's belly.

Suddenly aware of the mistake he'd made, Marc swung to hit his wife. The gunshots seemed to go off simultaneously in what sounded like cannon fire in the hospital room.

Gillian saw Marc's reaction when both Austin and Rebecca fired. He took both bullets, seeming surprised and at the same time almost relieved, she thought. Before he hit the floor, she thought she saw him smile. But he could have been grimacing with pain. It was something she didn't intend to think about as Austin got to his feet and she rushed to her sister.

In that instant, the door to the hospital room banged open as it was broken down. Marshal Hud Savage burst into the room, gun drawn. Within minutes the room was filled with uniformed officers of the law.

Chapter Twenty-Five

Christmas lights twinkled to the sound of holiday music and voices. Suddenly, a hush fell over the Cardwell Ranch living room. The only sound was the crackle of the fire. Dana saw the children all look toward the door. She had heard it, as well.

"Are those sleigh bells?" she asked in a surprised whisper.

The Cardwell brothers all exchanged a look.

Dana glanced over at Hud. "Did you—?"

"Not my doing," he said, but Dana was suspicious. She knew her husband was keeping something from all of them.

She felt a shiver of concern as she heard the sound of heavy boots on the wooden porch. A moment later, the front door flew open, bringing with it a gust of icy air and the smell of winter pine.

A man she'd never seen before stomped his boots just outside the doorway before stepping in. Because he looked so much like his brothers, though, she knew he had to be Austin Cardwell.

He carried a huge sack that appeared to be filled with presents. The children began to scream, all running to him.

"I told you Austin would be here for Christmas," she

said as she got to her feet with more relief than she wanted to admit. "I'm your cousin Dana," she said. "Come on in."

It was then that she saw the woman with Austin. She was dark haired and pretty. Dana thought she recognized her as the jeweler who lived up the road, although they'd never officially met.

She knew at once, though, that this was the woman Austin had met in the middle of the highway and the reason he'd been missing the past few days.

"This is Gillian Cooper," Austin said as he set down the large bag and put an arm around the woman.

Dana knew love when she saw it. There was intimacy between the two as well as something electric. She smiled to herself. "Come on in where it's warm. We have plenty of hot apple cider."

She ushered them into the large old farmhouse and then stood hugging herself as she looked around the room at her wonderful extended family. Having lost her family for a while years ago, she couldn't bear not having them around her now.

Her sister Stacy took their coats as Austin's brothers pulled up more chairs for them to sit in.

The children were huddled around the large bag with the presents spilling out of it.

Mugs of hot cider were poured, Christmas cookies eaten. An excited bunch of children was ushered to bed though Dana doubted any of them would be able to sleep.

"They think you're Santa Claus," she told Austin.

"Not hardly," he said.

"I'm amazed that you remembered it was Christmas," Tag teased him. "At least you didn't miss the grand opening."

"Wouldn't have missed it for the world," Austin said and they all laughed.

"Gillian," Laramie said. "Please stay safe until after New Year's. We want all five brothers together."

Austin looked over at Gillian. They'd just busted a huge drug ring. Arrests were still being made from the names in Marc's book. Rebecca and her son were finally safe. It was over, and yet something else was just beginning.

"We'll be there."

SNOW HAD BEGUN to fall as Gillian left the ranch house later that Christmas Eve night with Austin. They walked through the falling snow a short way up to a cabin on the mountainside. Austin had talked her into staying, saying it was late and Dana had a big early breakfast planned.

"It should just be you and your family," Gillian had protested.

But Dana had refused to hear it. "Do you have other plans?" Before Gillian could answer, Austin's cousin had said, "I didn't think so. Great. Austin is staying in a cabin on the hill. There is one right next to it you can stay in."

Gillian had looked into the woman's eyes and known she was playing matchmaker and this wasn't the first time. Three of Austin's brothers had come to Montana and were now either married or headed that way. She suspected Dana Cardwell Savage had had a hand in it.

Gillian was touched by Dana's matchmaking, not that it was needed. Fate had thrown her and Austin together. In a few days, they had lived what felt like a lifetime together. But they lived in different worlds, and while maybe Austin's other brothers could leave their beloved Texas, Austin was a true Texan with a job that was his life.

"Did you have fun?" Austin asked, interrupting her

thoughts as they walked toward the cabins up on the mountainside.

"I can't remember the last time I had that much fun," Gillian answered honestly.

He smiled over at her as he took her hand. "I'm glad you like my family."

"They're amazing. I don't know what makes you think you're the black sheep. Clearly, they all adore you. I think several of them are jealous of your exciting life."

Austin laughed. "They were just being polite in front of you. That's why I begged you to come with me. They couldn't be mad at me on Christmas Eve—not with you there."

"Is that why you wanted me here?"

He put his arm around her. "You know why I wanted you with me. Making my brothers behave in front of you was just icing on the cake. You're okay staying here?"

"Your cousin does know I won't be staying in that cabin by myself, doesn't she?"

"Of course. I saw the look in her eyes. She knows how I feel about you."

"She does, does she?" Gillian felt her heart beat a little faster.

Austin stopped walking. Snow fell around them in a cold white curtain. "I'm crazy about you."

"You're crazy, that much I know."

He pulled off his gloves and cupped her face in his hands. His gaze locked with hers. "I love you, Gillian."

"We have only known each other—"

He kissed her, cutting off the rest of her words. When the kiss ended, he drew back to look at her. "Tell me you don't know me."

She knew him, probably better than he knew himself. "I know you," she whispered and he pulled her close as they climbed the rest of the way to his cabin. To neither of their surprise, a fire had been lit in the stone fireplace. There was a bottle of wine and some more Christmas cookies on the hearth nearby.

"It looks as if your cousin has thought of everything," Gillian said, feeling an ache at heart level. She was falling in love with his family. She'd already fallen for Austin. Both, she knew, would end up breaking her heart when Austin returned to Texas.

She should never have let him talk her into coming here tonight. Hadn't she known it would only make things harder when the two of them went their separate ways?

She looked around the wonderfully cozy cabin, before settling her gaze on Austin. It was Christmas Eve. She couldn't spoil this night for either of them. He'd promised to stay until the grand opening of the restaurant. In the meantime, she would enjoy this. She would pretend that Austin was her Christmas present, one she could keep forever. Not one that would have to be returned once the magic of the season was over.

Because naked in Austin's arms in front of the roaring fire, it *was* pure magic. In his touch, his gaze, his softly spoken words, she felt the depth of his love and returned it with both body and heart.

THE NIGHT OF the grand opening, Austin was surprised by the sense of pride he felt as Laramie turned on the sign in front of the first Texas Boys Barbecue restaurant in Montana.

He felt a lump form in his throat as the doors were opened and people began to stream in. The welcoming crowd was huge. A lot of that he knew was Dana's doing. She was a one-woman promotion team.

"This barbecue is amazing," Gillian said as Austin

joined her and her sister and nephew. He ruffled the boy's thick dark hair and met Gillian's gaze across the table. Andy had made it through the holidays unscathed.

As soon as Rebecca was strong enough, the Bakers had brought him down to Big Sky, where the two were staying with Gillian. Rebecca had healed. Just being around her son and sister had made her get well faster, he thought. Marc was dead and gone. That had to give her a sense of peace—maybe more so because she'd had a hand in seeing that he never hurt anyone again. She was one strong woman—not unlike her sister.

"Everything is delicious," Rebecca agreed. "And what a great turnout."

Austin looked around the room, but his gaze quickly came back to Gillian. He felt her sister watching him and was sure Rebecca knew how he felt. He was in love. It still bowled him over since he'd never felt like this before. It made him want to laugh, probably because he'd given his brothers Hayes, Jackson and Tag such a hard time for going to Montana and falling in love with not only a woman but the state. He had wondered what had happened to those Texas boys.

Now he knew.

DANA THREW A New Year's party at the ranch for family and friends. Austin got to meet them all, including his cousin Jordan and his wife, Liza, Stacy's daughter, Ella, as well as cousin Clay, who'd flown up from California. The house was filled with kids and their laughter. His nephew Ford was in seventh heaven and had become quite the horseman, along with his new sister, Natalie.

As Austin looked at all of them, he felt a warmth inside him that had nothing to do with the holidays. He'd spent way too many holidays away from his family, he realized. What had changed?

He looked over to where Gillian was visiting with Stacy. Love had changed him—something he would never admit to his brothers. He would never be able to live it down if he did.

Suddenly, Dana announced that it was almost midnight. Everyone began the countdown. Ten. Nine. Eight. Austin worked his way to Gillian. Seven. Six. Five. She smiled up at him as he pulled her close. Four. Three. Two. One.

Glitter shot into the air as noisemakers shrieked. Wrapping his arms around her, he looked at the woman he was about to promise his heart to. Just the thought should have made his boots head for the door.

Instead, he kissed her. "Marry me," he whispered against her lips.

Gillian drew back, tears filled her eyes.

"I'm in love with you."

She shook her head. "I've heard all the stories your brothers tell about you. *All Austin needs is a woman in distress and it's the last we see of him.* Austin, you've spent your life rescuing people, especially women. I'm just one in a long list. I bet you fell in love with all of them."

"You're wrong about that," he said as he cupped her face in his hands. "And don't listen to my brothers," he said with a laugh. "You can't believe anything they tell you, especially about me."

"I suspect your brothers are just as bad as you. After listening to how they met their wives, I'd say saving damsels in distress runs in this family."

He grinned. "You're the one who saved me."

Her eyes filled with tears.

"Remember our first kiss?" he asked.

"Of course I do."

"I knew right then you were the one. Come on, you felt it, didn't you?"

Gillian hated to admit it. "I felt...*something.*"

He laughed as he drew her closer and dropped his mouth to hers for another slow, tantalizing kiss. It would have been so easy to lose herself in his kiss.

She pushed him back. True, the holidays had been wonderful beyond imagination. She'd fallen more deeply in love with Austin. But her life was here in Big Sky, especially since she couldn't leave her sister and Andy. Not now.

She said as much to him, adding, "You love being a sheriff's deputy and you know it."

He dragged off his Stetson and raked a hand through his thick dark hair. Those dark eyes grew black with emotion. "I did love it. It was my life. Then I fell in love with you."

She shook her head. "What about the next woman in distress? You'll jump on your white horse and—"

"Laramie needs someone to keep an eye on the restaurant up here. I've volunteered."

She stared at him in shock. "You wouldn't last a week. You'd miss being where the action is. I can't let you—"

"I've been where the action is. For so long, it was all I've had. Then I met you. I'm through with risking my life. I have something more important to do now." He dropped to one knee. "Marry me and have my children."

"*Our* children," she said.

"I'm thinking four, but if you want more..."

She looked into his handsome face. "You're serious?"

"Dead serious. You may not know this, but I was the driving force originally behind my brothers and I opening the first barbecue joint. I can oversee the restaurant—and take care of you and kids and maybe a small ranch with horses and pigs and chickens—"

Just then, they both realized that the huge room had grown deathly quiet. As they turned, they saw that everyone was watching.

Austin shook his head at his brothers not even caring about the ribbing he would get. He turned his attention back to Gillian. "Say you'll marry me or my brothers will never let me live this down," he joked, then turned serious. "I don't want to spend another day without you. Even if it isn't your life's dream to become a Cardwell—"

"I can't wait to be a Cardwell," she said and pulled him to his feet. "Yes!" she cried, throwing herself into his arms. He kissed her as the crowd burst into applause.

From in the crowd, Dana Cardwell Savage looked to where her cousin Laramie was standing. "One more cousin to go," she said under her breath and then smiled to herself.

* * * * *

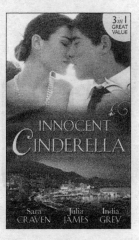